Two Days in Moscow

A Spy Thriller

By Lawrence Scofield

Acknowledgments

This book would not have been possible without the efforts of Judy, my wonderful editor. To Jennifer, who gave me the idea in the first place, my love and humble thanks are very much in order. My thanks and love extend to the rest of my family: Elizabeth, Daniel and John. They're the best.

Neither products nor brand names used in this novel represent or imply any relationship with, or endorsement by, the author or publisher.

Copyright Notice and Disclosures

Contents

Two Days in Moscow

A Spy Thriller

Prologue

THE CALL ORIGINATED from somewhere along the North African coast in the summer of 1986. Viktor Petrovsky, Chairman of the Soviet Union's Committee for State Security, sat in his office overlooking Dzerzhinsky Square in central Moscow and heard his secretary, Irina, answer the call.

"Lubyanka Building, Chairman Petrovsky's office, how may I assist you?"

"The Colonel wishes to speak with the Chairman."

"One moment, please." She put the line on hold and pressed a second line, "Chairman, sorry to interrupt you. I have the head of ..."

Petrovsky interrupted her. "Yes, Irina, I know who he is. Put him through."

"Of course, Sir."

"Good morning, Colonel," Petrovsky said after pushing the blinking button on his phone.

"Salam, Chairman. I pray Allah blesses you with health and good fortune."

"Thank you. How may I help you?"

"I have concerns about a mutual enemy, Chairman. A CIA agent named Laura Messier."

"Wait a minute while I pull the file."

Petrovsky was well acquainted with Laura Messier.

1

She murdered two Soviet agents in 1984. He pulled the file from his credenza. "Colonel, I have the woman's file in front of me. I see she killed one of your agents last spring in Paris. Why should the KGB become involved in a dispute between you and Shewolf?"

"Shewolf?" the Colonel asked. "I'm not familiar with the name."

"It's a code name we've given Messier. Her file is the largest of any agent we watch."

"Then I do not need to tell you this woman's misdeeds. I would just mention the attack last spring."

"Shewolf's involvement in that illegal act is well known to us."

"She stole the codes to the S-200 missile installations from my briefcase before the attack."

"I understand." Petrovsky hesitated before he spoke again. "What are you asking for, Colonel?"

"I want her killed."

Petrovsky laughed as though he'd been told a joke. "The problem with assassination isn't the killing, Colonel. It's finding someone to do it. It would take an extraordinary amount of money."

"How much?"

"Ten million U.S. dollars."

"I can transfer that sum immediately."

"One moment." Petrovsky withdrew a folder from the middle drawer of his desk and found the number of a Swiss bank account he used to divert funds. "Copy down this account number: 1479752230. The bank is Credit Suisse in Zurich. As soon as the transfer is made, the bank will notify me and I'll make the arrangements."

"Thank you, Chairman. You are a great friend of our

nation. Salam, Chairman."

Petrovsky hung up the phone and walked into his outer office. "Irina, would you find Ivan Ilitch? I've got a job for him. And contact Yuri Volkov in Paris. Tell him to call me."

"Yes, Sir. Right away."

Chapter One

IT WAS A warm and sunny September afternoon in 1986 when Laura Messier stepped out of a taxi onto a crowded sidewalk in the Marais district of Paris. The Marais, located across the Seine from the Cathedrale Notre-Dame, was home to a plethora of art galleries and upscale restaurants. Laura had arranged to meet Jean Broussard, the owner of a trendy nightclub in the district. Broussard's ownership of the club was something of a cover, though. Jean was one of the best intelligence men in Europe.

To all outward appearances, Messier and Broussard were an odd couple. Messier, in her early thirties, was tall, thin and drop dead gorgeous. However, her blond hair and cover girl looks were deceiving. Messier was generally regarded as the best martial arts specialist in the Central Intelligence Agency. Broussard, on the other hand, was not a fighter. In his mid-sixties, Broussard was a quintessential French gentleman; handsome, suave and clever. Short, slight of build with a graying goatee and a fondness for expensive clothing, Broussard had a magnetic personality. People loved him.

Laura scanned the club as she entered. She nodded to the maître d' as she walked past and sat at a booth along the wall where she could view the entire room. *No danger here*, Laura thought, studying the lunch crowd at the bar.

Of course, there wouldn't be. Despite the club's friendly atmosphere, Jean's security staff was ex-military. Although Laura moved around Paris without worry, one could never be too careful. The purported leak at CIA headquarters in Langley, Virginia, was real.

Jean walked through the club with a big smile as he approached her. "The most beautiful woman in the world just walked into my club. Mademoiselle, it's so wonderful to see you again." They hugged each other. Laura smelled his cologne. It reminded her of her father. They air kissed in the usual French manner.

"Jean, you look well."

"And you look so much better than the last time I saw you," Jean said. Indeed she did, for Jean had visited Laura in the hospital last spring where she convalesced following two gunshot wounds at the hands of an assassin. "Let's get out of here," he said. "I'm in serious need of espresso."

They left the club and strolled leisurely down the sidewalk arm in arm as two lovers might have done. "So, you're back?" Jean asked.

"Yes. Two weeks ago. I spent the summer in the States after I got out of the hospital. I also got married. You remember Steve Tilton, don't you?"

"Monsieur Tilton is a good man. You've chosen well," Jean said. "Did he resign from CIA?"

"That's what he claims, but I still see classified files around the house. I think he uses his new business as a cover."

"Are you still working at the Ministry?" The CIA had embedded Laura in the Foreign Ministry of the Republic of

France, where she worked as a personal aide to the Minister himself.

"No.   Minister Raimond replaced me during my absence."

"I'm sorry to hear that. What are your plans?"

"I'll be working out of the Embassy for a while. Special projects for the station chief."

They came upon a cafe where Jean led her to a patio table in front of the shop. Laura sat with her back to the street, sensing Jean would watch the street in case of trouble.

"The man across the street with sunglasses," Jean said. "He followed us from the club. He's your man?"

"Yes, Rick Williams, head of security at the American Embassy. Rick's become something of a bodyguard."

"I remember him from the hospital. I didn't recognize him with the sunglasses."

"You come here often?" Laura asked, as she scanned the patio and peered through the window into the cafe itself.

"The Mademoiselle is quite right.   I've become predictable in my old age. Perhaps I should change my habits."

The waiter spotted them and arrived to take their order. "I'll have a double espresso and the lady will take heavy cream and sugar in her coffee," Jean said.

"Very good, Sir." The waiter nodded before leaving.

"I wouldn't have thought I needed a bodyguard a year ago," Laura continued.   "But after Libya, the idea is growing on me. The Soviets have taken an unusual interest in me."

Jean smiled. "You helped destroy several of their MIG fighter jets. That's not something they'll soon forget. I wouldn't underestimate them if I were you," Jean cautioned.

"I learned that lesson in '84 when Volkov sent two men to kill me. They nearly did."

"You remember escaping into the French Embassy with the Tripoli Police shooting at us? At the time, I thought we were dead."

"We probably should have been," she said.

"As I recall, they ruined your dress."

"A bullet hole right between my legs," Laura said with a smile.

By the time the waiter arrived with their drinks, Jean was digging into his shoulder bag. He moved the bag onto his lap to allow the waiter to set the drinks before them. Jean found a picture and pushed it across the small table. "Do you know this man?"

"Ramirez Sanchez. The press calls him Carlos the Jackal. This is Paris in the background. Are you watching him?"

"When we can find him. He disappears and emerges from time to time."

Laura stared at the Hispanic man in the picture. "Some think he works for the KGB." She lifted her purse onto the table and placed the picture inside.

"Quite possibly. If you hear anything, even the smallest item, I'd appreciate knowing it."

"Would you like the CIA file on him?"

"Thank you, but no. Our information is better than yours. What we need are eyes on the street."

Laura shifted her gaze from the picture to her coffee. She reached for the cup and hesitated momentarily. She quickly looked around the patio. Jean caught her eye movement. "Something wrong?" Jean lifted his espresso cup.

"Stop," Laura said abruptly. "Don't drink it. Take a look at the liquid and tell me what you see."

"I see a nice cup of hot espresso. What else is there?"

Laura's eyes focused on one man sitting inside the shop at the window, reading a newspaper. "Can you see the reflection of the sun in the espresso?"

Jean moved his cup slightly until he could see the sun shining off the liquid. "Of course. Is there a problem?"

"The sun's reflection should not disperse into a rainbow, Jean. It should be a direct reflection of sunlight. There seems to be a clear liquid sitting on top. Do you see it in yours, too?"

"Yes, I believe I do."

This is when Laura appreciated Jean the most. Jean was a rock, never changing his demeanor under pressure. "Are you suggesting a foreign substance has been added to our drinks?" he asked.

"Maybe," she replied. "Don't turn and look, but a man sitting at the window inside the cafe is of Eastern European descent. He's reading a newspaper, but glances at me frequently."

"There's another standing behind you off your left shoulder leaning against a parked car."

"I hope we don't have a problem, Jean, but poison is one of the KGB's favorite methods of assassination." Laura took off her sun hat and ran her fingers through her hair. Upon seeing that sign, Rick Williams, stationed across the street, drew the service revolver from his shoulder holster and placed it underneath the folded newspaper he carried. Laura began discreetly attaching the suppressor onto the barrel of the Sig Sauer P226 inside her purse.

"Do you have a plan at this point?" Jean asked with a smile, as though poisoning was a common occurrence.

Laura returned the hat to her head. "Let me ask one more question. Have you seen this waiter before?"

"No. I think he's new."

"Bring the waiter over. If we have a problem, Rick will take the man behind my back. I have a direct line of sight with the man inside the cafe. If we've walked into a trap, it will be my third gun battle on the streets of Paris in three years, Jean. Besides which, they tend to be very tough on my nails." She held out one hand for Jean to see.

Jean smiled. "You have something of a reputation with the Paris Police about such things. Not your nails, of course."

"The waiter's your man. Lean to your right when he approaches to make sure I keep line of sight with the man inside. Ask the waiter to sip your espresso. If he refuses, insist. He'll probably offer to remove it. You need to force him to taste the liquid. If he runs back into the cafe, he'll exit the rear of the building. I'll move to the alley and stop him. Ready?"

"Yes, Mademoiselle."

Jean raised his hand and caught the attention of the waiter, who walked to their table. If Laura intended to shoot, she'd do it through her purse, so she raised her purse slightly off the table to line up her shot. "Yes, Sir, may I get you something else?" the waiter asked, standing over Jean.

"There seems to be a problem with my espresso. Would you mind tasting it and telling me what you think?"

"I'm sorry, but I'm not allowed to taste test. I'd be happy to remove it and bring a fresh cup for you."

The waiter reached for the cup. Jean grabbed his forearm and held it. The waiter looked worried. Beads of sweat appeared on his forehead.

"You're new here, aren't you?" Jean asked.

"Please let go of my arm, Monsieur. If you have a complaint, I'd be happy to bring over the manager." Jean tightened his grip and pulled the waiter close. "I'm an officer with French Intelligence, the DST. If you don't taste my drink, you'll be taken downtown for questioning while the contents of the drink are analyzed."

The man inside the cafe put his newspaper down on the table and reached inside his breast pocket. *It'll take two shots*, Laura thought; *maybe three to bring him down*. She dared not look to her right, afraid to reveal Rick Williams' position across the street.

The waiter tried to wrest his arm from Jean's grip. Jean used his other hand to remove the billfold from his breast pocket. He showed the waiter his DST identification. "I'm afraid I must ask you a few questions. What's your name?"

"I have nothing to say."

The waiter tore his arm from Jean's grip and sprinted into the cafe. Jean rose and followed him. Laura saw the man inside remove his weapon and aim it directly at her. She fired two quick shots through her purse, then a third. She saw him slump forward. Luckily, she managed to get three rounds off before people on the patio began screaming. The scene quickly erupted into chaos. Patrons knocked over tables and sent chairs flying as they fled. Laura heard two shots ring out from across the street. She looked behind her and saw a man lying on the sidewalk with a pistol next to him. She glanced at Rick, who pointed to his left. That meant he wanted Laura to go left, but she didn't.

She walked to the shattered window to make sure her man was down. Then, she turned left and ran down the sidewalk to the end of the block where she turned up a side street hoping to find an alley entrance. Laura pulled the weapon from her purse as she ran. Pedestrians saw the weapon and moved out of her way. Rick ran to the right and entered an alleyway parallel to the building.

The waiter threw chairs into Jean's path as he ran through the cafe. He burst through double doors into the kitchen. The chairs slowed Jean's pursuit and the waiter had disappeared by the time Jean entered the kitchen. "Which way?" Jean asked, shouting at the closest worker. The man pointed to a door at the rear of the kitchen. Jean carefully made his way to the back of the building, through a storage area and found the open back door. Still, he checked the storage area in case the man hid there. Once in the alley, Jean looked left and saw Laura running toward him. To his right, the waiter had run directly into Rick Williams. Rick stopped him, wrestled him to the ground and trained his weapon on him as Jean and Laura approached. Rick's chiseled six-five frame towered over the man

"Take him Laura," Rick said. "I've got to call this in. We need a team here."

"Let me call my men, Mr. Williams. Then I'll call DST," Jean said. Jean looked at Rick and pointed down the alley. "Secure that end of the alley."

After Jean placed the calls, he turned to Laura. "DST's on their way. My men will be here within a minute. I'm going back to the patio to retrieve one of the cups as evidence."

"Go ahead; I don't expect this gentleman will give me a problem. I'd be delighted if he did." Her malevolent expression froze the man in place. Rick took his position up the alley to guard the entrance from the street. Laura was alone with her subject.

"Perhaps, you have something to say now. What's your name?" Laura asked harshly.

"Pierre."

"Full name."

"Pierre Michel."

"Do you have identification with you, Mr. Michel?"

He started to retrieve a billfold from his pants pocket.

"Stop!" Laura ordered. "Do it with the other hand across your body. Do it slowly. If I see any quick movements, you're dead. You don't want to die today, Mr. Michel." The man complied. "Now, open it and hand it to me. You make any other movement; you even look anywhere else, I'll kill you." The man opened his billfold and held it high for Laura.

Jean's security arrived on the scene first armed with Uzi sub-machine guns. He sent several to the front of the cafe, others to cordon off the alley, and the rest to guard the area in case the enemy, whoever they were, still had men on the scene. Jean retrieved the cups from the patio. Although their table had been overturned, the cups still contained a portion of the liquid in question.

Rick walked down the alley toward her. "DST is here, Laura. They're cleaning up the scene in front. I expect them around back anytime now. You have, maybe, one more minute with your suspect."

"Thanks." Turning her eyes back onto her subject, she reached for the billfold. Inside were ordinary identification cards; a driver's license, a health card, and a Paris server's license which allowed the man to work in restaurants. "Who hired you Mr. Michel?" she asked. He said nothing. "I'll ask only once more. Who hired you?"

"They'll kill me if I tell you." Laura aimed her weapon and shot him in the leg. He screamed.

"I'll kill you if you don't."

"Wait, Laura," Rick said. "This isn't the way to do this."

"Believe me," Laura said to the man, ignoring Rick, "if you don't give me the information I want, you're of no value to me. Who hired you?"

Rick talked to the suspect. "Better do as she says. I think she means it."

"I was hired early this morning by a man sitting in the

cafe," the waiter said, grimacing from the pain of the gunshot wound. "I do not know his name."

"The man I shot?" Laura asked.

"Yes."

"What did he ask you to do?"

"He said you would order coffee and he would come into the kitchen and drop something into the cups before I served them. I have no idea what he put in the drinks."

Jean's men allowed the DST officers pass through the cordon. "For God's sake, don't shoot him again in front of French Intelligence," Rick said.

The man who led the DST contingent approached Laura. "Ms. Messier, is that correct?"

"Yes. I don't know you."

"I'm Paul Perrin. I worked with Henri Thomas last April apprehending the Libyans who followed you back to Paris."

"Understood, Mr. Perrin," Laura said. "Nice to meet you."

"And you as well. Do you mind if we take over the interrogation?"

"Go ahead." Laura put her weapon back in her purse.

"How did this man get shot?" Perrin asked.

"I shot him."

"Why?"

"He moved," she said in a matter of fact tone of voice.

Perrin spoke to the man. "Monsieur, take my advice. Don't move." His words were convincing. The waiter was paralyzed with fear. Perrin addressed his next comment to Laura. "We'll take him to American Hospital, have his wound dressed, then escort him to lock-up. If you'd like to continue your interrogation, he'll be available to you in a few hours."

"Thank you, Mr. Perrin. I think I've gotten what I need." She put her weapon back in her purse. "The men in front, they're dead?"

"Yes, Mademoiselle."

"I'd like to know their identities."

"We'd be happy to share that information," Perrin said.

"Forward it to Paris Station at the American Embassy."

"Of course."

"Am I free to leave?"

"Yes. If we need a statement, we'll contact the Embassy, but I spoke briefly with Mr. Broussard just a moment ago. It's clear what happened.

"Do you have the liquid we preserved as evidence?"

"Yes, we've secured it."

"I have reason to believe it contains some type of poison. Be careful how it's handled. It may be dangerous."

"Thank you, Mademoiselle. If you need an escort, we'd be happy to accompany you."

"Thanks, Mr. Perrin, but we'll manage. I'll be at the Embassy if you need me. Good day."

Laura, Rick and Jean exited the alley and walked past the front of the cafe. It had been cleared of bodies, but tables and chairs were strewn about the sidewalk and glass from the broken window was scattered everywhere. "Fucking bastards," she said.

Rick took Laura by the arm and led her to the front of the cafe. "I've got a car here. Jean, can we drop you somewhere?"

"No, thank you. My club's a block away. I'll walk."

Laura and Rick hopped in Rick's unmarked Embassy vehicle. "You think it was the Soviets?" Rick asked.

"I know it was," Laura responded. "I'm going to have to think of a way to stop them."

"I'm with you on this one hundred percent."

"I'm not sure the agency will help," Laura said, looking out the window. "This may be something I do on my own."

***

Laura and Rick were silent on the short drive back to the Embassy, northwest on Voltaire Boulevard and then west on Haussmann. A kind of shock had set in, the kind that one encounters after a near miss traffic accident. The after effect lingers and neither could dispense with the feeling. Rick stopped in front of the rear embassy gate; the guard recognized him and waved him through. They parked in the drive and walked in the back entrance where the duty officer mentioned that both were wanted in the Ambassador's office immediately.

As they rode up the elevator, neither seemed concerned with being called into the Ambassador's office. They were more concerned with protecting themselves. "Rick, I need a sniper rifle."

"I have a few in the armory. What are you looking for?"

"I trained on the M21 at the Farm." The Farm was the CIA's training facility near Williamsburg, Virginia.

"I have a couple. I'll give you the best one of the two and plenty of cartridges."

"You have a case for it?"

Rick thought for a minute as the elevator door opened. "There's a luggage maker we use in town. I'll give you his contact info."

They reached the Ambassador's office. "Laura Messier and Rick Williams to see Ambassador Wilcox," Rick said to the secretary.

"Go on in. You're expected."

They went inside the inner office and found the Ambassador talking on the phone. He motioned them to the stuffed chairs which sat adjacent to a coffee table. Laura and Rick continued their conversation.

"I need a couple more side arms, too. Can you arrange that?"

"I have several more Sigs."

"I want to keep them in a couple of different rooms in the apartment."

"Good idea. After we're done, walk with me to the basement and I'll get you fixed up."

They looked up to see the Ambassador had ended his phone call. He was listening to their conversation. "Are both of you okay?"

"Yes, Sir," Rick replied.

"Well, I've heard the French version. I'd like to hear yours." Laura and Rick looked at each other. Rick took the lead and explained the incident.

"That corroborates what I heard from DST. Do you

have anything to add, Ms. Messier?"

"No, Sir."

"The French are taking the lead in the investigation. Technically, we have no jurisdiction. They have decided this was an attack on a French citizen, a Mr. Broussard. You, Ms. Messier, and you, Captain Williams, will be considered bystanders whose participation was involuntary. The DST's controlling the release of information. There will be no mention of it in the press. Neither of you will be reprimanded and aren't under any sort of investigation. With any luck, the entire incident will go away."

"Are we free to go, Sir?" Rick asked Wilcox.

"John would like to speak with you in his office."

"We'll go there now, Sir."

"Very good. I'm glad you're unhurt and I wish you a pleasant afternoon," Wilcox said as he returned to his duties.

Rick accompanied Laura to John Brownley's office, the CIA Station Chief. "Thanks for taking over in there, Rick."

"No problem."

"If you don't mind, let me handle John."

"You got it."

Arriving at Brownley's office, his secretary, Jillian, greeted them cheerfully. "Good afternoon, Laura. Hi, Captain."

"Is he ready for us?" Laura asked.

"Go on in."

Brownley gave them a stare of aggravation and motioned them to the chairs in front of his desk. He was involved in a "Yes, Sir. Okay, Sir," kind of phone conversation with someone, apparently above his pay grade. He hung up.

"Well, you folks certainly have blown up my phone today. It's been ringing off the hook since about one o'clock."

"Nice to see you, too, John," Laura said pleasantly.

"Don't start that crap, Messier. You've been back in Paris two weeks and there's already a gun battle on the streets and dead bodies in the gutter."

"They were bad guys, John."

Brownley looked like a volcano ready to explode. "Don't you dare be flippant with me."

Laura hesitated. "Sorry. I didn't have time to worry about it."

"You better hope poison is found in those cups, Ms. Messier, or I guarantee you'll be fired. And, you!" Brownley shouted turning to Rick. "What the hell were you doing shooting across a crowded street, through traffic, right into a crowded sidewalk? Are you nuts?"

"Well ..." Rick began, but Brownley cut him off.

"Your job is the Embassy grounds, Captain Williams. We leave the street work to those qualified to do it."

"If I could just explain, Sir ..."

"Hell, no! There's no explanation that would legitimately place you on the scene this afternoon." Brownley slammed his fist on the desk. "Tape stop!"

Laura placed her hand on Rick's arm. "Okay, the show's over." John and Laura started laughing and Rick's confusion only encouraged them. "What's going on here?" Rick asked to no one in particular.

"That entire exchange was a charade for Langley.

19

We're off the record now," Laura explained.

Still confused, Rick said, "What?"

"Rick, everything we say here is recorded and sent back to Langley," John said. "Sorry I couldn't tell you. We're off the record now. What the hell happened?"

Laura proceeded to describe the incident in detail. "So, how did the waiter get shot?" Brownley asked. "The French say he was unarmed."

"He didn't give me the information I wanted."

"You shot him while you interrogated him?"

"He refused to answer a question, so I shot him."

"That's contrary to the Code of Conduct, Laura," John said.

"It's a gray area, John. He participated in an attempted assassination," Laura said with a shrug.

"What did the DST say about it?"

"Nothing."

"Friends of yours?"

"Well, sort of. Perrin and I knew each other by reputation."

"Well, I just got off the phone with the French. The waiter was a local kid, but the shooters were KGB special ops. Spetsnaz. They flew in two days ago from Poland. It'll take some time to analyze the liquid, but they think it contains poison and both you and Broussard were targets. We don't think the Soviets will claim the bodies."

"Of course not," Laura said.

"This does raise an issue, Laura. You can't have your own personal war against the KGB here in Paris. I've already talked with Langley. They want both of you on a plane tomorrow morning back to Washington."

"That's just what the Soviets want, John. They want me out of Paris."

"Well, they're going to temporarily get their wish. Jillian's making your travel arrangements as we speak."

"Isn't there any way to fight this?" Laura asked.

"One thing we're required to do is follow orders, Laura. Make sure you're on the plane. You, too, Rick."

"Yes, Sir," Rick said.

"That's all I have for you," Brownley said dismissively.

Rick led Laura to the armory where he stuffed an M21 sniper rifle into a soft bag, along with a suppressor and two boxes of cartridges. In a second bag, he put two Sig Sauer P226 pistols with suppressors and several more boxes of ammunition. "There, I think that'll keep you well stocked for a while. Can I give you a lift home?"

"Yeah, I don't think I should take a taxi with this stuff."

"No problem," Rick said as he lifted the bags. "Here, let me help you."

"You don't have to treat me like a girl."

"Just accept the help, Laura," Rick said as he shook his head. "Geez, you are a girl. Sometimes you need to act like one."

"I'm going to ignore that. I wouldn't want to rough you up again in the gym," she said with a smirk.

Rick knew the truth in that statement. The first time he worked out with Laura in the gym last spring, he was surprised at her hand to hand combat skill. Rick had been trained at Quantico, yet as proficient as he was at hand to hand combat, he had his hands full sparring with Laura.

Rick loaded the weapons into the trunk of the unmarked embassy vehicle and drove Laura the short distance across the river to her apartment in the 7th Arrondissement. As they passed the coffee shop a block away, Laura noticed the blue chalk mark at the base of the building, a warning from Markus Wolf, the East German spymaster with whom Laura had friendly relations. "Rick, when you get to the apartment, don't stop. Make a pass around the block. Something's wrong."

As they passed Laura's apartment at 51 Rue Cler, she noticed a man standing in a doorway across the street. *It could be nothing*, she thought, but as Rick turned onto the side street to go around the block, Laura peered into the alley behind her apartment where another man stood, leaning against a building, smoking. "We need to go to the coffee shop. I want to call up to the apartment. Steve should be there. I want to make sure he's okay."

"You see something out of place?" Rick asked.

"Something's not right."

"You might be a little sensitive after what just happened."

"Perhaps. It could be nothing."

"I'll go around the block and park at the coffee shop to avoid doubling back in front of the apartment. If it's surveillance, they'll notice the car a second time."

Rick parked in a space near the shop where Laura hopped out to use a pay phone. She called the apartment. The phone was picked up and after a short pause, Steve said, "Hello?"

"Hi, honey."

"Hi, Laura." *Steve never uses my name*, she thought.

"Are you fixing dinner?" she asked

"It'll be ready in ten minutes." Steve never prepared dinner. Laura and Steve used a system for communicating status. The first number, ten, meant the threat level was at maximum.

"I could probably make it sooner. I want to stop by the market first."

"Ten minutes would be fine." The second number, also a ten, meant that the coercion level was at maximum.

"Can I bring you something from the market?" Laura asked.

"Nope, we don't need a thing. Zero. I went shopping earlier in the day." The third number, a zero, meant Steve was unhurt.

"I'll see you in a few. Bye."

"Bye." *Something is definitely wrong*, she thought.

Laura walked back to the car. "Something's wrong in the apartment, Rick," Laura said looking at Rick. "Steve gave me a 10-10-0 status report."

"People inside the apartment? A hostage situation?" Rick asked.

"That's what I'm thinking."

"I'm calling Ops." Rick used the pay phone inside to dial CIA Paris Station.

"Operations," the voice said.

"74974," Rick replied.

"One moment please." Operations ran all callers through a voice print analysis. "This is Stan Kramer, Captain. What do you need?"

"Stan, I have a possible 10-31 at 51 Rue Cler. Second

floor apartment."

"What's the problem?"

"Possible hostage situation. An American, Steve Tilton, husband of Paris Station employee, Laura Messier," Rick said.

"Your staging area?"

"We'll use the lobby of the hotel at the corner of Rue Cler and Avenue de la Motte-Picquet. Approach from the northeast along Motte-Picquet. Enter the lobby from the Motte-Picquet side to avoid line of sight observation. Four men, street clothes, armed."

"I'll have to call the Paris Police, Captain."

"Negative, Stan. Strictly in-house on this."

"Then I'll have to get station chief approval. Hang on a minute." Kramer came back on the line within a minute. "Brownley will coordinate with DST. We'll send four men to the scene. You have permission to proceed."

Rick purchased two coffees to go and walked back to the car. "What's the plan?" Laura asked.

"Ops is sending a team. We'll use the lobby of the hotel down the street as a staging area. Let's move out before we're recognized." Rick pulled away from the curb and found a place near the hotel to park. The Ops team arrived shortly after Rick and Laura entered the hotel. The group sat around a coffee table in the lobby and watched Rick draw a map of the surrounding blocks.

"I need two of you to walk up Rue Cler," he said pointing to the map, "and apprehend the suspect across the street from the apartment. What's he look like, Laura?"

"Tan coat, blond hair," Laura replied.

"Make sure he doesn't use his radio. We want no

information going into the apartment."

"What if we're seen out the window of the apartment?" one of the men asked.

"We'll have to take that risk. Get the guy, secure his radio and get him off the street. No shots fired. Understand?"

"Yes, Sir," the man said.

"You two," Rick said to the others, "walk up the next street to the northeast, Rue Duvivier, to the alley entrance. Apprehend the guy standing in the alley. What's he look like, Laura?"

"Same description, Rick. All those bastards look alike."

Rick was amused by her answer. "Okay, once we've secured the surveillance, we're going to need to plan a breach, unless you want to negotiate with these guys. Any thoughts, Laura?"

"We're not negotiating with these guys. If they're Soviet Embassy employees, we've got to catch them in the act to have any chance at a prosecution. You remember the apartment layout, right?"

"Yes."

"Three man breach," she said. "One goes through the back door, one through the front. I'll access the roof, climb down the drain pipe on the front of the building and go in through the bedroom window. We keep it unlocked."

"Are you sure?" Rick asked with a look of disbelief on his face.

Laura gave Rick a serious look. "I'm sure."

"Okay. How will you access the roof?"

"The fire escape at the end of the block. From there, I'll hop from roof to roof. I've done it before," Laura said.

"Why am I not surprised at that," Rick said. "But we're short one guy."

Paul Perrin arrived with a team from the DST. "No, you're not," Paul Perrin said as he moved closer to the table.

"Mr. Perrin, it's good to see you. Okay, we've got our third guy," Rick said.

"Before we go in," Perrin said, "we're going to need eyes inside the apartment. How do we do that?"

"After the surveillance is rolled up," Laura said, "I can climb down the drain pipe on the back side of the building and look in the dining room window. I can see into the living room and the kitchen, too," Laura said.

"Fine," Perrin said. "Does the front door open into the living room?"

"Yes," Laura said.

"Whoever goes in the front will probably take fire. I've got body armor. I'll take that door."

"You'll take the back, Rick?" Laura asked.

"Yes. Do you keep it unlocked?"

"Usually. If it's locked, you can take a credit card and slide it between the door and the jamb. That will open it."

"How do we communicate?" Rick asked.

Perrin opened his shoulder bag. "I brought comm gear. I've got four sets, one for each of the three making the breach. Who gets the other one?"

"Give it to one of the guys going into the alley. We ought to be able to see the men in front," Rick said. Rick turned to Perrin, "What have you done to secure the area?"

"We've got men at every street corner. We're letting auto and foot traffic in for now, but we can cordon off the area on notice."

"What about timing?"

"They'll expect an entry through the door," Laura said. "If I go through the window and make my way down the hallway, we'll have an element of surprise."

None of the men around the table were comfortable with Laura leading a breach. It could be seen from the concern on their faces. "Look," Rick said. Everyone paused to allow Rick to present a better idea. "I'll go through the kitchen door. They won't expect an entrance from the rear."

"No. I'll go in through the front," Perrin said. "That'll give Captain Williams and Ms. Messier time to flank them."

"You could take a hell of a lot of fire," Rick said.

"I'll take my chances. Breaking the door down will draw attention away from you two," Perrin said, nodding at Laura and Rick.

Judging by the hesitation around the table, it became apparent that none of the options were preferable. Laura saw an opportunity to press her case. "Look, I can get inside unseen. The bedroom window slides up easily. There won't be any noise. I'll make my way down the hallway, let you guys know I'm in and both of you enter together. It's the best plan."

The men looked at each other and their silence indicated their assent. "Okay," Rick said reluctantly. "Let's gear up."

DST closed the surrounding area to auto and pedestrian

traffic as Perrin unpacked the comm equipment. Perrin fitted himself with an ear piece and microphone, handed the others to Laura, Rick and one of the men taking the back alley. The equipment was tested until each person could hear and talk without difficulty. Laura's weaponry was brought inside and she decided to carry an additional Sig besides the one in her purse. Rick gave her a shoulder harness for each handgun. "You'll have to wear these, Laura, to keep your hands free to climb."

"Ouch, these things hurt," she said as she pulled both harnesses over her shoulders and adjusted the straps. "The front straps lie right on top of my breasts. Can't I just stuff the Sigs in the elastic band on my pants?"

"You can't risk losing them as you climb. You'll just have to deal with it."

He looked at Laura's chest, then looked away. "What are you thinking, you pervert," Laura said.

Rick smiled. "I've seen women wear these before. It's just that you're ..."

Laura smiled. "Can you keep your mind on your work for a few minutes?"

Rick's face became flush with embarrassment. He looked at his feet.

Laura smiled. "The next time we're in the gym, Captain, I'm going to make you pay for that."

The exchange served to loosen the grim attitude and after a weapons check, Rick turned to the group. "Everyone ready?" He surveyed his group. "Okay, let's saddle up, people. Two man teams, start your approach up the street. Laura, get up the fire escape and in position."

Laura scampered up the fire escape and onto the roof

easily. She negotiated the waist high retaining walls between roofs, treading lightly across the roof above her apartment. She kneeled below the façade and watched as the man in front was apprehended without a shot. He struggled and reached for his radio, but the agents caught him by surprise and were able to confiscate his weapon and radio. They led him away quickly. "Man in front taken into custody," Laura said into the mic.

"Copy that, Laura," Perrin said.

"Hold until the second guy is rolled up," Rick said.

Soon after, two agents began walking down the alley, talking and laughing among themselves. They headed toward the butcher shop directly across from Laura's rear door. The surveillance man eyed them carefully, but did nothing as they approached. At the last moment, they lunged and took the man down. He struggled and tried to pull his weapon, but the agents were able to disarm him and hit him over the head with a pistol handle, knocking him unconscious. They pulled him into the butcher shop. *Poor Louis,* Laura thought, thinking of her butcher. *He puts up with so much from me. I'll have to buy something nice for him.*

"Guy in alley apprehended," Laura said into the mic.

"Hurry down the drain pipe before they know something's wrong," Perrin responded. "Captain Williams, go ahead and access the back entrance. I'll enter the front stairwell."

One of Laura's favorite pastimes was rock climbing around Ouray, Colorado, where she and her husband, Steve, vacationed each summer. She made her way down the pipe easily using the supports drilled into the brick. Incredibly, right above her dining room window, she turned herself upside down, wedging one of her feet between the pipe and wall. She grabbed one of the supports and slid her other hand down the pipe to support herself. She lowered herself just enough to see inside. Steve was in the middle of the living room bound to a chair with duct tape. The man who stood above him holding a gun looked like Yuri Volkov, the KGB man at the Soviet Embassy.

What the hell is he doing here, she asked herself. *He's not an ops guy*.

She saw two others sitting on the sofa holding automatic weapons. Their radios were lying on the coffee table. The men appeared to be talking among themselves. If they happened to look out the window and see the man on the street missing, surprise would be lost.

She raised herself up slightly and shifted to the other side of the pipe for a look in the kitchen window. She saw a man walking in the hallway toward the living room. *He must have used the bathroom*, she thought. She climbed back up the pipe. "Steve's tied to a chair in the living room. I count four men inside. All are in the living room and they appear to be armed."

"Are you ready to go, Ms. Messier?" Perrin asked.

"Walking across the roof to the front of the building now. I'll let you know when I'm inside the apartment."

"Go when ready."

Laura checked her weapons one last time. The mags on both her Sigs were full. She made her way down the front drain pipe and looked in the bedroom window. It was empty, the door open. She slipped her fingers underneath the window and opened it easily. She quietly hoisted herself inside, closing the window behind her. She moved to the opposite wall, out of sight of the doorway and whispered into the mic, "I'm in."

She heard Rick's voice in her earpiece. "Perrin, proceed up the front stairs. I'm going up the back stairs now. Laura, hold till we're ready."

"Check," Laura said.

Perrin quietly climbed the front stairs placing himself adjacent to the door, out of the line of fire. Rick climbed the back stairs and knelt below the window in the back door. He twisted the handle. It was locked. The doorjamb was loose and he slid a credit card between the door and the jamb. He worked the card up and down until he felt the latch move, then pushed the card farther until the lock released. He held the door closed. "In position," he said.

"In position here," Perrin replied.

She heard Rick talk to her. "You're good to go, Laura."

"In hallway now," Laura said as she drew her weapons and moved into the hall. She paused briefly to collect herself. Her hands were sweating profusely. She slowed her breathing. "Relax," she said under her breath. "Trust your instincts. Point and shoot, just like you were trained." When Laura felt herself under control, she crept down the hallway, both Sigs barrel up in firing position. She looked to her right, checking the bathroom. The door was open. It was empty. The second bedroom door was ajar. The room appeared empty, but she didn't want to be outflanked, so she stuck her head inside. It was empty.

She heard Rick speak softly in the mic, "Perrin, when

Laura fires, it's a go for both of us."

As she crept down the hallway, hugging the wall for protection, she saw Steve directly ahead of her. The wall kept her hidden from the men sitting on the sofa, but as she crept closer to the living room, her view of the room widened. The sofa was not yet in view, but someone had moved an additional chair into the room where a man sat next to Steve. She could see half his profile. When Steve saw her, his eyes widened, but he made no movement. She held the barrel of one weapon to her lips, indicating that Steve should remain quiet. She heard the assailants speaking among themselves in Russian. Someone would eventually start moving. Time to go.

Then the shooting started. One of the men suddenly appeared directly in front of her. He shouted and raised his weapon, but was far too slow. Laura fired once, then again. She kept firing, driving him back into the living room where he collapsed. Laura stepped over his body and into the living room.

Every subsequent action happened nearly simultaneously. She heard Rick kick the kitchen door open, smashing its window and heard firing in the kitchen. There must have been an additional man unseen by her. The two men on the sofa stood up and began firing. She dove to the ground and began pouring fire into the men. They aimed too high. Volkov turned his gun from Steve toward Laura. At that instant, Laura figured she was dead. It was one against three until Perrin crashed through the front door. Although wounded, the two men standing in front of the sofa were still dangerous. They redirected their fire at Perrin, who came through the door firing shot after shot. In a hail of gunfire, both men went down. Rick made his way through the dining room and immediately trained his weapon on Volkov. "Don't fire or you're a dead man," he said. Laura poured several additional shots into the men lying in front of the sofa. "That's enough, Laura," Rick said.

"Nothing's ever enough," Laura said viciously, turning her weapons onto Volkov.

"Don't shoot him," Rick said. Volkov quickly turned his weapon back to Steve. There appeared to be a stalemate.

Volkov smiled as though he were entertaining a dinner party. "Good evening, Ms. Messier."

"Well, well, well, if it isn't piece of shit Yuri Volkov," she replied. "You're out of your depth here, Yuri. I've never known you to be a shooter."

"I am tonight, Ms. Messier, if you don't drop your weapon. Tell your partner to drop his as well."

Laura spoke to Rick without looking away from Volkov. "Don't put your weapon down, Rick. It seems Yuri will never leave this room alive."

She then spoke to Volkov. "My husband is keeping you alive, Yuri. He dies, you die."

Volkov smiled. "I have diplomatic immunity, Ms. Messier. I cannot be touched."

Perrin stepped toward Volkov, his weapon trained on him. "You don't have immunity for this, Mr. Volkov. Legally, you can be killed and the Soviet government can't do anything about it, except file a protest."

"I think not, Mr. Policeman. No government would risk an international incident by killing a diplomat."

"You think I won't kill you right here, right now?" Laura asked.

Volkov turned his head toward Laura. He knew she was serious. He began to show signs of stress, his face turning a bright red. "Not if you want to see your husband alive. Put down your weapon, Messier, and your husband lives." He glanced at Rick. "You, too, Marine man."

"Nobody's putting their weapons down, Yuri," Laura growled. "You have no options left. Give up and you walk away with your life." Laura dared not look at Perrin directly on her left. Rick was somewhat in her field of vision.

"Here's my offer. I will allow your husband to go free and you will replace him," Yuri replied. "I have a van waiting around the corner. You will call them; they will pull the van in front of your apartment. I will take you into Soviet custody. Some very important people in Moscow want to talk to you."

While listening to Volkov speak, Laura wondered how to end the situation. She and Rick could possibly fire simultaneously. Rick, by far the better shooter, would go for Volkov's head, while Laura would try to shoot Volkov's gun hand. Volkov's hand was exposed as he held the gun barrel against Steve's skull. But how to communicate that to Rick?

"Very good, let's call your van," Laura said as though she accepted his proposal. "What's the number?" She walked toward the phone on an end table. Setting one weapon aside for a moment, she dialed as Volkov recited the number. She told the man who answered to pull his vehicle up to the front of the apartment.

Perrin spoke into his microphone. "Team two, grab the men pulling up to the apartment in the van. Kill them if they resist." Volkov frowned.

"What's the matter, Yuri? You thought you were going to get out of here?" Laura taunted.

Rick Williams, a combat veteran, was accustomed to hand signals. Laura hoped he would understand hers. Rick and Laura worked unusually well together. They trained in the Embassy gym several times a week. Laura was pretty sure Rick would get the message.

Volkov spoke again. "The men in the van are Soviet Embassy employees. By law, they cannot be touched. Stand down, Mr. Policeman. Make your decision, Messier. I have other business to attend to this evening. You will lower your weapons and allow me to secure your hands behind your back. The choice is a heroic one. Will it be your husband's life or yours?"

Laura used her right hand to momentarily take her index finger from the trigger and she lay two fingers against the gun housing, a signal to Rick that both of them should fire. Rick was fully experienced in tactics. She thought he'd get the message. She saw Rick smile slightly. That was all she needed. She fired. The round bounced off the gun handle, knocking the gun from Volkov's hand. It fell to the floor. Volkov's hand began to bleed.

Rick immediately changed his position to give himself an unobstructed shot, but didn't shoot when he saw the gun fly out of Volkov's hand. "Don't move, Mr. Volkov. Stay perfectly still," Rick said. Rick walked into the room holding his gun on Volkov. Perrin moved closer and trained his weapon on him as well.

"Laura, go ahead and release Steve," Rick said.

She laid her weapons down, walked behind Steve and began to release his hands.

"Mr. Volkov," Perrin said, "kidnapping is not an activity protected under the Geneva Convention. I'm placing you under arrest. You've been instructed to remain still and I advise you to do so." Volkov said nothing and seemed to believe that both Rick and Perrin might kill him. He didn't move.

Steve rubbed his wrists while Laura gently peeled the duct tape from his mouth. She smiled. "You really should have told me we had guests for dinner, honey." Steve rose and hugged her. "Do you know how much I love you," he said.

"I've got a pretty good idea."

Perrin spoke into his microphone. "Situation in the apartment is secure. Send a four man team up to take one perp into custody. And bring a paramedic. The perp's injured."

An ambulance was allowed through the cordon and stopped in front of the apartment. By now, darkness had fallen and Laura saw the flashing lights of emergency vehicles through the front window.

Volkov spoke again, this time with a mixture of pain

and frustration. "Messier, your government will recall you tomorrow. You've shot a diplomat. You'll lose your job."

"My dear Yuri," Laura said with a sarcastic smile, "I'll go back to the States where I'll sit on a warm beach somewhere, drinking gin and tonic and laugh at the thought of your government sending you to a gulag in Siberia. You're not a field agent, Yuri. You should have stayed in your office."

DST agents, paramedics and police entered the apartment. Paramedics bandaged Volkov's bleeding hand and checked the bodies scattered about the room to make sure no one was left alive. Volkov was handcuffed and led downstairs to a police van.

Rick walked over and hugged her. "Hell of a shot, Laura. Hell of a shot," he said. She spoke into his ear. "You're a good teacher." She kissed him on the cheek.

"We make a good team," Rick said.

"Well, Mr. Marine man, are you going to call this in or should I?" Laura asked.

Rick laughed. "Let me do it. You're in enough trouble already. You have a scrambler here?"

"In the closet."

Laura retrieved her scrambler and attached it to the phone line. Rick placed the call.

"Operations," the voice answered.

"Go secure, please."

"One moment." After a brief pause, the voice said, "Switch to red, then green please." Rick toggled the switch. After a short delay, the call continued. "Yes, how can I help you?"

"74974."

"Are you reporting status, Captain Williams?"

"Yes. Laura Messier's apartment, 51 Rue Cler. The DST and Paris Police have secured the premises and instituted a press blackout, but I need a team here immediately. Four dead, foreign nationals, probably Russian. Three more taken into custody by the DST."

"We'll do it immediately, Sir. American injuries?"

"No. Foreign nationals only. I'll stay at the scene until your team arrives."

"Very good, Sir. Should be five minutes or so."

"We need a carpenter and a locksmith to repair the doors, too."

"No problem."

"Thanks. Over and out," Rick said. Rick turned to Laura and Steve. "Why don't you get out of here? Otherwise, the Chief is going to want a statement."

"Thanks, Rick. You okay to leave, Steve?"

"Let me wash up in the bathroom first."

Laura and Steve were well away by the time the CIA team arrived. Information was exchanged, bodies photographed and prints were taken. After the bodies were removed by the police, the CIA team began to clean and repair the apartment.

Rick arrived back at the Embassy late that evening. He pulled through the gate and entered the back entrance where a guard cleared him to enter. "Evening, Captain," the guard nodded.

"Corporal. Anything happen I need to know about?"

"I have a couple of messages for you. The Chief wants

to talk with you immediately and Laura Messier left a number at the Paris Marriott."

"Thanks." Rick returned the salute and walked upstairs to Brownley's office where he gave him a briefing. Then, he dialed Laura. "Hi, Laura, Rick here. Brownley gave me our plane information for tomorrow. It's an Air Force transport out of the private gates, 8:00 tomorrow morning. Let's meet in the parking lot at 7:15. There's no ticket for Steve, by the way."

"That's fine. I didn't think there would be. He'll fly commercial."

"It'd be safer if he went with you to the airport. I'll have a couple of guards look after him until his flight leaves."

"Thanks," Laura said. "See you in the morning."

"Right."

Chapter Two

THE FOLLOWING MORNING, the taxi stopped in front of the private terminal where Laura and Steve met Rick. "Hi guys. Everyone okay this morning?" Rick asked.

"We're fine, Rick," Laura said. "Tough day yesterday."

"Yes, it was." Rick glanced at Steve. "You're coming with us. I was able to get you on the flight. It's safer if we stay together."

"Good. I think that's best," Steve replied.

Military personnel handled the passenger manifest procedure, after which the three of them walked across the tarmac to their ride home. "I thought this was supposed to be a military transport," Laura said.

"It is. It's one of the new Gulfstream IV's. I'm not even sure it has civilian certification yet. The top brass flew into Brussels for NATO meetings a couple of days ago. They stopped to pick us up on the way back." Rick laughed. "We get to see how generals travel."

"They serve food on this thing?" she asked, climbing the stairs.

"Yeah, generals food. Not your typical military menu."

The Air Force lieutenant welcomed them by name and showed them to plush seats near the front of the cabin, nicer than any first class cabin on a commercial flight. Several upper level military men sat in back, deep in conversation. The lieutenant drew a drapery across the cabin, giving the military men a measure of privacy. "Lieutenant, do you have refreshments aboard this morning?" Laura asked.

"Yes, Ma'am. Once we're in the air, I'll be serving a full breakfast. Can I get you a cup of coffee now?"

"Heavy cream and sugar for her," Steve said. "I take mine black. Rick?"

"Black's fine for me."

"Right away," the Lieutenant said.

Once the flight was airborne and breakfast had been served, Steve began his inquiry. "So, Laura, why did Volkov come after you all of a sudden? What's changed?"

"This wasn't Volkov, Steve. Volkov and I had an understanding. After his men attacked me in '84, we came to an arrangement. We'd leave each other alone. Moscow ordered this."

"Why?" Steve asked.

Rick answered for her. "Three Soviet MIGS destroyed at Bennina Airfield last April. A transport, too, wasn't there, Laura?"

"I think so," she replied.

"This was retaliation?" Steve asked.

"Yeah. Laura shut down the Libyan long range radars before the attack. That's a hundred million in Soviet military hardware. That's not counting the damage to the Libyans, which was pretty extensive," Rick said.

Steve thought for a moment. "Could very well be possible."

"I'm sure of it," Laura said.

"I saw Brownley last night when he handed me the flight passes," Rick said.

"What did he say?" Laura asked.

"Not much. I think he's under orders to keep quiet. He shrugged his shoulders and said we'd be debriefed at Langley once we got back."

"Volkov was right about one thing," Laura admitted.

"What's that?" Rick asked.

"Shooting a diplomatic officer is a big deal. I think the agency is about to put me on the bench for a while. If the Soviets wanted me out of Paris, I think they just got their wish."

"No one on the French side is blaming us, Laura. I don't think there's a problem," Rick said.

"We shot a lot of people," Laura said pointedly.

"Something else happen earlier?" Steve asked.

"She didn't tell you?" Rick asked.

"No."

"You want to tell him?" Rick asked Laura.

"Go ahead. I don't want to get angry again."

Rick explained the incident at the cafe with Jean Broussard.

Steve's alarm showed in his face. "Maybe they should put you on the bench for a while," he said looking at Laura. "Will the Soviets drop the matter after this?" Steve asked.

"I doubt it."

"Then, you're safer in Washington. They won't make an attempt in D.C."

Laura eventually fell asleep while Rick and Steve continued to talk as the Gulfstream made its way across the Atlantic. It was late in the evening when they arrived at

Washington National. Rick left to check in at the Watergate Hotel, while Laura and Steve caught a taxi to their home in Georgetown.

***

Laura and Steve traveled from their row house in Georgetown to CIA Headquarters in Langley, Virginia the next day. It was a pretty drive along George Washington Memorial Parkway. Laura watched for glimpses of the Potomac as they made their way northwest out of downtown. It was a familiar trip for both. Steve had worked as an Assistant Deputy for Intelligence at the agency and made the trip every day during his tenure. Laura, stationed in Paris, rode with Steve whenever she was in town. While the early morning trip was routine, the presence of a security team wasn't. Two men guarded the residence the previous evening and followed in a chase vehicle.

Rick Williams, unfamiliar with CIA headquarters, took an expensive taxi ride to Langley from the Watergate Hotel. He had no idea where it was located. He mumbled something to the driver about wanting to go to CIA headquarters and the driver cautioned the trip would be expensive. Rick figured he'd turn in the receipt for reimbursement, so he nodded okay.

Rick signed in at the front entrance, was given a pass for the day and told to report to Jim Tunney's office, the

Deputy Director of Operations. Upon entering Tunney's outer office, Rick found he was expected. "You must be Captain Williams," Linda, Jim's secretary said.

"Yes, Ma'am," he responded.

She smiled. "Let me take you to the conference room where you'll be meeting with the Deputy Director this morning. Can I get you something to drink?" she asked as she led Rick through the office suite into the conference room.

"Black coffee would be fine." Linda poured Rick coffee from the food service tray in the corner.

"Deputy Director Tunney will be with you shortly. Please make yourself comfortable. Restrooms are down the hall and I'll be at my desk if you need anything."

"Thanks," Rick said. He walked over to the large windows that looked out upon the rolling, forested hills of the grounds. *The view is pretty*, he thought, wondering in the back of his mind why he'd been summoned. Rick worked for Diplomatic Security, not the CIA.

Laura and Steve parked in front of the building, showed their passes at the security station and proceeded upstairs. "What are you doing with a building pass?" Laura asked as they walked toward the bank of elevators. "You still work here?" Steve's face became flush and he looked at the floor. "You told me you resigned."

"You're right, I did say that," Steve admitted.

"It's not a crime to inform your spouse of your employment, you know."

"I intended to tell you. I was waiting for an appropriate time."

"That's bullshit," Laura said with aggravation in her

voice as they exited the elevator on the seventh floor.

"I've got a meeting with Bill Bates so I'll leave you here," Steve said.

"Meeting the Director? The people on this floor lie for a living, Steve. Apparently, you're just like them."

Steve gave her an embarrassed look. "I'll see you later."

Laura walked into Jim Tunney's office and was greeted warmly by Jim's secretary. "Hi Laura. Welcome back."

"Hi Linda. Where are we meeting?"

"The conference room. Captain Williams is already here and Jim will be with you momentarily."

"Thanks." Laura opened the door to the conference room and found Rick staring out the windows. "Sleep well, Rick?" Rick turned around.

"Oh, hi Laura. Didn't hear you come in. Yes, the Watergate's nice." Laura walked over to the windows beside him.

"Pretty isn't it."

"I was trying to figure out how one might watch the place from those hills over there."

"It would be difficult. The entire complex is full of security devices. Someone told me they've got dogs up there, although I've never seen them."

"Wouldn't surprise me," Rick said. Rick knocked on the window gently with his knuckles. "Bulletproof glass?"

"I think so. They've closed most of the holes in security, but not all."

"What do you mean?"

"I think the problems in Paris came from here."

"A leak?"

"Yes."

"How do you know?"

"Brownley demands agents inform him of their meetings in advance. He puts them on a schedule and sends it to Langley. I put the Broussard meeting on his schedule a week ago. I suspect someone at Langley leaked it."

Jim Tunney entered the room smiling broadly. "Good morning, Laura. Thanks for coming. How was the trip?"

"Fine, Jim."

"It's good to see you in one piece after the other day." Tunney turned to Rick. "Captain Williams, I'm Jim Tunney, Deputy Director for Operations here at the agency. It's a pleasure to meet you."

Rick reached out and shook Jim's hand firmly. "Good to meet you, Sir."

"Why don't we sit at the table?" Tunney took a spot at the end while Rick and Laura sat on either side of him. Tunney looked like an administrator, nothing distinguishing him from any other; mid-fifties, short gray hair, glasses, a bland suit. His cologne was a cheap drugstore musk. He picked up the receiver on a phone sitting on the table and pushed a button. "Linda, would you have food service replenish the food tray, please? Thanks." Tunney looked at the two of them. "Doughnut anyone?"

"No, thanks, Jim."

Tunney set the manila file folders he carried on the table and opened the one resting on top. He read for a moment and then began talking to Rick without looking up. "Captain Williams, I took the liberty of pulling your file from State. I've asked that you be temporarily transferred to the agency. You'll serve under me." Tunny kept his elbows on the table and held a pen, which he pushed in and out continuously. He continued to read the file, skimming each page briefly, once in a while stopping to read something carefully.

"Am I to understand this transfer is mandatory?" Rick asked.

Tunney looked up from the file. "I'm afraid so, Mr. Williams."

"It's Captain Williams."

"During your time at the agency, you'll be identified as Mr. Williams to keep your status at State and with the Marine Corps a secret."

"So, this is a demotion?" Rick asked.

"No, Mr. Williams, it's nothing of the sort. You'll be on special assignment by arrangement with the Marine Corps and the State Department. You'll retain all seniority, rank and salary levels you've earned. You'll be working with us for a while."

"I see." Rick looked at the floor, interpreting it as a punishment for his actions the previous day.

"Why were you with Ms. Messier yesterday? Isn't your job protecting the Embassy grounds?"

"She asked for assistance and, yes, my job is to command the security detachment at the Embassy."

Tunney turned his attention to Laura. "Why'd you request Mr. Williams, Laura? Wouldn't it have been appropriate to ask Brownley for back-up?"

"Brownley's employees are administrative. They

couldn't have handled things yesterday."

"As you probably have guessed, the shooting of Volkov raised the incident to an international level. The Soviet Union made an official protest to the State Department this morning. They've threatened to reduce our staff in Moscow for what they call a military attack due to the involvement of Mr. Williams. Both you and Mr. Williams will make your statements as soon as we're done here. Once we have those, we'll turn everything over to the State Department and the White House. They'll figure out an appropriate response."

"Jim, none of it was our fault. We defended ourselves against attacks that were meant to kill us. If there is any blame to be assessed, it should fall on the Soviets."

"No one here is blaming you, Laura, or you, Mr. Williams. As I said, once we have your statements, we'll have a better understanding of what happened and be able to fashion an appropriate response. According to the French, you and Mr. Williams killed six KGB personnel yesterday, wounded two others and apprehended two more. The Soviets have decided to portray themselves as victims."

"Victims? That's bullshit!" Laura said raising her voice in anger. "They attacked us, Jim, twice in one day. During the second attack, Volkov broke into in my apartment and pointed a gun at my husband's head."

"French statements corroborate that. For the time being, we're recalling both of you pending an investigation."

"You're giving them just what they want. They want me out of Paris."

"You and Mr. Williams just killed, wounded or captured

every KGB agent stationed in Paris. You shot their entire office, Laura. I'm quite sure they want you dead. We're bringing you home to protect you," Tunney said firmly.

"How'd they know I was meeting Broussard yesterday?"

Tunney looked uncomfortable at hearing the question. "That's something we'll have to look into." He looked at his watch. "You're due in Assistant Director Pratt's office at the top of the hour to give your statements. Take a few minutes, collect yourselves and give us the material we need to go after these guys diplomatically. Okay?"

"Fine!" Laura said sharply, frustrated at Tunney's attitude.

"Yes, Sir," Rick said.

"Very good. We'll talk later."

After official statements were given and information about the incident had been analyzed, French, American and Soviet diplomats argued back and forth for weeks, but no reductions in the staffs at embassies occurred. The incident receded from memory. Rick Williams left Washington to teach the hand to hand combat class at the Farm. Laura was assigned to a low level position as an analyst on the European desk at headquarters.

***

As the holiday season fell upon Washington, Laura and Steve spent Thanksgiving with Steve's parents in Brookline, Massachusetts and then Christmas with Laura's parents in Des Plaines, Illinois. As had been their pattern for several years, they left immediately after Christmas for a week at one of their favorite vacation spots, Key West. Upon their return in early January, Laura sensed something different in her environment; something she couldn't quite identify. Experienced field agents develop a sixth sense about danger. Although she felt she was being watched, Laura couldn't find any evidence of it.

Laura arrived home from her gym workout on a chilly January afternoon ready to prepare the evening meal. She looked out the kitchen window and thought about how early the light was lost in January. She casually flipped on the kitchen light and opened the refrigerator to begin dinner preparations when she heard the sound. Two sounds, actually; one immediately following another. A high pitched tick, then a dull thud. She recognized the sound immediately. She instinctively dove to the floor and crawled behind the center island keeping it between herself and the window. As the refrigerator door swung closed, she saw the round had penetrated the stainless steel door. She looked at the floor where milk was leaking from the refrigerator. *Fuck*, she thought. She glanced at the window and saw a small hole in the glass. The shot had been taken, she judged, from the roof of a building a few blocks away. It was the kind of shot a marksman would make, at twilight, through the trees, the window, and into the kitchen where she had suddenly opened the refrigerator door, spoiling what would have been a kill shot.

Her only weapon was kept in the upstairs master bedroom. She crawled through the dining room as another shot came rocketing through the kitchen and into the dining room where it bounced off the floor and lodged itself in a wall. *He can still see me*, she thought. She ran into the foyer as a third shot came through the house. Once in the foyer, she knew she was out of the line of fire, so she bounded up the stairs into the bedroom where she retrieved her Sig Sauer P226 from the night stand. The agent guarding the front of the house heard the shots and came through the front door, calling out. "Laura, we've got an active shooter somewhere. Stay away from the windows."

"Jack, I'm in the upstairs master bedroom. He's shooting at the house from somewhere out back. Where's Pete?" she asked, referring to the guard stationed in the backyard. At that moment, another shot rang out.

"Pete, what's your location?" Jack said into his intercom. Nothing but static came over the earpiece. "Pete. Come in, Pete. Active shooter on a rooftop somewhere around 30th Street Northwest." Again, nothing. Jack yelled, "Laura, I'm calling D.C. Metro. Stay away from the windows." Jack pushed a button on his radio. "D.C. Metro, come in."

"D.C. Metro, identify yourself and location." the voice demanded.

"Jack Mason, CIA. 1339 29th Street. We've got an active shooter somewhere around 30th Street Northwest and O Street. Request immediate assistance,"

"Copy that, we've got two black and whites in the area."

Keeping herself from the windows, Laura made her way through the hallway and into the second bedroom right above the kitchen. She knew a round would not penetrate the outer brick wall so she stood next to the window where she thought she might be closer to eye level with the shooter. She peered out and was immediately showered with glass as the shooter put a round through the window pane an inch from her head. *Fuck*, Laura thought, *this guy's good.* "Jack," she yelled, "I think Pete's down in back." Jack called D.C. Metro a second time.

"D.C. Metro, Jack Mason, CIA. We've got a man down in the backyard."

"Copy that, we've got two squad cars rolling up to the scene. Please watch for them as they move through the yard," the voice answered.

"Tell them to be careful. Shots are being fired."

Laura sat on the floor next to the shattered window with the barrel of her weapon pointed at the ceiling. *He's gone by now*, she thought. Still, she kept her finger near the trigger in case a stranger appeared in the doorway. The scene began to unfold in slow motion, first the sirens, then voices in the backyard, and after a while, finally she heard Jack speak. "Laura, I'm coming up the stairs." He appeared in the doorway. "You okay?"

"Yes. How's Pete?"

"He took a round in the vest. It knocked him completely off his feet. They're loading him in an ambulance. He may have a broken rib or two."

"The shooter?" Laura asked.

"Metro's looking."

"He's a sniper, Jack. He knows what he's doing. I'll bet the rounds match a Soviet Dragunov."

"Why would you think that?"

"Just a hunch. He's probably in a taxi riding to Dulles

right now to catch a flight out of town. Probably ditched the rifle somewhere," Laura said. Jack offered a hand to Laura.

"Let me help you up. We called Steve. He's still at the office. Come on, we're getting you out of here. You'll spend the next couple of nights at the Watergate."

"Thanks, Jack. Let me know if they keep Pete overnight. I want to visit him."

"I'm sure he'd appreciate that," Jack said as he led Laura downstairs into a waiting car. She looked at Jack as she climbed in the car.

"Thanks, again, Jack. You're the best."

"You bet."

In the days that followed, Laura had the glass repaired in the windows, the woodwork and walls patched. She bought a new refrigerator. She put heavy shades on the windows in the house, installed tint on the auto glass and was careful about venturing outside the home. She began to carry a weapon. The agency assigned two extra guards at the house, but the precautions weren't needed. The shooter vanished.

A rifle discovered in a nearby trash can proved to be a Dragunov sniper rifle, a weapon made in the Soviet Union. The rounds found at the house were linked to the rifle. A full thumb print was found on its stock. However, D.C. Metro came up with no matches for the print. The CIA and FBI didn't, either. Metro traced the weapon to a gun show in rural Virginia where it was purchased with a fake Virginia driver's license. Laura helped with the investigation, viewing airline passenger manifests at Dulles and National Airport, cross checking them with CIA files of active KGB and Stazi agents. But no trace of the shooter could be found.

The idea that came to her was more of a feeling at first. It was a feeling that she had not been an active participant in her own protection. The layoff had dulled her street sense which was now heightened after the attempt on her life. Her first phone call was made in the middle of the day from a pay phone at a gas station in McLean, Virginia. She brought several rolls of quarters and fed the phone each time the recorded message asked for more change. The number she called was committed to memory as no record of it existed. She waited for the answering machine message which requested the party leave a message. "Wanglestrasse," she said and then left the number of the pay phone. She waited about fifteen minutes before the phone rang. "Wanglestrasse," the voice said in German.

"Guten tag, Markus."

"Ah, I recognize the voice. How are you, Shewolf?"

"I'm fine. How's the East Berlin weather?"

"Winter's tough on old men, my young girl. These bones are always cold. I must use a space heater underneath my desk at work."

"I keep telling you to defect. They'd give you a house on the beach with young blond women running around in bikinis."

"Ivan Ilitch. That's the name you're looking for."

"You have a picture?"

"No. He's a ghost."

"Tell me about him."

"He lives in Moscow, mid-thirties, has no wife or

children. He works special projects for Petrovsky."

"Speaks English?"

"Yes, among other languages. He's Spetsnaz. Their best sniper. Highly skilled. Can get in and out of places they'd send no one else."

"I'm one of Petrovsky's special projects?" Laura asked.

"Apparently, you are, although it's a waste of their time and manpower. I told them you'd kill anyone they sent."

"Ilitch got close because I was lazy."

"Then stop being lazy, my dear girl. Just because CIA withdrew you from Paris doesn't mean you're retired. No one ever leaves this business. You know that."

"It's good to hear your voice, Markus."

"And yours as well. Be careful Shewolf. There are those who would harm you."

"May I call you again?" Laura asked.

"Of course, my dear. It's always a pleasure to hear from you." She heard the disconnection and the line went dead.

The second call was placed from her bedroom at home with the window open so the carillon at the church down the street could be easily heard over the phone. She attached the scrambler into the phone line, waited for the carillon to begin at the top of the hour and then made the call. She held the receiver toward the window so the bells could be heard on the message machine. She hung up. Jean Broussard returned the call the following morning. "Good day, Mademoiselle"

"Thanks for calling back."

"Hearing your voice, Mademoiselle, brings me much happiness. Are you planning a return to Paris?"

"Soon and I'd like to meet."

"Of course," Jean said. "Meet me at the Marais club before it opens."

"It'll be nice to see you again."

"You, too. Goodbye."

She made one last call, this time to an agency line at the Farm. She knew Rick's weapons class at the CIA training school would be ending soon. Since the call went to a secure line, she used agency protocol. "47992, calling for 74974," she said.

"Callback number?" the receptionist asked.

"None."

"Thank you. I'll let them know."

Rick called back late that evening. "Hi Laura. How are things going with you?"

"Pretty good, Rick. Keeping busy out there in the woods?"

"Boring as hell. I can't even get the ball scores."

"When does your class end?"

"Friday."

"Have you made living arrangements in town?" Laura asked.

"Nope."

"Steve and I want you to stay with us. We've got a spare bedroom, plenty of space and we'd enjoy your company."

"Thanks for that, but I don't want to impose."

"It's no trouble, Rick. It's settled. You get back, what? Saturday?"

"Yes, we'll wrap things up Friday and I should be back at Langley sometime Saturday afternoon."

"Good. Call me. I'll drive out and pick you up."

"Thanks, Laura. That's very kind of you."
"See you on Saturday."

Rick arrived over the weekend and proved to be a pleasant houseguest. Laura enjoyed the conversation between Steve and Rick at the dinner table each evening. Rick temporarily used an agency car to travel to and from Langley each day where he worked on the Intelligence side.

Laura drove to Langley each day, but didn't do any meaningful agency work. She studied maps of the transit system in Moscow, highways leading in and out of the city, border crossings and rail routes through Eastern Europe. She asked for and received access to satellite data and studied the transcripts of interviews with defectors. She reviewed customs procedures at airports in the Soviet Union and East Germany. None of this escaped the attention of Jim Tunney who knew she was searching for an assassin. If the hunt satisfied her need for closure, Jim was willing to permit it.

She resumed combat training with a martial arts instructor in D.C. She began the study of Aikido, a Japanese form of self-defense. She sought out an expert with knives. She also practiced with weapons at a rifle range in McLean two days a week, which on the surface wasn't out of the ordinary for an agency field agent, but Rick had seen this behavior from Laura prior to her Libya mission. He volunteered to ride along with her to the rifle range to learn more about what her activities meant.

Upon entering the gun shop, the owner greeted Laura

warmly. "Good morning, Laura. Great to see you."

"You, too, Harry. Is the locker room open?"

"Sure."

"Can my friend and I use one of the golf carts?"

"Absolutely," the owner said, gesturing out the back door. "You know where they are."

"Harry, this is Captain Rick Williams, United States Marine Corps. Rick, meet Harry Lapp, owner of this fine establishment."

"Pleasure to meet you Captain. Semper Fi. Always happy to serve the Corp at my range."

"Thank you, Sir. Great to meet you."

"You better be on your game today," Harry said with a smile. "Laura's one of the best we have around here."

Laura laughed. "Harry, I'm an amateur compared to this guy. He's a marksman."

"Well, I was about to show him your last sheet from 400 yards, but I think I'll leave it in the drawer then," Lapp said with a chuckle.

Laura turned to Rick. "Come on, follow me." Rick followed Laura into the locker room where Laura opened a large locker stuffed with weapons.

"Geez, Laura, where did you get these? You could start a war with this stuff."

Laura smiled as though she'd just shared a secret. "Friends, Rick. It pays to have friends. Here, what do you think of this?" She handed him a sniper rifle.

Rick held it this way and that, studying the weapon. "It looks like a Remington 700, but it's different."

"It's not in production yet. It's designed on the 700, but it's a proto-type of the new M24 the Army's going to buy."

"Wow!"

"Want to try it?"

"I'd love to."

"I'm going to use this," Laura said as she took out the Soviet Dragunov and showed it to him. "What do you think of it?"

"You don't see many of these in the States. Wasn't this used by the sniper who attacked you?"

"Yes, although I'm not nearly as good with it as he is."

"Why do you need to practice with his weapon?"

"If you want to think like your enemy, it's good to emulate him."

Laura grabbed a handful of paper targets from a tray as they made their way out the back of the shop and onto the range. "Let's use a cart," she said as she motioned to a golf cart. "Can we start at, say 200 yards and work our way out?"

"Why do I think I've just been issued a challenge?"

"Oh come on, you can beat me with your eyes closed."

They set their targets and then made their way back to the sheltered area at the top of the range where they each fired a clip at their targets. They drove down to targets where Rick observed Laura's target. "Really nice spread, Laura. You've improved."

"Thanks. Harry's been helping me a little. You're still better, though. How about we extend the shot a little? You up for that?"

Rick shrugged his shoulders. "Sure. The M24 takes getting used to, but it's one hell of a weapon, that's for sure."

"I think it's better than the Dragunov, don't you think?"

"Don't know, never used a Dragunov. Have you used

it?" Rick asked, holding up the M24.

"A little, but the Dragunov is keeping me busy. I'm trying to make it my own. I've never been good with weapons. You know that."

Setting their targets at 400 yards, they fired another round and viewed the results. "Damn, you're good," Laura said.

"Nah, just lucky. Not a lot of wind today. You did nicely, though. You've been practicing," Rick said with a smile.

"Let's do one more round."

"Sure," Rick said.

"Want to extend to 600 yards?"

"Well, I doubt I can hit anything, but it'll be fun to try."

After placing the targets, they fired another clip, viewed the results and then made their way back to the locker room. "Laura, I'm impressed," Rick said as they cleaned their weapons. "That's a damn good spread at 600. You're as good as a military sniper."

"You're still better, though."

"Well, I've done it for real. That's a big difference."

On the return trip back to town, Laura and Rick continued the conversation. "In a combat situation, Laura, you'd have a spotter for most work. They're a tremendous help."

"I'm not a confident shooter, Rick. You know that."

"Well, it does take a certain mentality. A calmness, a certain amount of conviction and that's really where practice becomes important. Permission to speak freely?"

"Rick, as long as I've known you, we've always been honest with each other. Say whatever you want."

"Why are you doing this? What are you practicing for?"

Laura hesitated. "I'm not sure why I'm doing it."

"Tell me what's going on."

"Nothing."

"Nothing yet, right?"

"That's right, nothing yet," Laura answered.

"You've found him, haven't you?"

"Who?"

"The sniper."

Laura paused, thinking of the manner in which she wanted to phrase her response. "I know who he is. I just don't know where he is."

It slowly dawned on Rick what Laura's intentions were. "You're going to find him?" he asked.

"He's buried so deep, I don't know if that's possible."

"If you need me, just ask."

"I will," Laura said quietly.

At dinner the following evening, Laura decided to tell Steve she'd be going out of town. Due to the classified work Laura and Steve engaged in, it wasn't always possible to be completely forthcoming, but each of them tried, whenever possible, to tell the truth.

"Steve, I want to let you know I'm going out of town for a few days," she casually mentioned.

"Going to see your parents?"

"No, I'm going back to Paris."

Steve stared at her, shocked she would suggest it.

"You're not safe there."

"I'm a field agent, Steve. I know how to take care of myself."

"Is the trip sanctioned by the agency?"

"No. I'm going as a private citizen."

"You haven't informed the agency?"

"No."

"You going to tell them?"

"No. What is this? Some sort of interrogation?"

"This puts me in a hell of a spot, Laura."

"Puts you in a hell of a spot? Who am I speaking with? My husband or an agency employee."

Steve hesitated for a moment, thinking about his answer. "I'm your husband. I have a right to ask and you have a responsibility to tell me."

Laura thought about that far longer than was comfortable. "When we talk," Laura started, "sometimes I wonder if I'm talking to the agency."

"I've never divulged our conversations to the agency. Ever!"

"Can I trust you now?"

This time, Steve's answer was immediate. "Yes."

"Okay, I believe you. I have a lead on the shooter."

Now it was Steve's turn to hesitate. Laura could see the wheels turning in his mind. An agent conducting an operation apart from the agency would be contrary to the Code of Conduct. It could result in criminal charges against her.

"How could you possibly find him when the intelligence community can't?" he asked.

"I have better sources."

"Impossible. Have you considered the possibility you're being set up?"

"My source is reliable," Laura said flatly.

"So the shooter's in Paris?"

"No. The shooter's in a place where the CIA can't get to him."

"Then, why go to Paris?"

"I'm hoping the French will help me."

"Why can't you let go of this? It's over, Laura. He's gone," Steve said, raising his voice.

"It's not over. He'll be back, Steve."

"How in the hell would you know he'll come back? Perhaps it was just a random shooting. Did you ever consider that?" Steve was simmering, close to boiling over.

"He's a hunter, Steve. He'll come back to finish the job."

"Oh, come on, Laura. You don't know this guy," Steve responded sarcastically.

"He left the Dragunov."

"He left the rifle? Because of that, you know something about this guy?" Steve sounded like an attorney cross examining a witness. "He left it because he was in a hurry to get out of the area."

"That's what I thought at first, too," Laura replied, "but once I started practicing with a Dragunov, it opened my mind. He thinks I can't find him. He's arrogant that way. Yes, I know him."

"Good Lord, you're consumed by this. You can't let it go," Steve said bluntly.

Laura waited a minute before speaking again. *This is what the shooter wants*, she thought. *He wants to sow panic and fear.* When she spoke again, it was almost as though she was divorced from any reality. She looked away as she spoke. "He thinks he can't be defeated. That could be his weakness."

"You're going to try to kill him?" Steve asked.

"Yes."

"Where does he live?"

"Moscow."

Steve paused for a moment, hardly believing what he was hearing. "Going into Moscow without agency support is just crazy. Are you my loving wife or an out of control rogue agent?"

"I'm your wife and I love you more than anything in life. But I also know this. When Nazari tried to kill me in the hospital, he killed a DST agent, two nurses and a Marine guard to get to me. This assassin shot Pete just because he was in the backyard and looked in his general direction. The next time he comes, he'll kill anyone and everyone to get to me. He's got to be stopped, Steve, and if the agency won't do it, I will."

Steve ameliorated his anger hearing that comment. He remembered Laura lying in the hospital the day after she'd been shot twice. "Look, I understand where you're coming from. But you can't fight every battle, Laura. You can't win at everything you do."

"Winning and losing in our kind of work can mean life or death." She looked him squarely in his face. "I'm going to do this Steve. I have to. If you won't help me, then don't hurt me. I'm sure the agency will find out about it sooner or later, but allow me to develop it without interference. Please!"

Steve pushed himself back from the table as though he were separating himself from the conversation and their relationship. He looked at her with the eye of a seasoned intelligence professional. "You've won an Intelligence Star, Laura. Only a handful of people have ever been awarded that honor. You've sat with the President of the United States at a State dinner. You're the best in the world at what you do. But even you won't be successful going into Moscow. What you're thinking about is impossible. You'll be caught and even if by some miracle you're able to survive it, you'll face charges once you get home." He paused before continuing. "I won't help you, but I won't hurt you, either. I'll keep it confidential within the agency. But know this: If you follow through with this, the damage you cause quite possibly cannot be repaired."

"I understand," she replied softly. "Thank you."

***

When the agency informed Laura of the withdrawal of her protective detail, she considered it fortuitous timing. Although she had established a great relationship with the men who watched her, Laura was relieved they would no longer be in the house. With her privacy intact, she used the basement area, which served as the security station, to establish a work space for her planning. However, to keep the illusion within the agency that she was dependent on the protection, she stopped by the Assistant Deputy Director of Operations office.

Mike Pratt's office was nestled into a corner of the operations center and since he had no secretary, she simply walked into his office where she found him studying briefing reports. Mike looked up with a cheerful smile, as though he were glad to see her. He wasn't, but Mike figured he could hide behind a shallow expression. "Hi, Laura. Haven't seen you in a while. How are things going?"

"I'm fine, Mike, except the agency removed the protective detail at my house."

"I'm sorry, Laura, I had no idea."

Laura smiled at the thinly veiled lie. "Mike, I'm in no mood for administrative bullshit. Why'd you pull them off?"

"Okay," Pratt said, closing the file he'd been reading. "Would you like to sit down?" he asked, motioning to chairs in front of his desk.

"No. I want to know why you pulled the security."

"Because we saw no further threat."

"What's the matter? The Nicaraguan rebels getting expensive?"

"You know I can't talk about that," Pratt said.

"I thought you were selling arms under the table to pay for that."

"I really can't talk about it," Pratt said as though it was a closely guarded secret.

"What happens in Washington is important, too, Mike. An assassination attempt on a CIA operative right in your own backyard? Come on, Mike, cut the bullshit."

"Laura, we looked for the guy," Pratt said, spreading his arms out as though they had done their best. "We found nothing. D.C Metro considers it a random shooting. They might be right."

"Might?" Laura asked.

"Look, we don't think a sniper would take that shot. The angle was wrong, the shooting position was flawed. Four-hundred yards through trees? It's a low percentage shot."

"That's the type of shot a marksman would make. He made it look random. And don't even begin to claim nothing was found."

"We don't think the rifle means anything. It was purchased at a gun show for crying out loud. It's over, Laura. Forget about it. We left the security system for you. You're safe."

"Until I'm not."

"If anything else happens, report it to operations and we'll go back out there. Until then, our people have other duties."

Laura had finally disguised her point well enough to pose the question. "So, I'm on my own. Is that the deal?"

"You're as safe as any citizen in D.C., Laura. Just keep an eye out for anything unusual and phone it in."

"I want to hear you say it. You're not watching the house any longer?"

"No."

"Thanks for nothing."

Laura walked out of Pratt's office smiling to herself. Pratt, on the other hand, watched her walk out and muttered under his breath, "God, that woman's a bitch. A pain in the fucking ass."

After withdrawing money from an account Laura created using the clandestine cover name, Irene Thomas, she used a sidewalk pay phone outside the bank to give Jean Broussard advance notice of her arrival in Paris. She waited until the top of the hour for the clock across the street to ring the hour of day. Two rings meant she'd meet Jean in two days. Rick watched from a distance as she placed the call. The following day, instead of going to headquarters, Rick dropped her off at the train station where she paid cash for a fare to New York City. He watched until her train pulled out of the station, then brought the car back to the house to avoid any suspicion she might be gone. However, unknown to Laura, Rick called a taxi afterwards and traveled to Dulles to take a flight to JFK, where he planned to guard Laura before her flight to Paris.

The train ride was uneventful. She was overlooked by the early morning business crowd and sensed no danger. Once she arrived at Penn Station, Laura took a shuttle to JFK, where she used an Irene Thomas credit card to pay for her flight to Paris. She had a couple of hours before the flight, so she walked through the terminal to a coffee shop. She began to get the uncomfortable feeling she was being watched. She immediately entered a restroom with two entrances, leaving by the second exit. She slipped behind a food cart to watch the foot traffic in the terminal. When she saw Rick Williams, she was furious. She circled around and came up behind him. "What in the hell are you doing here?"

A surprised Rick Williams spun around. "Shit. You scared me."

"Two of us make a larger target."

"Steve and I wanted to make sure you're safe."

"No offense, Rick, but you're like a walking advertisement for spies. You attract attention."

Rick stiffened his resolve. "Well, get used to it because I'm following you to Paris."

"Oh God, please tell me this is some sort of joke."

"This is an arrangement I have with Steve and you'll just have to deal with it."

"Well, I'm taking the Concorde so I'll be long gone by the time you arrive."

"So am I," Rick countered.

"Fuck!" Laura nearly shouted. "You've been an immense help in the past and I'm grateful for it, but this time, I need to be alone."

"And you will be. Trust me; I'll only be there if you need me. Otherwise, I'll be in the background. You won't even know I'm there."

"Not know you're there? How'd I manage to get the drop on you?" Laura asked. Rick's face turned red from embarrassment. "Look, I don't mean to insult you," Laura continued, "but any good field agent could have done that."

"Let's just leave it at that. I'm going to turn my back and walk away. I'll see you on the plane." Rick smiled. He'd seen Laura's outbursts in the past. She was brilliant, a star within the agency, but with that brilliance came a volatility that took a bit of patience to endure.

As Laura Messier walked through Charles de Gaulle airport in Paris late that evening, she remembered the events of last fall. She sensed that Ilitch wouldn't stop. Checking into the Paris Marriott, she decided to act unafraid. An appearance in Paris would be unexpected by her enemies. Speed would be her ally. She'd be in Paris and then gone before her opponents could react.

Chapter Three

MAXIM KHOZIN LAY on his stomach at the crest of a hill about a hundred kilometers east of Vladikavkas, Chechnya, at dawn on a cold February morning. It was windy and damp in this God forsaken wilderness, miles from the nearest road, accessible only by horseback. Except, Khozin and his partner, Ivan Ilitch, didn't have horses. They had driven a Soviet issue Jeep until there were no roads left to follow, then walked for two days to arrive precisely at this spot where informants had told them their targets would be sleeping in a small cabin. Khozin and Ilitch had been sent to kill the men responsible for a raid on the Soviet military outpost in Vladikavkas some weeks before. With eight Soviet personnel dead, killed as they slept, and the building that housed them burned to the ground, a Soviet government response was required. However, sending a large detachment of troops nearly two thousand kilometers from Moscow to maintain order could incite open rebellion in a region long known for its resistance to outside rule. There was a tacit admission by the Soviet government, which had few resources in the region, that the population was largely ungovernable. To do nothing would encourage further violence against the small number of officials the Soviets sent to Vladikavkas from Grozny. Instead, they turned the matter over to the KGB, who sent their top sharpshooting team, Maxim

Khozin and Ivan Ilitch, to kill the commander of the rebel group responsible for the attack. That reprisal should be enough, the KGB reasoned, to send a strong message to the population that the Soviet presence should be tolerated.

Khozin and Ilitch had picked a spot among the rocks above the valley floor where the cabin and its associated outbuildings, a barn and an outhouse, were located. They had watched the cabin for three days to learn the patterns of the men living there. Saddling horses in the morning, riding off to unknown places and returning before sunset, Khozin and Ilitch counted four men, one of whom stayed to guard the cabin during the daytime. Khozin had no idea where they rode each morning, but they arrived back at the cabin each evening with supplies strung over their horses. Either the local population was supporting them or they were robbing the few farms in the area. Khozin thought the former was true. These men were true partisans, a throwback to previous generations of hardscrabble men who lived off the land and were suspicious of authority. They were tough, hard men who knew how to fight.

The men in the cabin drew their water from a small creek that ran the length of the valley, runoff from the melting snow on the mountains nearby. Upon returning at dusk each evening from wherever they had gone, they'd carry water from the creek back to the cabin and clean their weapons while sitting on stumps of newly felled trees. They'd unsaddle their horses and lead them to the dilapidated barn a few meters from the cabin. Afterward, Khozin would see smoke from the chimney, and when the wind blew in his direction, smelled food the men prepared for themselves. Khozin had no idea whether these men were responsible for the attack on the military outpost, but it seemed likely. Their voices carried far beyond the cabin and Khozin heard them laughing about the Soviets they had killed as they relaxed in the evening outside the cabin, smoking rolled tobacco and eating food off Soviet issue mess kits they had somehow acquired. They were loud because they thought themselves to be safe and Khozin gave them no reason to think otherwise. He didn't use his scope in the evening, afraid the glint from the glass might give his position away. Khozin and Ilitch had covered themselves with a brown tarp to blend into the rocks. They moved as infrequently as possible to avoid any sound or movement that might compromise them. They ate relatively little, only the rations that ordinary Soviet soldiers carried in the field. They drank even less, each drawing only two canteens of water upstream from the same creek the partisans used. Khozin and Ilitch were careful because the partisans often patrolled the valley, galloping up and down the creek for miles, looking for signs of human presence. The men had seen nothing, of course, because Khozin and Ilitch were professional killers, the best the Soviet system could produce.

Maxim Khozin was the spotter for Ilitch, and Khozin knew the best way to kill these men would be from a distance. Luckily, Ilitch was the best marksman Khozin had ever worked with, perhaps the best in all the Soviet Union. Khozin respected Ilitch, a young man driven to succeed and eager to escape the shadow of his illustrious forefathers. They had known each other since childhood, both coming to Moscow University from Leningrad. Khozin was a famous name in the Soviet Union. Maxim's grandfather helped lead the defense of Leningrad during the Second World War. Ivan's grandfather fought right beside him. Ivan's father had risen through the ranks of the Communist Party to occupy a seat in the Politburo. Ivan and Maxim were determined to make names for themselves at any cost, from their distinguished service in Afghanistan to their present duties doing contract work for the KGB. They would endure any hardship, overcome any obstacle and take whatever risk was required to complete their missions. There were plenty of hardships to overcome on this mission. Khozin and Ilitch had carried their supplies for nearly 40 kilometers over rough terrain, sleeping in the open without a campfire, picking up their litter to leave no trace for those who might follow them. Once arriving at the cabin, they had rarely moved a muscle under their tarp. They ate, slept, urinated and defecated all within a meter of where they lay. Through rain, the snow that had covered them the night before, the wind and cold, Khozin and Ilitch were as tough and hard as the men they watched.

Ilitch planned to attack shortly after dawn when the targets would be sleepy and ill prepared to defend themselves. The shooting position above the cabin was to the east so Ilitch's targets would be looking into the rising sun to return fire. The men would be closely grouped, saddling their horses, which the guard brought from the barn each morning and tied to a hitching post in front of the cabin. With a ten round capacity Dragunov sniper rifle, Ilitch was confident he could take all four men at once. If he happened to miss, he knew they'd grab their rifles and he'd be in a firefight, so he was determined to give himself every advantage. *Today is the day*, he thought. Clear sky, no wind, and the men unaware they were being watched. No further advantage could be found.

The sun had risen, but had not yet reached the valley floor; that would take another fifteen minutes or so. Khozin could see smoke rising from the cabin chimney. "Ivan, they're awake."

"What's the guard doing?" Ilitch asked.

"He's in the outhouse."

"Soon to be followed by the others, no doubt," Ilitch said.

"Unless they piss outside the door again."

"How long until they saddle the horses?"

"About twenty minutes."

"We should get ready," Ilitch said.

"Today's the day?"

"Yes. I've seen enough. Let's get this business done and get the hell out of here."

"Thank you. I'm tired of shitting in my pants," Khozin responded with a chuckle. He pulled his own rifle off his back and quietly unpacked a third, making sure both were fully loaded with ammunition. They now had three Dragunov sniper rifles ready. Khozin was not nearly the marksman that Ilitch was, but he could fight, if needed. Khozin picked up his scope and stared. "The guard left the outhouse and is bringing the horses out of the barn."

"Where are the saddles?"

"Right where they were yesterday, thrown up against the side of the cabin."

"Position of the sun?" Ilitch asked. He dared not turn

around and look to the sun himself. It would take too long for his vision to re-adjust.

"Ten minutes to reach the valley floor."

"Let's hope they take their time. I need the light." For the first time this morning, Ilitch surveyed the scene through the scope on his rifle. "Wind?" he asked.

"Wind is calm," Khozin responded.

"Range to target?"

"510."

"A fair day's work, I think," Ilitch said.

"I've seen you hit targets at twice that distance."

"Yes, but four in a row? All within seconds? What the hell does Moscow expect of me?"

"Look at it this way. If we don't kill them, they'll track us down with the horses," Khozin said.

"I guess I better not miss," Ilitch said with a smile.

"Could you find a better mission for us next time?"

"Work will pick up now that spring is approaching," Ilitch answered. "Petrovsky will keep us busy. Remember, we've got unfinished business in Washington."

"Think you could book us a vacation in the Bahamas after Washington?" Khozin asked.

"What's the matter? Cuba not good enough for you?"

"The hotels are dirty, the women are fat and the liquor sucks. Only thing good about it is the cigars. The sun should reach the cabin in five minutes." Ilitch looked through his scope again.

"Two days walking, three days watching, eating nothing but fucking military rations. I'm ready to get back to Moscow," Ilitch complained.

"The guard has gone inside the cabin," Khozin reported.

"Okay, reach around and grab the comms out of the knapsack just in case we get separated."

Khozin rolled on his side and unpacked the battery operated headsets. "Here," Khozin said, as he handed one to Ilitch. Both men put them around their heads and turned them on. "Check," Khozin whispered into his microphone.

"Copy," Ilitch said. "Maxim, when these guys come out, one or more will head to the outhouse. They'll take their weapons with them. The others will prop them against the cabin while they saddle the horses. I'm going to take the last guy out of the cabin first, right in the doorway. I should get a second shot before they hear the sound of the first. Hopefully, two of them will be down by the time they realize what's happening. The other two will grab their weapons and try to get back in the cabin. I need you to pour fire into the doorway to prevent that. You think you can put something into a target that small?"

"I'll do my best," Khozin said, doubtful that he could actually do it.

"Well, you don't need to hit anything. Just shoot at the doorway. If they get back in that cabin, we'll never get them out."

"Done."

"Just so you know, if I miss and they use the horses as shields, I'll have to shoot them, too, so be prepared for a long walk back to the Jeep," Ilitch said with a bit of sarcasm.

"Well, don't miss then. I'm so fucking tired of walking," Khozin complained. "The sun has reached the roof of the cabin. They should be coming out any moment."

Ilitch used the door to the cabin as a target to focus his shot. "Make sure you have the other rifle ready. You just keep shooting at the doorway with yours."

"Got it."

"I can't believe that fucking woman opened the refrigerator door right as I squeezed off the round," Ilitch said.

"You talking about Washington?"

"Yes."

"Bad luck."

"It could be nasty business next time," Ilitch warned. "I'm going to have to take her at close range."

"Why would that be a problem?"

"Petrovsky says she's as good as we are. It could get messy."

"Tell him to forget the woman," Khozin said.

"He won't. I have no idea why, but he insists we finish the job."

"The cabin door just opened."

"Yes, I see it," Ilitch said. "Let's go."

The first man stepped out of the cabin and headed to the outhouse. The second and third men came out nearly together, stepped off the stoop and turned to saddle the horses. The fourth man appeared in the doorway and stood there for a second, adjusting his vision to the bright sunlight. He looked around before stepping off the stoop. *That's their leader*, Ilitch thought, as he squeezed off the first shot. It hit the man in the stomach and Ilitch instinctively shifted his aim just a bit and shot another of the men dead center in the back as he propped his weapon against the cabin. He went down immediately. The remaining men reacted quickly when they heard the shots. The man walking to the outhouse sprinted behind it, while the only man left in front of the cabin moved behind one of the horses. Ilitch put two more rounds into the man in the doorway, now doubled over in pain. He fell on the stoop and didn't move. Ilitch put two rounds into the horse which protected the man hiding behind it, and the horse began to fall, leaving the man exposed. Ilitch didn't get an opportunity to put his kill shot into him as the man behind the outhouse began firing at the rocks. His aim was precise and the rounds hit the rocks immediately below Khozin and Ilitch.

"Damn, that guy's good," Ilitch said, as they were sprayed with rock fragments. "Looks like we're in a firefight." The man behind the falling horse was able to guide the animal to the ground and established a position lying on the ground using the horse to protect himself. "We've got to outflank them. Take my Dragunov. I'll use my sidearm," Ilitch said, handing his rifle to Khozin. "You've got three rifles. Keep them busy while I circle around and get behind the cabin."

"Yes, Sir," Khozin said, and he began firing alternatively at each of the two men. "I'll hold them in place."

Ilitch pushed himself back from the crest of the rock outcropping and ran around the backside of the rocks to a point where he could run down the hill behind the cabin. "Maxim!" he shouted into the comm. "Keep the guy at the outhouse busy. I'm in his line of sight." Khozin began firing repeatedly at the corner of the outhouse where he'd seen the man shoot. But the man had moved to the opposite corner and shot at Ilitch as he ran down the hill. He fired twice in succession and Ilitch felt the breeze of the rounds as they whizzed by.

"Fuck," Ilitch muttered as he took cover behind the cabin.

"They're talking to each other," Khozin said into the comm. "The guy in front knows you're behind him."

"Copy that," Ilitch responded. Ilitch entered the back door of the cabin. He moved through the cabin to a small window right above where the man lay behind his dead horse. The target had turned himself around and was waiting for Ilitch to appear around the corner. Ilitch shot him twice through the window. As soon as he fired, two shots came smashing through the window from the outhouse. "Who is that fucking guy?" Ivan asked. "Maxim, I think the guy in front is down, but I'm not sure. I'm going around back and come up behind him to make sure."

Ilitch retraced his steps, went out the back door of the cabin and made his way around to the front hoping he'd have a shot at the one remaining man. He glanced quickly around the corner and withdrew. The man put a round right at the corner where Ilitch hid. Ilitch was showered with splinters. Two horses were still tied to the hitching post, straining at the reins, trying to break free and bolt. "Maxim, the man in front is dead. When I give you the word, put as much ammo as you can right into the outhouse. I think the rounds are going all the way through, so he'll have to keep low. Wait until I give you the word."

"Yes, Sir," Khozin replied.

Ilitch got on his stomach and crawled along the front

wall of the cabin, using the horses to shield him from view. He reached up and untied one of the horses. Slowly standing up, he stroked the horse to calm him. "There, there now, fellow. Nobody's going to hurt you." He firmly took the horse by the halter and began walking toward the outhouse using the horse for protection.

"Now, Maxim, now!"

Khozin poured fire into the outhouse, but the man saw Ilitch's approach and immediately shot the horse. As the horse began to fall, Ilitch had a choice to either go down to the ground with the horse and use its body for protection or keep standing to get a clear shot at his opponent. Ilitch chose the latter and for a brief second, both men stared at each other. The man had an easy shot at Ilitch standing in the open and raised his rifle into firing position. That's all the time Ilitch needed. He had already gauged distance, height and body position. Ilitch fired twice and the man's head exploded in blood. He fell to the ground, dead instantly.

"We got him. All clear," Ilitch said into the comm. "I'm going to walk around to make sure everyone's dead. Come down and bring our stuff with you. Leave nothing behind."

Ilitch kept his sidearm in firing position as he checked the man behind the outhouse. Although the man was dead, Ilitch spoke to him briefly. "You were a worthy opponent, my friend. In another life, perhaps we'll know each other. Forgive this one last transgression." He shot the man one last time and then proceeded to approach the men lying in front of the cabin. The leader, sprawled in the doorway, was still breathing. He looked up at Ilitch.

"Who are you?" he asked.

"No one you'd know," Ilitch answered, right before giving the man a round in the head. The other two were dead. Khozin came running down from the rocks. "Damn, you exposed yourself on that last shot, Ivan."

"Nothing else to do. I had to end it quickly. Anyone within hearing distance will be here soon and they won't be friendly. Saddle the horse left at the hitch and there should be another in the barn. I'll search the cabin for intel. Let's get the fuck out of here before anyone arrives."

"One question?" Khozin asked.

"What?"

"How the fuck do you saddle a horse?"

"Jesus, Maxim. Didn't they teach you anything at KGB training? Search the house, I'll saddle the horses. If you find food, bring it and fill the canteens, too. Quickly."

Khozin and Ilitch mounted the horses, rode to where they had hidden their Jeep and arrived back in Vladikavkas late the following day, where they transferred their belongings to an auto they had driven from Grozny. The townspeople took no notice of them, but they hurried nonetheless. They drove back to the Soviet military base in Grozny where they enjoyed their first shower and hot meal in a week. They hitched a ride on a Soviet military transport headed for Moscow a day later and once aboard, they disappeared because no official file existed for either Khozin or Ilitch anywhere at KGB headquarters. They worked directly for Viktor Petrovsky, the Chairman of the KGB, under verbal orders only. They were ghosts.

***

Laura woke early on Thursday morning at the Paris Marriott wondering if she'd ever call Paris home again. She and Steve still owned the property at 51 Rue Cler in the Seventh Arrondissement, but Steve had made arrangements with a management company to rent the upper floor apartments to tourists. Laura fought the urge to drive by the place.

She wondered whether she should make an appearance at the American Embassy. Wherever she appeared, sooner or later, Ivan Ilitch would find out. She knew she needed to be seen to confuse the Soviets as to her whereabouts, but she couldn't stay in Paris long enough to expose herself to danger.

She had a croissant and coffee in the hotel restaurant, half expecting to be recognized, but this was a slow week for diplomats in Paris. No dignitaries were present in the hotel. The hotel restaurant was filled with businessmen and what few tourists visited during the winter. *Winter is a good time to visit Paris*, she thought. Hotel prices are at their lowest. She caught a glimpse of Rick Williams standing in the lobby, but he didn't bother her. She felt more relaxed than at any time since she'd returned to Washington. Paris was her home.

Laura exited the front entrance of the hotel. Looking for surveillance and finding none, she took a taxi to the Marais district to visit Jean. His club didn't open until lunch time, but she knew Jean arrived each morning well before it opened. When the bouncer unlocked the door, he motioned for her to come in. She followed him to the bar, where the bartender was restocking for the daily opening.

"Please have a seat at the bar and Mr. Broussard will be with you shortly."

The bartender looked up. "Can I get you something to drink, Mademoiselle?" Laura heard Jean answer him over her shoulder.

"Franz, she takes coffee with heavy cream and sugar. Am I right, Mademoiselle?"

"Jean," Laura said, spinning around on the bar stool. He put his arms around her and gave her a hug followed by a kiss on each cheek. "And yes, you're right; heavy cream and sugar."

"You grow more beautiful every time I see you. Monsieur Tilton is a lucky man."

"It's so good to see you, old friend," Laura said. "You're looking well."

"It's wise of you to come with a bit of protection, I think."

"You spotted him?"

"Captain Williams? Yes, he's on the roof of the building across the street. Well, he was on the roof. We captured him and brought him inside to avoid attracting attention."

"How'd you see him so fast?" Laura asked.

Jean laughed. "Trade secrets, Mademoiselle. Spies never tell all we know," Jean said with a wry smile. "Why don't we invite him to meet with us?"

Laura giggled. "Why not?"

The bartender returned with cups of coffee for Laura and Jean. Jean motioned with his hand and two security guards walked Rick into the room, hands cuffed behind his back.

"They got the drop on me," he said sheepishly. Laura and Jean began laughing. The guards released him. "Do you have to laugh about it?"

"Don't feel bad, Rick. Jean's one of the best agents in the world. Even I couldn't outsmart him."

"No, but you could seduce me," Jean said with a smile.

"Jean, you are a delightful man."

"Captain Williams, may we serve you something to drink?"

"No thank you, Mr. Broussard. I'm fine."

Jean turned his attention back to Laura. "Yes, it's true that I'm a wonderful man," he said teasingly. "Now, what brings you all the way from Washington on a false passport?"

"How do you know I traveled on a false passport?" Laura asked.

"Because to do otherwise would be a risk unworthy of you, Mademoiselle."

Laura smiled, "You know me too well, Jean. I'm here looking for someone."

"Aha! And this man is to become a future lover?"

She laughed, "Nothing that exciting, I'm afraid."

"Then tell me about this man you're looking for."

"His name is Ivan Ilitch."

"That name is unknown to me." He thought for a moment. "I do not believe he exists in DST files. He's Russian?"

"Yes. He tried to kill me in Washington a few months

ago. It's only by luck that I'm still alive."

Jean paused before he spoke again. "Did the CIA investigate the attack?"

"They think the assassination attempt was a random act of violence," Laura said.

"So, they don't believe Ilitch had anything to do with it?"

"They don't know about Ilitch."

"They didn't investigate thoroughly?"

"They relied on the Washington D.C. Police Department to do the investigation. I found Ilitch's name by calling a source I have in the East German Stazi. He identified Ilitch as the shooter."

"And you trust this source, Mademoiselle?"

"Implicitly."

"I see," Jean said. "So you didn't mention Ilitch's name at the CIA?"

"No. There's a Soviet mole at CIA and I was concerned about a leak. I'm going to find him on my own."

"Mademoiselle, you have dual citizenship. Legally, you are a French citizen. The Republic of France does not look kindly upon attempts to kill its citizens. I suggest we run this through the DST. Let's get them interested. Perhaps we'll obtain the legal authority we need to find him."

"What about CIA?"

"Let's leave them on the sidelines for the moment. The Republic of France does not need the permission of the United States to protect one of its citizens. If the CIA believes you were the victim of a random act of violence, we shall do nothing to persuade them otherwise."

"Thank you, Jean. I knew you'd help."

"No need for thanks, Mademoiselle. It's in the interest

of the French government to look for this man. We've heard rumors for years that Petrovsky uses assassination squads. They don't exist in KGB files. They're carefully hidden and impossible to find. What else did the source tell you?"

"He's in his thirties, single, no children. Lives in Moscow."

"That's it?"

"Not much to start with, I know. CIA did get a thumb print off the rifle he left behind. Ran it through every database they've got. It turned up nothing."

"Well, perhaps we can match it to a cold case somewhere. What kind of rifle?"

"A Dragunov."

"A Russian sniper weapon, isn't it?"

"Yes," she replied

"What are you doing tomorrow?"

"I was going to get in touch with Fareed Hassan."

"Hassan has retired to an estate in Tuscany. His position in the Libyan government became unstable after the bombing last year."

"He was your source inside the Libyan government?"

"Yes, he was our double agent. In what manner do you believe Hassan could help you?" Jean asked.

"He has contacts. He may know of Ilitch."

"If Ilitch is the man we're seeking, we shouldn't spread any word of it. Any mention of his name could find its way back to Moscow. Can you and Captain Williams meet me at DST Headquarters in the morning?" Jean asked.

"Of course."

"Let's meet in the lobby at 10:00 am. I'll talk to my superiors and find out if they want to pursue it."

"Thank you, Jean."

"You're welcome. May I suggest something else, Mademoiselle?"

"Of course," Laura said.

"You're probably thinking you should avoid the American Embassy, correct?"

"The CIA would be highly displeased if they knew I was in Paris."

"I think you should walk right in the front door this afternoon. Make no attempt to conceal yourself. We might have a better chance of finding Ilitch if he were actively looking for you in Paris. Meet me tomorrow morning and we'll discuss it further."

Laura and Rick caught a taxi to the American Embassy where they knew they'd be seen by foreign intelligence agencies that monitor foot traffic in and out of the building. "Let's hope someone doesn't take a shot at us," Rick said, looking around as they exited the taxi.

"The Soviets don't go to the bathroom without permission. It's unlikely they'll bother us until they get orders from Moscow."

"I hope you're right," Rick said nervously.

Inside the entrance, both were recognized and welcomed by the staff. "Captain Williams, such a pleasure to see you back in town," the guard said. "You too, Ms. Messier."

"Hi, Jeff. Is Chief Brownley upstairs?" Laura asked.

"Yes, Ma'am. Let me call up and let him know you're here." Once they'd been cleared, they walked through the lobby and around the corner to the elevator as they had done so often in the past.

"Kind of good to be back," Rick said.

"Yes, it is," Laura replied.

Once upstairs, Brownley's secretary greeted them and ushered them into his office. "Hang on a minute," Brownley said, motioning them to chairs in front of his desk. Laura and Rick sat down. Brownley pushed a button underneath his desk, "Tape stop," he said. He turned to Laura. "Well, this is a surprise. Does Langley know you're here?"

"I'm afraid not, John."

"It's good to see you. How are you doing?"

"I think we're both doing well," Laura answered.

"How's life as an intelligence man, Rick?"

"Boring, Sir. I've been doing hand to hand combat instruction at the Farm."

Brownley laughed. "And you, Laura? Keeping busy?"

"Doing research at Langley when I'm not being shot at."

"Shot at?" asked Brownley.

"Someone tried to kill me in Washington."

"Who?"

"Well, D.C. Metro never found him," Laura explained. "They determined it was a random act of violence."

"That doesn't sound right, not after what happened last fall."

"I didn't agree with it, but the agency dropped it."

"Let me guess," Brownley said. "You're doing your own investigation."

"I am, but don't worry. I'm not asking for help."

"I'm more concerned for your welfare. We don't have the manpower to protect you."

"We're not asking for anything," Rick said. "This is

89

more of a ..." Rick thought for a moment, "... a social visit."

"In other words, you want to be seen entering the embassy," Brownley surmised.

"That's right."

Brownley looked at Laura. "You realize I'm supposed to report your presence to Langley, don't you?"

"I expected you would," Laura answered.

"Well, I won't. If there's anything I can do to help, let me know."

"You're a good man, John. Thanks."

"Are you staying at the apartment?"

"No," she said, "we're at the Marriott downtown."

"Want a man in the lobby? I can probably spare one."

"No, I think we'll be fine. As Rick said, this is just a courtesy call to let you know we're in town. We'll be leaving Saturday morning."

"You have our emergency number? You're still an agency employee."

"Of course," Laura said. "We'll take no more of your time today, John."

"All right then. Use the emergency number if you need it."

Laura and Rick entered the front entrance at DST Headquarters promptly at 10:00 am the following morning. "Smile, Rick. Your picture's being taken," Laura said with a chuckle as they exited the taxi.

"By whom?" Rick asked.

"The Soviets, East Germans, Mossad, even the Brits. Someone will get a visual on us. I guess that makes you an intelligence officer."

"Not a bad way to make a living. As far as I can tell,

you guys don't do much," Rick said with a smile.

"Not really funny," she said as Rick opened the door for her.

Jean Broussard was waiting in the lobby and after giving a firm handshake to Rick, he greeted Laura warmly. She smelled that cologne again. She'd never told him how much she liked it. "Good morning, Mademoiselle, good morning. You look more beautiful each time I see you. If only I were thirty years younger, no?"

"I just might have to steal you away from your wealthy lover in the south of France," Laura said with a smile.

"Come; let's meet another old friend of yours."

After clearing security, Jean led them to a conference room where Laura found Jacques Martin, the DST representative at the French Embassy in Tripoli who helped Laura escape Libya the previous April. "Jacques, how wonderful to see you," Laura said. "This is my associate, Captain Rick Williams, United States Marine Corp."

Jacques Martin looked like a college professor, round metal framed glasses, medium build, and dark hair. He had a calm, studious manner about him. Jacques was a thinker. He greeted both of them warmly. "It's my pleasure to see you again, Laura, and nice to meet you, Captain Williams."

"You've been re-assigned to Paris?" Laura asked.

"Yes. We rotate in and out of the country from time to time. I'm happy to be home for a couple of years. Can I offer you refreshments?"

"No thanks, I'm fine."

"Captain Williams?" Jacques asked.

"No thank you."

"Please sit. We're expecting one more person, but let's go ahead and get started."

They sat at a beautiful conference table adorned with a fresh flower arrangement. *Typically French*, Laura thought. *CIA could use some of their ambiance*. Before they began, a fifth person entered the room, Henri Thomas, the man who escorted Laura back to Paris last April.

"Oh my God! It's Henri." Henri was a huge man, very strong with gray speckled hair and a wonderful smile. He was one of the kindest people Laura had ever met. He gave Laura a hug. Henri's big arms enveloped her, just as they had when they'd left Tripoli. She felt safe with Henri around.

"It is wonderful to see you, Laura. Sorry I'm late, Jacques."

"This is Captain Rick Williams, Henri," Jacques said.

"Good to see you again, Rick."

"You know each other?" Jacques asked.

"Yes," Rick said. "Henri and I worked together at the hospital last April."

"Ah, I remember now. Rashid Nazari. That was nasty business," Jacques said.

"Very," Rick said.

"Let's get down to business, shall we? This will comprise a working group charged with doing a preliminary investigation into an attempted assassination of a French citizen. This group has the status of an official investigation and I'm required to report its findings to the Director. Let's start by asking you to describe what happened, Laura."

"A shot was fired from a Soviet made Dragunov sniper

rifle into my Washington residence last November from a distance of about 500 meters, an extraordinary shot made over rooftops, through trees and a window. It was taken by a first class marksman, Jacques. Subsequent shots were fired at the windows of my home and a CIA employee was wounded. We never found the shooter, although the weapon was recovered in a trash bin a day later."

"Jean told me the investigation was done by the local police. Is that true?" Jacques asked.

"Yes."

"Strange. The CIA did no investigation at all?"

"Just a search through their records for a thumb print found on the weapon. The D.C. police concluded it was a random act of violence. When CIA couldn't match the print, they accepted the finding and dropped the case."

"Obviously, you thought differently. You believed it to be another attempt by the Soviets to kill you, something they've tried in the past. You did an investigation of your own and came up with a name?"

"Ivan Ilitch."

"Have you informed the CIA of this name?"

"No," Laura replied.

"May I ask why?"

"There's a Soviet mole at CIA, Jacques. I was afraid the information might be passed to the Soviets and I'd lose my chance to find him."

"Can you reveal how you obtained Ilitch's name?"

"I have a highly placed source within the East German Stazi, Markus Wolf. I called him for help and he identified Ilitch."

"Why would he do that?"

"I suspect that he's looking for friends in the West in

case he needs to defect."

"Laura, we experience political assassinations in France from time to time that are never solved. In fact, Interpol has a long list of such incidents around Europe. We've long suspected Soviet involvement, but we've never had a name before. We'd like to pursue it. Since you're a French citizen, we can legally act upon it."

"I'd appreciate your assistance, Jacques."

"Let's set some rules for the investigation. First, we keep it in-house. In other words, if we decide to go outside the DST, we make that decision as a group. Second, I must get the approval of our director for any action we take. Do we have agreement on those points?"

"Yes, absolutely," Laura said.

"You, Captain Williams?"

"Yes, of course," Rick said.

"We're going to need to meet as new information is discovered," Jacques continued. "Has the CIA restricted your ability to travel?"

"I can travel as a private citizen."

"Good. I did a bit of research, Mademoiselle, and found that your employment with the French government was covered under an unusual arrangement with the CIA. That agreement is ongoing so I took the liberty of having you transferred from the Foreign Ministry to us. You'll receive compensation as any other DST agent and we'll pay your travel expenses for the period of the investigation. I'm sorry I cannot extend that status to you, Captain, but we have a special category called ex-officio under which we can pay your travel expenses. Is that satisfactory to both of you?"

"That's very generous, Jacques," Laura said.

"Captain Williams?
"Thank you, Mr. Martin. I accept."

Jacques hesitated, thinking about administrative details before he continued. "I'll ask our Director to call the CIA to inform them of our investigation and request that you and Captain Williams be available to us as needed. To insure secrecy, we're giving each of you French passports to travel under assumed names. Following this meeting, please accompany Jean to have passport photos taken. We'll drop the passports off at your hotel, along with the underlying documents. Make sure you retrieve them before you leave."

"Thank you," Laura said.

"Now, regarding the investigation. We've had time for a preliminary search of our files, but we've learned we may be looking for two men, not one. We've found a person who seems to be closely associated with Ivan Ilitch, a man named Maxim Khozin. We believe both Ilitch and Khozin to be thirty-three years of age and may have known each other as children. Ilitch's family moved to Moscow so the father could serve on the Soviet Central Committee and subsequently in the Politburo. We believe both men became reacquainted at university in Moscow. Both served in the Red Army upon graduation and served in the same unit in Afghanistan. Here is a picture of what we think is both of them together during their time in the Army."

Jacques removed a picture from a file folder. It was passed around the table. Ilitch and Khozin were circled in red pencil. "After a year in Afghanistan," he continued, "they disappeared. There are no records to be found for either of them. This, we suspect, is when they entered the Soviet Special Forces."

"This is excellent research," Laura observed.

"Thank you. From this point, its conjecture, but we suspect Ilitch was trained to be a sniper and Khozin his spotter. We believe they work as an assassination team for the Chairman of the Committee for State Security, Viktor Petrovsky. We've got people trying to put together a history of their movements using dates of unsolved assassinations as a starting point."

"What can we do to help?" Laura asked.

"We need irrefutable evidence that Ilitch is our man. The burden of proof is very high for something of this nature."

"I understand," Laura said.

"We'll ask the Washington Police to share information about their investigation and I'd ask the two of you," Jacques said referring to Laura and Rick, "to do whatever research is possible at Langley so we can pull together profiles of Ilitch and Khozin. We need the information quickly. I would imagine Ilitch will attempt to finish his assignment with regards to you, Laura, rather soon."

"When do you want us back?" Laura asked.

"One week from today. We'll have another meeting to gauge our progress. By the way, credit cards will be enclosed with your identification. We've established a budget for the investigation and you can charge your travel to those cards."

"Thank you so very much, Jacques."

"Now, Laura, I'm going to ask you to do a bit of public relations work."

"I don't understand," Laura said.

"We want to make sure you're seen in Paris, so we're going to make it obvious. The Soviet Ambassador takes his lunch near here, so we've asked Foreign Minister Raimond to lunch there also and include you in his party. Can you do that for us?"

"Absolutely. Monsieur Raimond is a dear friend of mine."

"Good. We've got a car waiting for you downstairs. Have a great lunch and I expect to see both of you next Friday morning."

Lunch with Foreign Minister Raimond went smoothly and although the Soviet Ambassador was in the room, it was impossible to ascertain whether Laura was noticed. Rick, looking out the back window of the taxi on the way back to the hotel, asked, "Are we okay here?"

"What do you mean?" Laura asked.

"Is anyone following us?"

"Relax, Rick. If we had picked up a tail, I'd know about it," Laura said.

"You sure about that?"

"Rick, you've been doing this for a couple of months. I've done it for ten years. Yes, I'm sure."

Leaving the hotel Saturday morning, Laura and Rick picked up the package of documents from the concierge and while waiting, Laura found herself instinctively scanning the lobby. She found nothing unusual, nor did she notice anything out of place at the airport. It seemed to be a routine travel day.

***

After arriving back in Washington, a message awaited Laura on Monday morning at the CIA security station asking her to report to Director Bill Bates. Arriving at his office on the seventh floor, she was ushered in immediately. "Hi Bill, what's up?"

Bill looked up from his desk. "I received a call from French Intelligence this morning informing me you'll be working with them on a part-time basis. We also received a note from D.C. Metro. They forwarded records from the shooting at your house. Is DST investigating the attack on you?"

"I asked them for help."

"Why?"

"Isn't it obvious? I'm unhappy with the job Metro did."

"Laura, not every act of violence can be explained. Has Steve hired private security?"

"Yes, of course."

"Then you've taken the precautions you need." Bates leaned back in his chair and looked away for a minute, thinking of what he wanted to say. "The French have asked for our cooperation and, of course, they'll receive it. Personally, I think it's a waste of time. Any work you do on this must be your own time. Understand?"

"Yes, Sir."

Laura walked out of Bates' office frustrated by his inaction. *Another agency whitewash*, she thought. *On the other hand, he doesn't know about Ilitch*, she reasoned. *Give Bates a break. He's just trying to do his job.*

Laura began the arduous task of combing CIA files again, this time armed with new information. She mistakenly ignored the history of the name Ilitch because it didn't help her find any current information. Once she began researching name histories, she found some of the same family information the French had uncovered. Khozin, as it turned out, was a famous name in Soviet history dating back to World War II. Current records showed nothing, however. The CIA concentrated more on Afghan rebels than the Red Army. The CIA had been providing arms and logistical support to the rebels. She found nothing that would lead her to Ivan Ilitch or Maxim Khozin.

The following week, Laura discovered the French working group had uncovered nothing new, either. "Jacques, we're at a dead end here," Jean said bluntly at the next meeting. "To take this investigation further, we need to use our source in the Kremlin."

"Sorry, Jean," Jacques responded. "We can't burn him."

"What are we waiting for, Jacques? Another assassination?"

"Jean, I'll make the request, but frankly, the information we obtain from that source is too valuable to risk exposure. We've got to look at other alternatives." The room was silent for a minute before Jean pressed his point further.

"We've got a name, Jacques, something we never had before," Jean said with urgency in his voice. "This is an opportunity to solve a number of high profile assassinations."

"Jean, as I said, I'll look into the matter. That's all I'm prepared to say at this point." There was silence in the room again as people wondered if the investigation had come to an end.

"Suppose we staged a mock assassination," Laura began.

"And hire the Soviets to carry it out?" Jacques asked Laura, relieved that someone had another idea.

"Yes."

"An assassination of you?"

"That's the idea," Laura answered.

"You're thinking they'd send Ilitch?"

"He failed the first time, so yes, I think they'd send him again."

"How do we hire the Soviets to kill you?" Jacques asked. "That sounds strange." That brought laughter to the group.

"We'd need an intermediary, Jacques," Jean said. "Someone the Soviets trust." He turned to Laura, "Does the Mademoiselle have anyone in mind?"

"Gaddafi," she said simply.

"How would we convince ..." Jacques didn't finish the question. He merely smiled and said, "Fareed Hassan," after he realized the answer.

"Exactly," Laura said.

"Fareed Hassan?" Rick asked.

"Former head of Libyan Intelligence," Laura answered. "French double agent. He left Libya right before the bombing last spring."

"Hassan is not to be trusted, Jacques," Jean warned.

"I believe that's what the Mademoiselle is counting on, Jean," Jacques said.

Turning to Jean, Laura said, "Hassan must have some kind of agreement with Gaddafi to remain safe. Otherwise,

Gaddafi would have him killed. My guess is they're still in contact. Does anyone know where we can find him?"

"He runs his wife's farm outside Monteriggioni, Italy," Jacques added.

"His wife's Italian?"

"Yes."

"Where's Monteriggioni?" Laura asked.

"A small town in Tuscany, south of Florence," Jacques explained.

"Jean, if I arranged to meet Hassan somewhere, say in Monteriggioni, would he report the meeting to Gaddafi?" Laura asked.

"He might," Jean said, "but I don't think he'd take the meeting."

"Why not?"

"He doesn't need anything from you. He took millions of dollars out of the country. He's not going to get involved. I think it's a dead end."

Henri, who had been silent in the meetings, spoke for the first time. "With all due respect, Laura, it's too risky. Jacques and I know Hassan personally. Jean's right. Hassan's played both sides so long we'd never be able to trust him. I believe we have only two options. Either we give up our source or Laura goes back to her source in Stazi. My feeling is we must use our own."

Jacques knew Henri's judgment was sound. "All right," he said reluctantly. "Our source is an electronics expert named Jack Postl. He's 26, originally from Czechoslovakia, worked for the Communist Party in Prague and was transferred to Moscow to build computer systems for Kremlin offices. He's something of a genius.

He builds computers small enough to sit on a desk and, apparently, he's been successful connecting these devices together in networks," Jacques said.

"And he wants out," Jean added.

"That's correct. He reached out to us a year ago using a computer network connected to a telephone line. He's been passing electronic records to us ever since with the hope we'll get him out."

"I think it's time we went and got him, Jacques," Jean said.

"As I said before, the Director will be reluctant to pull out our only source in the Kremlin."

"Are we to leave him there until he gets caught? He's an amateur, Jacques."

"I see your point, Jean. The decision isn't mine to make. For the Director to consider an exfil, I'd have to present a plan to show him how we'd do it. What do you have in mind?" Jacques asked.

"If we can meet again tomorrow, we'll have time to come up with something," Jean said.

"Good. Let's meet again tomorrow morning at ten o'clock."

"Excellent. Jacques, could you have a car swing around and pick us up? We need transportation to my club. We'll use it as a meeting place this afternoon. Mademoiselle, Captain Williams and Mr. Thomas, is that satisfactory?" The group nodded in the affirmative.

"Very good, Jean. There'll be a car waiting by the time you get downstairs."

The group had a pleasant lunch at a cafe near the DST building and then proceeded to Jean's nightclub. As they entered the club, Henri looked around the room. Jean smiled and rested his hand on Henri's arm. "Henri, my men do a sweep every week. No worries. We're totally secure."

Henri chuckled. "You read my mind, Jean."

Jean's club had closed after serving lunch to prepare for the evening's business. Jean's bartender lowered the blinds over the front windows to prevent pedestrians from peering into the club. The group sat at a large table in the middle of the room where Jean's bartender served drinks.

"Let's get to work, shall we?" Jean asked. "How would we exfil someone from Moscow?"

"What's the source's name again?" Laura asked.

"Jack Postl," Jean replied.

"Have you met him?"

"Once. Very intelligent. He's someone we can work with."

"Does he have physical skills?"

"He was a boxer. He received training in the Czech Olympic program. But his intellect is his real gift, Mademoiselle."

"Can he shoot?" Laura asked.

"Not that I know of, but I wouldn't want to get him angry. He's an imposing presence."

"That could be useful, I suppose."

"I think the Mademoiselle would like him."

"We've got to get a set of eyes on Ilitch, Jean. Would Postl be in a position to do that?" Laura asked.

"We should go talk to him. Let's ask him to travel home next weekend."

"To Czechoslovakia?"

"Yes," Jean replied. "His parents live in Prague."

"Here's the way I see this," Laura said. "There's a subway station underneath Lubyanka, but your people in Moscow could stand in the station forever and never know Ilitch got off a train. If we could get Postl inside the building, and identify Ilitch, then your men could follow him."

"Do you gentlemen have any comments?" Jean asked the others.

"I'd like to know who our Russian speakers are, besides me," Henri said. "If we have to go in there, we need to speak the language."

"I speak it well enough, but I doubt the Mademoiselle or Captain Williams do." Jean looked at Rick and Laura.

"Not me," Rick said.

"I only know the basics," Laura added.

"As long as two of us speak it, we can get by," Henri said.

"Postl will be fluent, so there are three of us," Jean said. "But we must give Jacques a plan." He looked at Laura. "Do you have any ideas?"

"If Postl builds computers, where does he get the parts?"

"We send them to him from a front company."

"Perfect. What if he tells his superiors that he's had parts damaged during shipping? He tells them he wants the parts shipped to, say, East Berlin, so he can travel there to personally check the shipment. Surely, they'd allow him travel there. We could bring him out through a checkpoint."

"How would we get him through the Brandenburg Gate?" Henri asked.

"I haven't figured that out yet." That brought a laugh to

the group.

"Every good plan has a little mystery in it, doesn't it?" Jean said with a chuckle. "Unless someone has a better idea, let's go with that one. We'll meet downtown tomorrow at ten and see what Jacques says," Jean said in summary.

The following morning, Jacques listened carefully to Laura and Jean explain their plan. "Look, here's my reaction," Jacques said. "Everyone understands Postl's got a shelf life that's coming to an end. He'll have to come out eventually. Maybe now is the time. But we ought to bring him out directly from Moscow. There are too many variables otherwise. I'll speak with the Director and present the idea that we need to get him. If we go ahead with this, we're going to have to meet with Postl first. Let's start with that. I'll contact everyone once the Director comes to a decision."

***

Back in Washington a few days later, Laura heard that a plan to rendezvous with Postl had been approved. The message instructed her to come to Paris immediately and accompany Jean to Prague. After an appropriate explanation to Steve, she took a flight from Dulles to Toronto, where she caught a connecting flight to Paris. She arrived early the next morning and took a taxi directly to DST headquarters. Laura met Jacques in his office. "Good morning, Jacques."

"Good morning. Thanks for coming so quickly, Mademoiselle. Jean should be here any moment. We've got you on a flight to Prague this afternoon. When Jean arrives, we'll discuss your cover, then have a car drop you at de Gaulle."

Jean arrived shortly after and apologized for being late. "Sorry, Jacques. Traffic."

Jacques glanced at his watch. "No worries. We've got enough time. The Director has approved a mission to exfil Postl directly from Moscow. We're sending you to Prague to discuss it with Postl. This is something he needs to hear in person. Let's go over your covers and get you on your way. You'll be computer sales people from Inline Computer Manufacturing, here in Paris. Inline is our front company. To the authorities, you'll say you're giving Postl a sales pitch on the company's newest line of products. Here's the literature you'll show customs if they ask." Jacques handed each of them copies. "Here are the rest of the documents you need to travel, plane tickets, hotel reservation, passports, credit cards and currency."

"Thank you, Jacques," Jean said.

"Be prepared to have your bags searched at customs. Make sure you carry no contraband, nothing except clothing and toiletries. You'll be shadowed by Czech Internal Security. They won't bother you, but don't venture out of the hotel alone. Postl knows you're coming. He'll have figured out how to meet, so follow his instructions. If for some reason he doesn't contact you, don't try to contact him. Stay in the hotel until your return flight and come home. Understood?"

"Yes," Jean said.

"One more thing, it's common for people from the West

to go through an interrogation at the airport. It doesn't mean anything's wrong. Stick to your cover and mention that they can verify your employment by calling the company phone number listed on your business cards. We have a receptionist at that location to accept calls and she can connect to a supervisor, a Mr. Pierre Dumont. You can mention him if you need a name. If you're detained, the French Embassy knows you're coming and will assist you. Any questions?"

"No. You've done a wonderful job, Jacques. Thank you," Laura said.

"Very good. Let's get you on your way. There should be a car downstairs to take you to the airport. Good luck."

Chapter Four

JACK POSTL ARRIVED at work promptly at eight o'clock on Monday morning, March 23rd, to find a note on his desk. He was summoned to the Kremlin to see his supervisor, Nikolai Gradovich, head of the ElectroTechnical Ministry. ElectroTechnical was responsible for the installation and maintenance of the computer systems used in government buildings across Moscow. Postl was head of one of the departments within the Ministry, a small group of computer technicians and programmers that worked solely on desktop computers. His office, tucked away in the basement of a building two blocks away, served as a workshop where he and his colleagues built the machines, programmed and tested their software.

Postl was well known in the offices of the Kremlin. His good looks and affable nature served him well as he made his way in and out of the various Ministries. He not only built and installed the machines, he also trained office personnel how to use them. His training courses were entertaining and informative, filled with suggestions about how to make the routine of administrative work easier using computer technology.

He usually drove a small truck filled with computer gear onto the Kremlin grounds each morning, which prompted guards at the gate to search his truck, but they had become accustomed to the routine of Postl driving through the gate. Over time, they had begun waving him through as he gained the trust of those who protected the complex. This morning, however, Postl decided to walk through the gate carrying only a briefcase.

"Morning, Mr. Postl," the guard at the entrance said.

"Good morning, Alex. How are you?"

"Very well, Sir, and you?"

"Great now that the weather's warming up," Postl replied as he handed the guard his identification.

"You're not bringing the truck in this morning?"

"I'll be driving in later today, but right now I'm due in the Minister's office for a meeting." The guard handed Postl's identification back.

"Very good, Sir. Have a pleasant day." The guard lifted the gate and Postl walked through onto the grounds.

Jack viewed the panorama of brightly painted domes and huge monolithic buildings as he walked. It was a gorgeous scene. *Lots of history around this place*, he thought. *The Czars, Napoleon, the revolution; this place is steeped in historical significance.* As Postl walked among the buildings, he thought about the path that had brought him from a small apartment in Prague to the seat of the Soviet empire.

Jack was the son of John and Esther Postl. His father, ambitious and talented, had founded a string of health clubs in Prague and made many contacts among the elite in the Communist Party. Jack took advantage of his father's contacts to gain a position in electronics with the

Communist Party following his graduation from university with a degree in electrical engineering. While working on Czech mainframe computers, Jack began to study the advanced computer technology emanating from the West.

Once Jack figured out how to access a computer network outside the country using telephone lines and a modem, he found a firm in France that would ship him the latest desktop computer parts from California. Using those parts, Jack and his staff began building desktop machines. Officials in Moscow were impressed enough to transfer Jack to the Kremlin where he installed the machines in Ministry offices. Authorities were more excited about the technology Jack gave them and less concerned with the manner in which Jack obtained it. Jack's backdoor communications with the West were ignored. Even a visit by a Western computer salesman from France, a man named Jean Broussard, was overlooked.

Jack wasn't political in the sense that he believed Communist Party propaganda. He didn't think about politics. He was enamored with emerging technologies, especially the work being done in Silicon Valley. When Jack inquired about the possibility of relocating to the West, he found a receptive partner in Broussard. They made a deal. Jack would send documents to the French in exchange for safe passage to the West. The arrangement turned out to be one sided, however. Jack had sent documents for a year without the French ever lifting a finger to bring him out of the country.

Although he was an expert at disguising illegal

downloads from the Kremlin's mainframe computers, Jack knew he'd eventually be caught. The people who ran the mainframes were bright; they'd figure it out. It was only a matter of time. Jack had begun investigating the possibility of obtaining parts directly from China and Malaysia. If he could find a reliable supplier, he didn't need the French. He'd find another way to leave the Soviet Union.

Before Jack left the office for his Monday morning meeting with the Minister, he checked his online computer account and found another message from France. Jean Broussard wanted to meet in Prague next weekend. Jack decided he'd inform the Minister he wished to travel home to Prague next weekend to visit his parents. He'd meet Broussard one last time before he severed the relationship.

As Jack bounded up the stairs to the Ministry Building, he was already eager to leave for the weekend. He wondered whether he could leave on Thursday to give himself extra time with his parents, who he hadn't seen in nearly a year.

"Good morning, Natasha," he said as he smiled at the Minister's secretary.

"Hi Jack. You're right on time. The Minister's expecting you."

"Can I go on in?"

"Sure. Let me tell him you're here." She punched the intercom button on her phone. "Mr. Gradovich, Mr. Postl is here to see you." The Minister answered, "Yes, please send him in." Gradovich walked around his desk toward the door as Jack entered. "Jack, thanks for coming over. What a lovely spring day."

"Yes, Sir. I walked over from the office."

The Minister motioned to a chair as he made his way around to sit behind his desk. "You've become so popular around here that I'm taking requests for your services," Gradovich said with a chuckle.

"I'm glad to help, Sir."

"We've received a request from the Lubyanka Building. They want you to wire the entire building for desktops." Gradovich thought about electronics in terms of wiring for telephones. He hadn't the faintest idea what computer technology meant. He thought of these machines as electronic typewriters, but if they were popular among administrative staff, he was determined to give them whatever made them happy.

"Do you have schematics for the building?" Jack asked. Gradovich pulled several large, folded prints from a file folder.

"Here are the blueprints." He spread them across his desk. He ran his finger over the diagram. "I'm thinking you should run the wiring through the elevator shafts here," he said, pointing at the diagram, "and into the rooms above the false ceilings. You can drop the wires via conduit to the floor."

"Where's their mainframe?"

"On the first floor. Boris Novotny is the man you need to see over there. He knows you're coming."

"That's a big building. I'm going to need several weeks, just so you know," Jack said.

"We're reassigning you. Those people have a lot of political muscle and they've been screaming for this stuff, so we're redirecting your efforts. They have a tendency to get very noisy."

"It's going to take a couple of weeks to finish our current project. When do they want us to start?"

"You need to meet with Novotny this week. They want you to start right away."

"I can send a couple of technicians over now to get started. I'm headed out of town this weekend. I'm going to see my parents in Prague and meet with the computer salesman I do business with."

"I have no problem with that, Jack. Just keep the KGB off my back," Gradovich said.

"I can do that, Sir."

"Sounds great, Jack. Give my regards to your parents."

"Thank you, Sir."

***

Ivan Ilitch and Maxim Khozin were sitting at a window on the eighth floor of a new downtown Lisbon, Portugal high rise. The bottom floors of the ten story structure were occupied, but the top three floors remained unfinished. They had been enclosed, but lacked drywall, lighting and plumbing fixtures. Construction workers simply vanished one day and never returned.

The shooting position Ilitch and Khozin had chosen overlooked a nearby plaza which was being used for political rallies. Portuguese national elections were to be held the following week. The right-wing presidential candidate, Diego Amal, was scheduled to speak and the plaza was packed with people hours ahead of his appearance. Amal was far ahead in the polls and would likely win the presidency at the end of March.

It was important to the Soviet Union that Amal's opponent, Mario Sorrentos, be elected or so went the explanation Ilitch received before being sent to Lisbon last Thursday. If elected president, Amal would deny the Soviets port privileges in the Atlantic. Portugal would join the fledgling European Economic Community and promote closer ties with the United States. It was vital to Soviet interests that none of those things occur, so Chairman Petrovsky sent Maxim Khozin and Ivan Ilitch to assassinate Amal and throw the election to Sorrentos, the Socialist candidate.

Sitting in front of a window that faced the plaza, Ilitch had become irritable. This was the third day they'd watched the plaza. "What's our exit strategy?" Ilitch asked.

"We've been over it a hundred times," Khozin replied.

"Let's fucking go over it again!" The lack of amenities was contributing to Ilitch's foul mood.

"Relax, Ivan. We've got the service elevator stopped on our floor. No one else will use it. We'll go directly to the ground floor without stopping. We'll go out the back entrance to the car in the alley. It's fast and it's clean."

"Go check and see if the car's still there."

"It's still there, Ivan."

"Go fucking check, Maxim. I want to know for sure." Khozin sighed, stood up, and walked over to the east side of the building where he looked down at the street. He walked back.

"It's there. Would you relax?" Maxim asked.

"It's a long way, Maxim."

"Where? To the target?"

"No. Back to Moscow when I fuck this up."

"You're not going to fuck this up," Maxim said. Part of Khozin's job was to address the psychology of his shooter; calm him, take away distractions and give him confidence.

"The wind is swirling down there. I'll be lucky to get anywhere near the target."

"No, it isn't. The wind is blowing away from us about five knots. See the flags? You get the trajectory right, you're going to be fine."

"It's a fucking insane shot, Maxim. Six-hundred fifty meters to hit a target on the ground from eight floors up. It can't be done."

"It's not 650 meters, Ivan. Don't exaggerate. It's 610. Look, you've got time for three shots before anyone realizes what's happening. You'll get him."

"What time is it?" Ivan asked.

"Ten-fifteen. Amal speaks at Noon. Relax," Maxim replied. "Want more coffee?" Sitting on the floor, Ilitch leaned back against a concrete support.

"No. You realize if we keep doing this, we're going to get caught," he said.

"Not today. We drive out of town, meet the plane at the air strip and we're out of the country. We can relax a few days in Spain before we go back. It's an easy job, Ivan."

"Yeah, I know. It just doesn't feel right."

"What doesn't feel right?" Maxim asked.

"The job, Maxim. What the fuck do you think I'm talking about? Something doesn't feel right about it. Can't put my finger on it."

"Does it ever feel right?" Maxim asked, wondering

whether Ivan was mentally ready to complete the assignment.

"No."

"Then don't worry about it. We kill the guy or we don't. Either way, we're out of the country in a couple of hours."

"Yeah, you're right. Fuck it. If I miss, I miss. We'll tell Petrovsky it couldn't be done," Ivan said. Maxim noticed his shooter relax. *He's the best shooter on the planet*, Maxim thought. *If Ilitch can't do it, no one can.*

"Is it too early to cut the hole in the window?" Maxim asked.

"No, go ahead. Nobody's going to notice. Too far away."

Khozin held a piece of paper up to the window. "Where do you want it?" Ilitch glanced at the paper.

"Lower. Almost to the floor." Khozin moved it down.

"Here?"

"That's fine."

Khozin traced a hole about the size of a pie plate, then attached a suction cup to the glass in the middle of the circle and used a glass cutter to carve the circle. Afterward, he pulled on the suction cup and the circular piece pulled away. "Here, feel this," Khozin said, holding his hand in front of the hole.

Ilitch stood up, walked over and put his hand down in front of the hole. "The air blowing out? That's the air pressure in the building. It's higher than the outside air."

"Is that going to affect the shot?"

"It shouldn't. I guess I better set up the Dragunov." Ilitch unlocked the weapon case and began to assemble the weapon. He lay down and looked at the podium through its scope. "We need the tripod," he said. Khozin pulled the tripod from the case; Ilitch set the weapon on it and looked through the scope again. "Don't pack the stuff afterward. Just wipe everything down. Remind me to wipe the rifle."

"Remember, we've got to wipe the elevator buttons and door handles, too."

"Yeah, you're right," Ilitch said.

The two fell silent for a while as the minutes ticked down to noon. The crowd continued to build and at eleven forty-five, a roar from the plaza could be heard through the window. Maxim looked through a set of binoculars. "The target just arrived. He's exiting the car and moving through the crowd to the podium. His security team is looking around at the buildings."

"Better move away from the window," Ilitch said. Khozin stepped back and sat on the floor. "Remember Afghanistan?" Ilitch asked.

"Remember it? How could I forget it?"

"Remember those firefights? Everything is fast. You shoot without thinking. Line it up, squeeze it off and look for the next target."

"Yeah, so what?" Khozin asked.

"This is war in slow motion. Kill someone, wait a month, kill someone else."

"You're only realizing this now? I mean, we've been at this for years, Ivan." Both of them laughed.

"Oh, I almost forgot," Ilitch said. He dug into his shoulder bag, pulled out a pistol and handed it to Khozin. "Take this in case we run into a problem getting out of here. Take the suppressor, too."

"What's this? You've never used anything like this

before."

"It's a Sig Sauer P226. It's what the bitch uses."

"What bitch?"

"The fucking bitch in Washington." There was a roar from the crowd below. Someone began speaking into the microphone at the podium. Khozin got up and peeked out the window.

"That's the speaker before our guy," Maxim said.

"These fucking guys talk forever," Ilitch complained. "Longest speeches I've ever heard. Maybe I should do the crowd a favor and take this guy out, too." Both of them laughed. Ilitch got up and took his firing position. He looked through his scope. "I see you, you little bastard," Ilitch said, thinking out loud.

"What bitch in Washington?" Khozin asked.

"The one we fucked up on last fall."

"I heard she's not in Washington anymore."

"Yeah, Petrovsky told me," Ilitch said. "We're going to have to hunt her down." Ilitch took three rounds out of his pocket, loaded one in the chamber and two others in the magazine. "Three ought to do it," he said. "That bitch is looking for me, I guarantee it."

"How do you know that?" Khozin asked.

"I don't. I can just feel it. She's good, Maxim. Petrovsky told me she took out the entire KGB unit in Paris. Six men, Maxim; all in one day."

"Those guys are idiots. They're not real fighters."

"Well, she is."

They heard a huge roar coming from the crowd below. Khozin grabbed his binoculars and stared at the speaker's platform. "Okay, our man's coming up to the podium. You ready?"

"Yep."

Ilitch and Khozin watched Amal walk to the podium and accept the cheers of the large crowd that spilled out onto the streets around the plaza. "Thank you. Thank you, everyone," Amal said into the microphone. He held his arms out wide.

"Range to target?" Ilitch asked.

"610."

"Wind?"

"Judging from the flags, no cross wind. We're in good shape," Khozin said.

The crowd was still cheering as Amal turned one way, then the other with his arms held high in the air. "Turn this way one more time, you bastard," Ilitch whispered. Just as he said it, Amal turned to give Ilitch a full frontal target. Ilitch shot and Amal's head exploded in blood. He slumped to the ground. "Confirm it," Ilitch said." Khozin looked through the binoculars.

"Kill shot in the forehead."

"Let's get the fuck out of here." Ilitch wiped the gun, left it on the floor and picked up his shoulder bag. They calmly walked to the elevator where Khozin pushed the ground floor button with the sleeve of his jacket. The two of them walked out of the building a minute later and casually got into a car.

"You know where you're going?" Ilitch asked.

"Yes," Khozin said, pulling away from the curb. Two minutes later, they turned onto the main highway and headed out of town. "See, I told you. Clean."

One hour later, they turned onto a gravel road that led to a rural air strip where a small plane was idling on the dirt runway. Khozin pulled next to the plane. They exited the car and bounded up the stairs. "You fellows need a ride today?" the pilot asked.

"Sure do. Get us out of here," Khozin said.

"Spanish Riviera okay with you?"

"Anywhere but here," Ilitch said.

"Good enough," the pilot said as he revved the engine. "We all closed up and strapped in back there?"

"Yes, Sir," Khozin said.

"We're on our way." The pilot gained speed down the runway, took off and headed toward Valencia, Spain, where Ivan Ilitch and Maxim Khozin disappeared once again.

Chapter Five

LAURA MESSIER AND Jean Broussard stepped off an Air France flight at Prague Ruzyne Airport early Thursday evening, March 28th. Laura had little trouble passing through customs with the explanation that the purpose of her visit was business. She waited nearly an hour in the terminal for Jean, though. His computer equipment was heavily scrutinized by customs officials, piece by piece. Jean's language skills were flawless as he kept explaining over and over to each inspector that the parts were harmless. He showed them company documents, the hotel reservation and even gave them Jack Postl's name as his business contact. Eventually, his passport was stamped and he showed up in the terminal with the boxes having been re-taped and strapped to a dolly. They found a taxi waiting curbside and as usual, Jean communicated well with the driver. They traveled to the city center where they checked into the Hotel Paris Prague.

They met at the hotel restaurant for a late dinner. "Why are you doing this to me?" Laura asked.

"Doing what?" Jean asked with a mischievous grin.

"Speaking Dutch. I haven't used Dutch since the last time I was in Brussels two years ago."

"The correct name of the language, Mademoiselle, is Nederlands. Our conversation may be overheard. This gives us some measure of privacy."

"Can't we just speak German?"

"I prefer a small amount of elegance to my methods," Jean said laughing. "Would you prefer this?" Jean said in Arabic.

"Oh God, no. I've heard enough Arabic to last a lifetime."

"My apologies, Madam." Jean switched back to Dutch. "This is an excellent restaurant, one of the best in the city. May I order for you?"

"Just avoid that horrible seafood you ordered for me that night in Tripoli."

"Terrible dish as I remember," Jean said.

Jean questioned the waiter in Czech about the menu and settled for roast duck with a very expensive wine. "Jacques will complain about the price of the meal," Laura said in German with a smile.

"We're playing the role of rich Westerners for the surveillance team in the lobby. It's the small details that sell a cover, Mademoiselle."

"Well, I like the idea of a great meal on the company credit card. Can we please pick a common language?"

"How about Spanish?" Jean asked with a grin.

"Multa," Laura replied.

After dinner, Laura and Jean stopped in the hotel bar for a nightcap and it was there Laura noticed the two men sitting at the bar. "Their surveillance team drinks heavily," she said.

"Yes, I told the waiter to run a tab and put their bill on my room," Jean said. That brought a hearty laugh and one of the men at the bar, hearing their laughter, looked in their direction. Jean raised his glass in salute and the men at the bar nodded, raised their glasses and it became something of a moment between them.

Laura rolled her eyes. "Oh God, Jean, don't you ever stop with the humor? I'd rather shoot those two and be done with it."

"The Mademoiselle seems a bit out of sorts this evening."

"I fear walking into a 7.62 round."

"Ah, Ivan Ilitch is still on your mind."

"Yes, and I hope I'm on his. He knows I'm looking for him," Laura said.

"How could you possibly know that?"

"I can feel it."

"You have a fair amount of instinct for this kind of work."

"Fear sharpens instinct."

"Then Mr. Ilitch's instincts ought to be very sharp because I'm sitting with the best in the business. And she's got nice legs, too." Jean laughed loudly at his own joke.

"You're a sexist."

"It's my French upbringing, Mademoiselle, and I make no apology for it."

"It's part of your charm, I suppose."

"Before I embarrass myself further, I'm retiring for the evening. May I escort you to your room?"

"Please do before I kill those two with my bare hands," she said, sneaking a peek at the surveillance team.

Laura slept late the following morning and was in the shower when Jean knocked on her door. She answered with an oversized towel wrapped about her body and her hair wrapped in another. "Come on in," she said as she left the door open. "I'll be with you in a minute." Jean entered and Laura disappeared into the bathroom. Jean heard the hair dryer running, then the smell of perfume and in a few minutes, Laura appeared fully dressed and ready for the day.

"The alcohol last night buoyed your spirits, Mademoiselle."

"I feel great this morning. You're looking dapper as usual."

Jean wore slacks, a black turtleneck and a tweed blazer. "Are you ready to meet Mr. Postl?"

"Let me grab my purse and coat."

"You mean these?" Jean held out her coat and purse.

"Oops, I guess you saw the Sig."

"How'd you slip it through customs?"

"A short skirt and lots of make-up."

"It's the Mademoiselle who is sexist, no?"

"One must use one's assets." Laura said with a sly smile.

"Of which you have many, my lady. Let's go introduce you to Postl."

Jean asked the valet to carry his computer boxes to the curb where a taxi was waiting. They drove into a nearby area of fashionable homes. Laura kept looking out the back window.

"No need to look. We lost our tail," Jean commented.

"How'd you manage that?" Laura asked.

"The bar opened early. I left the bartender with instructions to keep their glasses full. I would imagine our friends are busy with their vodka."

"You're a man of many talents, Mr. Broussard."

"I believe our friends would sooner die of liver problems than at the hands of, shall we say, a femme fatale?"

"Is that what I am?"

"Yes and that's a very dangerous thing for a man. Mr. Ilitch will have met his match, I think."

The driver pulled up to a lavish home by Eastern Bloc standards. "I thought the Postls lived in an apartment?" Laura asked.

"Jack does, but his parents are Party elites. They're quite wealthy by Czech standards and the Party is happy to allow it."

Jack Postl opened the front door with a big smile as they were exiting the taxi. He walked to meet them at the curb, arms spread wide apart. "Mr. Broussard, it's so nice to see you again. Thank you for coming. I've not had the honor of meeting your lovely companion." Jack held out his hand. "Ma'am, I'm Jack Postl. It's a pleasure to meet you."

"Jack, this is Laura Messier, one of the more interesting women you'll ever meet."

"Lovely to meet you, Jack," she said, grabbing his hand. Tall, well built, with blond hair and blue eyes, Postl was quite attractive, Laura thought.

"Let me help with the boxes," Jack offered. He picked up both quite easily, stacking one on top of the other and carried them into the house. Laura whispered, "Those things are heavy, Jean."

"A weightlifter," Jean whispered back.

Once inside, Laura and Jean met Jack's parents, Esther

and John, who were not your typical dour East European couple. John had a crinkle in his eyes, a jovial manner and was a very good accordion player as they soon learned. He insisted on performing Czech folk tunes. Jean was an eager accomplice, singing loudly off key. It would have been an embarrassing moment, except the two were immune from any self-reflection.

Jack's mother, Esther, was a perfect foil for her exuberant husband, adding little bits and pieces of conversation much like the straight man in a two person comedy team. Later, in thinking about the Postls, Laura thought how wonderful it would have been to have such parents. Much of their happiness had been transferred to Jack as he was a charming fellow with an inquisitive mind. He also had a surprising amount of knowledge of the United States.

"Where did you get your knowledge of the States?" Laura asked, sitting in the living room enjoying Esther's finger food.

"I read Western magazines I purchase on the black market. I also have an uncle who lives in Chicago," Jack said. Laura stole a glance at Jean, who was happily munching Esther's hors d'oeuvres. *Was Jack asking that his parents be transported to the West, too*, she wondered?

"I didn't realize you had relatives in the States," Laura said

"My brother immigrated to the States before the Communists came," John said. "He owns a string of health clubs in Chicago."

"Is the Party aware of this?" Laura asked.

"Oh my heavens, no. I shudder at the thought of them

finding out. Esther, dear, you're not about to go blabbing about Uncle Charlie to the neighbor ladies, are you?"

"Oh yes, dear. I'm going on radio tomorrow to announce it to the entire Communist Party." John nearly doubled over in laughter.

"That's my girl for you," he said amid the giggles.

"Have you ever considered emigrating to live near your brother?" Jean asked.

"Us? For goodness sake, no. A vacation would be nice, but to start over on the other side of the world? We've got everything we want here in Prague. Why would we want to move? Moving to America is for young folks like Jack."

Over the next hour, John and Esther made their guests feel like a part of their family; chatting, eating and telling stories. Jean finally turned the conversation to business. "Jack, why don't we go into the den where I can display the computer parts I've brought for you." Jack rubbed his hands together.

"Exactly what I've been waiting for."

Much to Laura's amazement, Jean seemed to have an in-depth knowledge of computer technology. Laura felt completely helpless and decided to help Esther clear the dishes from the living room. She glanced out the front window where a late model black sedan sat across the street. Apparently, they hadn't lost their surveillance after all.

At the end of their visit, Jack offered to drive Laura and Jean back to the hotel. It was during the trip that Jean made his overture. "Jack, I think you and Laura should spend some time together. She'd be a good person to know. I suggest you pick her up outside the hotel later this evening."

"Sure. Laura, ten this evening okay?"

"Uh," she hesitated. She looked to Jean for guidance, but received only a smile in return. "Yes, uh, I guess that would be fine," she stammered. "How about picking me up at the rear entrance?"

"Certainly."

Before exiting the car, Jean was quick to add, "The parts are yours to keep Jack and don't hesitate to place an order. There are plenty more where those came from."

"I'll be sure and do that, Mr. Broussard. Thank you so much for the visit and I'll see you later this evening, Laura."

Jean walked Laura into her hotel room. "We made great progress selling equipment today, didn't we?" Jean asked, looking at the ceiling light fixture where he suspected a listening device was installed. "Let's celebrate with an early dinner downstairs."

"Great. Give me a minute to change." She used the restroom to change into tight jeans and a dark stretch top, black leather jacket and sneakers. She spent a minute or two at the mirror refreshing her make-up and combing out her hair.

They proceeded downstairs to the hotel restaurant, where Jean spoke Dutch again. "I suggest a nice cut of prime rib this evening. Does that suit you, Mademoiselle?"

"I wasn't expecting to meet Postl alone."

"I take that as a 'Yes' for the prime rib. You see how pleasant it is when you allow me to order for you," Jean said with a grin.

"Still sexist, I see."

"I call it chivalry."

"It makes it hard when you improvise like you did this afternoon."

"You mean about meeting Jack? The Mademoiselle is one of the greatest intelligence agents in the world. But she gets lazy at times. My job is to push her into performing her best."

"How am I supposed to lose the surveillance?" Laura asked.

"Judging from the Mademoiselle's evening wear, I believe she's already come up with a solution."

"So you'd like me to ditch the surveillance, meet Postl and figure out how to exfil him in about three hours?"

"No. Right now, we're having dinner. Then, we'll have drinks. You'll have …" Jean thought for a moment "… an hour at most."

"You're impossible, do you know that?"

"Yes, quite," Jean said with a hint of a smile.

Laura opened the window in her fourth floor suite at 9:50 pm. She climbed out the window, closed it behind her and stood on the ledge outside the window. She began climbing down the facade toward the ground. The ornate facade offered numerous handholds and she had little trouble making her way across and down, back and forth, working her way to the ground floor where she leaped to the sidewalk. She took a handkerchief from the purse and wiped her hands. *Easier than I expected*, she thought. *I didn't even break a nail.*

She walked around the corner to the back of the hotel and found Postl waiting in the same car he used earlier. He got out and opened the passenger door. "Good evening, Laura."

"Hi Jack. Can you speak English?"

"Sure," he said.

"Lovely evening for a workout, don't you think?"

"Are you saying you want to see my dad's health club?"

"Why not."

"He's got a club downtown. It shouldn't take long to get there."

Jack drove the short distance and parked in an employee space. He used a pass key to gain entry to the facility which had closed for the evening. Once inside, Laura found a very nice weightlifting facility. "Come," Jack said motioning for her to follow. "I'll show you the swimming pool, sauna and boxing ring.

"Are you a boxer?" she asked walking through the next room past the ring.

Jack looked hesitant. "Yes. Why do you ask?"

"Let's put the gloves on and find out how good you are."

Jack laughed as though the idea of fighting a woman was ridiculous. "Sorry, I don't fight women."

"Too bad. I would have loved to knock you down a few times."

"Are you joking?" Jack asked.

"Do I sound like I'm joking?"

Jack thought for a minute before answering. "Well, I suppose I could show you a few moves if you want to learn how to box."

Laura laughed. "You do that," she said cynically.

They donned head gear, vests and gloves and then climbed into the ring. Jack stood there without moving.

"Are you sure you want to do this?" he asked.

"What are you waiting for?" Laura asked, dancing around, pounding her gloves together. She dropped her gloves and pointed at her chin. "Give me your best shot right here." Jack backed away.

"I'm not going to throw a punch. Are you crazy?"

"I'll strike first then," she said.

In the blink of an eye, Laura took the initiative and with blinding speed, she hit Jack with several punches to the face and body. Jack was unprepared for the attack. He kept backing up until he was leaning against the ropes. Laura pelted him with hard punches. Jack had no choice, except to cover up. Laura stopped and backed away.

"Had enough?" she asked.

Jack took a minute to clear his head before he spoke. It wasn't that he'd been punched that bothered him. Jack had to wrap his mind around the notion that she could fight. "You're good. I had no idea you could do that."

"It wasn't a fair fight," Laura said.

"What do you mean?"

"I've done this kind of thing for years."

"You mean fight in competitions?" Jack asked.

"I don't fight for recreation, Jack. I fight for my life."

Jack paused, looking her up and down. "You're an intelligence agent, aren't you?" Laura shrugged in response. "And I don't think you're French. You're American." Laura just shrugged again.

They peeled off their gear and walked to the vending machines. "Juice?" Jack asked.

"Sure."

Jack took a key out of his pocket, opened the machine and pulled out two orange juices. "Are you here to bring me to the West?"

"Possibly."

"What do you mean 'possibly'?"

"It depends on what you're willing to do for me," Laura said.

"You want something from me first, right?"

"That's the way the world works, Jack."

"You want information?"

"Yep. That's what I want. Information"

"Why is it you people always want something?" Jack asked harshly.

"Don't judge me by your relationship with Broussard," Laura shot back.

"I satisfy request after request from the French and nobody ever brings me out."

"I'll be the one bringing you out, Jack. That's why I'm here. Do you know what's involved in getting you out? It's not that easy."

"I've been waiting for over a year," Jack said. "You think I'm not ready? Oh, that's funny." Laura saw Jack's anger begin to build.

"Then, show me."

"What do you mean?"

Laura pointed to the ring. "Show me in there."

"You want to fight again?" Jack asked.

"No, not fight. I want you to defeat me. Things could get difficult bringing you out. I must know you're willing to do whatever's necessary."

"No problem." Jack walked over and began putting on the sparring equipment. He continued to talk as he prepared. "You want something from me? You sound just like the French. I'll tell you what. You can request your documents lying on the canvas. I'm a trained boxer." That's when Laura saw a different part of Jack's personality; his anger.

"Your training won't help you against me," she said, amused at Jack's braggadocio. She quickly donned the protective equipment.

"We'll see about that," Jack retorted.

When she was ready, Jack attacked her with a fierceness that belied his affable personality. He stalked her, pushed her, tried to punch her, yet nothing worked. He tried to find a weakness and found none. Laura was too quick, too experienced and too patient. The pop of the gloves hitting each other echoed in the room. She'd block one punch, then another. Jack could never land a solid hit. She allowed him to expend his energy, retreating time and time again when he'd move forward, turning herself to avoid getting caught on the ropes. Dancing, moving, giving him a target that disappeared by the time he punched, she gauged Jack's moves as a large cat would its prey. She didn't so much watch him as she anticipated him. It was as though she could read his thoughts. Then, without warning, she ended it, switching from fighting right-handed, to left-handed, confusing Jack. Leading with her hip, Laura delivered a power left handed shot to the jaw, knocking him to the floor. Laura untied her gloves as Jack lay there stunned. She stepped through the ropes and picked up a bucket of water. Climbing back into the ring, she dribbled water on his face.

"Here, let me help you up," she said, offering her arm.

"No! I can do it myself," he said in anger.

"Jack!" she said sharply. He climbed to his feet and began walking around the ring. He refused to look at her. "Jack!" she repeated.

Jack finally looked at her. "What!" he yelled.

"Walk with me," she said, taking off the gear. Jack was reluctant to follow, but climbed out of the ring and took off his gear. He followed her across the gym. They sat again in the folding chairs pushed against the wall. "Look," she said, gesturing toward the ring, "for all I know, you could be setting me up. You could turn me in to the authorities."

"I wouldn't do that."

"I've heard you that seek greater employment opportunities in the West. That sounds odd to me. Most people want out for political reasons, Jack. I need the truth or I'll kill you right now." Jack wondered whether she was serious. One look in her eyes convinced him the threat was real. *She's just as tough as the Soviets*, he thought.

"Computer technology's going to change the world, Miss Messier," Jack explained. "I want my life's work to mean something. All the new technology comes from the West. I want to be part of that. That's why I want to leave."

She thought about her next few questions, looking again at the ring and remembering how Jack fought. "Broussard gives you all those computer parts, doesn't he?"

"Yes, Ma'am."

"What do you give him in exchange?" she asked.

"Information off the computers."

"Information from which departments?"

Jack seemed perplexed by the question. "All of them. I have access to everything."

"Don't they monitor who looks at files?" Laura asked.

"Of course. It's dangerous to go snooping around classified material. They're not fools. They'll catch me eventually."

"But if I wanted something, you could get it for me?" Laura asked.

"Maybe. What do you want?"

"I'm looking for an employee of the KGB."

"I can probably find him. I'm working in that building for the next few weeks."

"The Lubyanka Building?"

"Yes," Jack answered. "What's the employee's name?"

"Ivan Ilitch."

"How do you spell it?" Jack asked. He walked to the counter, retrieved a business card and a pen. "Here, write it on the back of this."

She wrote the name and handed it to him. "I'll look around and see what I can find."

"I need more than documents, Jack."

"What do you need?"

"He doesn't work in the building. He's sort of a freelance worker. He meets with the Chairman from time to time. If you see him, I'd appreciate knowing it."

"What does he looks like?"

"See if you can find a picture in a file somewhere," Laura said. "Just let me know if you see him."

"That's it?"

"That's all I need."

"How do I contact you?"

"You can't," Laura said. "Keep communicating with the French. Let them know if you see Ilitch."

"How are you going to get me out? And when?"

"Talk to me about the computer parts you order."

"There's not much to talk about, really. I order the parts from Mr. Broussard. When they arrive, we assemble the machines."

"I'm specifically referring to problems you might have with the orders."

Jack thought for a minute. "Well, some of the parts get damaged during shipping because they're delicate. We have to return them. And we never have enough parts. We can build a machine in a day, but it takes weeks to get the parts. So, we're faced with constant shortages and delays."

"I see. Would they allow you to travel to inspect the parts before they're shipped?"

"I don't know. I've never asked."

"Are the machines popular?" Laura wondered.

"Once we put one in an office, everyone in the building wants one. We can't keep up with all the requests."

"If they're in demand, perhaps the Minister could make a travel request on your behalf. It would look legitimate coming from him."

"Possibly," Jack said.

"If not, we could always forge travel documents, but it would be better if you could get an official approval."

"They're careful about who they allow to travel."

Laura hesitated for a moment, thinking. "Get me the information on Ilitch. After that, I want you to ask the authorities for permission to travel. Have the Minister do it for you. When everything's in place, I'll come into Moscow to get you.

"Okay. I'll work on it."

"There's something else you need to know."

"Yes?" Jack asked.

"I risked my life coming here to talk with you. That's how serious I am. Do you believe me?"

"Yes, Ma'am."

"Good. You better take me back to the hotel. I shouldn't be gone too long," Laura said.

When Laura got out of the car, she leaned back in before she closed the door. "The next time you see me, Jack, I'll be bringing you out. Best of luck until then." She closed the door and walked away.

***

After returning from his assignment in Lisbon, Ivan Ilitch gave KGB Chairman Petrovsky a report on the mission. He took the Red Line subway from the Kazansky Station near his apartment to the Lubyanka Station, where he climbed the stairs into the building. As he entered the Chairman's outer office, he found a man lying on the floor underneath the secretary's desk. Jack stuck his head out from under the desk, "Can I help you?"

"Where's the secretary?"

"Irina? She's got the day off while I run computer wire through her office."

"Who are you?" Ilitch asked. Postl rose, walked over and extended his hand.

"I'm Jack Postl, from the ElectroTechnical Ministry.

I'm installing computers in the building."

Ilitch didn't offer his hand. He simply stared at Jack, assessing the truthfulness of his statement. "I'm here to see the Chairman."

"Let me find the phone. I'll ring his office and tell him you're here. Didn't catch your name."

"Ivan Ilitch."

Postl's eyes widened and looked away to hide the shock of seeing the subject of his search face to face. He searched for the phone. "Ah, there it is," he said. He picked up the receiver and pressed the intercom. "Mr. Chairman, sorry for the interruption. There's someone here to see you."

"Well, out with it. Who is it?" Petrovsky replied tersely. He wished Irina hadn't taken the day off.

"A Mr. Ivan Ilitch."

"Send him in." Jack hung up and turned to Ilitch, "The Chairman will see you now."

As Ilitch walked toward the door leading into Petrovsky's office, Jack watched him. *I'll send the French a note tonight*, he thought. Jack crawled back underneath the desk and resumed working. Ilitch shut the Chairman's door behind him and Petrovsky looked up from his paperwork. "How did the Lisbon business go?"

"I'm sure you've heard, by now. We were successful, Sir."

Petrovsky didn't ask him to sit. *It'll be a short conversation*, Ilitch thought. The room reeked of cigarette smoke. Petrovsky laid his cigarette in an already full ashtray and leaned back in his chair.

"Yes, I did hear that. Did you enjoy your holiday in

Valencia?"

"Yes, Sir. Very much. Thanks for the time off," Ilitch responded.

"I have new information about Shewolf, Ivan."

"You mean the woman in Washington?"

"Who else would I be speaking of?" Petrovsky asked, raising his voice. Petrovsky paused for a moment to give emphasis to his next statement. "It's time to clean up this mess you created. She's been seen in Paris attending meetings at French Intelligence headquarters. The meetings are held on Mondays, so travel to Paris and correct your mistake."

"Where does she stay in Paris?"

Petrovsky's face became flush. He shouted, "How the fuck would I know? Do I look like my job is walking around the street finding people?"

Ilitch looked at the floor. Petrovsky was unpredictable; a volcano ready to explode at the slightest provocation. Ilitch knew he must be careful to show the proper amount of contrition. "No, Sir. My apologies," he said.

"You go to Paris and take care of this business, Captain Ilitch. And I remind you, if you'd done your job the first time, this trip wouldn't be necessary." He slammed his hand on the desktop. "No one kills the entire staff of the KGB in Paris and gets away with it. It's an insult to the Soviet people that she's still alive!"

"Yes, Sir. I'll go this weekend."

Petrovsky changed his voice to a more hospitable, yet still menacing tone. "I have one additional request, Ivan. Do not take her anywhere near the DST building. Wherever else you choose is fine, but I repeat, not right in front of the French. Do you understand?"

"Yes, Sir."

"Then be on your way," Petrovsky said tersely.

"Thank you, Sir." Ilitch bowed slightly and turned to leave the office.

"And tell that idiot computer man to get in here. Now!" Petrovsky shouted.

"Yes, Sir." Ilitch walked past Jack on his way out. "Hey, idiot computer man. The boss wants to see you." Jack poked his head out from under the desk.

"I'm sorry. What did you say?"

"The boss wants to see you. If I were you, I'd go in there now."

Jack walked to the doorway. "You wanted to see me, Sir?"

"How long are you going to be here?" Petrovsky demanded.

"Two weeks, Sir."

"Remind me again why you're here."

"I'm installing computers for yourself and your secretary," Jack said.

"And how is that supposed to help me? Make it short. Two sentences in plain Russian."

"You'll be able to keep confidential files on your own computer. No one can see them, but you." Petrovsky seemed pleased by that statement. "Good. What's your name, again?"

"Postl. It's Jack Postl, Sir."

"Carry on with your work. And shut the door on your way out."

Jack returned to his installation while Petrovsky

wondered whether he should check Postl's credentials. *Having people work in close proximity to state secrets without proper vetting could be dangerous*, he thought. He picked up the phone and called Novotny, the computer technician who ran the mainframe at Lubyanka. "Novotny, its Petrovsky."

"Yes, Sir. Good morning. How can I help you?"

"This fellow you've got working up here in my office. What's his name?"

"Jack Postl, Sir. The Ministry sent him over to install desktop computers in the building."

"Postl said my confidential files would be put on my own computer. Is that true?" Petrovsky asked.

"If that's what you'd like to do, yes, of course. Once he's installed everything, he can take whatever you want off the mainframe and put it on your personal machine."

"Can this Postl be trusted?"

"As far as I know, Sir. He comes highly recommended. He's worked for many other Ministries in the Kremlin. We thought it best to get him over here as soon as possible."

"When these files are transferred to the machine in my office, will it be Postl who does it?"

"Yes, Sir. Postl will make the transfer himself," Novotny assured Petrovsky. "No one else will be involved. He'll set up a password that only you know. It'll be an extra layer of security we've never had before."

"How are we supposed to operate these machines? Isn't this something Irina would do?"

"Irina will have one on her desk, too, but we thought you'd prefer handling your most secret files yourself. Postl does all the training and by the time he's done, I think you'll be pleased with the new system. And, the mainframe will still be available to you."

"Good. I want this completed as soon as possible. Tell Postl to finish my office and Irina's before he moves on."

"Yes, Sir. That's why Postl suggested we start with your office ..." Petrovsky interrupted Novotny.

"Wait a minute. It was Postl who suggested starting with my office?"

"Yes, Sir. That's what he's done in the other ministries. Get the executive offices up and running first. I spoke with the Minister over at ElectroTechnical and we feel good about the plan. We'll get it done as quickly as we can." Petrovsky hung up the phone, leaned back in his chair and lit another cigarette. *I'm going to get Postl's dossier*, he thought, *just to be sure*.

Chapter Six

THE PORTUGUESE INVESTIGATION into the assassination of presidential candidate Diego Amal was transferred from the Ministerio Pulbico to the SIS, the intelligence branch, as soon as foreign involvement was suspected. The SIS received a bit of luck when a clean fingerprint showed up on one of the elevator buttons in the service elevator. That print, however, turned up no matches either in Portuguese records or at Interpol. The only other lead was a Soviet made Dragunov sniper rifle left at the crime scene. No purchase or registration records for the weapon could be found. At that point, the investigation stalled.

It took a few days for Jacques Martin to learn the details of the Portuguese assassination through Interpol, but he immediately recognized similarities to the attempt on Messier's life. He telephoned a contact within the SIS and received permission to view their investigative records. He took a copy of the fingerprint found at the scene and compared it to French arrest records. No matches were found. However, a diplomatic bag from the French Embassy in Moscow arrived the following week containing a Red Army registration for Ivan Ilitch which included a full set of fingerprints. When Jacques compared the fingerprint from the Portuguese assassination with Ivan Ilitch's Red Army registration, it turned up a match. It was the first positive proof that Ivan Ilitch could be linked to an unsolved assassination.

At that point, Jacques had the match he needed to substantiate his investigation, but he knew further evidence was needed to get a mission approved by the DST. He began looking at cold cases. A second match was found from a print left at the scene of a 1984 French diplomat's murder outside a Paris restaurant.

With two confirmed kills by Ivan Ilitch, one conducted on French soil, Jacques compared the prints with the thumb print found on the rifle used in the assassination attempt on Messier. Once again, a positive match was found. With this documentation, Jacques received permission to pursue a mission to capture or kill Ivan Ilitch. Jacques' working group was scheduled to meet the following Monday, April 6th, at DST headquarters.

***

Maxim Khozin and Ivan Ilitch arrived in Paris Saturday morning, April 4th using forged Swiss passports. They had little trouble passing through customs. They declared the purpose of their visit to be business and custom agents gave them only a cursory examination. They hired a taxi to take them to the Soviet Embassy where they questioned KGB Chief Denis Melinin about the whereabouts of Laura Messier.

"We know she attends meetings at French Intelligence

on Monday mornings, but not every week," Melinin said.

"Will she be there this Monday?" Khozin asked.

Melinin laughed, "If we knew that, we would be mind readers, wouldn't we?"

"So, you don't know?" Ilitch asked.

"That's correct. We know when we see her."

"Does she stay in her apartment or in a hotel?" Khozin asked.

"She uses hotels, a different one each time. Sometimes, she doesn't use a hotel. She flies straight in and out. It's random."

"What name does she use?" Ilitch asked.

"Again, she uses several."

"Does she travel alone?" Khozin followed.

"She travels with a male companion most of the time."

"You're not much help," Ilitch said.

"We have no instructions from Moscow to make her a priority."

"How do we find her?"

"Do what we do," Melinin suggested. "Watch the front entrance to the DST building Monday morning around ten and see if she shows up. We have a safe house close to the entrance. You're welcome to use it."

"Do you have weapons for us?"

"No. You'll to have obtain them separately." Melinin searched the rolodex until he found a name. He copied the name and phone number. "Here's a contact you can use."

Khozin and Ilitch left the Embassy shaking their heads. "Did he even know we were coming?" Khozin asked.

"It didn't sound like it. He's a typical government bureaucrat; doesn't know, doesn't care," Ilitch replied.

"What do you want to do?"

"We should sleep in the safe house to avoid hotels. Let's drop off our bags and find one of those American fast food places. I'm in the mood for a couple of cheeseburgers"

They found the safe house and discovered the view of the DST building to be virtually useless. Ilitch picked up the pair of binoculars left on the window sill overlooking the street. "How long has it been since they used these things?" Ilitch asked, blowing dust from the lenses. He looked down the street and found the building. "The place is a fucking block away, Maxim. I can't see shit from this angle. I don't know how they can tell she even goes in there."

"Can we stand on the street somewhere closer?"

"Oh yeah. Let's stand across the street and hold up signs. 'We're Soviets and we're here to kill you. Have a nice fucking day.'" Both of them laughed. "Even if we see her, by the time we run downstairs and flag down a taxi, she'll be gone. We'll never find her."

"Go back and tell Petrovsky it can't be done," Khozin said.

Ilitch gave Khozin a look of frustration. "You tell him. The other day I thought he was going to post us to Siberia." They both laughed again. "Fuck this. Let's go get a cheeseburger," Ilitch said.

Laura and Rick checked into the Renaissance Hotel late Sunday evening and took a taxi to DST headquarters the following morning. As they emerged from the taxi at the front entrance, Laura stopped and looked at the surrounding buildings. "What's wrong?" Rick asked.

146

"Something's changed."

"What are you talking about?"

"I'm not sure, but something's different," she said.

"What's different? Cars, pedestrians; what?"

Laura stared down the block in the direction of the safe house. "Someone's watching."

"We should get off the street then before someone takes a shot at us."

"You're right. Let's get inside," she said.

At the safe house, Khozin watched her get out of the taxi. "I've got her, Ivan. She's getting out of a taxi."

"Here, let me see." Ilitch reached for the binoculars and watched her look straight at his position. "Does she know we're here?"

"She probably knows she's being watched, but I can't believe she knows it's us," Khozin said as he picked up a camera.

"She's just standing there looking at us. Beautiful, isn't she?"

"You falling in love with the mark?" Khozin asked.

Ilitch chuckled. "That isn't her husband with her. I'd love to be that guy, fucking her brains out every night."

Khozin snapped pictures until she was out of sight. "It would be an impossible shot from here, Ivan. What do you want to do?"

"The boss doesn't want us to take her in front of the building. Come on, let's get a taxi," Ilitch said, laying the binoculars back on the window sill. "We'll keep the meter running while she's in there and follow her when she leaves."

"Good morning, everyone," Jacques said after his working group had assembled. "I appreciate everyone attending this morning. We've had a break in the Ilitch case." Everyone leaned forward, eager to hear anything that would get the stalled investigation moving. Jacques explained the fingerprint evidence. "We were able to obtain a full set of prints for Ivan Ilitch. Comparing them to prints left at crime scenes, we've proven Ilitch's involvement in three crimes, two murders and the attempted assassination of Messier. We're going back through other cold cases as we speak to see if Ilitch can be linked to additional crimes. This is the proof we needed. We took the evidence to Director Picquet and he approved a mission to pursue Ilitch."

"Pursue him where?" Laura asked.

"Anywhere we can find him," Jacques answered.

"In Moscow?"

"Yes, if we must."

"How did we get the original set of prints?" Jean asked.

"Jack Postl accessed Red Army files, stole Ilitch's enlistment records and left them at a dead drop."

"He's an amateur, Jacques," Jean continued. "He's going to get caught."

"I agree, Jean. Have you come up with an exfil plan?"

"Using the airport option, we'll travel to Moscow and wine and dine the head of the ministry. We'll make it a real sales call; convince him our front company's a legitimate business. That's the key. If the minister's convinced we're real, he'll get a travel permit for Postl and we'll bring him out when we leave. However, we must make the front company look good here in Paris because they'll investigate us. Can you do that?" Jean asked.

"Yes, of course. We can paint trucks, fill a warehouse with computers, hire staff and create lots of paperwork. We can make it look good." Jacques looked around the room. "Questions?"

"Wouldn't it be easier to bring him out on forged papers?" Henri asked.

"Yes, we could do that," Jacques answered. "But, we're asking him to bring confidential files from Petrovsky's office with him. Postl's a high value asset. We must provide more assistance than forged papers. We'll use the forged papers as a back-up. Any more questions?" Jacques asked. He looked around the room. "Good," he said. "We'll send people to Moscow on a sales call and exfil Postl when they leave. Now, what about Ilitch? Laura, do you have any thoughts?"

"Has Postl been inside Lubyanka yet?" Laura asked.

Jacques smiled. "Yes, he's working in Petrovsky's office as we speak. And he's seen Ilitch. We didn't realize he'd see Ilitch so quickly, so he had no instructions from us. Next time, we'll follow Ilitch back to his home. Postl will be working in the vicinity of Petrovsky's office for a few weeks, so let's be patient. We think Ilitch will show up again." Jacques looked around the room. "Any objections to a tail on Ilitch?" He waited for a few seconds again. "Good. The next time Ilitch shows up at Lubyanka, we'll have men in position to follow him."

Laura and Rick left the meeting feeling progress had been made. They had a few hours before their flight back to Toronto, so Laura asked the taxi driver to take them to a favorite cafe near her old apartment. It had been months since Laura had been to Cafe La Flore where the owner, Pierre, was still the maître d'. He remembered Laura and welcomed her with a smile and a kiss. *It's nice to be back in the old neighborhood,* she thought. After a leisurely lunch, they stepped out into the sunshine of a nice day in Paris. Rick stepped to the curb to hail a taxi while Laura waited in the doorway until the taxi stopped in the street.

As she began walking toward the cab, the skateboarder came out of nowhere, skating around walkers at a high rate of speed. Laura quickly dodged a collision and felt the burn of a round in her arm before she heard the crack of the weapon. The round grazed her, then passed through the windshield of a parked car and wedged itself somewhere inside the vehicle. Upon hearing the sound, Rick turned and pounced on Laura, driving her to the ground. Blood began to seep through Laura's blouse.

"I'm hit, Rick," she said.

"I know. Someone will call an ambulance. With your permission, I'm going to pursue the shooter. I saw him."

"Go! I'll be fine."

"Fuck!" Ilitch said into his comm set. "The woman has nine lives! Fucking skateboarder! Maxim, you have the male companion?" Khozin had positioned himself across the street while Ilitch had stationed himself a few doors away from the cafe.

"It's not a clear shot, Ivan. We're done. Let's get out while we can."

Ilitch surveyed the scene. "Okay. Let's go." They turned and walked quickly in the opposite direction. Rick spotted both of them, the only people walking away from the commotion. He began running after them, dodging pedestrians while drawing the weapon from his shoulder holster as he ran.

Maxim looked over his shoulder. "The male companion made us, Ivan," he shouted into the comms. "We've got pursuit."

"Fuck!" Ilitch said in frustration. "Run!" As Ilitch ran, his headset fell to the ground, but he had no time to retrieve it. Rick picked up the comm set and continued the chase.

The pursuit wound its way through traffic, in storefronts, out the back into alleyways and along crowded sidewalks. The participants dodged automobiles, knocked over store displays and bumped into pedestrians. Ilitch and Khozin had a large head start and although Rick was a fast runner, he lost them within a few blocks. He holstered his weapon. "Damn it!" he said, out of breath. He stood motionless, looking for any sign of their presence. He saw none. He holstered his weapon and walked back to the scene where an ambulance had stopped in front of the cafe. The police arrived on the scene and stopped Rick as he approached, "I'm sorry, Sir. I cannot allow you to go farther."

Rick reached for his billfold and showed his ID. "United States Central Intelligence Agency. The woman is my partner."

The policeman took a look at Rick's ID. "Go ahead, Sir. My apologies."

As the paramedics wheeled Laura's stretcher to the back of the ambulance. Rick saw she was conscious. "Are you okay?" he asked.

"I'm fine, Rick," she said. "It's just a flesh wound. The

skateboarder saved me."

"Looks like you've lost blood."

"Excuse me, Sir," the paramedic said. Rick stepped aside while they lifted her into the back of the ambulance. "You can ride along if you wish."

"Thanks," Rick said, hopping in the back. The paramedics strapped an oxygen mask over Laura's mouth and nose. "Is she going to be okay?" he asked the paramedic.

Laura removed the mask. "Did you ..."

"Shhh ..." Rick said.

"Please, Mademoiselle. You need to keep it on until we arrive," the EMT said as he gently put the mask back over her mouth and nose. He pressed a bandage into Laura's arm to stem the bleeding.

"Relax, Laura," Rick said with a smile. "Is she going to be okay?" Rick asked the paramedic again.

"Yes. The bullet passed through flesh, which is good news. The doctor will check the wound for clothing fragments, clean it and do some stitching. A pressure bandage, a round of antibiotics and she'll be fine."

"Hear that, Laura?" Rick asked. Laura nodded her head. "Relax; close your eyes and rest."

The police took statements at the hospital and an hour later, Laura and Rick were ready to leave when Jean Broussard and Jacques Martin appeared in the waiting room. "We heard the news," Jacques said to Rick. "How is she?"

"I'm right here in the wheelchair, guys. I'm fine," Laura said with a bit of frustration. "I've been through worse."

"How closely did you see the shooter?" Jean asked

Rick.

"About fifty meters," Rick said. "There were two men, Jean. The shooter and a spotter across the street. Both ran when I gave chase. The guy across the street was much taller than the shooter. Both had dark hair. Light colored shirts, dark trousers; the shooter had a black leather jacket."

"Isn't Khozin taller than Ilitch?" Jean asked.

"Let's not jump to conclusions," Jacques said. "The police will do their interviews, recover the round and we'll see what we've got. We'll view whatever surveillance video we can find. There's a chance we'll pick them up."

"Sorry, I couldn't catch them," Rick said. "They had nearly a block head start, Jacques. Here." He reached into his pocket and gave the headset to Jacques. "The shooter dropped this during the chase."

Jacques took a handkerchief and wrapped the evidence. "Thanks. We'll see if we can get a print."

"Are we free to go ahead and travel today?" Rick asked.

"Yes. We've got a car to take you to the airport." Jacques brought four DST guards who secured the hospital's emergency exit while Laura and Rick were led to a heavy, bulletproof car. "I'm going to have a couple of men ride along, Laura. They'll be with you until you board this evening."

"Thank you, Jacques," she said.

"I'm sorry this happened. We should have been more careful."

"It couldn't be helped, Jacques."

"Rest up and I'll keep you informed."

The limousine had a car phone, so Rick called ahead and purchased two seats on the Concorde that left Charles

153

de Gaulle that evening bound for Washington Dulles. They were back in Washington late that evening. "What the hell happened to you?" Steve asked when he picked them up.

"I had a little problem today."

"Were you shot?"

"Yep."

Steve turned to Rick. "What happened?"

"We were ambushed by two men coming out of lunch after the meeting," he said. "I gave chase, but couldn't catch them. We did get a piece of evidence, though. One of them dropped a comm set."

"I'm going out to Langley in the morning," Steve said. "I'll speak with Bates. We can't have people taking shots at agency employees. It's totally unacceptable."

"I wasn't supposed to be in Paris in the first place," she said.

"Doesn't matter. You were attacked without provocation."

***

Bates was unable to meet with Steve for a couple of days and by then, Laura felt well enough to attend. Bates came out of his office to greet them. "I heard about what happened, Laura. I'm terribly sorry. Good morning, Steve."

"Morning, boss." Steve turned to Laura. "I'm going to run down to Roger's office for a few minutes. Will you be okay meeting with Bill alone?"

"Of course."

"I'll leave the two of you then," Steve said.

Bill motioned Laura into his office. "How are you feeling?"

"I'll be fine, Bill."

"Come in and sit down." Bates motioned for Laura to sit as he made his way around the desk. "What happened the other day?"

Laura explained the incident, which prompted Bates to ask further questions. "You say you have a pretty good hunch about the identity of the attackers?"

"We think it was the same people who conducted the attack in Washington last fall, Bill."

"What evidence do you have?"

"There may be a print on a comm set the shooter dropped during the pursuit. Remember the assassination of the Portuguese presidential candidate a couple of weeks ago?"

"Yes. It's my understanding that incident's unsolved."

"The French have linked a print from that crime scene to a man named Ivan Ilitch. The print from the rifle used in the attempt on me last fall matches Ilitch, too. He and his partner, Maxim Khozin, are a two man hit team that operates directly out of Petrovsky's office in Moscow. The French have been able to further identify Ilitch as the shooter in a second assassination of a French diplomat in '84."

"Very fine work, Laura. Congratulations."

"Well, the work was done by the DST, but that's not the end of the story," Laura said.

"Tell me."

"Ilitch's fingerprints were found among his Red Army enlistment documents. The source that retrieved them is in

Petrovsky's office."

"The French have a source that high up inside the KGB?" Bates looked incredulous.

"He's a computer technician who works on KGB computers," Laura said.

"Their computers are compromised?"

"This fellow has complete access."

"How do you know the source is trustworthy?"

"I met him last week in Czechoslovakia. He's legit."

The information was a revelation to Bates, who was taken by complete surprise. He hesitated before he spoke again, looking out the window at the forested areas of the complex. Bates was loath to admit that other intelligence services were equal to the CIA. "You've run a great investigation, Laura," Bates finally said.

"It's a French team, Bill. I'm just a small part of it."

"What are your plans?" he asked.

"As soon as my arm heals, we're going into Moscow to bring the source out. I'll also find Ivan Ilitch if I can."

"I see. Would you be offended if I confirmed this with the DST Director? I'd like to offer our assistance, but I want to make sure we're cooperating at the executive level first." Laura didn't respond. She stared at the Bates. It created an awkward moment between the two. Bates knew he had to tread lightly. Messier was high strung and prone to anger. "I mean no offense by double checking your information," Bill continued. "If we're going to be part of a mission in Moscow, I may need to get it approved by the White House. I have to be sure what we're getting into."

"Is this an admission you were wrong last fall to conclude the attack was a random act of violence?" Laura asked.

"Laura, please understand I must rely on the judgment of others."

"It's convenient when D.C. Metro can run your investigation, isn't it?"

"Look, there's no question you've done a fabulous job pursuing this. Sometimes, we get it wrong. I'm sorry." Bates looked at his schedule. "I've got another meeting to attend at the moment. Can we talk again in the morning, say nine?"

Walking toward the exit with Steve, Laura stepped on the eagle's head on the CIA emblem embedded in the floor inside the entrance. Steve noticed. "In all the years we've been coming in and out of the building, I've never seen you do that," he said.

"What are you talking about?"

"You stepped on the eagle."

"You'd make a good field agent, Steve. Yes, I did step on it and I meant to. I don't get a lot of respect around here. I'm treated far better across the pond."

"Come on, let's grab some lunch," Steve said with a smile.

"Sure. Thanks for coming with me. It's nice to have someone support me."

"Always."

The following morning, Laura and Steve checked in through the front entrance at 8:45 am. "Where are you going?" she asked as Steve got off the elevator.

"Sorry, I've got another meeting with Roger at nine-fifteen." Roger Wilson, the CIA Chief of Staff, was Steve's former boss.

"What'd they do, buck you all the way back to recruiter?" Laura smiled.

"Sorry, dear, the meeting's classified."

"You're full of bullshit."

"Have a good meeting, dear," Steve said with a patronizing smile as he got on a different elevator.

Laura exited on the seventh floor and headed to Bates' office. "Hi, Nancy," she said.

"Hi, Laura." Nancy pushed the intercom, "Director Bates, Ms. Messier is here."

The Director came through the doorway. "Good morning. How's the arm feeling?"

Laura flexed her arm. "Not too bad. I hate changing the damn bandage every morning."

Bates closed the door behind him and motioned her to chairs. "Let's sit here. How long before it's healed fully?"

"The doc said six weeks, but I'll have full use of the arm before then. Maybe, three. Why do you ask?"

"Word came through early this morning. The print on the comm set was a match with Ivan Ilitch."

"I was sure it would be."

"Mr. Martin needs you back in Paris as soon as you're feeling better. I'd like to offer you our assistance. How can we help?"

"I'm not sure about the timing yet, but there are logistics we need when we go in."

Bill found a legal pad on his desk and pulled a pen from his breast pocket. "What are you looking for?"

Laura thought for a minute. "A safe house. A place where there are no neighbors."

"And?"

"A car and driver who speaks English."

"What else?"

"Weapons and comm sets," she said.

"I'll make sure it's done."

"Thanks, Bill."

"Oh, and we've placed surveillance on your home. I know Steve has his own people, but I want to make sure we have a presence, too. Mr. Martin sent me a photo of Ilitch. If Ilitch comes in country, we'll get him."

"There's one more thing."

"Yes?"

"Please keep this confidential. I'm worried about leaks."

"I understand. We'll run this on a need to know basis."

"Thank you."

"I didn't get the pleasure of working with you on Eldorado Canyon last year, Laura. I'm glad to help you this time around." Bates walked Laura to the door. "Be careful and stay close to our guys. They'll protect you."

"Thanks, Bill."

***

It was over a week before Ivan Ilitch was summoned again to Petrovsky's office. He expected the delay as it was customary for Petrovsky to show displeasure by pushing aside those who participated in failed missions. When Ilitch arrived at the office, he found the inner door wide open and Jack Postl assembling a computer at the

Chairman's desk. "Excuse me," he said, after walking through the secretary's office and into the doorway. "Where's the Chairman?"

"He's working in a side office today," Postl said, nodding to a closed door along one of the side walls. "Let me tell him you're here. I saw you the other day, but I'm sorry, I don't remember your name."

"Ivan Ilitch."

"That's right. One moment," Postl said. He picked up Petrovsky's office phone. "Mr. Chairman, Ivan Ilitch is here to see you." He hung up the phone. "He'll be with you shortly. You're welcome to take a seat if you like." Ilitch sat in one of the two office chairs in front of the desk while Postl went back to working on the computer.

Ilitch waited nearly a half hour. When Petrovsky appeared through the door, he said, "Postl, I need to speak with Captain Ilitch privately."

"Of course, Sir."

"Shut the door behind you."

"Yes, Sir."

Petrovsky pushed several computer parts aside to clear space in the middle of his desk. "This idiot computer man is taking far too long building these computers," he said, pointing to the parts spread out on his desk. "I'm thinking a short stay in the prison downstairs will improve the speed with which he works."

Ilitch knew better than to respond. He looked straight down at the dark red carpet that blended with the dark colored mahogany walls. "Tell me, Captain Ilitch. Do you think a short stay in the prison would improve your marksmanship? I hear the woman still lives."

"She was wounded in the attempt, but you're right, Sir. She's still alive."

"So, you were beaten again by this woman?"

"I couldn't get a clear shot at her. She seems to be the luckiest person on the face of the earth."

Petrovsky studied Ilitch for a minute before responding. "I'm hearing nothing, but excuses, Captain. I want results. What are we to do? Surrender to the Americans?"

"No, Sir. I need to put together an infiltration team. Four men, all English speakers, all Special Forces. Give me that and I'll give you a successful result. I'm tired of being embarrassed by this woman."

Petrovsky nodded his agreement. "That's what I wanted to hear, Ivan." He slapped his hand down on the desk, knocking one of the computer parts to the floor. "You're finally taking this woman seriously. I'll give you whatever you need. Make a list and give it to me directly. Keep me fully informed regarding your timetable."

"Yes, Sir, and thank you."

"Now, get out of here and start your work, Captain."

Ilitch rose to attention, saluted his superior, turned and walked out of the office.

Jack, who had moved to the secretary's desk in the outer office, dialed a number which connected to a public phone in the subway station underneath Lubyanka. "Hello," the voice answered.

"Mother?" Postl asked.

"Board," the voice replied.

"He's on his way to you now. Blue shirt, jeans and black leather jacket."

"Thank you," the voice said before hanging up.

Petrovsky retrieved a computer part that had fallen to the floor and when laying it back on his desk, he happened to read the small sticker on the back, "Made in the U.S.A." What the hell is this, he asked himself? "Postl!" Petrovsky yelled.

"Yes, Sir," Postl said, sticking his head in the door.

"Come in here!"

"Yes, Sir." Postl stood in front of the desk.

"Where do you get these computer parts?"

A simple answer is best, Jack thought. *If Petrovsky thinks me an idiot, I'll give him no reason to think otherwise.* "I get them from a company in France," Postl replied innocently.

Petrovsky held up the part for Postl to look at. "This says it's made in the United States."

"I'm sure it was. That's where the latest equipment comes from."

"How do you find out about these parts?" Petrovsky asked.

"A company in France sends brochures to the Ministry."

"Let me see one of them."

"Sure. I think I have one in my bag." Jack retrieved his tool bag, opened it in front of Petrovsky and rummaged around until he found a brochure. It was crumpled, so Postl straightened it before handing it to him. Petrovsky opened the trifold and pointed to the last page.

"That's the name of the French company, 'Inline Computer Manufacturing?'"

"Yes, Sir," Postl replied.

"They're in Paris?"

"That's right. The address and phone are right there," Jack said, pointing to the brochure.

"I thought the West had a ban on sending electronic equipment to the Eastern Bloc."

"I don't know anything about that, Sir. You'd have to speak to the Minister."

"Don't we have computer companies here in Moscow?"

"With all due respect, Sir, the stuff they make isn't reliable. Everyone I know gets their equipment from the West," Postl said in a manner that suggested it was common knowledge.

"I see. Stay right there a minute."

Petrovsky picked up his phone and dialed the extension to the computer department in the Lubyanka Building.

"Technology. May I help you?" the receptionist asked.

"Get me Novotny. Petrovsky calling."

"One moment please."

Novotny picked up immediately. "Mr. Chairman, good day. How can I assist you?"

"Novotny, that big computer you use. Has it got a name?"

"It's an I.B.M. 4442 mainframe computer, Sir."

"What's I.B.M. stand for?"

"International Business Machines."

"Where was it made?"

"The United States."

"Why the hell do we get our equipment from America?" Petrovsky asked.

"The best equipment is made there, Sir."

"How do we circumvent the ban on electronic equipment?"

"We purchase from companies in France and Sweden. Is there a problem?" Novotny wondered whether Postl had caused a problem.

"Postl's working in my office. I saw one of his computer parts with an American label on it."

"Unfortunately, Sir, we have to rely on imports for much of our technology. Hopefully, we'll correct that in a few years."

"That's all I need." Petrovsky hung up and looked at Postl. "Apparently, you're correct. Has the ElectroTechnical Ministry done any kind of investigation into this company?"

Jack shrugged, "I think there's some kind of process to get on the approved vendor list, but honestly, I have no idea what's involved."

"Has anyone at the Ministry met these people?"

"Sure. They come to town once in a while. They give us lots of free samples."

"Free samples?" Petrovsky asked suspiciously. Petrovsky stared at Jack, trying to ascertain whether he had hidden motives. "I want to meet them the next time they're here. They're putting electronic devices in my headquarters. That's a concern."

"Yes, Sir. I understand."

"Good. Continue on with your work."

Petrovsky moved to an adjoining office. *Novotny's explanation wasn't convincing,* the Chairman thought. Petrovsky dialed a private number.

"Soviet Embassy, Paris," the voice answered.

"Get Denis Melinin on the phone. It's Petrovsky

calling from Moscow."

"Please wait."

Denis Melinin picked up immediately. "Greetings to you Mr. Chairman. How are you?"

"Melinin, I want you to investigate a computer company."

"A firm in Paris? What's the name?"

"Inline Computer Manufacturing. Find out everything you can and call me back personally."

"Very good, Sir."

Melinin was pleased for the opportunity to distinguish himself in the eyes of his boss. *I'll turn the company inside out if it means a promotion*, he thought.

Petrovsky searched his briefcase for the dossier that ElectroTechnical sent him regarding Jack Postl. He sensed something wrong, but couldn't quite figure out what his intuition told him. Finding the file, he decided to study it to allay his suspicion.

***

Ivan Ilitch would have preferred to drive to Lubyanka, but parking was difficult to find near the building, so Ilitch commonly walked from his apartment to the Kazansky rail station a few blocks away. He was at Lubyanka within minutes. The Red Line ran straight through the downtown area and past Lubyanka Square. It was popular in Moscow and trains were frequently packed with people, something that bothered Ilitch a great deal. Ivan was claustrophobic.

Standing elbow to elbow with others made him irritable, so he simply ignored passengers which made the three man job of following him easier. Ilitch walked downstairs to the subway station underneath Lubyanka. Three French agents spotted him as he waited on the platform. One man boarded the same car with Ilitch and the others boarded cars on either side. Their comm sets were concealed within the sleeves of their overcoats and no one noticed the men whispering into the newspapers they held in front of their faces. The men exited the train at Kazansky along with Ilitch and began a complicated series of overlaps so Ilitch never saw the same person more than once. They followed him to a newly built apartment building at 8 Basmannyy Pereulok, three blocks south of Kazansky. One of the men followed Ilitch into the building and waited alongside him for the elevator. Both men entered the elevator together. Ilitch exited at the fourth floor while the other man continued to the top floor. "Fourth floor exit," he said into his comm after Ilitch left the elevator. He waited on the top floor for instructions. The other two men, standing across the street, watched for lights in the windows of fourth floor apartments.

"Come back down, exit at four, and go right," one of the men across the street said into the microphone. What's the second apartment down that hallway?"

"404," came the reply a couple of minutes later.

"We got him. 8 Basmannyy Pereulok, Apartment 404."

The men waited for their colleague to exit the building. A dark colored van pulled to the curb in front of them seconds later. "Hop inside, gentlemen," the driver said, opening the side door. "We may have a long wait, so make yourselves comfortable." The van parked where the front entrance could be observed. They waited for Ilitch to exit the building, something that could have taken hours. They intended to identify the car Ilitch used. They didn't wait long as Ilitch exited the building only moments later, walking to a red Peugeot and driving away. One of them men snapped pictures.

"Are we following him?" the driver asked.

"No. We've got plenty of pictures. Let him go," the surveillance leader said. The French Intelligence team had done their job. The material would be sent by diplomatic bag to Paris, where Jacques Martin would view it in two days. Ivan Ilitch was known to French Intelligence.

***

The elderly man who spoke with a thick Russian accent lived alone in a rural cabin in the woods of Eastern Virginia. Colonel Fedor Belkin, a decorated Soviet soldier, had been imprisoned at Lubyanka for what the Soviet government called "subversive activities." His transgression? Repeated criticisms of Soviet involvement in Afghanistan. Upon his release after two years, he quietly left the country with the help of the CIA, staying briefly in Switzerland before being whisked off to the United States under cover. Belkin was granted a pension by the American government for his work advising the U.S. military and intelligence communities. The phone in his cabin rang in the early morning hours of a late April weekday. "Hello," the Colonel said.

"Colonel, it's Laura Messier calling," Laura said in Russian.

"What a pleasant surprise. I've not heard from you in quite some time, young lady. Have you been ill?"

"I was injured a few weeks ago, but I've recovered enough to resume my activities. How have you been feeling?"

"I'm doing quite well, thanks. Are you continuing your studies?" the Colonel asked.

"Yes, Sir, and I wondered if I could come for a visit."

"Of course, dear. Old men welcome visits from beautiful women. Come whenever you'd like," the Colonel said.

"Tomorrow morning?"

"Tomorrow would be fine."

Laura headed south the next morning on I-95, then southeast on Virginia Route 208 to Lewiston Road, eventually ending up on a long gravel drive that led to Belkin's cabin on the wooded shores of Lake Anna. Checking her rear view mirror frequently, she identified the chase car her surveillance team used. The Colonel was already working outside on his dock when Laura pulled up to the house. He waved and began walking toward the car. "Good morning," he shouted from a distance. As she opened the car door, Belkin's German shepherd began to bark furiously at something down the gravel drive. "Shhh, Igor," Belkin said as he walked toward the driveway. "A friend has come to visit."

"Hi Fedor. It's wonderful to see you again," Laura said in Russian. "Igor must be barking at the security team that followed me. They're probably parked somewhere down the driveway. I apologize, but I've come with a bit of an entourage today."

The Colonel laughed as he greeted Laura warmly. "I have no worries, young lady. Not with Igor around. He's a first class surveillance expert. My compliments on how much your Russian has improved. I can actually understand you now," the Colonel said, kissing her on both cheeks.

"It's great to see you doing so well, Fedor. Here," she said, handing him a picnic basket. "I thought we might enjoy lunch afterward."

"Very thoughtful of you. Let's set the basket inside while we work. I hope you don't mind that I asked Borys to join us this morning?"

"Oh no, not at all. Hi Borys," she said as they stepped into the cabin.

"Good morning, Miss Laura," he said. Borys was the bodyguard the CIA had assigned to Belkin, an athletic young man; a Russian speaker who'd been trained in the intricacies of Spetsnaz hand to hand combat. He'd serve as Laura's sparring partner. Colonel Belkin had helped developed the training program used by the Soviet Special Forces.

"Borys, would you bring the equipment from the shed?" the Colonel asked.

"Yes, Sir."

"We'll work on the grass in front of the cabin." Turning to Laura, he said, "Go ahead and get stretched out." Laura went outside and began a series of stretching exercises while Belkin retrieved a notebook and pen. Upon returning, his students had donned protective gear. "Are we ready?" Both nodded. "Very good. Let's begin with Advanced Level One," he said.

It was clear that Laura was the superior fighter, but not necessarily skilled in Belkin's techniques. Time and again, the Colonel corrected Laura when she broke from the Spetznas discipline.

"Borys keeps getting me angry and I want to smash his face," Laura said out of frustration. That brought laughter to Belkin. Borys didn't speak much English, but figured out the gist of what she said. He simply smiled.

"Aha! You cannot defeat him without resorting to other techniques," the Colonel observed.

"No, I can't," she admitted.

"Then, learn, my young friend."

However, Borys was simply too experienced in Spetsnaz technique and the battle ended up to be a stalemate, albeit one among friends.

Afterwards, Laura unpacked her lunch basket and the three of them sat on the grass eating sandwiches and potato salad. "You did a better job of remembering the sequences today. Your intensity was raised. Something has changed in you?" Belkin asked.

"I may be going on a mission soon."

"I see. You may face someone skilled in Soviet techniques?"

"Yes."

Belkin stared at Laura for a moment. He began to understand Laura's motivation. "The Soviet Union is the only place to find someone with greater skill than Borys." Belkin waited for a response.

Laura, hesitant to reveal operational details, finally said, "I'm not at liberty to comment on that."

Belkin gave her a hint of a smile as though he'd forced her to make a confession. "With all respect to Borys, your opponent will have greater skill. He'll certainly be more aggressive."

"So, how do I defeat him?" she asked.

"Give ground and counter strike. That's a good strategy for someone like yourself who has superior quickness, but is deficient in size and strength. Obviously, you have training in other disciplines you've not shown me. You'll be aware of his technique, but he won't know yours. So stay away from his strength and size advantage and wait for an opening. Then use your other training to disable your opponent."

"Thanks, I'll remember that." Could I change the subject and ask you a personal question?"

"Certainly, "Belkin said. "What would you like to know?"

"Why did you leave?"

"You mean the Soviet Union?"

"Yes," Laura answered.

Belkin hesitated, a hint of regret showing in his face. "None of us have the opportunity to pick the system we live under. I was born into a system and raised to believe in it. However, as we mature, we begin to see the flaws in our system of government. I'm sure you see flaws in the American system."

"Yes, of course."

"Then why don't you defect to the Soviet Union?"

"I like our system better," she said.

"So do I," Belkin said with a chuckle. "I saw a chance

to leave and how many times in life do we get a chance to start over?"

"Rarely."

"I had no wife, no children or family, so I took a chance. And now, here I am living on beautiful Lake Anna in a wonderful dacha I could never afford in Russia," he said, gesturing toward the lake and his cabin. "I have plenty of money and I'm talking with a beautiful woman. Life can be good if one is willing to take chances."

"Do you miss your country?"

"I miss the country of my youth, but not the country that exists now."

Laura glanced at her watch. "I'm afraid I must leave now. I'll give you a call when I return."

"Wait one moment, please. I have something to give you," Belkin said. He rose and walked into the cabin, reappearing a minute later with a black leather pouch and a scrap of paper upon which a note was written. He handed the paper to Laura, "Where you're going, you'll need help. Here is the name and phone number of a friend. I'll contact him to let him know of your visit. He'll ask a favor in return for his help. When you call him, you'll need this." He handed over the pouch.

Laura memorized the information on the paper scrap. She handed it back to the Colonel. "Thank you, Fedor. I appreciate everything you've done," Laura said.

"You're welcome. Now, leave an old man to his fishing," he said, waving his hand toward the lake. "A young woman must have hundreds of more important things to do than talk with an old man like me."

Laura kissed him on the cheek. "Stay well, my friend,"

she said.

***

Jack Postl turned on his computer before leaving for work on Monday, May 4th and found a message marked "Urgent!" It read:

"*Delete any records of communication between us. Destroy the hard drive and modem. You will be contacted at the dead drop in Sokolniki Park. Check the drop Mondays and Thursdays.*"

Jack sat frozen in front of the terminal. For the first time since he began communicating with the French, he became frightened. Are they going to search the apartment? Arrest me? He frantically searched his closet until he found a replacement hard drive and modem, installed them on his machine, and re-installed the operating system. He prepared for work and slipped the old drive and modem into his backpack. He discarded them in a trash bin on his way to work. He looked around frequently, thinking he may have been followed, but nothing seemed out of the ordinary.

The phone rang at the secretary's desk Monday morning, May 4th. "Chairman Petrovsky's office," Irina said.
"Denis Melinin from Paris calling for the Chairman."
"One moment please." She pushed the intercom,

"Chairman, I have Denis Melinin on hold for you."

"Put him through," Petrovsky said. "Melinin, what do you have?"

"Mr. Chairman, we investigated the Inline firm you asked about. We entered the office and spoke with the receptionist last Wednesday, but were unable to meet with the manager. We penetrated their office Thursday night, took a look at their files and saw a number of purchase orders and shipping documentation, some of it for the ElectroTechnical Ministry. We entered the storage area and found a number of computers and parts."

"You think they're a legitimate company?"

"Yes, Sir, as far as we can tell. We checked their corporate records and found them properly filed. They have a small warehouse out by the airport. It was filled with computers and parts. The truck parked in front had the company name on it. It's hard to believe they're a shell company."

"Did the corporate paperwork list shareholders?" Petrovsky asked.

"Yes, Sir. Some of them appear in the Paris phone directory."

"I need you to drive by those addresses. I need to know those shareholders are real people."

"We'll do it today."

"Very good."

Petrovsky hung up, thought for a moment and then punched the intercom. "Irina, get Serge on the phone, please."

"Yes, at once, Sir." She hung up and dialed upstairs.

"Assistant Director Orlov," the Director said.

"Mr. Orlov, it's Irina from downstairs. The Chairman would like to speak with you."

"Of course. Put him through." Kristina connected the lines. "Good morning, Mr. Chairman," Orlov said.

"Serge, I want to investigate someone working in the building. His name's Jack Postl. He's from ElectroTechnical and he's installing computers over here. Find out everything you can. Turn his life upside down if you have to. And send a couple of men to search his apartment."

"Yes, Sir. We'll do it today."

Chapter Seven

IVAN ILITCH GATHERED his men in the warehouse he rented across the street from his apartment. It was where he'd built a shooting range, a workout facility and a small office. "Maxim," he said to Khozin, "this is Oleg and Timofei, friends from my Red Army days. Oleg, Timofei, meet my partner, Maxim." The men shook hands and sat in folding chairs. Ilitch pulled a bulletin board in front of them.

"Our target is this woman," Ilitch began, pinning Messier's picture on the board. "Her name is Laura Messier. She lives in Washington, D.C."

Oleg whistled. "Damn, Ivan, she's fucking hot. Can we keep her locked up and fuck her for a while before we kill her?"

"This isn't a joke, Oleg. She'd kick your ass in two seconds. She killed the entire staff of the KGB in Paris last fall. She's dangerous. And she knows we're coming." That brought silence to the room.

"Why don't you set up a sniper position and take her out?" Timofei asked.

"I tried twice. We're going to have to take her at close range."

"Can I fuck her first?" Oleg asked, still chuckling from his last comment.

"You want the job or not?" an annoyed Ilitch asked.

"How much does it pay?" Oleg asked.

"The KGB will pay each of you five million rubles if we're successful."

"Fuck, yes, I want the job."

"Then shut the fuck up and listen," Ilitch demanded.

"Sorry. Go ahead."

"Messier attends meetings in Paris at the DST headquarters on Monday mornings," Ilitch continued. "You and Timofei are going to stake out the place."

"What do we do if we see her?" Oleg asked.

"She'll fly back to Washington after the meeting. Follow her. Maxim and I will already be there. Once you arrive, we'll cut the power and phone line in the middle of the night," Ilitch said pointing to her house on a map, "then we'll enter the house and kill everyone. It's a one day job."

"She have an alarm system?" Timofei asked.

"Yes, but it's turned off."

"Why?"

"Because she's got two full-time guards. They go in and out of the house frequently, so they leave it off."

"It sounds messy, Ivan," Timofei said. "A lot of shit could go wrong. How many people inside?"

"Besides her? Probably the husband and a military guard, but we'll watch to get a count. I'm not counting two guards outside who patrol the perimeter."

"We're outnumbered, Ivan, at least 5-4, by my count," Timofei said. "Not good odds if she knows we're coming."

"That's why we take the outside security first before we enter the house. If we're unable to do that, the mission is a no go."

"You have a floor plan of the house?"

"We'll go over the operational details at the safe house when you arrive."

"She got a dog?" Timofei asked.

"No dogs."

"I hate fucking dogs."

"How do we get out of there afterward?" Oleg asked.

"We'll go directly to the airport. You two," Ilitch said, nodding to Oleg and Timofei, "will take the first flight out to Paris. Maxim and I will go through Geneva. We'll be out of the country by the time anyone discovers the bodies."

"What about documents, credit cards and cash?" Oleg asked.

"Maxim's got everything you need. He has the address of the target if you lose her and the phone and address of the safe house. Remember, Maxim and I will already be there watching her residence. If you need to contact us, call the safe house. Anything else?"

The men looked at each other. "I think that covers it," Timofei said.

"Maxim, you have anything to add?" Ilitch asked.

"I have an envelope for each of you," Khozin said, "with everything you need." He passed an oversize envelope to each man.

"One more thing," Ilitch said. "Both of you are English speakers so once you board the flight to Washington, it's English only, even when speaking with each other. Got it?"

"Yeah, sure. No problem," Oleg said.

"You can work out here at the warehouse before you leave. Use the gun range, lift weights, anything you like. Suppressors only when you use the range. Maxim's got keys to give you. Let yourselves in and out. If I don't hear from you, we'll meet late Monday night in Washington. Be prepared in case we have to fight, gentlemen. I hear she's really good."

***

"Where'd you go this morning, sweetie?" Steve asked at dinner. "You rolled out of bed pretty early."

"You know the Soviet defector Belkin?"

"We got him out a couple of years ago."

"He lives down on Lake Anna. I drove down for a visit."

"And?"

"And what?" Laura asked.

"What'd you talk about?"

"He's coaching me in Spetsnaz hand to hand combat."

"That's it?"

"I took a picnic lunch for us. Why are you asking?"

"You realize you're talking to an Associate Director?" Steve asked.

"You realize I've got a gun? Stop with the questions."

"Get prepared to answer some," Steve said, frustrated by Laura's evasion. "Bates wants to see you in the morning. You, too, Rick."

"Hey, leave me out of this," Rick said. "I'm minding my own business. Great roast, by the way, Laura."

"He wants to see both of you. I'll be sitting in on the meeting, so you might as well tell me about Belkin," Steve said.

"Thanks, Rick. That was awfully nice of you to say." Laura turned to Steve. "You don't like the roast?"

"The roast is very good. Now, tell me."

"I've said all I'm going to say," Laura said, rising from the table. "Your turn to do the dishes."

The three of them arrived promptly at 9:30 am in Director Bates' office the next morning, Thursday, May 7th. "Good morning everyone," Bates' secretary said. "The Director's waiting."

"Ah, there you are," Bates said as he walked around his desk to meet them. "Come on in and let's chat for a bit. Good morning, Steve."

"Morning, boss," Steve said.

"Laura. Rick," Bates said, acknowledging them with the plastic smile administrator's use when feigning politeness. "Let's pull up an extra chair for Steve and get into this thing, shall we? Can I get coffee for anyone?" After a pause, Bates said, "No? Okay. Laura, I've been told you visited Fedor Belkin. Would you mind telling me the details of your discussion?"

"Fedor and I are friends. He's been coaching me in Spetsnaz training methods."

"What else?"

"I made a picnic lunch. We sat on his lawn and ate after my workout," Laura said.

"I find it hard to believe that was the extent of your visit. It's my understanding he gave you something."

Laura looked Bates straight in the eye. "Yes, he gave me a gift. As I said, we're friends. You can make up whatever story fits your narrative, Bill, but I've seen Fedor several times over the past couple of years. This isn't anything new."

"Nothing else was discussed?"

"No."

Bates didn't believe her, but he knew she'd never divulge more. "Okay, let's move on," he said. "The French have informed me your mission will go active next week."

"Good. I'm ready." Laura said.

"We have a scheduling problem. The Secretary of State will be visiting Moscow next week for talks. The trip's been on the books for months. Steve will be a part of SecState's delegation. Having you and Steve there at the same time is a problem.

"Did I hear you correctly? Steve will be in Moscow next week?"

"Yes."

"Steve neglected to mention it," she said, casting a glance at Steve. "Will he be anywhere near where we're conducting ops?" Laura asked.

"Possibly," Bates said.

"What I hear you saying is, if something happens, let's say the mission goes sideways, they could use Steve as leverage," Laura said.

"That's our concern. The DST moved their timetable up because the Soviets have taken a sudden interest in the front company they're using. They don't believe the Soviets have turned up anything, but they're not sure."

"Their source could be close to being exposed," Laura said. "Did you ask the French to delay the mission?"

"Yes."

"And they refused?"

"That's right."

"So you're asking me to stay home?"

"I'm sorry," Bates said.

"This is a French mission, Bill. The State Department

181

talks have nothing to do with me."

"The Soviets may believe they're linked," Bates said. "Let's just say we want better coordination."

"Well, if the French are going ahead with the op, then I'm required to go. The solution to your problem is simple. Steve stays home and you send someone else," Laura said.

"Steve's required to attend. He'll be meeting Serge Orlov, his equivalent rank in the KGB. We must send someone of equal rank."

"It's been long established that I work with the French, Bill. It's been that way ever since I started here. I didn't pick the date for the mission. If you've got a problem, it's with them, not me."

Bates' frustration showed in his face and tone of voice. "I'm trying to avoid a confrontation, Laura. The issues at stake in these talks are global. We can't afford to risk an embarrassment while the Secretary's in Moscow."

"I guess you're saying that I'd be an embarrassment."

"No, that's not what I said."

"Look, Ivan Ilitch is important. He'll be back, Bill, and this time he'll bring a team with him. Everyone will be at risk; Steve, Rick, the guards you placed at the house. Everyone. Ilitch is a pro and he'll kill everyone in the house."

"I understand your concern, but we simply can't have one of our agents doing an op in Moscow while SecState's there. It's out of the question. I'm giving you an official order to stand down."

"I suppose this is where I say I'm a French citizen and you have no authority to stop me."

"Steve, talk to her," Bates said, looking at Steve.

"Honey, Bill's just asking for a delay."

"I see you're taking his side of things," Laura replied with the tension rising in her voice. She was visibly upset. Steve taking Bates' side of the issue was a betrayal. "And don't ever 'honey' me inside this building." She turned to Bates. "I work for the DST. If they say the mission is a go, then I'm going."

"I can prevent you from going, you know," Bates said ominously.

"What are you going to do? Arrest me?"

"Yes, if it comes to that."

There was an uncomfortable silence in the room before Laura spoke again. She couldn't fight the entire agency, she reasoned, but Bates had gone too far. She gave Bates an admonition. "You'd find it difficult to arrest me, Bill, if I resisted. Do you really want to go down that road?"

Bates recognized her anger and sought to lessen the tension. He lowered his voice. "Laura, I'm sorry. You can't go."

Laura hesitated again, realizing she'd met a brick wall. She decided the solution was to simply lie. "Here's what I'm willing to do. I'll delay my mission one week. Is that satisfactory?"

"Yes," Bates said, relief showing on his face. "Do I have your word on that?"

"Of course."

"Then I accept you at your word and no further action's necessary."

Laura rose as if to leave, but she reached in her bag and pulled out her pistol. She leaned over the desk and pointed it at Bates. "One more thing, though," she said. Bates froze at the sight of the weapon. Whether it was fear or surprise or just not knowing how to react, Bates was motionless. "I don't like to be threatened," she hissed, just loud enough for Bates to hear.

"I apologize, Laura."

"I didn't ask for an apology. Just be aware that I don't react well to threats." She put the Sig back in her purse. "You've got your week. Now, with your permission, Mr. Williams and I are leaving. Will we have any trouble on our way out?"

"No, you're free to go."

"Thank you."

Steve walked Laura to the elevator. He stood there speechless, shocked by Laura pointing a gun at the Director.

"I'll see you tonight at the house," Laura said coldly.

"Okay," he said. He tried to kiss her on the cheek, but she pushed him away.

"Stop!" she said. "No more playing nice."

"I just thought ..." Steve began to say, but Laura interrupted him.

"Just go back to work." The elevator opened and she, along with Rick, left the building.

Once Laura and Rick arrived home, Laura carried Belkin's pouch into the house. It contained a Soviet telephone scrambler. She wired it into her bedroom phone and placed a call.

"Da?" the voice asked.

"Please go to secure," Laura responded in Russian.

"One moment." There was about a ten second delay.

"Go ahead, please."

"I need to speak with Arkady Tonov."

"Who should I say is calling?"

"A friend of Fedor Belkin," she said.

"I'm Admiral Tonov. And you are?'"

"Shewolf."

"Your reputation precedes you."

"Fedor told me to call."

"How can I assist you?"

"I have a list of needs."

Tonov listened to the list. "Those things will be difficult to acquire, but not impossible. I'm prepared to help if funds are available."

"I can provide the funds."

"Shall we settle on $50,000 U.S. dollars cash?"

"That's fair. Fedor mentioned you needed something else?" Laura asked.

"Yes."

"What if I told you I could satisfy that request?"

"Then we have a deal, Shewolf. I'll have the items ready. What's your arrival date?"

"Next Monday."

"Goodbye," Tonov said abruptly, breaking the connection.

Laura wasn't quite sure how to satisfy the Admiral's request, but no mission ever unfolds precisely as planned. *I'll just have to improvise a solution when I get there*, she said to herself.

Laura unplugged the scrambler and called her bank. "Laura Messier calling. I need to make a large cash withdrawal."

When she stated the amount, the officer asked, "When will you arrive?"

"Thirty minutes."

"We'll have it ready."

She came downstairs and asked Rick to take her to a luggage store. "Of course. I know just the place," Rick replied. The shop had a selection of leather luggage and Laura bought a sturdy travel bag.

She hopped back in the car. "Could you drop me by the bank for a minute?"

"Sure."

Rick waited in the car while Laura withdrew $50,000 from her own account and another $50,000 from the joint account she shared with Steve. She handed the travel bag to the bank officer. "Please put eighty in this and I'll put the other twenty in my purse."

Once they arrived home, Laura began to pack.

"You're going to Paris?" Rick asked.

"Right now before they try to stop me."

"I'm coming with you."

"No. Bates will fire you for it," Laura said.

"To hell with Bates. I'm coming."

"Rick, if Bates fires me, I can work for DST. You've got to keep your job."

"I can always go back to the Marines, Laura."

"You've got a clean record. Don't mess it up. Stay here and smooth things over with Steve for me, will you?"

"You'll need back-up over there," Rick said.

"DST will shadow me."

"I'll stay tonight and think it over. You might see me at

Monday's meeting. Just so you know."

"Fine. Stay here over the weekend, talk to Steve and make peace with Bates if he calls."

Laura pulled her own black box from a closet and called the secure line at DST headquarters in Paris. "Is Jacques Martin still in the office this evening?" she asked. "Laura Messier calling."

"One moment," the receptionist said. After a brief delay, Jacques answered, "Hi, Laura. I guess you heard about the mission. It's a go for next week."

"Yes, I heard. I'm coming into Paris early. Tonight, in fact. I'm coming in on my Eileen Thomas ID. It will be the last Concorde flight from Dulles, arriving de Gaulle around 4:00 am. Can you arrange to have someone there to walk me through customs?"

"Yes, we'll have someone meet you at the gate."

"One more thing. I'm sending a black travel bag by diplomatic pouch. Hold it for me."

"I'll keep an eye out for it."

"Thanks, Jacques. See you Monday."

Laura called the property management company that looked after the building Laura and Steve owned in Paris. The receptionist answered, "Premiere Property Management."

"Marie, please."

After a moment's delay, "This is Marie. How can I help you?"

"Marie, its Laura Messier. Do you have anyone in the apartment on Rue Cler?"

"No, not right now."

"I'm going to need to use it for a while."

"When will you arrive?"

"I know it's kind of short notice, but I'll be there tonight."

"I'll send someone over to make sure it's ready for you."

"Thank you, Marie."

An hour later, Rick helped Laura load luggage into her car. "I've got to run by the French Embassy first, then to Dulles."

"No problem ..." He stopped mid-sentence and stood motionless in the driveway.

"What?" she asked.

"I saw a reflection in one of the upper floors of that high rise over there. Just a flash, then it was gone. Take a look."

Laura stared at the building three blocks away, a fifteen story condo building that rose above the surrounding houses. "There! See it?" Rick asked. "That's a scope."

"It would be a tough shot from there," Laura said. "Four hundred yards into the sun with a crosswind."

"If that's Ilitch, will he follow you to Moscow?" Rick asked.

"Wouldn't you? What do they call it, the home field advantage?"

"You think he'd actually bring a team to D.C.?"

"That's what I'd do."

"You got a plan?" Rick asked.

"I'm going to kill every last one of them."

"Fuck," Maxim said. "I think they made us. Come, take a look, Ivan." Ilitch walked to the window, took the rifle and peered over the rooftops and into the driveway of Messier's home. He saw Messier and her male companion stare at the building.

"I think you're right," Ilitch said. "Reflection off the scope." He pulled the rifle back and looked at the scope. "Yep." He trained it on Messier again. "Hello, sexy lady. We're going to have a little surprise for you when you get back." He put down the rifle. "Looks like they're getting ready to leave. Let's go snooping around after they've gone. Find the phone and electric lines going into the house."

"We can use those work shirts with 'Acme Electric' on them," Khozin said.

Ilitch chuckled. "Yeah, just like those American cartoons with the coyote. I love those."

Laura asked Rick to wait at the curb in front of the Embassy of the Republic of France. She stuffed the Soviet scrambler into the travel bag along with the money, entered the Embassy and showed her French passport to the guard. "What's your business today, Ms. Messier?" he asked in French.

"I need to see the head of DST station."

"What's in the bag?"

"Classified material to be sent by diplomatic pouch to Paris."

"Do you know where the office is?"

"Of course."

"Go on up."

Andre LaPointe met Laura in his outer office. LaPointe looked like many public servants, devoid of personality, unassuming in appearance. Short with gray hair, overweight, early 50s, there was nothing distinguishing about him, probably by design. "Good afternoon, Ms. Messier. You're sending something by pouch?"

"Yes, Sir. I need to send this bag to DST Station Paris and it must arrive ASAP to the attention of Jacques Martin."

"I'll need to see what's inside."

Laura opened the bag. LaPointe's eyes widened when he saw the cash, but otherwise just said, "I see. We're going to call this Top Secret." He took three classified stickers, placed one on the side of the bag and used the other two as a seal overlapping the top. He put an address sticker on it. "Jacques will have it late tomorrow afternoon."

Laura took a sheet of stationery and wrote a short note to Jacques. "Would you put this in an envelope and send it to Jacques as well?"

"Certainly, Ma'am."

Laura hurried back to the car. "You've got driving skills, Rick. Get me to Dulles fast. I've got to go through the line at the ticket counter."

"We need to wait a minute," Rick replied.

"Why?"

"You'll see." A Metro squad car rolled up beside them. The officer got out and motioned for Rick to roll down the driver's side window.

"Are you Rick Williams?"

"Yes, officer." He showed his CIA issue ID. "Official government business. I need an escort to Dulles."

"You got it." The officer turned on his flashers and siren. Laura was at Dulles in twenty minutes and made her flight to Paris.

***

Thursday evening, Jack arrived home to find his apartment ransacked. The contents of his kitchen drawers had been emptied onto the floor. The refrigerator door had been left open. Jack's clothing had been scattered around the bedroom and the mattress cut open. The living room furniture had been overturned; the cushions ripped open with a knife. His computer was missing. The computer parts on his work bench had vanished. *They've discovered I'm working with the French*, Jack thought. *No, if they knew that, they'd arrest me. They only suspect something.*

Jack immediately left the apartment and walked to the Ohotny Ryad stop on the Red Line and took the subway north to the Sokolniki station. It was a warm May afternoon, perfect for a walk, but Jack hardly noticed the weather. His worry was being followed. He saw no one as he loitered outside the park. He entered the park and walked down a footpath to a picnic table atop a hill, a few hundred meters into the park. Jack's dead drop was a rotted hole in an old tree not far into the woods. Jack sat at the table while hikers passed until he found himself alone. He walked into the woods, found the tree, reached into the space and pulled out a message. It read:

"Submit a large purchase order Friday for the Lubyanka Building. Request permission to travel to Paris to inspect the machines before delivery. Inline has informed the Ministry their personnel will arrive Monday evening for talks. You will accompany them back to Paris Tuesday. Copy all files from the Chairman's computer before you leave."

Jack walked back to the train station, deposited the note in a trash bin outside the station and returned home.

The following morning, Friday, May 8th, Jack began his workday by stopping at the ElectroTechnical Ministry. He walked in Minister Gradovich's office where Natasha, the secretary, smiled broadly. "Hi, Jack. What brings you over this morning?" she asked.

"I need a blank purchase order." She walked to a filing cabinet and rummaged around inside until she found the form. "Would you like to fill it out now and leave it?"

"Is he in this morning?" Jack asked.

"Yes. I'll let him know you're here."

She pushed her intercom button, "Minister, Jack is here to see you." She looked up at Jack, "He says to come in."

"Thanks."

Jack walked in Gradovich's office with the purchase order in hand. "Good morning, Sir."

"I'm glad you stopped by, Jack. I was going to call you this morning. Inline is sending sales reps to Moscow on Monday."

"I'm glad you'll get a chance to meet them. I need to order parts for twelve desktop machines to complete the Lubyanka job. Should we hold the PO and give it to them in person?"

"Yes, there's no sense in mailing it. Here, let me see it," Gradovich said holding out his hand.

"I haven't filled it out yet, but if you have time, I'd like to sit down and complete it so I can get your signature."

"Use part of my desk," Gradovich said pointing to one end of his desk. "We can talk while you're filling out the order. I thought we'd take them to dinner on Monday night."

"My social calendar is empty."

"Empty? A young man like you? We've got to get you a girlfriend, Jack. Natasha likes you."

"I had no idea. I'll have to ask her out some time."

"She's smart, pretty and someone's going to catch her eye. Be quick about it."

Jack completed the purchase order and handed it to Gradovich. "I'd like to ask a favor." Jack said as Gradovich signed the PO.

"How can I help?"

"I'd like to travel to Paris and inspect the shipment before it's delivered. Obtaining replacement parts slows up the installation. The Lubyanka people seem to be in a hurry."

"Don't they test everything before it's sent out?" Gradovich asked.

"I'm sure they do, but I ask for upgrades. I'd like to test those upgrades right at the warehouse."

Gradovich hesitated, thinking for a minute. "How long would you need?"

"A couple of days. It could save us weeks waiting for parts."

"When would you leave?"

"When are the Inline people leaving?"

"They're flying out Tuesday night."

"Could I leave when they do?"

"Where are we on the Lubyanka install?"

"The two machines in the Chairman's office are up and running. I've got two more going in one of the Director's offices. After that, I don't have any parts left. If I'm at the warehouse, I can hurry them up a bit."

"I can't authorize travel, Jack. I'll have to put in a request with the Deputy Chairman. The KGB might need to approve the request. I'll call today and get the process started. Just so you know, if it's approved, they'll send a security officer along with you."

"I don't have a problem with that."

"Good. Give me a call before the end of the day and I'll let you know."

Serge Orlov stopped by Petrovsky's office Friday morning. "Is the boss here?"

Irina pushed the intercom, "Mr. Chairman, Director Orlov is here to see you."

"Thank you, Irina. Send him in."

Orlov entered the office where Petrovsky had pulled two chairs together. "What have you got for me, Serge?"

"I wanted to brief you about the Americans coming in town next week."

"You mean the Foreign Ministry meeting?"

"Yes. We rented a conference room over at the National. The Americans are staying there and we want to keep them confined inside the hotel."

Petrovsky laughed. "Good. What's the agenda?"

"They sent an advisory out about the meeting. Did you happen to see it?"

"It's probably around here somewhere. Just tell me."

"The Americans want to complain about our involvement in Central and South America, specifically Nicaragua. We'll refuse to discuss it. They'll ask for more cooperation in Europe. Maybe a drawdown of forces. That's something we can discuss. They're going to complain about Soviet submarine traffic off the east coast of North America and electronic eavesdropping in the Bering Sea, among other things. They'd also like to discuss African politics, which is interesting, considering they've ignored the continent."

"The goals on our side?" Petrovsky asked.

"We'd like more cooperation with their space program and establish regular communications between our bases in the Antarctic. We'd like advance notice of ice breaker movements in the Arctic. We'll review new verification protocols for Salt II, ask for elimination of their electronic surveillance in the Black Sea and the shadowing of our ships in the Mediterranean. I'm sure they'll bring up terrorism and various security issues of minor importance. Defense will send someone over and the Foreign Secretary will run the meeting."

"What do we know about the official you'll be meeting with?"

"They're sending Steven Tilton, a career analyst. He's one of Bates' associate directors. Experienced, smart; he's married to one of their field agents in Europe, Laura Messier. Their defense rep will be James Donaldson. Career military; Army Brigadier General from the Pentagon. Nuclear expert."

"I'm surprised they'd send Tilton. We've had a contract out on his wife for months."

"CIA doesn't believe it. They think Messier's been the subject of random violence," Orlov said.

"Good."

Orlov smiled. He liked Petrovsky's brusque manner. "I also wanted to brief you on the investigation of this computer worker, Jack Postl."

"Find anything interesting?" Petrovsky asked.

"He's clean. We turned his apartment upside down. Found nothing. We took his computer to Novotny. He didn't find anything, either. We poked around his personal life. No girlfriend, no extra income, no bad habits. There's nothing we can use as leverage."

"What about the family?"

"I investigated his parents in Prague," Orlov said. "Called party officials there. They've got nothing on the family. The father is popular among party officials."

"So, we've got nothing to worry about?"

"I don't think so. He seems completely normal."

"Good work, Serge. Anything else?"

"I see they put one of those computers on your desk," Orlov said. "They put one in my office, too. What do you think of them?"

"I haven't turned mine on yet. How about you?"

"I didn't understand a word Postl said during the training. I have no idea how to use it."

"Me either. It's Soviet progress, Serge," Petrovsky said. "Installing machines no one can use." Both men laughed.

Later that afternoon, Denis Melinin picked up the phone in Paris and called Moscow. "Denis Melinin calling for the Chairman."

"I'm sorry, Mr. Melinin, but the Chairman's left for the weekend. He'll be back Monday morning. Can I take a message?"

"I need to speak to him about Inline Computer Company in Paris."

"Very good. I'll give him the message."

"Thank you, Irina. Have a pleasant weekend."

"You, too, Mr. Melinin."

Jack drove to Lubyanka Friday afternoon and backed his small truck up to a loading dock at the rear of the building. "Good afternoon, Mr. Postl," the guard said as Jack raised the cargo door. "Loading in today?"

"Yeah, I've got a computer printer to install in the building," Jack said, as he opened the back of the truck.

"Sorry, but I've got to check the box."

"No problem." Jack set the box down and pulled a box cutter out of his tool pouch. "Here, I've got something to open it with." Jack sliced open the packing tape, opened the box and allowed the guard to inspect the contents.

"You're good. Go ahead," the guard said. "You need help getting it in the building?"

"No, I can handle it. I'll run it up on the dolly."

"Have a great weekend, Mr. Postl," the guard said, noting the delivery on his clipboard before returning to the desk inside the door.

Jack took the printer to Petrovsky's office where he asked Irina for access. "I'm sorry, Jack, the Chairman's left for the weekend. I'm not supposed to allow anyone inside."

"Can I leave it in your office over the weekend?"

Irina looked around. "There's really no place for it out here. Go ahead and put it in his office."

"It'll only take a minute or two. I'm going to unpack it so I can take the box back with me."

"That's fine."

Jack entered Petrovsky's office, turned on the machine, waited for it to boot and then slid a floppy disk into the disk drive. He used his administrative password to gain full access and entered the commands to copy the files previously downloaded from the mainframe. While waiting, he began to unpack the printer. After a couple of minutes, Irina appeared in the doorway. "Need anything, Jack?"

"Can I move the end table next to the desk? I need to set the printer close enough so I can run a cable to the computer."

"Sure, go ahead. If he doesn't like it, he can move it back on Monday."

Irina returned to her desk while Jack slipped a second floppy into the computer. He moved the end table next to Petrovsky's desk, set the printer on top and began to unpack the printer cable and power cord. Jack removed the second floppy and inserted a third into the machine.

"Irina, could you come here a moment?" Jack asked loudly.

She appeared in the doorway. "Yes, Jack?"

"I can't reach the electrical outlet underneath his desk. The power cord is too short. Do you have an extension cord I can use?"

"Maybe. Let me look."

Jack removed the third floppy and inserted the fourth.

Irina returned with an extension cord in her hand. "Will this do?" she asked.

"Perfect. Thanks." Jack ran the cord underneath Petrovsky's desk to extend the printer's power cord to the outlet underneath the desk. He removed the fourth floppy disk and inserted the fifth. He gathered the packing materials and placed them inside the printer box. He set the box in Irina's outer office. "I just need another minute, Irina. I want to make sure the printer turns on properly."

Irina smiled. "No problem, Jack."

When the last file had been transferred, Jack removed the floppy, logged off the system and shut down the computer. He slid the floppies into his jacket and turned off the machine. *Only Novotny would know I accessed the system*, he thought. *If he looks.*

Jack loaded the empty box on his dolly and exited Petrovsky's office. "I'm done. You want me to turn out the lights?" Jack asked.

"No, that's fine," Irina replied. "I'll do it when I leave this afternoon. Doing anything interesting this weekend?"

"I don't have enough money to do anything interesting."

"I know the feeling. Oh, by the way, Novotny's looking for you. He told me to tell you."

"Thanks," Jack said, panicked by the thought that Novotny had checked his computer and found something incriminating.

"Have a nice weekend, Jack," Irina said.

"You, too."

Jack stopped by Novotny's office on the way out of the building. "Hey, you wanted to see me?"

"Don't get angry, Jack. I had nothing to do with it." Novotny pointed at the ceiling. "Those bastards upstairs gave me your computer. It's in the back room if you'd like it back."

"Could I take it with me now?"

"No problem. Hang on and I'll get it for you." Novotny returned carrying Jack's computer. "Here, I'll put it on the dolly." He set the machine in the printer box. "They tear up your place?"

"How'd you know?"

"When they showed up with your computer, I figured as much. They did the same thing to me when I started here. There's nothing to worry about."

"They tore the apartment up, Boris. I can't afford to replace that stuff."

"Bunch of paranoid bastards, Jack," Novotny said. "Don't complain or you'll make it worse. It happens a lot around here. Just pretend it never happened."

"That's what I thought, too. Thanks for the machine."

"Not a problem."

"Would you mind if I used your phone?" Jack asked. "I need to call the Ministry." He picked up Novotny's phone.

"Minister Gradovich's office. May I help you?"

"Natasha, its Jack. I need to speak with the Minister."

"Sure. Hang on," the secretary said.

"Yes," Gradovich said.

"Did you hear about the travel request?"

"They want to see it in writing. Natasha's typing it now. We'll run it over to the Deputy Chairman's office before the end of the day. We should know something on Monday."

"Thanks a lot."

"I want you to understand something. If the request is denied, it has nothing to do with you. It's expensive to send bodyguards on trips. And they must send someone because Western spies often kidnap people."

"I understand. Thanks."

"I'll see you Monday. Remember, we've got Inline coming in."

"Yes, Sir."

***

"Go to secure," Steve said. Laura had already set up the scrambler on the phone at the Paris apartment.

"Go ahead, Steve," she said.

"What are you doing in Paris? I waited for you last night. What's going on?"

"I needed to get out of town for a while."

"You're not safe in Paris."

"I'm as safe as I am in D.C. There was Soviet surveillance at the house."

"But we have security here. In Paris, you've got nothing."

"The agents at the house, Steve, are only there to keep an eye on me."

"That's absolutely false and you know it," Steve said.

"I'm not going to argue with you. The DST will check on me from time to time. Have a good meeting in Moscow and I'll see you when you get back."

"That's it? Tell me you're not going on that mission next week."

"I'm not going, but I need to tell them in person."

Steve thought about that for a moment. "I understand. Please be careful. Keep your head down and I'll stop off on my way back to D.C. Bye."

Laura hoped she'd be safe at the apartment. The management company had put a string of tourists in the apartment since Laura had returned to the States. The locals ignored them. Nevertheless, she kept a low profile over the weekend, avoiding her friends in the neighborhood.

As was her custom before a mission, Laura calmed herself by visiting tourist attractions. She visited the Louvre, the Musee Rodin and the Tuileries Gardens. She enjoyed the sights, the spring weather and the anonymity that public places provided. Watching children play in the Gardens, she wondered whether she'd ever have a family of her own. She longed for the kind of familial bonds that she'd never felt as a child. The beauty of childlike innocence was attractive. *My life is far too complicated*, Laura thought. She pledged to change her life upon her return. By Monday morning, she felt a peace that normally escaped her in dealing with the complexities of life. She was ready.

***

Laura stepped out of a taxi Monday morning at DST headquarters and although she suspected the building was under surveillance, she felt no immediate threat. Laura paused on the sidewalk in front of the building for a moment. The urban landscape looked normal for a Monday morning. The auto traffic, pedestrians, the light rain that dampened the street; it was a typical spring day. She avoided looking directly at the building down the street which she guessed housed a Soviet safe house because she wanted her watchers to believe they went unnoticed. The overwhelming feeling Laura experienced that morning was relief. Her ordeal was about to end, one way or another. As she entered the building, she felt a confidence that is only derived from experience. *This is just another mission*, she thought; *no more or less dangerous than what I've experienced before.*

Jean and Jacques were talking quietly in the hallway as she approached. "Great to see you, Mademoiselle," Jean said, giving her a kiss on each cheek. "You look stunning this morning."

Jacques clasped her hand in both of his. "I'm so glad you came. Your employers in Washington asked us to delay the mission. Did they make the same request of you?"

"Yes. I was called into the Director's office and told to stay home."

"We told them 'no' and, obviously, you did as well," Jacques said.

"You were kind enough to take my investigation seriously, Jacques. I thought I needed to be here."

"Good. Let's go in and get started," Jacques said.

Not only was Rick absent from the meeting, but Henri

Thomas as well. "Where's Henri?" Laura asked.

"Henri's been posing as a corporate official at our Inline location and as you probably know by now, the Soviets have taken a sudden interest in the company. We felt Henri was at risk, so he's staying home."

"Probably for the best. Jean and I made the Prague trip. We've played the roles before."

"Precisely," Jean said.

"We did acquiesce to one request by the Americans," Jacques said. "We're now staying at the Berlin to avoid the American delegation."

"Excellent," Jean said. "I've always enjoyed the Berlin. Best hospitality in Moscow."

"I thought you'd like it, Jean. We received word that Postl's trying to receive government approval for travel to Paris. He's asked to leave on Tuesday."

"They'll send a bodyguard along with him, won't they?" Laura asked.

"If the request is approved, yes. We'll have Paul Perrin at the gate when he arrives. He'll separate Postl from his handler."

Jacques stared at both Laura and Jean to gain eye contact. "This is important. If they let Postl go, they'll use Aeroflot. You're flying Air France. I've left your return flight open. After you confirm Postl's left the country, you must take the next Air France flight. Once Postl lands in Paris and is taken into custody, it won't take them long to figure out what we've done."

"As I recall," Jean said. "Aeroflot and Air France fly out of different terminals. The terminals aren't connected, Jacques. How will we know he's left?"

"We'll have someone trail Postl. Once he's gone, they'll page you in your terminal. When you hear that, you must leave immediately."

"What happens if Postl's travel is denied?" Jean asked.

"We're giving you a forged travel permit. We'll have someone trailing him to see if he's able to use it. If not, you must consider his exfil a failure and leave as quickly as possible."

"Good," Jean said.

"The difficult part for you two will be the dinner Minister Gradovich has scheduled for this evening. He's well versed in computer technology. Do you know enough to fool him, Jean?"

"We'll be fine, Jacques."

"Laura, you're going to have to follow Jean's lead."

"Jean and I work together well. I don't anticipate a problem," she said.

"The Mademoiselle plays the role of the dumb blonde to perfection," Jean said to laughter.

"Now," Jacques said, "let's discuss Ivan Ilitch for a moment. He's put a team together for his next mission which appears to be your residence in Washington, Laura."

"I suspected as much," Laura responded.

"That's where we have a problem. Ivan Ilitch may have already begun the mission. He took a flight to Switzerland early last week and hasn't been seen since. Obviously, there's nothing we can do if he's not in town," Jacques said.

"He'll return as soon as he knows I've flown to Moscow."

"Probably so, but you won't have much time to wait. Whether Postl gets out or not, you must leave Moscow Tuesday night. I can't stress that enough."

"I understand," Laura affirmed.

"Good. Its ten thirty-five right now. That leaves you time to stop at Operations and pick up your identities, plane tickets and cash. Jean, we have a briefcase full of sales material for you to take along. There's a car waiting at the back of the building. You have a one-thirty flight."

"One more thing, Jacques," Laura mentioned. "Did you receive the bag I sent from Washington?"

"Yes, it's in my office."

"I need you to forward that to the embassy in Moscow. It must be there tonight. I hope that's possible. I absolutely need it."

"I'll send it on the same flight you're on. I'll notify the embassy that it's coming."

"Thanks."

"I think we're ready," Jacques said. "Good luck."

During the trip to the airport, Jean and Laura studied their dossiers. Jean was Gaston Joubert, president and CEO of Inline Computers. Laura was Claire Petit, his administrative assistant. Inside the envelopes were passports, various documents and family histories. The DST placed paperwork within various government offices to substantiate the dossiers.

"I see a problem already," Laura said.

Jean chuckled. "And that would be?"

"The ID's are not the same as the Prague ID's. If anyone checks ..." her voice trailed off. Jean completed her sentence, "and Postl says at dinner, 'Nice to see you again,' it could be an issue."

"Exactly."

"Well, there's nothing we can do now. If we act our

roles well, there won't be a problem," Jean said.

The driver pulled into the departure area at de Gaulle, "Air France?" he asked.

"Yes. You can pull over here if you like," Jean said. "We don't mind walking."

The driver lifted their overnight bags from the trunk. "Good luck," he said.

As they walked through the terminal, Jean studied his ticket. "They have us checked all the way to the gate. We need to go this way," he said, pointing down one of the hallways.

"We're being followed."

"That's why I asked the driver to let us off early."

"Whoever those men are, they're not even trying to hide," she said.

"KGB goons. They're completely without training," Jean said.

Oleg and Timofei followed Laura to the airport and became confused when she didn't take a flight back to D.C. They watched the complete boarding sequence without obtaining tickets for the flight.

"What do we do now?" Oleg asked Timofei after boarding had closed. "They're not going to Washington."

"We better call Ivan."

They walked back to the terminal where they used a credit card to place a long distance call to Washington. Khozin answered the phone at the safe house. "Yes?"

"Maxim, this is Oleg. We followed Messier to the airport like Ivan asked, but she's not flying to Washington."

"Hang on a minute. I'll get Ivan."

Ivan came on the line a moment later. "Where's she going, Oleg?" he asked.

"If you can believe this, she's going to Moscow."

"Are you shitting me?"

"No, I'm serious. She just left for Moscow. She wasn't with that male guard of hers; she left with an older man."

"You didn't get on the flight?"

"No. We didn't know what to do."

"Oleg, you're an idiot. Take the next flight back to Moscow. Maxim and I will leave now. We'll meet at the warehouse tomorrow."

"One thing, Ivan. Are we going to get into trouble for using the credit card to eat American fast food over the weekend?"

"Put Timofei on the phone," Ilitch said.

Oleg turned to Timofei. "He wants to talk to you." Timofei took the phone.

"Yes, Ivan?"

"Take the fucking credit card away from Oleg. He's an idiot. Catch the next flight back to Moscow. We'll meet tomorrow at the warehouse. Okay?"

"Yes, Sir."

Ivan slammed the phone down. Frustrated, he looked at Maxim. "She went to Moscow. Let's get the fuck out of here. We've got a chance to get her in Moscow if we can find her." In less than ten minutes, Ilitch and Khozin were on their way to Dulles.

Chapter Eight

SHEREMETYEVO INTERNATIONAL AIRPORT is the main commercial airport serving the metropolitan Moscow area. Located northwest of the city well beyond the outer ring road, its two separate terminal complexes serve Moscow's international and domestic carriers. Clean and efficient, it contains none of the amenities, nor any of the commercial advertising, one would typically find in the West.

Laura saw only one restaurant and gift shop upon her arrival. She and Jean arrived late Monday afternoon where they were met at the gate by a tall, serious looking man in a black suit. Well-muscled, blond hair, early 40s; he was an imposing figure. He held a sign that read, "Inline."

"Are you looking for us" Jean asked?

"Petit and Joubert?" When Jean nodded in the affirmative, the man said, "Follow me, please," as though there were any other choice.

"Where are we going," Laura asked.

"I'm Inspector Sokoloff, Moscow Police. We have a special customs procedure for foreign guests." They were led on a long walk out of the gate area to customs, where they were subjected to a body pat down and asked to open their bags. The customs agent asked the purpose of their visit, when they planned to return and frowned when Jean said they had not yet booked a return flight.

"You'll have to book your return at this time," the agent said, stamping their passports. "The Inspector will take you to the Air France ticket counter in the other terminal." Their passports were returned and they were driven to the second terminal, where Jean booked a return the following evening at 8:00 pm. Once that was completed, they were led outside where an official from the ElectroTechnical Ministry was waiting.

"Inline Computers? I'm Valerie Utkin. Here, let me take your bags," he said to Laura.

He piled their luggage in the trunk of a green, late model Soviet made compact car parked at the curb. He opened the back door and they squeezed into the small seat for the ride to the hotel. "I've been instructed to take you to the Berlin. Is that correct?" he asked.

"Yes. We appreciate your assistance," Jean said in perfect Russian.

The austere nature of the airport was a preamble to Moscow itself, a functional city devoid of the kind of commercial establishments one would see in the West. Driving into the downtown area, though, the Kremlin loomed large with its many beautiful buildings and palaces bathed in light. They could see the tops of the Ivan the Great Bell Tower, the Cathedral of the Annunciation and St. Basil's rising above the Kremlin Wall. The wall was a beautiful red color with watch towers every few hundred meters. It gave the appearance of a fortress.

"Pretty, isn't it?" Jean asked.

"Absolutely beautiful," Laura replied.

"The wall of the Kremlin has been around since the 15th century," Utkin said. "Back then, there was a moat around the place that's been replaced, of course, but one can imagine how imposing it looked back then."

Utkin parked in front of the Berlin Hotel, a building with an ornate exterior that had the look of something that had been around for a century. "Allow me to help you inside," Utkin said as the doorman opened the car door for them. Utkin deposited their bags on the sidewalk. "I'll wait in the lobby while you freshen up for dinner. You have a 7:30 pm dinner with Minister Gradovich at the National Hotel."

"I was hoping we'd dine here at the Berlin," Jean said. "The chef here is one of the best in Europe."

"As you probably know, Mr. Joubert, hotels that cater to Westerners serve the best food in Moscow. It's called, 'keeping up the appearance of prosperity.' I think you'll find the restaurant in the National to be equally good to the Berlin."

"I shall look forward to an excellent meal."

That short conversation on the sidewalk gave Laura time to study the architecture of the building. She knew the only way to avoid the KGB tomorrow morning would be to scale down the outside of the building as she'd done in Prague. She studied the various routes, the handholds and ledges until Utkin finally said, "It's one of the beautiful, old buildings in Moscow. Are you a student of architecture, Ma'am?"

"Me? Oh, no. I'm just enjoying the sights and sounds of your beautiful country. I've never been to Moscow before."

"I hope you have a pleasant stay, Ma'am. The doorman will lead you to the check-in counter and I'll wait in the

211

lobby until you're ready for dinner."

A bellhop escorted them to their 5th floor rooms. *Lucky*, Laura thought. *The ledge outside the 5th floor windows will be helpful.* On the way up in the elevator, Laura spoke in Dutch to Jean. "I was rather hoping to avoid the National."

"Yes, I imagine you were, Mademoiselle. I can see you've been studying," Jean replied in Dutch with a smile.

Laura laughed. "You mean Dutch?"

"Nederlands, Mademoiselle. It's Nederlands. I'll make a world traveler out of you yet," Jean replied with a wry smile.

Both hotels, the Berlin and the National, had an old world charm about them. The Berlin had the ambiance of a boutique hotel; a small, plush lobby with expensive looking marble, carved woodwork and polished brass. It was furnished in what Laura guessed was Czarist period furniture; beautifully padded chairs, sofas and finished wood table tops. When they arrived at the National, Laura found the lobby to be a bit larger, but it retained all the intimate feel of the Berlin, except for the massive chandelier that dominated the lobby. That was a showpiece that Laura suspected was as old as the hotel itself. The restaurant at the National occupied a prominent place off the lobby where Utkin led them to a short, plump man standing in the restaurant foyer. Late fifties, bald, wearing a black suit, he had a friendly face and relaxed manner. He smiled broadly and held out his hand as they approached. He spoke in Russian. "Welcome to Moscow, Mr. Joubert and Ms. Petit, I'm Nikolai Gradovich, the ElectroTechnical Minister."

Jean shook his hand vigorously and answered in equally fluent Russian. "So nice to meet you, Minister Gradovich. I'm Gaston Joubert and this is my assistant, Claire Petit." Laura offered her hand. Gradovich was taken aback by Laura's beauty. A former fashion model, Laura decided to play up the dumb blonde look by wearing heavy make-up and expensive, stylish clothing.

"It's a pleasure to meet both of you. Ms. Petit, you're absolutely beautiful."

"Thank you, Minister," Laura said in acceptable Russian. "It's exciting to visit your beautiful country."

"I've got a table ready for us. I think you'll find the dining here to rival the finest restaurants in Paris." The maître d' led them to a table where Jack Postl was already seated. "This is Jack Postl, the computer expert who's ordered so much of your equipment."

Postl stood, smiled and held out his hand. "Hello. It's nice to see both of you again."

"You've met?" a surprised Gradovich asked.

"These were the officials who visited me in Prague," Jack said.

"Ah, yes. I'd forgotten."

Laura winced imperceptibly, but Gradovich seemed to accept Jack's assertion and Laura hoped the mistake would go unnoticed.

"I have gifts for each of you," Jack said. "Tokens of your visit to Moscow." He handed each of them a small ceramic replica of St. Basil's Cathedral and gave Laura a box of chocolates.

"How thoughtful of you, Mr. Postl," Laura said.

The restaurant was busy; guests were seated at every table. In the middle of the room, tables had been pushed together in a long rectangle for a large party. Laura glanced at the U.S. Secretary of State and his entourage. Steve, two chairs away from the Secretary, saw Laura immediately and stared at her as she walked through the room. "Stay calm, Mademoiselle," Jean whispered in her ear. "Look straight ahead." He took her by the arm and forced her to look away.

Unfortunately, the maître d' seated Laura with her back to the wall. Steve, in her direct line of sight, continued to stare while she tried to ignore him. "I've been informed that the two of you are guests from the Republic of France," the maître d' said leaning over slightly, "so I took the liberty of providing menus in your native language," handing each of them a menu.

Modeling for the Ford Agency in New York prior to joining the CIA was something of a finishing school in grace and etiquette for Laura. She was the perfect complement to Jean as he worked his magic with Gradovich over the next hour and a half. Jean was convincing as a corporate head, portraying himself as a savvy, smart businessman. After the second bottle of wine, Gradovich and Jean entered their own little world of jokes and stories. It became obvious the two men genuinely liked each other. *That is Jean's greatest gift*, Laura thought watching him work. *He's likeable.* She managed to follow the conversation, laugh when required and answer politely when asked a question. Otherwise, she stayed out of the way and avoided Steve's stare. The dinner was a huge success and when Gradovich walked them to the curb afterwards, Laura and Jean knew their ruse had been successful.

"Mr. Utkin will pick you up at 8:00 am," Gradovich said, "and bring you inside the Kremlin where I'll personally give you a tour. I'll show you some of Mr. Postl's work as well."

"Wonderful," Jean said. "Looking forward to it. Thank you, Nikolai. We'll see you in the morning."

Utkin dropped them off at the Berlin where Laura, once again, studied the building facade as she walked toward the front door. Jean persuaded her to accept a nightcap in the bar before returning to their rooms. They spoke to the bartender in Russian, but spoke to each other in Dutch. "Mademoiselle, you were magnificent this evening," Jean said.

"Likewise, Mr. Joubert. Nicely done."

"The two men reading across the lobby? One of them is Sokoloff."

"Yes, I see him," Laura said. "He's working late this evening."

"Will he be a problem?"

Laura laughed. "No, not at all. However, I do have a problem. I feel one of my migraines coming on. If it keeps building, I may have to skip the tour tomorrow."

"That would be unfortunate," Jean said with a wry smile. "Perhaps, the front desk stocks pain reliever."

"I'll ask on my way to the room. So thoughtful of Mr. Postl to bring gifts. Something to show my friends back in Paris," she said.

Jean raised an eyebrow at the suggestion. "I'm sure

they'll be pleased. It's time I retired for the evening. If you aren't feeling well in the morning, call my room and let me know."

"Have a pleasant evening, Mr. Joubert," Laura said as they parted.

Laura returned to her room and inspected the box of chocolates, which seemed a bit too heavy. Under the bottom lining lay five computer disks. She removed them and put them in her shoulder bag. She called the front desk and left a message for Mr. Joubert that she wasn't feeling well and would be staying in her room in the morning. She set the alarm to 4:30 am on the bedside clock and after removing her make-up and evening wear, she waited for the pain reliever to be delivered, then fell into bed and slept.

***

The alarm sounded softly, but Laura was already up, showered and dressed. She wore a pair of black jeans, a dark blue silk blouse and a black leather jacket. She wore her favorite sneakers, the type she used rock climbing in Colorado. Her Claire Petit passport was held at the front desk, so she checked that her Messier passport was hidden in the lining of her shoulder bag.

Laura looked out the window. It was still dark. She figured she had another half-hour before the sky began to lighten. *That should be plenty of time*, she thought. She wiped down the room to remove her fingerprints in case she didn't return. She took a piece of hotel stationery and scratched out a note in French:

Went to find pain medication. Be right back.

She left the note on the bed. *That ought to confuse the KGB*, she thought.

Laura unlocked the 5th floor window and climbed out onto the ledge, shutting the window behind her. She took chalk from her shoulder bag and rubbed her fingers white. A delivery truck went rumbling by, brakes squealing at the stoplight on the corner. *Sounds seem louder at night*, she thought. The ledge was wide and easy to negotiate. *Too bad it's the only ledge between me and the second floor*, she said to herself looking down. As she made her way around the corner of the facade to the side of the building, she encountered wind. Laura quickly grabbed the nearest window frame to balance herself. It wasn't enough wind to prevent climbing, but it was a hindrance. Carefully passing a room where the draperies had been left open, she peeked in the window and found the room's occupant asleep on the bed. *Probably passed out after a night of drinking,* she thought. She moved the shoulder bag to her back. *It's a little unbalanced*, she thought, *but there's nothing I can do about it. I need a spot where all the windows underneath are dark.* She grabbed a window frame and peered over the ledge. When she found a good spot to begin her climb, she sat down on the ledge with her feet dangling off. *Not many handholds*, she thought, looking down. *Just the window framing until the second floor. It should be enough,*

217

hopefully.

Facing the building, Laura lowered herself off the ledge, hanging by her hands. She reached out with one foot, trying to make contact with the window directly below. When she felt the window frame, she moved her opposite foot to the other side. She wedged both feet into the frame, pressing her toes into the sides and then lowered one hand to grab the top of the window. *Three points*, she thought. Releasing her top hand, she lowered her body in front of the window below. Laura quickly grabbed the top of the frame with both hands and slid her feet down until she felt the bottom of the sill. *Four points; I'm okay*, she thought. The window framing was better than some of the handholds she'd used on cliffs around Ouray. Laura repeated the process all the way down to the second floor where she stood up straight on another ledge. She lowered herself off that ledge until she was hanging by her fingertips and then dropped to the sidewalk below, being careful to keep her knees bent to cushion her fall. She landed and thrust her hands in front of her, falling forward onto all fours. Standing up, she did a quick check. *Nothing hurt*, she thought. Laura looked around and saw no one on the sidewalk. Another delivery truck rumbled by. *Morning grocery deliveries*, she thought. She checked her watch. 4:50 am. Right on time. She walked across the street where a black Mercedes flashed its parking lights.

Laura walked to the driver's door, where a man rolled down the window. "Shewolf?" he asked.
"And you are?"
"Vladimir Tonov, the Admiral's son. Hop in back," he

said in English.

Laura slid into the back seat. "Nice car," she responded in English.

Vladimir laughed. "It's my father's. Rank does have its privileges." He reached over the seat and held out his hand. "Call me Vlad."

They shook hands, which amazingly enough, was a tradition here in the Soviet Union. "I watched you come down the side of the building. Damn, that was good." Laura couldn't tell much about Vlad in the dark, except that he was young, mid 20s, had dark hair and a pleasant smile. "Where we going?" he asked.

"Know a pastry shop close by?"

"Sure," Vlad said.

"Coffee and pastry is on me."

Vlad drove three blocks to a shop where Laura saw workers inside preparing for the day's business. The street was quiet. Only the pastry shop showed any activity this early. "They don't open until five, so we've got a couple of minutes. What can I get you?"

"They have apple turnovers in Moscow?"

"The best you'll ever eat."

"Get me one and a large coffee, cream and sugar. Get whatever you want for yourself." She handed him a fist full of cash.

"This is too much money," Vlad said.

"Buy a mix of everything and leave a big tip."

"I like your style, Shewolf," he said with a smile.

Vlad hopped out as soon as he saw one of the workers unlock the door. He returned to the car with the best pastry

Laura had ever enjoyed. "It's still hot," she said.

"They prepare everything right before they open. The place is packed by seven, so we picked a good time."

"Good coffee, too. I need to go to the French Embassy. Know where that is?"

"Sure. I know Moscow well." He looked in the rear view mirror. "We've got company. Don't worry. I know these guys. Just keep quiet. They're here for the pastry."

Laura turned around and saw a Moscow police car behind them. The officer walked to Vlad's door and knocked on the window. Vlad rolled it down.

"Morning, Vlad. What brings you out so early?" the officer asked.

"I'm taking my father's whore home. He wanted her out of the house before the neighbors woke up."

The policeman shined his flashlight into the back seat. "Okay, Vlad. Drive safely." Vlad started the engine and pulled away from the curb.

"See, no problem," Vlad said looking in the rear view mirror.

"That had me worried for a minute. When you get to the Embassy, drive around back. You'll see a wrought iron gate next to a guard house. Pull up to the gate."

"Yes, Ma'am."

Laura tugged at the lining of her shoulder bag and pulled out her Messier passport. When Vlad pulled up to the gate, she said, "Keep the car running, I'll be back in a minute."

She walked up to the guard house and passed her Messier passport to the attendant. He riffled through the pages. "I need to enter the Embassy to retrieve a diplomatic pouch," she said.

"I'm sorry, Mademoiselle, the Embassy doesn't open until 8. You'll have to return then."

"I'm with the DST. We're running an op in Moscow. Call operations and give them my name."

The guard picked up the phone, read Messier's name aloud for Operations, then hung up. "Who's your driver?"

"Vladimir Tonov, son of Admiral Tonov, Soviet Navy."

"We'll have to search him."

"Fine. Just let us in," Laura said.

The electronic gate opened and Laura motioned for Vlad to drive through. Four guards came out of the building and surrounded the car. One of them knocked on Vlad's window. "Please exit the car." Vlad climbed out. "Please turn around and put your hands on top of the car." The guard did a quick pat down while another looked inside the Mercedes. He turned to Laura. "What's in the box?"

"Pastry. Would you like some?"

"No."

"I had a black bag sent here yesterday from Paris. I need to retrieve it."

"Come inside, please," the guard said.

"Vlad, wait here. I won't be long."

Laura was led into a room with bulletproof glass separating the counter from the lobby, reminding Laura of a bank. The room was painted an ugly green with linoleum tile on the floor and overhead fluorescent lighting. It had a strong smell of cleaning solution. The guard who accompanied Laura slid her passport underneath the glass. An attendant sitting at the window studied it. "You have no entry stamp," he said to Laura.

"I didn't come in country on that passport."

"What did you use?"

"That's not important. I need a black leather bag Jacques Martin sent from DST Paris yesterday."

"Have that person contact us to confirm it," the attendant said flatly.

"I'm here on official business. You're holding a bag for me. I need it now, with all due respect."

The attendant looked resolute. He stared at Laura. "We're closed until eight. Come back then, we'll get verbal confirmation and release the bag." He pushed the passport back underneath the glass.

"Let me make this real simple. I use that phone over there," she said, pointing to a phone on the wall of the lobby, "and call Paris Operations. They wake up your Ambassador and tell him some junior grade is stopping an op that's been planned for months. Then, I get my bag and you get fired. Get the fucking bag."

The attendant looked frustrated. He made a phone call and then looked at Laura. "Wait here for a moment."

He was gone about fifteen minutes, but she recognized the bag when he returned. The seal had not been broken. "We'll have to check the contents before we release it," the attendant said.

"Read the label, genius. It says 'Top Secret.' It's none of your business," Laura said with impatience.

The guard gave her a look of anger, but pushed it into a box built into the glass. Once he shut the inside door, the outer door unlocked. The guard accompanying Laura opened the door and handed it over.

"You'll have to sign for it," the attendant said from behind the glass. He pushed a clipboard underneath.

She scratched an illegible signature. "Have a pleasant day, gentlemen."

Out in the parking lot, she found Vlad leaning up against the car, smoking. "Do you have the equipment I asked for?"

Sure," he said with a shrug. "It's in the trunk."

Laura handed Vlad the bag. "Put this in the trunk while you've got it open."

Vlad opened the driver's door, reached in and pushed a button that unlocked the trunk. He threw her bag in the trunk and withdrew a briefcase which he laid on the hood of the car. She removed her jacket, opened the briefcase and found two Sig Sauer P226s. She pulled the shoulder holsters over her head and then inspected the weapons. "These ever been fired?"

Vlad shrugged again. "Don't know, but the Admiral always gets the best stuff."

"They look new. You have a couple of extra clips for me?"

"I brought four. Here's a holder to attach them to your belt."

Laura smiled. "Atta boy, Vlad. I'm liking you more and more all the time." She fastened the clips to her belt.

She looked at Vlad and asked, "Ready?"

Vlad slammed the trunk shut. "Always, Ma'am."

One of the guards opened the car door for her. "You starting a war?" he asked.

"If I do my job well, Sergeant, maybe we don't have to

fight wars. Good day, Sergeant." She turned to Vlad. "Vlad, let's get the hell out of here."

Vlad pulled through the gate and onto the street. "Where to now, boss lady?"

"I need to see your father."

"We're on our way."

The trip took them to the outskirts of Moscow, where Tonov owned a blue bungalow with white trim and a detached garage. The house sat well off the road on a large parcel of land, hidden by a row of trees along the roadway. Vlad drove into the circle drive and parked at the front door. "I'm going to need the bag in the trunk, Vlad."

Vlad popped the trunk and handed it to her. "Come on in, boss lady."

Admiral of the Fleet Arkady Tonov, the Soviet Union's second highest ranking naval officer, was sitting at his kitchen table drinking coffee and reading one of the Moscow dailies. He rose when Laura and Vlad entered the room. *He's really attractive*, Laura thought. *Not at all what I expected.* Early 60s, tall, muscular, with short gray hair and blue piercing eyes, Tonov had a commanding presence about him. He wore a military sweater with gold insignia embroidered into the fabric of the shoulders. *He looks like Admiralty*, she thought.

"You must be Shewolf," he said, smiling warmly. "Very nice to meet you."

"Honored to meet you, Sir." They shook hands.

"I need to know your real name."

"Laura Messier."

"How do you spell it?"

Laura spelled the name for him.

"Thank you. Do you have something for me?"

"Yes." She laid her bag on the table, opened it and stacked $50,000 U.S. dollars on the table.

"Do you have contingency funds?"

"Some."

He frowned. "How many people will you bring?" Arkady asked.

"Four."

"I'm making documents for all your people. Can you give me descriptions?"

Laura described the people who would be traveling later in the day.

"The pictures will be intentionally blurred, but the passports won't be checked closely. Vladimir knows where to meet us at the airport." He turned to Vlad. "Have them there no later than 5:00 pm. Earlier, if possible." He turned back to Laura. "Be careful, Shewolf."

"I will. Would you allow me to use your phone? I'm sorry, but I must place a call."

"Certainly. It's over there," Arkady said, pointing to the kitchen counter.

Laura looked at the rotary dial phone and found the Admiral's number on a small plastic insert below the dial. She phoned the Berlin Hotel and asked to speak with Mr. Joubert.

"Yes," Jean answered his room phone.

"Call back at this number," Laura said, reciting the number. She hung up.

Jean hurried to the lobby, where he picked up a house phone. "Outside line, please," he said. As soon as he heard the tone, he dialed the number. Laura picked up.

"Yes?"

"How can I help you?" Jean asked.

"Change of plans. Check out after lunch, walk to the National and I'll pick you up there. Tell our Czech colleague we've made other travel arrangements. He should not board his scheduled flight."

"Thank you."

She hung up. "Sorry, Arkady, just a bit of housekeeping."

"Not a problem. We'll see you at the appointed time?"

"Yes. Good day, Sir."

***

The two KGB men sitting in the lobby of the Berlin walked to the lobby counter. They flashed their ID badges to the clerk.

"A man with a goatee just placed a call from the house phone over there. Can you tell us who he called?"

"Let me see if I can pull up the phone log." He called the operator, explained the situation and listened to her lecture him that it was impossible to monitor house phones because the calls weren't included in room charges.

"Tell them the call was placed to the laundry."

"Okay."

The clerk turned to the men. "He called the hotel laundry, Sir."

"Thank you."

***

After they pulled out of the drive, Vlad said, "Don't worry about the money."

"I got a bit frightened at the look on his face."

"No worries. The Admiral has money stashed all over Europe. Where to now, boss lady?"

"8 Basmannyy Pereulok. You know where it is?"

"Give me a landmark."

"Kazansky rail station."

"Other side of town. I think I can find it."

Forty minutes later, they passed the rail station. "I'm guessing its south of the station, but the side streets wind around back here. It might take a couple of minutes to find," Vlad said as he turned onto a side street just south of the station. He made several more turns. "I think it's down a little farther." Vlad slowed to look for building numbers. "Should be the next block. Maybe that green apartment building coming up on the right."

"Don't slow down. This one?"

"Yeah, that's it. Pretty nice place."

"Go around the block. Find a parking spot no one's going to notice."

"People always spot a Benz. Can't do anything about that. You want to watch the building?"

"Yes."

Vlad drove around the block. "How about here?" he asked. "End of the block. We can leave fast if we need to."

"That's fine." Laura looked at her watch. 8:30 am.

Vlad looked at the street sign. "No parking zone? Not

a problem. No one's going to question a Mercedes with military plates."

"Good. Go ahead and shut it off. Now, we wait."

"Okay, boss lady. Whatever you say."

Laura watched the black van circle the block twice. The third time, it flashed its lights and stopped by Vlad's car. Vlad rolled down the window. "You guys need something?"

."We're looking for someone," the driver said.

Vlad looked in his rear view mirror at Laura. "You know these guys?"

"Maybe. Tell him 'Bastille.'"

Vlad said the password and the driver said, "Day," in return.

"I've got to talk with these men." Laura rolled down her window.

"Messier here."

"Montaigne. Four of us here. They meet in that warehouse across the street. Two went in early this morning. We haven't seen Ilitch."

"If he shows up, it'll be later. Maybe early afternoon. Have you been in the warehouse?"

"Yes."

"What's the layout?"

"The front door's the one they use. There's a back entrance off the alley, but it's locked from the inside. We've never seen them use it. If you go in the front, there's one big room. Everything's right in front of you. They've set themselves up in the middle. Chairs, table, bulletin board, that sort of thing. They keep the overhead lights on right above them, so you'll get a clean look."

"Weapons?"

"Lots. Don't exactly know what you'll be facing, but we've got some firepower of our own. We can do a tactical assault if you want. Lob some flashbangs in those windows up there. Come in both doors," Montaigne said.

"No, too loud. This has to be quiet. Tell you what. Have your men cover the back in case anyone escapes. I'll go in the front."

"You don't want us to go in with you?"

"No. I like to work alone."

"I've heard that about you. You sure? You'll be taking down four armed men."

"If I need you, I'll yell."

"We'll be around if you need us."

"You guys want some pastry?" Laura asked.

"Sure. Pass them over."

Vlad handed the box out the window.

"Thanks."

"Relax for a while and let's see if Ilitch shows up."

The van pulled away and turned the corner.

***

Valerie Utkin left the engine running in front of the Berlin. He told the doorman he'd be right back. He picked up the house phone and asked the operator for Gaston Joubert's room. Jean picked up. "Hello?"

"Mr. Joubert, its Valerie Utkin. I'm here to pick you up."

"I'll be right down." Jean looked at his watch, eight-forty. *She's probably at Ilitch's apartment by now*, he thought.

Jean wore the casual business attire he was accustomed to using. Slacks, dark turtle neck and tweed jacket. He looked in the mirror. *Time to put on my game face*, he thought. He smiled warmly stepping off the elevator and extended his hand when he saw Utkin. "Good morning, Valerie."

Utkin was pleased Joubert remembered his name. "I've got a car out front. Where's Ms. Petit?"

"Headache. She's asleep in her room."

"She's not coming?" Utkin asked.

Jean laughed. "No, I'm afraid not. Women can be difficult travel partners."

"Minister Gradovich will be disappointed."

Utkin stopped at the Kremlin main gate. He rolled down his window. "Name?" the guard asked.

"Valerie Utkin, ElectroTechnical with a guest to see Minister Gradovich."

"Guest name?"

"Gaston Joubert," Utkin said.

"I need to see his identification."

Jean passed forward his wallet. "Here," Utkin said, handing the wallet to the guard. He looked through the wallet, took a pen from his breast pocket and wrote Gaston Joubert on his clipboard.

"How long is he staying?"

"Noon."

"Give me a minute to get him a pass." The guard returned moments later. "Have your guest clip this to his jacket."

"Yes, Sir."

The guard motioned for the attendant to open the gate and Utkin drove through. "It's difficult to find parking inside. We might have to walk a block or so. Do you mind?"

"Not at all. It will give me time to look at the beautiful buildings," Jean said.

***

Jack entered the ElectroTechnical Ministry well before Jean arrived. "Good morning, Natasha," he said entering Gradovich's office.

"Hi, Jack." Natasha gave him a seductive smile. *I never noticed how nice she is*, he thought.

Gradovich's office door was open when Jack arrived. Natasha nodded toward the door. "He's expecting you."

"Good news, Jack," Gradovich said. "Your travel permit's been approved. Run over to the Deputy Chairman's office and pick it up. I'll give Joubert the tour and you can meet us for lunch over at the Berlin."

"Very good, Sir."

Upon entering Deputy Chairman Rostov's office, Jack was asked to wait in the lobby while the deputy's assistants addressed the needs of dozens of people. Assistants called numbers in a queue. Jack took a number and waited ... and waited ... and waited. Twice, he went up to the counter and twice was told to wait his turn. Jack thought this was precisely what was wrong with the Soviet system of government. The entire nation's business was ultimately channeled into about a dozen offices. Nothing happened without government approval and bureaucracy ground to a halt because of the sheer volume of paperwork.

After waiting almost three hours, Jack was finally called to the counter where an overbearing, overweight and overly suspicious clerk found his paperwork among a large stack of travel requests on the desk behind him. He held the deputy's signature stamp above the document, ready to put a seal of approval on Jack's permission to live a better life. A number of boxes on the form had yet to be completed. "Is your travel related to a sporting competition?" the clerk asked.

"No."

The clerk checked the appropriate box. "Are you part of a touring arts organization?"

"No."

Another box checked. "Are you taking part in a government seminar or convention?"

"No."

"What's your reason for travel?"

"Its work related."

"What Ministry?"

"ElectroTechnical."

"What's your job there?"

"Computers."

"Where are you going?"

"Paris, France. It says Paris right there on the paper."

"Why are you going again?"

"Its work related."

"Relating to what?"

"We're buying computers."

"In France?"

"Yes."

"When will you return?"

"Day after tomorrow," Jack said.

While the clerk played a real life game of twenty questions, Jack watched the minutes tick away. *As though the clerk has any authority to deny my travel*, Jack thought. Finally, the clerk stamped the document with enough force to go through a dozen carbons. He tore off the top copy and handed it to Jack. "Your flight is at 6:00 pm today, Aeroflot #676, out of Sheremetyevo. Meet Inspector Romanov at Customs in the International Terminal. He'll have your itinerary, passport and ticket. He'll accompany you on the trip. Show him this document. Arrive at least two hours before your flight. Your permission is granted."

"Thank you very much," Jack said.

"Next!" the clerk shouted loudly to no one in particular.

Jack looked at the clock. It was 12:15 pm.

***

Jack hurried to the Berlin and caught the end of lunch. "Sorry I'm late, Minister. It took forever at the deputy's office. Hi, Mr. Joubert. Good to see you."

"Glad you could make it," Jean said.

"Please enjoy dessert with us," Gradovich suggested, motioning to an empty chair.

"Absolutely, Sir." Jack sat.

"Did you get your travel documents in order?"

"Yes, Sir. I'm flying out on Aeroflot at six o'clock tonight."

"Why don't you take the rest of the day off? Go home and get ready. Can't be late for air travel these days."

"Thank you, Sir."

"I wanted to wait until you arrived to give Mr. Joubert the purchase order." He turned to Jean and handed him the order. "We're pleased to buy more computer equipment, Gaston. And, Jack will be there to pick it out for us."

"Wonderful news, Nikolai," Jean said, looking at the order. "Just wonderful. We'll be delighted to host Mr. Postl at our facility."

"I'm glad you came to visit, Gaston. We've begun what I hope will be a long standing relationship between us."

"It's refreshing to lay politics aside and work together as businessmen, isn't it?" Jean asked.

"Quite right, Gaston. Business is still business." Gradovich glanced at his watch. "I'm afraid time has gotten away from me, my friend. I must return to the office. Gaston, it's been a pleasure to meet you. Please convey my best wishes to Ms. Petit. Such a charming woman."

"I'll pass that along," Jean said as they stood to leave. "Here's a parting gift for each of you." Jean handed them thank you cards purchased in the gift shop. "It's not much, but we wanted to do something."

"Have a safe trip home," Gradovich said. They shook hands and gave a good grasp of each other's arm. "What time is your flight this afternoon?"

"8:00 pm this evening."

"I'll have Valerie pick you and Ms. Petit up at 6:00 pm."

"Thank you so very much, Nikolai. Goodbye," Jean

said.

While Jean waited in the lobby for Utkin to retrieve the car, Gradovich and Jack walked out of the hotel together. "If I could, Sir," Jack said, "I'll leave now."

"Have a great trip. Pick out some nice machines for us."

"Yes, Sir."

Walking away from the hotel entrance, Jack opened the card Jean had given him. Inside was a note:

"Arrive at the International Terminal by 4:00 pm. Do not approach the ticket counter or Customs. Do not talk to anyone. When you hear a page for Mr. Schmitt, go to the house phone and answer the call. I'll have further instructions for you."

Jack threw the card in a trash can.

***

The KGB men sitting in the hotel lobby hadn't seen the woman registered as Claire Petit all day. "I haven't seen her since last night," Sokoloff said.

His partner, Dmitri Krupin, shook his head. "We would have seen her leave the hotel. Let's call her room."

Krupin walked to a house phone along the wall on an end table. "Please connect me with ..." He put his palm over the headset and turned to Sokoloff. "What's her room number?"

"506," Sokoloff said.

"... 506, operator." The call went unanswered. "She's not answering. Let's go up and knock on the door."

They knocked on her door several times and waited. "I've got a master," Sokoloff said, opening the room with a hotel master key. They entered and looked around. "Clothes still here. Check the bathroom."

Krupin opened the bathroom door. "Make-up is here."

Sokoloff read the note on the bed. "Looks like we missed her walking through the lobby. She went to find a medicine shop."

"Maybe the doorman saw which way she went." They went downstairs and stopped at the front desk. "The guest in 506. She hasn't checked out, has she?" Sokoloff asked the clerk.

The clerk looked at the register. "You're referring to Ms. Petit?"

"Yes."

"Not yet. She asked for a late checkout. 2:00 pm."

"Any medicine shops within walking distance of the hotel?"

"Yes. Go outside and turn left. Two blocks."

"Thank you." The men walked outside and approached the doorman. "Have you seen a blond woman, early 30s, attractive, walk out of the hotel this morning?" Sokoloff asked.

The doorman, wary of questions, decided to remain neutral. "I've seen several women fitting that description come and go today."

"She checked in with an older man yesterday evening. Do you remember her?"

"I get off at three. I wasn't here."

"Thank you," Sokoloff said. The men walked down the street.

"Two blocks this way," Krupin said.

Jean watched the men leave the hotel. He quickly went upstairs and packed his clothing. He used a pen knife and paper clip to pick the lock to Laura's room, where he gathered her personal items as well. He went back downstairs, checked out of the hotel and walked out the front entrance. "Pardon me," he said to the doorman, "but could you give me directions?"

"Sure. How may I help you?"

"I'm meeting someone at the National Hotel. Is it within walking distance?"

"Yes. Walk down to Teatralnyy. Turn right and you can't miss it. It's about 6 blocks. Are you sure you want to walk? There's a taxi waiting right there," he said, pointing. He held up his hand and snapped his fingers. The taxi driver, hanging around hotels looking for fares, pulled up immediately. The driver hopped out and opened his trunk.

"Run this gentleman over to the National."

"Yes, Sir."

"How nice of you," Jean said to the doorman as the driver loaded Jean's bags into the trunk.

"Have a pleasant day, Sir," the doorman said. Jean handed him double an ordinary tip.

As the taxi pulled away from the curb, Jean saw the KGB men walking briskly back toward the hotel, heads down, talking intently with each other. Jean chuckled. *These men have no idea what we're doing.*

Jean entered the National and immediately found the

concierge desk. "Pardon me, Ma'am."

"Yes, Sir?"

"I'm meeting someone this afternoon. Do you mind if I wait in the lobby?"

"Not at all. Can I have coffee or tea sent over?"

"Coffee would be wonderful," Jean said. "Would you mind keeping my bags here at the desk?" He laid a large tip on her desk.

"No trouble at all." She walked around her desk, picked up his bags and put them behind her. "Let me know if I can assist you further."

Jean made himself comfortable on a plush sofa in the lobby. He picked up a European edition of Pravda and began reading. It was only a few minutes later he noticed a large, noisy group of people walking through the lobby from the restaurant. They spoke English. *The American delegation*, Jean thought. *Steve Tilton could become a problem.*

Chapter Nine

"HEY, BOSS LADY," Vlad said. "You awake?"

"I see them. Unloading luggage out of the red Peugeot."

"Those your guys?" Vlad asked.

"Yep." Laura looked at the clock on the dashboard. "2:15 pm. Right on time."

"What you do want to do?"

"Let's wait. They'll walk up to the apartment. In a few minutes, they'll come back down and walk across the street to meet their buddies. I want them all together."

"What'd these people do to piss you off?" Vlad asked.

"They're professional assassins, Vlad. They murder innocent people."

"So, you're just going to walk in there and kill all four?"

"That's the idea."

"Four against one? Bad odds, boss lady."

"That's true. They need more men."

"You're kidding, right?" Vlad asked.

"No, I'm not."

Vlad checked his side mirror. "Looks like your friends saw them, too. They went around behind the warehouse."

Laura checked her weapons again, pulling the mags to make sure they were fully loaded, then snapped them back in place. She looked down the barrels at the sights. She slipped on skin tight black leather gloves to avoid leaving fingerprints. *Something Ilitch should have done in Portugal*, she thought. "I think we're ready."

"You sound like you've done this before."

"Never like this. This will be a first."

"Why not let your friends handle it? You stay back and watch," Vlad suggested.

"This is personal."

"Need some help? I've got a Lugar in the glove box."

"Ever killed anyone, Vlad."

"No."

"Do yourself a favor. Stay out of it."

"Whatever you say, boss lady."

He started the engine. "Turn it off, Vlad," Laura said. "They'll notice."

"Whatever you say." He shut down the engine. "I thought you'd like a quick get-away."

"If I do this right, we won't need one."

"Whatever you say, boss lady."

Maxim Khozin and Ivan Ilitch piled their luggage in Ivan's apartment. "Oleg and Timofei should be at the warehouse. You want to go over there?" Khozin asked.

"Let's go. Just leave the stuff here. We'll deal with it later. I want to get that bitch."

They quickly walked across the street, eyes straight ahead, and entered the warehouse. Oleg and Timofei were finishing sandwiches that had been delivered earlier. "Hey, Ivan, you're back," Oleg said.

"Did you guys try to find that bitch?" Ilitch asked.

"No. You said meet at the warehouse."

"Not a problem. Let's get started. Maxim, would you turn on more lights?"

Maxim walked over and flipped a switch. Another bank of lights came on. "Thanks," Ilitch said. "Oleg, hand me that map of Moscow on my desk." Oleg searched through the paperwork and found it.

"Here."

Ilitch unfolded the accordion map and pinned it to the bulletin board. "All right. We know she's in Moscow so let's start with the downtown hotels. She likes fancy hotels. We've got the National here ..." Ilitch put a pin in the map, "the Berlin, the Metropol and the Marriott, all within walking distance of each other." Ilitch pinned each location. "Chances are she's at one of them. Let's each pick one." He pointed to her picture on the board. "Memorize her face. You've got permission to shoot her on sight. She's been classified as an enemy of the State."

"What if she's not at any of them?" Timofei asked. "Wouldn't it be better to call Lubyanka and get some help?"

"No," Ilitch said. "I don't want to share the bounty on this bitch. No one takes our money. Okay?"

"Fine," Timofei answered.

"Who wants which hotel?" Ilitch asked.

Laura slipped in the warehouse door. It was dark inside the entrance. Only the lights in the middle of the room were lit. She hung back for a moment, watching. *Montaigne was right*, she thought. *They're all grouped in the middle, just like he described.* She silently drew her weapons, holding them at her side. She studied the scene; Ilitch was talking. Two men were sitting in front of the bulletin board. She'd take them first. The one on the right, then the left. After that, she'd take Khozin, just an arm's length from Ilitch at the bulletin board. He'd be third in the

241

sequence. Finally, she'd take Ilitch standing at the board, talking. He'll be the most difficult because he'll have time to react. She slowed the sequence down and imagined it in her mind. *Aim slow, shoot slow*, she thought. *Aim slow, shoot slow*. She quietly moved forward.

"Hello!" a feminine voice called out. "Could you guys help me? I'm lost." The men looked in the direction of the voice. She raised her weapons and walked into the light. She fired with her right at the first man seated. Hit him in the forehead. Nearly simultaneously, she fired with her left and hit the second man in the forehead. Both slumped over, dead instantly.

Khozin was the first to react. He made a move toward the desk, where a pistol lay on top of Ilitch's paperwork. Laura fired with her right at Khozin. The round hit him in the chest. The impact threw him backwards. She fired a second time, then a third, all while pointing the weapon in her left hand at Ilitch. Khozin went down.

Ilitch bent over to unsnap his ankle holster. "Stop!" Laura shouted. "You'll be dead before you unsnap, Ivan." Ilitch froze and looked at her.
"Stand up."
"Fuck you, bitch" he said.
Laura's anger turned to rage. She shot him in the right shoulder. "Fuck me?" she asked. "Fuck you, asshole! Stand the fuck up." Ilitch was hurt, but managed to rise. Laura walked toward him. Ilitch looked in her eyes and judged that she'd want to talk, giving him time to think of a

plan to escape.

Laura saw the calculation in Ilitch's eyes. She smiled, amused that Ilitch thought an escape might be possible. She calmly said, "No. It's over." She shot him in the forehead with her left. He slumped to the ground. Laura walked over and stood looking at him. "Lady Liberty says hello, Ivan."

She glanced at the two men who had fallen from their chairs. They appeared to be dead. She looked back at Ilitch. His eyes were twitching. "If you can hear me, Ivan, this is for ruining my stainless steel refrigerator." She shot him again in the head.

She walked to Khozin, lying on the floor still clinging to life. He was bleeding badly from the chest and mouth.
"I should look you in the eyes when I kill you, Maxim, but I don't want blood splashing on my jeans. I've got a plane to catch." She shot him in the head from six feet away. She surveyed the scene for a moment. "Fucking bastards," she said, looking at her picture pinned to the bulletin board.

Laura walked to the back door. She yelled, "Hey Montaigne, its Messier. Can you hear me?"
"Yes," she heard him shout through the door.
"I'm opening the door. Don't fucking shoot me. Everything's secure." She opened the back door. "Come on in, fellas. It's over."

The French team entered with weapons drawn, but put

243

them away when they saw the scene. The mood turned somber as the men walked forward and quietly analyzed the carnage. Montaigne turned to his men. "Pull the van up to the back door." Laura put the weapons back into her shoulder holsters and walked around the room with Montaigne. "We'll get the place clean," Montaigne said. "Remove the bodies, shells, casings. Wipe everything down. They'll be no evidence to find." Montaigne stopped and looked at her. "Four against one," he said. "Fucking amazing."

"These two," Laura said, pointing at Ilitch and Khozin, "were the best assassination team the Soviets had. Without you boys, we'd have never found them. Thank you. You're the best."

"You're welcome."

"I'm afraid I must leave."

"Go. We've got this under control."

"Take care," she said.

"You, too."

Laura slipped out the front door and slowly walked to Vlad's car, sickened by what she'd just done. *This isn't who I am*, she thought. *This isn't what I want.* She was disgusted by the rage she felt inside the warehouse. A profound sense of sadness overcame her. She heard Vlad unlock the car and she climbed in the back seat.

"Pop the trunk and get my bag for me, will you?"

"Sure," Vlad said, before retrieving the bag from the trunk. He climbed back into the driver's seat.

"Well?" Vlad asked, passing the bag over the seat.

"What are you waiting for? Let's get out of here."

Vlad pulled away from the curb. He looked at Laura in

the rear view mirror. "What happened?"

"I fucking killed them, Vlad. What do you think happened?" she asked, showing anger in her voice.

"Sorry," Vlad said, looking at her in the mirror. "It must have been hard to do."

"It always is."

"Where to now?"

"The National Hotel."

"Okay, boss lady. Whatever you say."

Vlad headed downtown while Laura looked out the window, trembling at the memory of what she'd just done. *Forget about it*, she told herself. *Don't let it affect you. This isn't over yet. Concentrate on your job.*

***

Irina brought the chairman a message. "Sir, Denis Melinin called again from Paris. He called Friday after you'd left for the weekend."

"Thanks. I'll give him a call."

Petrovsky suspected Melinin was trying to position himself for a promotion. *I should have never contacted him,* he thought. He picked up the phone and dialed Melinin's number.

"Melinin here," he answered.

"Petrovsky, returning your call."

"Hello, Sir. More information on Inline Computers. We suspect the manager, a man named Pierre, is actually a DST agent."

"What's your evidence?"

"The address listed for him is an empty lot."

"Maybe he moved."

"We considered that. We took pictures of him going in and out of their building and compared them with pictures of known DST agents. We came up with a match. We believe he's Henri Thomas, a long time DST employee."

"Lots of people look alike, Denis. That doesn't make them spies."

"We believe they're the same person. It's possible that Inline is a front for French Intelligence."

"All right. We'll check it out."

He hung up and asked Irina to step into the office. "Would you find Jack Postl and ask him to stop by my office?"

"Yes, Sir."

Jack heard his apartment phone ring. *Don't talk to anyone*, he remembered the note saying. He didn't answer. He packed his favorite clothes in a backpack, threw in what photos he wanted to keep and looked around the apartment. He closed the door behind him for the last time and headed to the bank to withdraw money.

Irina returned minutes later. "Sir, no one's seen Jack around the building today. I called his apartment, but couldn't get an answer."

"Get his boss on the phone. Gradovich knows where he is."

Natasha picked up Irina's call. "Minister Gradovich's office."

"I've got Chairman Petrovsky on the line for the

Minister."

"One moment please."

"Good afternoon, Chairman," Gradovich said.

"Hello, Nikolai. I need to speak with your computer man, Postl. Where is he?"

"He's out of town for a couple of days. He should be back Friday."

"Out of town?" Petrovsky was surprised. "Where'd he go?"

"Actually, he hasn't left yet. He's flying to Paris this afternoon; buying computers for us."

"Did he clear it with the travel office?" Petrovsky asked.

"Yes, he has a travel permit."

"What time's his flight?"

"6:00 pm. Is he in any kind of trouble?" Gradovich asked.

"I've got a few questions about the company he's buying computers from."

"You're talking about Inline?"

"Yes," Petrovsky answered.

"They're here in town."

"They're in Moscow?"

"Yes. Two of them," Gradovich said.

"You met them?"

"Yes. We've had meetings the last two days."

"Who are they?"

"A man and a woman. Gaston Joubert and Claire Petit," Gradovich answered.

"You say one of them is a woman?"

"Yes."

"How long will they be here?"

"They're leaving this evening."

"So, Postl's leaving this afternoon and so are the people from Inline?"

"Yes," Gradovich replied.

"That's a strange coincidence."

"I suppose it is."

"Nikolai, stay close to your phone this afternoon. I'm going to have one of my assistant directors, Grisha Pasternik, give you a call. We're going to hold Postl and the Inline people at the airport until we find out what's going on."

"I'd be happy to help in any way I can."

"Good."

Petrovsky dialed Pasternik's office. "Grisha, can you come down to my office for a minute? I've got a job for you."

"Certainly, Sir."

Pasternik walked into the chairman's outer office where Irina nodded. He knocked on the chairman's door and then entered. "What do you have for me, Sir?"

"You know Jack Postl?"

"Yeah, the computer fellow."

"He's leaving town in a few hours. I need him stopped at the airport."

"I'll have it done immediately."

"Find out who's assigned to escort him. Let him know we're putting a temporary hold on Postl's travel."

"Anything else?" Pasternik asked.

"There are two foreign nationals visiting Moscow from a computer company in Paris. They're flying out this afternoon, too. Call Nikolai Gradovich over at the

ElectroTechnical Ministry and find out what he knows about them. Then tell Customs we want a hold on their travel, too. Put all three in airport security. You go out there and find out why they're leaving together."

"Yes, Sir. I'll get right on it."

Petrovsky leaned back in his chair and looked out the window. He lit another cigarette and thought for a moment. *It's probably nothing*, he thought. *Melinin's such an idiot. On the other hand, why are two foreigners taking Postl out of the country? Sounds like an exfil, except Postl went through channels to arrange his travel. He hasn't tried to hide anything. Well, we'll hold everyone at the airport until we get to the bottom of it, whatever it is. If it turns out to be nothing and I've got to pay to re-book these people on flights, then I'm firing Melinin's ass.*

Pasternik hurried to his office and pulled out an administrative directory where he found Deputy Chairman Rostov's office number. He placed the call. "Deputy Chairman's office," the voice said.

"This is Assistant Director Pasternik of the KGB calling. Connect me with whoever handles travel."

"Connecting you now."

A second voice came on the line. "How may I help you?"

"What's your name, young man?"

"Gregoriev, Sir. Dima Gregoriev.

"Dima, I'm one of the Directors for the KGB. Pasternik is my name. I want you to look up a travel permit for someone traveling this afternoon. The name's Jack Postl. Can you do that while I wait?"

"No need to look it up, Mr. Pasternik. It's right here on my desk. He picked up his copy a couple of hours ago."

"What's his flight information?"

"Aeroflot number 676 to Paris, France, leaving Sheremetyevo at 6:00 pm this evening."

"What's the name of the person accompanying him?"

"Inspector Romanov. Anything wrong, Sir."

"No, not at all. Thank you."

Pasternik called the ElectroTechnical Ministry. "This is Director Pasternik from the KGB calling for the minister."

"One moment," Natasha said.

"Director Pasternik, good to speak with you," Gradovich said.

"Would you mind answering a few questions about a couple of foreign nationals you've met the last couple of days?"

"Not at all. Go ahead."

"How do you know these people?"

"They're from a computer company in Paris."

"Why are they in town?"

"They're selling us new computers. Is there a problem?"

"This is just routine. What are their names?

"Gaston Joubert and Claire Petit."

"How do you spell their names?"

Gradovich spelled them out.

"They flew in a couple of days ago?"

"Yesterday."

"Do you happen to know what airline?"

"Air France."

"Could you describe them for me?"

"You mean what they look like?" Gradovich asked.

"Yes."

"Joubert is short, has gray hair and a goatee. He's in his 60s. His assistant, Ms. Petit, is pretty. Tall, thin, long blond hair; she's in her 30s."

"What hotel are they using?"

"The Berlin."

"Would you happen to know what time their flight leaves this evening?"

"They told me 8:00 pm. We're supposed to pick them up at their hotel around six and take them to the airport."

"No need to pick them up. We'll do it for you."

"Am I in any trouble here?" Gradovich asked.

"You? No. We just check on foreign guests from time to time. Nothing to worry about."

"Do I need to stay by the phone any longer?"

"No. We have all the information we need. Have a nice afternoon."

Pasternik used his administrative directory again to find the phone number for the Customs office at Sheremetyevo airport. "Customs," the voice said.

"This is Assistant Director Pasternik of the KGB. Has a Soviet man named Jack Postl gone through Customs this afternoon?"

"Hang on a minute. I'll check," the woman said. She came back on the line immediately. "What's the spelling?"

Pasternik spelled the name for her.

"No one by that name has been checked through."

"How about two French nationals, Gaston Joubert or Claire Petit?" This time, Pasternik spelled the names before she could ask.

"One moment." She came back on the line. "Neither of them have come through today."

"I need a travel hold on all three. You need the names again?"

"No. I've got them."

"Ask airport security to take them to the security office in the Aeroflot terminal whenever they show up. We'll have someone there to conduct interviews."

"We'll see that it's done, Sir."

Pasternik picked up the phone again, this time dialing the Aeroflot ticket counter at Sheremetyevo.

"Aeroflot counter. May I help you?"

"Yes, this is Director Pasternik of the KGB. This is official government business. Can you page someone in the terminal?"

"Of course, Sir. What's the name?"

"Inspector Romanov."

"Do you want to hold or leave a message?"

"I'll hold."

"One moment." Pasternik heard traditional Russian patriotic songs while on hold. That stuff is terrible, he muttered to himself.

***

Alexander Romanov arrived at the airport early. He looked at his watch; just past three. He'd packed a small carry-on bag, ready to follow a Soviet businessman around Paris for a couple of days. It would be a nice trip. Perhaps he could sneak out to a club after putting his man to bed. Sitting outside Customs reading a magazine, he heard his name over the public address system. He found the Customs manager. "I'm Inspector Romanov. I just heard my name on the loudspeaker, saying there was a call for me. Can you patch me through?"

"It's not possible from here," the Customs clerk said. "You'll have to walk out to the terminal and look for a house phone. You'll see them scattered around."

Romanov walked back to the terminal and picked up a phone mounted on the wall next to the ticket counter. "This is Inspector Romanov. I heard my name on the loudspeaker."

"Yes, Sir. You have a call waiting."

"Can I take the call from this phone?"

"Yes, absolutely. Let me connect you." A moment later she said, "Your call is connected. Thank you for using Aeroflot Airlines."

"This is Romanov."

"Romanov, this is Director Pasternik calling from KGB headquarters. Are you waiting for a man named Jack Postl?"

"Yes, Sir. I haven't seen him yet."

"When he shows up, take him to the security office. We need to question him before we allow him to travel.

"When he shows up at Customs, you want me to take him to security?"

"That's correct, but if you see him beforehand at the ticket counter or in the terminal, grab him."

"Okay. What's he look like?" Romanov asked.

"Tall, blond, blue eyes, 30s."

"I'll do my best."

"Once you've got him, I need you to find two more people."

"Who are they?"

"Both French. Gaston Joubert, short, gray, with a goatee, 60s and Claire Petit, pretty, long blond hair, in her 30s. They're leaving later this evening. We blocked them at Customs so they can't leave. When you find them, take them to the security office, too."

"Hang on a minute while I write their names down. How do you spell them?"

Pasternik spelled out the names.

"Are they flying Aeroflot, too?" Romanov asked.

"No. Those two are Air France."

"That's a different terminal."

"So?"

"You want me to find Postl first, then walk to another terminal and find the other two?"

"You have an objection to walking?"

"I can't be in two places at once. It's a big place. I'm not even sure I can find Postl. Look, I'm not responsible for the other two. They weren't part of my orders."

"I understand that, Romanov. We're going to get you some help, but just start looking."

"Yes, Sir."

"Thank you!" Pasternik said. He slammed the phone down. What in the hell is wrong with these people, he asked himself.

Pasternik called the basement office at Lubyanka. "Security," the desk clerk answered.

"It's Pasternik from upstairs."

"Yes?"

"I need two men to run an errand for me."

"Sure. What do you need?"

"I need two foreigners picked up at the Berlin Hotel at six pm."

"Names?"

"Gaston Joubert and a woman, Claire Petit. Both are French."

"Brief description?"

"The man is short, gray, in his 60s. The woman is tall, blond, in her 30s"

"No problem. Where are we taking them?"

"They're supposed to travel tonight, so take them to the airport and escort them to the security office inside the Aeroflot Terminal. We'll have someone there to conduct an interview before we release them to travel this evening."

"The Moscow Police usually assigns someone to follow foreigners around the city. Would you like me to notify whoever they've assigned?"

"Good idea. Just make sure they end up in the security office out at the airport."

"Very good, Sir."

I think I've got this wrapped up, Pasternik said to himself. *One more call*. "Chairman Petrovsky's office. May I help you?"

"Sorry, it's Grisha again, Irina. Can I speak with the Chairman?"

"Sure."

Petrovsky picked up the line. "What's going on, Grisha?"

"We've got all three blocked at Customs. When they

show up, they'll be taken to the security office. Can you give me some background before I drive out there?" Petrovsky proceeded to tell Pasternik what he knew of the situation. "Do you mind if I squeeze them?"

"Go ahead," Petrovsky said. "We've got to find out what's going on."

"I'll call you tonight at home if I find anything interesting. Do I have your permission to release them if there's nothing wrong?"

"Yes, absolutely."

Pasternik called back a moment later. Petrovsky picked up his own line. "Yes?"

"Sorry to bother you, Sir. It's Grisha again. I had a thought. Something about Gradovich's description of the woman bothered me."

"Go on."

What American agent do we know who's blond, pretty and in her 30s?"

"Shewolf?"

"Yes, Sir. We know she's been attending weekly meetings at DST headquarters. Suppose the French and Americans have mounted a mission in Moscow and used the Soviet-American talks as a cover? I know it's farfetched, but it's possible."

"To what end? Postl? He's not important enough, Grisha."

"But if Postl stole information from KGB computers, that would be important enough, wouldn't it?"

"He can't get access to sensitive files."

"You sure about that?"

"We had the kid checked out. Searched his apartment, his computer. He's clean. What are you suggesting?" Petrovsky asked.

"When they arrive at the airport, let's subject them to a real interrogation. Put them in separate rooms, go from room to room, rough them up and see what we get."

"Postl and the older man might break, but if it's Shewolf, forget about it. My sources tell me she's impossible to break."

"With all due respect, I'd like to try," Pasternik said confidently.

"Fine. Go ahead. I've another way to investigate Shewolf. I'll get that going, too."

"Her husband's in town for the talks. Why don't we pick him up on a suspicion charge and shake him down, too."

"You mean pull him out of the talks?"

"Yes," Pasternik answered.

"He's got diplomatic immunity. We can't prosecute him for spitting on the sidewalk."

"It would embarrass the Americans, Sir. Lots of press hanging around the talks."

"You're right. Have the Moscow Police do it. To make something stick, you've got to find his wife. Go find her, Grisha."

"I'm on my way to the airport."

"Good luck."

Petrovsky opened his safe and pulled out a list of addresses and phone numbers. He dialed the apartment of Ivan Ilitch. No answer. He dialed the phone in the warehouse across the street. No answer there, either. He dialed Maxim Khozin's apartment. Again, no answer. Finally, he called Assistant Director Moldova's office. "Moldova? It's Petrovsky."

"Yes, Sir."

"Leo, I've got a job for you. Can you come down to my office for a minute?"

"Sure. I'll be right down."

Leo Moldova walked in. "How can I help?"

"I need two things, Leo. First, ask the police to send a couple of squad cars to the National Hotel. Find an American involved in the Soviet-American talks going on at the hotel. His name is Steven Tilton. Apprehend him right in front of the press as the talks are ending. Take him downtown to Police Headquarters for questioning."

"It's as good as done, Sir."

"Second, I need you to locate someone for me."

"No problem."

"The name is Ivan Ilitch. Here's his address and phone. Go to his apartment. Don't send anyone else. You do it. If he doesn't answer, enter the apartment. If he's not there, go to the warehouse across the street. Same thing, go in and look around. Call my private line with a report."

"Yes, Sir."

Petrovsky pushed his intercom button. "Irina, it looks like it's going to be a late night. Do you mind staying for a while?"

"Of course not."

"Why don't you bring in food for us?"

"Great. I'll have someone bring something up from the cafeteria."

"Could you bring me a cup of coffee?"

"Sure. Coming right up."

Petrovsky emptied his ashtray into the wastebasket below his desk. He noticed one of the computer cords unplugged. *What the hell is this*, he thought. *Doesn't Postl plug in his equipment*? He leaned back in his chair and lit a cigarette. *It's going to be a long night*, he said to himself.

Chapter Ten

VLAD TOOK SIDE streets to avoid the traffic, which had been building toward the evening rush hour. When Laura noticed the circuitous route toward downtown, she forced herself to focus. *Snap out of it*, she told herself. *You want to change your life, do it later. Right now, you've got a job to do.*

"It's after three, Vlad. Where are we?" she asked.

"It's taking longer than expected due to traffic, boss lady. I'm doing the best I can to avoid the ring road. We should be pulling up to the hotel in a couple of minutes. How long are you going to be?" Vlad asked.

"Just a couple of minutes."

"I've got to come inside and make a call. I'll park a few meters from the entrance and leave the flashers on."

Within minutes, Vlad parked near the front of the hotel. "Welcome to the National," the doorman said, holding the door as Laura and Vlad entered. Inside the lobby, Laura scanned the room until she found Jean seated comfortably with his nose in a magazine. She walked over.

"Ready to go, Mr. Joubert?"

"There you are," Jean said. "Yes, I'm ready. However, we have a small problem. Your husband."

"I know. I've got to pull him out of the talks. There's a black Mercedes parked along the curb. The driver's name is Vlad. He's over there making a phone call," Laura said, nodding in the direction of Vlad. "Hop in the front and I'll be along in a minute."

Laura walked to the front desk. "There's a government meeting this afternoon between Soviet and American officials," she said to the clerk. "I must speak with one of the Americans. There's been a family emergency. Where are they meeting?"

"Second floor ballroom, but you won't be able to get close to the room. They have a security perimeter set up. Go up the staircase, turn left and speak with one of the staff."

"Thanks."

Vlad picked up a house phone and asked for an outside line. He dialed the number and a man picked up. "Hello?"

"Sammy, its Vlad. You and Katrina ready?"

"Yeah, no prob."

"Sammy, I'm serious. I need you on this."

"Not a problem, Vlad. Don't worry about it."

"You fuck this up, Sammy, and I'll have you banned from every club in Moscow."

"Relax. What do you say that shit for?"

"It's important."

"I got it, Vlad. I got it. Like I said, no worries."

"All right. Be ready."

Vlad hung up and walked back outside to the car. Jean was waiting at the curb.

Laura walked up the stairs to the second floor where she found a small lobby adjacent to the elevators. It was filled with reporters and camera men waiting for the meeting to end. She pushed her way through the crowd to a security desk that blocked access to the ballroom. Red velvet ropes were stretched across the hall, leaving only a small opening by the desk. A Soviet guard sitting at the desk checked the badges of people walking in and out. "I'm sorry, but this area is closed to the public," he said to Laura in Russian. "Use the elevators on the other side of the lobby."

She spoke English in return. "I need to speak to one of the Americans participating in the talks. He has a family emergency at home."

The guard handed her a notepad and pen. "Write a message on this and I'll make sure he gets it," he responded in English.

She saw a friendly face walking down the hallway. "Jack!" she shouted and waved. Jack Mason smiled and walked over.

"I'm going outside the perimeter for a minute," he said to the guard. "Walk with me, Ma'am," Jack said. He grabbed Laura's arm and pulled her away from the press. "What the hell are you doing here?" he asked in hushed tones.

"I was about to ask you the same question?"

"Bates sent me to look after Steve."

"I'm Claire Petit, by the way."

"Are you working?"

Laura nodded. "I need to pull Steve out of the meeting. It's an emergency, Jack, or I wouldn't ask."

Jack looked at his watch. "It's three twenty-five. The meeting's over in an hour and a half. Can it wait?"

"No. It's important. Can you get him for me?"

Jack knew Laura well enough to know she was serious.

"Wait here."

Laura watched Jack speak into his comm as he walked down the hallway toward the ballroom. In a couple of minutes, she saw him walk a red faced Steve back toward the lobby. Steve looked ready to boil over with anger. They stepped beyond the perimeter and were immediately besieged by reporters. "No questions," Steve said, holding up his hands.

"What's the status of the negotiations?" a reporter asked, notebook in hand.

"No comment at this time."

"Any comment on a potential reunification of Germany?"

"I'm sorry. No questions."

"Let's move away from the press," Jack said, pushing them through the media gathered around the security desk.

Steve spoke softly, but intently, as Jack led them behind a row of large tropical plants that separated the lobby area from a bank of elevators. "What the hell are you doing here?" he asked Laura.

"Jack, please keep the press away," Laura said.

"Sure. No problem, Ms. Petit."

"Can everyone give us some space, please?" Jack asked reporters who followed them.

"Ms. Petit?" Steve asked. "Tell me you're not working."

"Steve, there's trouble on the way. You need to leave."

"What the hell have you gotten yourself into?"

"You need to come with me. We need to go right now," Laura said with urgency in her voice.

"I will do no such thing. You're on your own."

"You want the authorities to arrest you in front of the press?"

"Both of you lower your voices," Jack said, glancing around the room. "You didn't ask for my opinion, Steve," Jack said, "but the press will eat you alive if you're taken in for questioning. It doesn't matter what she's done. Go! I'll explain it to SecState."

Steve looked as angry as Laura had ever seen him. His face flush, he looked down at the carpet and didn't say a word. "Steve, look at me," Laura said. Steve looked up, but refused to look at her. "Whatever you want to say, say it later. A situation is developing. To stay ahead of it, both of us need to leave right now."

"All right," he said. "I'll be back in a minute. I've got to get my briefcase."

"Leave it."

"Look, I've got to pack, check out and get my passport back. It's going to take a few minutes."

"Leave everything. We need to walk right now," Laura said.

Jack leaned in and grabbed Steve firmly by the arm. He pulled him close and the two men came nose to nose. "Steve, get the fuck out of here." Steve looked back and forth between Jack and Laura. He began to object, but Jack cut him off. "Go!" Jack said emphatically.

Steve relented. Laura took his arm, walked him out of the hotel and pushed him into the Mercedes back seat. She jumped in after him. "Ready to go, boss lady?" Vlad asked. She slammed the door.

"Get us the hell out of here, Vlad."

"Yes, Ma'am. To the airport?"

"As fast as you can."

Vlad performed like a Formula One driver, wheeling the Mercedes through lane changes, off and on ramps; even using the shoulder at times. Drivers would pull off to let him pass, thinking the luxury car with military plates was an official vehicle. Steve, however, was oblivious to the hard braking, acceleration and tailgating that Vlad used to force his way through traffic. "Do you know the damage you've done?" he asked Laura. "This can't be swept under the carpet."

"You're right. By the way, say hello to Gaston Joubert," Laura said, gesturing to the front seat. "You may know each other."

Jean looked back, "Monsieur."

"And, our driver is the son of the head of the Soviet Navy, Admiral Arkady Tonov."

Vlad looked in the rear view mirror. "The name's Vladimir. Call me Vlad."

"Vlad, this is my husband."

"Boss Lady's husband? Wow! Nice to meet you."

"What the hell ..." Laura put her hand to Steve's mouth. He stopped mid-sentence.

"We'll talk about it later." She leaned forward and put her hand on the front seat. "How long to get to the airport, Vlad?"

"Forty-five, give or take," Vlad said. "I can cut that to thirty-five."

"Would someone please tell me what's going on?" Steve continued.

"If you knew anything at all, Monsieur," Jean said,

putting his arm over the seat and looking back. "it would make you culpable. I suggest you feign ignorance."

"As far as you know, it was a family emergency, Steve," Laura said.

Jean looked at the clock on the dashboard, then back at Laura. "It's 3:50. I told him to be there at four. Surely, he can sit in the terminal for a while without getting in trouble."

"Maybe," she said.

***

Leo Moldova pounded on the apartment door until finally, he forced his way through a deadbolt to gain access to Ilitch's apartment. "Mind your own damn business," he shouted at an old man down the hall who peeked out of his door at the noise. Once inside, Moldova saw luggage sitting in the middle of the living room. *He's been here recently*, Moldova thought. *Ilitch must have been in a hurry. He dropped the bags off and left. Two types of luggage? Two people, maybe?* He checked the rest of the apartment; nothing.

Moldova walked across the street expecting the warehouse to be locked, but found the door opened easily when he pushed the handle. It was quiet, musty and dark inside. It was one of those old brick warehouses built before World War II. There were lots of them all over town. The overheads in the room's center were on and Moldova could see dust particles floating in the air underneath the lights. *Someone's been here recently*, he thought, instinctively drawing his sidearm. He didn't perceive anyone in the room, but he tensed when he saw overturned chairs. He walked into the light and saw dark red stains on the concrete floor. It appeared to be a crime scene hastily sanitized. As his eyes adjusted to the light, he saw chunks of the brick wall had fallen to the floor. Shots had been fired and rounds had bounced off the wall. Someone had picked up the casings. *This was a professional hit*, he thought.

Moldova inspected the rest of the warehouse. A barrel in a corner of the room leaked fluid from an ammo round. It hadn't been leaking long. He looked on the other side of the barrel; no exit hole. The round still inside. *Judging from the trajectory, the shooter entered like I did*, he thought. Moldova found a bulletin board behind the barrel, broken into pieces and thrown in the corner. The dark substance splashed on it looked like blood. The back door was unlocked. Moldova went outside. *This is where they would have removed the bodies*, he reasoned. He walked back in the building and lifted the receiver on the desk phone. Moldova phoned the Moscow Police, gave them the address and told them to bring a forensic team. They asked him to wait at the scene.

Moldova called Petrovsky's private line.
"Yes?" Petrovsky asked.
"It's Leo, Sir. I'm at the warehouse across the street from Ilitch's apartment. There's evidence of a shooting. It happened recently. Probably today."
"What about Ilitch?"

"I can't find him."

"What did you find in the apartment?"

"It appears Ilitch had just returned from a trip. Luggage was in the living room, but he wasn't there."

"Thank you, Leo."

"I'll stick around for the police to show up, then I'm on my way back to headquarters."

"Very good."

Petrovsky hung up the phone and leaned forward, putting both elbows on his desk. *Who's good enough to kill Ilitch and Khozin? She's not that good.* He called Moscow Police Headquarters, gave them Claire Petit's description and asked them to send extra personnel to the airport. *She can't get through Customs, so they'll eventually find her*, he said to himself.

***

Jack Postl arrived at Sheremetyevo a few minutes prior to 4:00 pm and sat in one of a long row of thinly padded chairs that were bolted to the terminal floor. They were courtesy chairs people used while waiting. The airport was busy; the terminal crowded with people. Every few minutes, another announcement blasted over the loudspeaker system. The line at the Aeroflot ticket counter extended beyond the rope line into the terminal walkway. People set their luggage on the floor, making it difficult to walk through the terminal.

Jack found a single seat and put his backpack on the floor between his legs. He closed his eyes, trying to not appear nervous. *I've not done anything wrong they know about*, he thought. *I'm just a ministry employee going on a business trip. Stick to that story if anyone questions me. I don't know anything else. Listen for the Schmitt announcement*. He looked at the wall clock next to the ticket counter; four-fifteen. He looked again a few minutes later; almost four-thirty. *No announcement*, Jack thought. *Is anything wrong?* He noticed a man in a black suit walking up and down the terminal stopping men with blond hair. The man watched people walk in and out of the terminal. He was looking for someone. *Don't make eye contact*, Jack thought. He opened a paperback novel and pretended to read.

***

Vlad pulled in front of the private aircraft terminal at Sheremetyevo at 4:30 pm. He glanced at the clock. "Not bad, considering the traffic." They unloaded their luggage onto the sidewalk. "Go inside, everyone. My dad should be waiting. Boss lady knows what he looks like. I'm going to pull the car around into one of the official government spots."

Laura, Jean and Steve walked inside the private terminal and found the head of the Soviet Navy, Admiral Arkady Tonov, sitting with a woman and a pilot. Tonov was wearing his full dress ceremonial uniform. "There you are," he said loudly, walking toward them as the three approached. He gave each of them a big bear hug, as though they were his best friends. "Such a pleasure to have my friends accompany me on the trip. This is Svetlana, our flight attendant and Dmitri, our pilot," gesturing toward them.

"Hello Gennady," Svetlana said to Jean. "So nice you're able to join us."

Jean picked up the ruse smoothly. He smiled as though he'd known her for years. "Ah, the beautiful Svetlana. You are the essence of beauty, my dear." He kissed her hand.

She turned to Steve, "And Peter. Wonderful to see you. I'm so sorry about your late wife."

Steve was speechless.

"I'm afraid Peter hasn't been the same since his wife died," Tonov said to the others. "Are you recovering well from your stroke, Peter?" the Admiral asked.

Steve had no idea what was said, but saw the Admiral nodding, so he said, "Yes," in return.

"The mountain air of Salzburg will rejuvenate you, my friend." Tonov slapped him on the back.

Tonov turned to Polzin and whispered. "What's the status of the plane, Dmitri?"

"The mechanics have finished the checklist. We're ready to go once they're finished fueling," Polzin said.

"How much for the fuel?"

"American dollars?"

"Yes." Polzin did a quick calculation in his mind. "Eighteen hundred, Admiral."

"Have you filed a flight plan?"

"Yes, Sir. If you'll give me the money for fuel, I'll pay them and board for my final instrument check." The Admiral handed him two thousand dollars. "Thanks," Polzin said. He glanced furtively around the terminal. "Hopefully, I'll see you in a few minutes."

Svetlana addressed Laura. "Hi, Nadia! Keeping track of that naughty son of the Admiral?"

Laura also handled the conversation well. "Hi, Svetlana. Vlad's a handful, isn't he?"

"He's a very bad boy!" Svetlana exclaimed.

"That's my Vlad, for you," Laura said. "Here he is now."

Vlad walked up, put his arm around Laura and kissed her flush on the lips. "I've missed you terribly, baby. I know you'd like to freshen up before the trip. I brought the things you left in the apartment last night."

"Thank you, Vlad. How considerate of you."

"Come, I'll show you to the ladies room."

Jean handed Laura's travel bag to her. "You might need this, Nadia," he said.

Vlad walked Laura to the ladies room. "Here's what's going on. We've got to sell you to Customs as the General Secretary's daughter. There's a black leather mini-skirt and black stockings in the bag. Also, dark red lipstick. Put your make-up on heavy, tease your hair up and you'll look exactly like her. I know her. She's a brat. Act the part and no one will question you."

"Got it. I'll be right back," Laura replied.

Laura quickly changed clothing and touched up her

271

make-up. She had brought along a pair of four inch black pumps, which she pulled from her travel bag, exchanging them for her sneakers. The black mini-skirt and stockings would match her black leather jacket well, she thought. She used Vlad's lipstick, took a comb from her purse and lifted her hair into a tousled look she sometimes used as a runway model years ago.

She removed the shoulder holsters and stowed them in her bag. However, she decided to keep one weapon with her, so she reloaded the clip and then pushed it behind her back into the band of her skirt. She donned the jacket, stood back from the mirror and looked at herself. The look needed a bit more cleavage, she thought, so she unbuttoned an additional button on her silk blouse. Not bad, she said. It's definitely a nightclub look, something young women might use in Paris.

Laura stepped into the lobby, where Vlad's jaw nearly dropped to the floor. "You look absolutely amazing, boss lady. You easily pass for the Secretary's daughter. Forgive me for putting my hands on you, but we must act the part at Customs."

"Don't worry about it, Vlad. If we're going to sell it, let's do it," she said with a smile.

Vlad put his arm around her and they walked back to the group.

**

While Laura dressed in the ladies room, Jean spotted a wall phone and excused himself to place a phone call. He asked to be connected to the Aeroflot ticket counter in the International Terminal. An Aeroflot ticket agent came on the line. "Aeroflot Airlines. How may I help you?"

"I need to speak with someone in the terminal who's traveling on Aeroflot this afternoon. Could you page that person for me?"

"Yes, Sir. What's the name?"

"Mr. Schmitt."

"One moment, please."

The agent put Jean on hold and made the announcement. Jack Postl, sitting inside the International Terminal, finally heard the announcement he expected. He picked up his backpack and walked to the Aeroflot ticket counter where agents were processing a long line of impatient customers. Ignored by the agents, Jack finally interrupted, "I'm sorry, but I just heard my name over the loudspeaker." The agent glanced at Jack and pointed to a courtesy phone on the wall next to the counter. "Over there," she said.

Jack picked up the phone and was connected to Jean. "This is Mr. Schmitt."

"Do not take your scheduled flight, Mr. Schmitt. Please go to the private aircraft terminal immediately."

"Thank you."

Chapter Eleven

AS JACK WALKED toward the exit, Inspector Romanov watched the young, blond man with the backpack walk across the lobby. Romanov stepped in front of him. "Excuse me. Are you Jack Postl?"

"Yes, Sir," Jack replied.

"I'm Inspector Romanov. I'm glad I found you. I've been assigned to accompany you on your trip. I thought we were supposed to meet at Customs?"

"I was waiting in the terminal for my girlfriend. She wanted to say goodbye before my flight. I'm afraid I haven't found her."

Romanov looked at his watch. "Your girlfriend will have to wait. I must ask you to accompany me to the security station. The authorities need to interview you before the flight."

"Is anything wrong?"

Romanov smiled. "No, it's routine. It won't take long and we should be able to make the flight if we hurry. Shall we go?" Romanov asked, extending his hand toward one end of the terminal.

"Yes, of course."

A man watching nearby phoned the French Embassy. "Subject A has been picked up for questioning," he said.

"Thank you," an unidentified voice said.

A phone call was then placed from the Embassy to the Air France ticket counter. "Air France. How may I assist you?" the phone clerk asked.

"I need to page a Mr. Joubert. He's a ticketed Air France passenger waiting in the terminal."

"Of course. Please wait on the line."

A page made over the loudspeaker system went unanswered. "I'm afraid Mr. Joubert is not answering," the clerk said after a five minute wait. "Please try again later."

"Thank you," the voice said. The man at the Embassy made one more call, this time to DST Headquarters in Paris. "Jacques Martin, please." The call was connected immediately.

"Hello, this is Jacques."

"Problems in Moscow. Subject A has been detained for questioning and Mr. Joubert is not answering a page."

"Thank you. Keep me informed."

Inspector Romanov took Jack to the far end of the terminal where a desk was positioned in front of a set of double doors. A uniformed airport security guard sitting at the desk looked up. "Yes?"

"I'm Inspector Romanov. KGB Director Pasternik asked me to bring a passenger to Security."

"Name of passenger?"

"Jack Postl."

The guard studied a clipboard, found Postl's name on a list and looked up. "Follow me." He led them through the double doors to the third room on the left. He unlocked it and held it open. "Wait here, please. Someone will be with you shortly."

"Have a seat, Mr. Postl," Romanov said, gesturing to a

chair. "The investigator will be here any minute."

"What's this about?" Jack asked.

Romanov shrugged. "I don't know. They just told me to bring you to Security."

Jack looked around the room. It looked like what he imagined a police interrogation room might look like. Secure metal door, no windows and a table in the middle with a chair on each side. Fluorescent lighting. The only thing missing was the two way mirror he'd seen in movies. He looked at his watch. Almost five o'clock.

Within minutes, a man walked into the room. Same kind of dark suit, Jack thought. All of them must wear dark suits. He shook hands with Romanov. "Pasternik, KGB."

"Inspector Alexander Romanov."

Pasternik looked down at Jack with a patronizing smile. "You must be Jack Postl."

"Yes, Sir."

Pasternik sat down opposite Jack. "Mr. Postl, my name is Pasternik," he said in a friendly manner. "I'm from the Committee for State Security. We're doing an investigation of two foreign nationals you may have come into contact with in the last couple of days. Could I see your identification, please?" Jack pulled out his billfold and gave it to Pasternik, who thumbed through it looking at each item. "You're the man working on computers at Lubyanka, aren't you?"

"Yes."

"I've seen you in the building. That's quite a bit of money to be taking on a two day trip, Mr. Postl," Pasternik said, pointing to the cash in Jack's billfold.

"The Ministry gave me a check for expenses. I cashed it on the way to the airport."

"I see." Pasternik handed the billfold back. "You have a reservation on a flight this evening to Paris?"

"Yes. In about an hour."

"Could I see the ticket?"

"I don't have it."

"I have it," Romanov said. He pulled it from the breast pocket of his jacket and handed it to Pasternik, who studied it.

Pasternik looked at Jack. "Why are you traveling to Paris?"

"The Ministry's sending me."

"That's the ElectroTechnical Ministry?"

"Yes."

Pasternik took his time between questions, studying Jack. He looked for anything in Jack's demeanor that indicated guilt. "Are you worried you're going to miss your flight?"

"Yes."

"Why?"

"I've never been to Paris before."

"That's understandable. So, what's the Ministry asking you to do in Paris?"

"They buy computers from a company there. I'm picking out the machines for them."

"What company?"

"Inline Computers."

"And they're sending you to pick them out?"

"Yes."

Jack looked too young to be representing a ministry.

"Why you?" Pasternik asked.

"I'm the one who installs them."

"I see."

Pasternik picked up the briefcase he'd carried into the room. He opened it and pulled out a picture. "I have a picture to show you." He slid the picture across the table. "Do you know this person?"

"That's Ms. Petit."

"How do you know her?"

"She came to Moscow to sell us computers."

"So, you met her?"

"Yes."

"She works for this company, Inline?"

"Yes." Jack glanced at his watch.

"It's 5:20, Jack," Pasternik said. "Don't worry about the flight. If you miss it, we can put you on a later one. Did anyone else from the Ministry meet this woman?"

"Minister Gradovich met her."

"Was she alone?"

"No, there was a man with her."

"What was his name?"

"I think it was Joubert."

***

While the group continued to wait in the private aircraft terminal, the Admiral walked over to Laura. "As soon as fuel is loaded, we're ready to go. You owe me two thousand for fuel, by the way."

"Can I pay you once we board?" Laura asked.

"Fine. I did a head count. We're missing one of your people."

"Yes."

"I want to take us through Customs together. How long before your last person arrives?" The Admiral looked at his watch. "It's 5:20. Our scheduled take-off time is 5:45 pm. We can't be late."

Jean watched the conversation and walked over. "Is there a problem?"

"We're ready to go through Customs, Jean and Postl's not here. I don't want to leave him."

She turned to the Admiral. "Do you have an ID for me?"

"Here," he said, handing her a passport.

"He's waiting in another terminal," she said to the Admiral. "I'll go get him."

The Admiral looked at his watch again. "You must hurry. We haven't much time."

"Mademoiselle, I'll go," Jean said.

"No, you won't," Laura replied. "I have a feeling it could get messy."

Jean grimaced. "Isn't it always?"

"I'm thirty years younger than you. Messy is a little easier for me."

"By the way," Jean said. "I meant to ask you, how was your afternoon meeting?"

"Very messy. Not for me, though."

Jean smiled. "Shewolf. That's what they call you, you know."

"Apparently, for good reason." Laura looked for Vlad. "Vlad? Would you come here for a second?"

Vlad walked over. "Yes, boss lady?"

"You've got to take me to another terminal. It won't take long."

"Whatever you say, boss lady."

***

Pasternik was prepared to question Jack as long as it took for him to admit wrongdoing. This was going to take a while, he thought. He tapped his finger on the picture. "Would it surprise you to know this woman's name isn't Ms. Petit?"

"That's the name she used," Jack said.

"Jack, you seem like a nice kid. I'm sure you're innocent in all this. The woman's a foreign intelligence agent. She manipulated you. I'm not sure why, but we're going to find out."

"What's her real name?"

"She's Laura Messier, an American intelligence agent. She's dangerous, Jack."

"She seemed so nice."

Pasternik laughed, wondering how anyone could believe that. He'd seen Messier's file. She was a monster. "They always are," he said. "This one, especially, because she's pretty. She's a con artist, Jack."

"I had no idea."

"I'm sure you didn't. Did she ask you for anything when you met her?"

"No."

"Did she ask you to bring anything with you on the flight?"

"No."

"Did she give you anything to take on the flight?"

"No."

"Did she slip something in your coat or your pocket?"

"Not to my knowledge."

"Do you mind if I search you?"

"No. Go right ahead."

Pasternik asked Jack to empty his pockets onto the table. He gave him a quick pat down. "Take off your shoes."

Pasternik looked inside Jack's shoes. "Okay. You can put them back on." He turned to Romanov. "Inspector, would you dump the contents of Mr. Postl's backpack on the table?"

Romanov unzipped the pack, turned it upside down and shook it. Jack's personal items spilled out onto the table. Pasternik searched through the contents. "Why all the pictures?"

"They're pictures of my parents, Sir. I wanted to carry them in case the plane crashed. I'm afraid of flying."

Pasternik laughed at Jack's feigned naivety. "So am I, Jack. So am I. Go ahead and put your things in your pack."

"Yes, Sir."

"So, she didn't give you anything or ask you to bring anything. Did she ask you to do anything for her? Favors or anything of that nature?"

"Not that I can recall."

"Did she ask you to copy anything, say from the KGB computer system, for example?"

"No."

"Have you ever copied files from the KGB

mainframe?"

"Only JCL files."

"What are those?" Pasternik asked, leaning forward.

"Those are instructions for the computer itself."

"What about data files?"

"Text files?" Jack asked.

"Yes."

"No. I don't manage data. At Lubyanka, that's Novotny's job."

"So, you wouldn't necessarily see those?"

"I can't. Not unless Novotny gives me the passwords."

"I see." Pasternik leaned back and thought for a minute.

"So, why did she ask you to come to Paris?"

"The woman in the photo?"

"Yes."

"She didn't. That was my idea," Jack said.

"Your idea?"

"Yes. Some of the computers they send us don't operate correctly. I wanted to test them before they're shipped."

"She didn't know you were going to Paris?"

"Not until she got here."

"Let's talk about the man for a minute. Were you involved with him at all?

"No. Minister Gradovich talked with him."

"I see." Pasternik paused again, thinking about how to crack Jack's story.

***

Vlad gunned the Mercedes out of the parking lot. "Where are we going, boss lady?"

"The International Terminal."

"Departures or arrivals?"

"Departures. Just pull up to the Aeroflot doors and wait. I'll be back in a minute."

Vlad pulled onto the outer road and turned into the International Terminal. He stopped under the Aeroflot sign. "Wow. Lots of police walking around. Something must be going on," Vlad said. He pulled to the curb. "This close enough?"

"Yep."

A policeman walked up as Laura got out of the car. He knocked on the passenger window. Vlad rolled it down. "You can't park here."

"I've got a VIP passenger, Officer. She'll be right back."

"Okay, but if it gets jammed up, I'll have to move you." He stopped Laura as she began to walk away. "Excuse me, can I see your ID?"

"Sure. No problem." Laura dug into her purse and produced the Soviet passport the Admiral had given her. The policeman looked at the ID and then looked at Laura. His eyes shifted back and forth until he finally asked, "Are you the General Secretary's daughter?"

"Last time I checked."

"I've seen you on TV."

"Do you mind if I run inside and say goodbye to my boyfriend? I'll be right back."

The officer gave her a friendly smile. "Go right ahead. Sorry to bother you, Ma'am."

Laura entered the terminal. The lobby was jammed with people. The Aeroflot ticket counter had a line of passengers stretching half the length of the lobby. The seats running the length of the lobby were full. People were walking up and down the terminal dragging luggage, herding children, and staring at the departure and arrival schedules monitors. It was noisy. *This is as bad as LaGuardia or Dulles*, she thought. She saw a sign pointing to Customs, so she walked half the length of the terminal only to find more lines at the Customs booths. She walked back the other direction. *I'll never find him in here*, she thought. At the opposite end of the terminal, she saw the sign, "Security," hanging from the ceiling. *That's the last place I want to go*, she thought, *but probably the best chance I have to find him. They can page him for me and if he were stopped for questioning, that's where they'd take him.* She slipped her leather gloves on again in case of trouble.

It took far longer than she expected to walk the length of the terminal, walking around people with luggage, dodging children and avoiding passengers standing in the aisle talking. As she approached Security, the guard sitting at the desk raised his eyes. "Can I help you?"

"I'm looking for my boyfriend."

He pointed toward the terminal. "Find a house phone and have him paged."

"Is he in one of your rooms?"

"Is he in trouble?"

"I don't think so," Laura said.

"Then, he wouldn't be back there, would he?"

"Mind if I have a look?"

"See the sign? It says 'Authorized Personnel Only.'"

"Don't you have a list or something you could check for me?"

The guard gave her an annoyed look. "What's the name?"

"Jack Postl."

"You'll have to wait." He pointed to seats out in the terminal. "Sit over there. He'll be out in a few minutes."

"No, thanks. I'll just go on back."

Laura walked around the desk and through the double doors. *Metal*, she thought. *That'll work just fine.*

"Hey! Stop!" the guard yelled. He ran after her, pushed through the doors and found Laura in the middle of the hallway, pointing a weapon at him.

"I'm sorry. I truly am," she said. She shot him in the forehead. The round went completely through his head, bounced off the metal door behind him and lodged itself in the ceiling. Thank heaven for the suppressor, she thought. Otherwise, I'd have the entire Moscow Police force running in this direction.

She unclipped the key chain from his belt and searched his set of keys. One with a large letter 'M' stamped on the face. She put her ear to the first door and, hearing nothing, unlocked the door. She drug the body into the room, searched his pockets, found a handkerchief and wiped the hallway floor as best she could. She threw the soiled hanky into the room, locked the door and proceeded down the hallway, putting her ear next to each door to listen. Hearing the murmur of voices from the third room, Laura held her weapon behind her and knocked.

"Inspector, would you get the door for me?" Pasternik

asked. "By the way, aren't you supposed to be out in the terminal looking for the other two?"

"Yes, Sir."

"Answer the door, then go out there and continue your search."

Romanov walked to the door. He opened it halfway. "Yes?"

Laura shot him in the head as soon as he opened the door. Blood splattered everywhere. As Romanov fell backwards, Laura gave him a shove. He landed on Pasternik. Laura pushed her way into the room, keeping the weapon pointed straight ahead. A surprised Pasternik struggled to push Romanov away and wipe the blood off his face. He stood up and recognized Shewolf, but was too late to offer any resistance. Laura shot him twice in the chest. He slumped to the floor on top of Romanov's body. Pasternik was still alive, eyes open, struggling to breath. Laura stood over him. "Sorry," she said. She shot him one last time in the head. She stuffed the pistol underneath her jacket. "Hi Jack. Ready to leave?" she asked with a smile.

"Shit!" Jack said, standing up and retreating to the back wall. "Shit! You just shot them." Jack stared at the bodies.

"Yes, I did. You ready to leave?"

Jack continued to stare at the bodies. "But … but … you just ..."

Laura cut him off. "Yeah, I shot them. So what? Come on, we've got to hurry."

"You just ..." He didn't finish.

Laura stepped over the bodies and slapped him. "That's right, they're dead. They're not going to bite. Step over them and let's go!"

Jack slowly began to move toward the door in a state of shock. "Jack! Pick up your backpack. We've got to get out of here!" Laura picked up his backpack, handed it to him and gave Jack a shove out the door. She locked the door behind her and led Jack up the hallway. He recoiled at the blood in the hallway and stopped. "Keep moving, Jack. Ignore the mess." She gave him another shove. Once through the double doors, Laura asked, "Do you see any police around?"

"No," Jack replied.

Laura took the master key and locked the double doors. She found paper on the desk and wrote a note, leaving it on the desktop: *"Be Right Back."*

"Come on," she said to Jack. "And, try to act normal, will you?" She led Jack through the terminal to the outer doors. "This way," she said, pointing to the terminal doors. She pushed him through the doors.

Once outside on the sidewalk, the fresh air revived Jack. He moved faster until he froze when he saw the policeman standing by Vlad's Mercedes. "You finally found him?" the policeman asked.

Laura laughed. "He was completely lost, I'm afraid. Wrong terminal." The policeman opened the back door. "Come on, honey," she said. Pushing Jack into the vehicle, Laura climbed in after him. She looked at the policeman and smiled. "Thanks."

He touched his cap. "Have a safe trip, Ma'am." He closed the door.

"Okay, Vlad. Get us the hell out of here."

"You got it, boss lady."

They pulled away from the curb. Vlad looked in the rear view mirror. "You go bang-bang again, boss lady?" Vlad asked, holding up his hand in the shape of a pistol.

"Yep," Laura replied.

"How many this time?"

"Just shut the fuck up, Vlad. Get us back to the terminal."

Vlad smiled. "You got it, boss lady."

***

The Admiral had a sense of relief at seeing Vlad and Laura walk through the door with the last passenger. He gathered the group together. "Are we ready to leave now?"

"I believe we are," Jean said.

"Good. Shewolf, hand me your passport."

"Here," she said.

"I'll run them over to Customs, have them stamped and be right back."

He walked to the Customs booth and demanded to see the manager. "Yes, Sir. I'll get him right away," the woman said, intimidated by the admiral's uniform and authoritarian manner. Tonov acted impatiently when she returned. "Is there a problem?" he asked.

"No, Sir. The manager will be with you in a minute."

The manager stepped to the window. "Yes, Sir?"

"Who are you?" the admiral demanded.

"Stepan Burkov, Sir. How may I help you?"

"Step out from behind the window."

The Customs manager opened the door and came out from behind the protective glass. "Yes, Sir. How can I help you?"

"I'm Admiral Tonov. We're very late leaving this afternoon, so I collected the passports of my friends over there." He pointed to the group. "We're all going to the same place; Austria for the Mozart Festival in Salzburg. If you'd be so kind to stamp them for us, we'll be on our way."

The Customs manager hesitated, wondering how to phrase his words to avoid upsetting an important man. "Sir, I must check everyone individually. I'm sorry, but it's the rules."

"Rules do not apply to high government officials, young man. Be quick about it. Our flight's due to leave."

"I'm sorry, Sir, but if you'd just have everyone line up, I'd be happy check them through personally."

"Do you see that young woman over there?" Tonov asked, pointing at Laura, who looked ready for an evening at one of Moscow's underground discotheques. "She's the daughter of the General Secretary." He pulled her passport out of the stack and showed it to the manager. "If you make her wait in line, the next place you're going is Lubyanka Prison."

Burkov looked at the passport, then looked at Laura and became nervous. His face became flush. "Yes, Sir, I've seen her on the television. But, Sir, my supervisor told me ..."

Tonov interrupted him as though Burkov was nothing more than a worthless enlisted man. "You're an idiot!"

Tonov gestured toward Laura. "Nadia, darling, would you come over here, please?" Vlad slipped her a phone number and whispered in her ear. "Use this number."

Laura glanced briefly at the number and sauntered over to the Customs booth. "What seems to be the problem, Admiral?"

"I promised your father you'd call him before we left. He wants to say goodbye."

Tonov looked at Burkov. "For heaven's sake, hand her a goddamn phone!" he shouted.

Burkov pulled a desk phone with a long cord out the door. "Here you are Ma'am."

"Is this a speaker phone?" Tonov asked.

"Yes, Sir," Burkov replied.

"Put it on speaker. You'll want to hear every word."

Laura dialed the number. "General Secretary's office. Katrina speaking. How may I help you?"

"Hi Katrina, its Nadia," Laura said playing along.

"I'll get your father. Hold on, Nadia."

A man with a deep, resonant voice came on the line. "My little Babushka. Did you call to tell me goodbye?"

"Yes, Daddy. I'll miss you."

"Have a great trip. I love you, Babushka."

"I love you, too, Daddy."

"Put the Admiral on the phone."

She handed the phone to the Admiral. "Yes, General Secretary?"

"Take good care of my daughter, Arkady. Since the death of my wife, she's all I have."

"I will take great care. I need a favor, Sir."

"Anything for you, Arkady. You're one of the great

heroes of the Soviet Union."

"There's a Customs official here who insists on interviewing your daughter before he allows her to travel."

"What?" he shouted. "Put that imbecile on the line."

"He wants to talk to you, Burkov," the Admiral said with a smirk.

Burkov was nervous as he put the receiver to his ear. "Yes, General Secretary?"

The General Secretary screamed, "Pass my daughter through Customs immediately, you idiot, or I'll have you shot in an hour! Do you understand me?"

Burkov could barely get the words out of him mouth. "Y...Y...Yes, Sir."

"What's your name?"

"Burkov, Sir."

He heard the General Secretary scream at Katrina. "Katrina, have the KGB pick up a man named Burkov in the Customs office at Sheremetyevo immediately! Have him taken to Lubyanka."

"Please, Sir. No. Please no," Burkov pleaded. "There's no need of that. Please forgive me."

"Then you give Admiral Tonov everything he asks for, no questions asked. If you keep my daughter waiting one minute longer, I'll have you executed by firing squad tonight."

"Yes, Sir. Right away, Sir." He hung up.

"Stamp them and be quick about it," Tonov said. "And consider yourself lucky."

Burkov took the passports and stamped each one without looking. He gave them back to the Admiral. "I'm sorry for the inconvenience, Sir. Have a great trip."

Lawrence Scofield

The admiral returned to the group with a big smile on his face. "We're cleared to leave, everyone. Gather your luggage and walk this way," he said, pointing to the doors leading to the tarmac. Outside, sitting on the tarmac, a beautiful Dassault Falcon 50 waited with its passenger door open.

An airport worker stood at the bottom of the stairs. "You can leave your luggage here if you like. I'll stow it in the cargo hold. Please be careful walking up the stairs." Svetlana boarded first and stood inside the door to direct passengers to their seats. After everyone boarded and took their seats, the worker climbed the stairs and stuck his head inside the cockpit. "Captain?"

Polzin looked over his shoulder. "Yes?"

"You're all ready to go. Have a safe flight."

"Thanks, Abram. We'll see you later." *A lot later*, Polzin thought. *Maybe never*.

The worker pushed the outside door shut as Svetlana walked to the front of the plane and locked it in place. She walked down the aisle to make sure passengers had their seat belts fastened.

Laura was surprised by the luxurious interior of the Dassault Falcon 50. Beige, leather stuffed chairs were near the front of the cabin; a three person sofa was further back. The restroom located at the rear of the plane was next to a small galley that contained a refrigerator and microwave oven. It was as nice as any plane Laura had ever traveled on. "My, gosh. I didn't expect something like this," she said to Tonov.

"Thank you, Shewolf. She's got some flight hours on

her, but she's a solid plane in perfect condition."

Svetlana walked up to the cockpit. "Captain, the cabin is secure."

"Thanks, Svetlana. You can leave the cockpit door open, but lock it in place for me."

"Of course, Captain." Svetlana latched the door to the cockpit wall, then took the closest seat and belted herself in.

Laura leaned over to the admiral. "Is Svetlana the captain's wife?"

Tonov laughed. "How did you know? Authorities won't allow a pilot's family to leave the country for fear they'll defect," he said. "She works for Aeroflot. By the way, I promised them $5,000 U.S. dollars to make the trip today. I hope you've got more cash in that bag of yours."

It was Laura's turn to laugh. "I think I can arrange something, Admiral. They're worth every penny."

"That's one of the things I like about you, Shewolf. Besides being young and attractive, you're a pro. It's nice to work with professionals."

Laura heard the engines increase intensity and felt the plane begin to move. She looked out the window where an airport worker stood on the tarmac using orange flashlights to direct the plane. She heard Polzin on his radio.

"Flight control, this is Falcon five-zero, one-niner-zero-eight, pushing away from the gate."

Laura heard the radio crackle. "Falcon five-zero, one-niner-zero-eight, this is flight control, you're cleared to taxi. Runway two-two. We've got one ahead of you."

The Admiral looked at Laura. "Keep your fingers

crossed. If we get airborne, there's a pretty good chance we'll get out of here."

The plane taxied to the end of the runway, then began a 180 degree turn. As Dmitri turned the plane, Laura could see one aircraft directly ahead. She heard that plane's engines roar and looked up the aisle through the cockpit window. It had taken off.

"Falcon five-zero, one-niner-zero-eight, you are now cleared for take-off."

"Roger that, flight control. Falcon five-zero, one-niner-zero-eight cleared for take-off," Polzin repeated into his headset.

Laura felt the plane surge and accelerate down the runway. In a few seconds, the plane was airborne and she heard the mechanical sound of the wheels being folded into the fuselage.

"Falcon five-zero, turn to heading one-eight-zero and hold at five-thousand feet."

"Roger that, flight control. Turn to heading one-eight-zero and hold at five-thousand feet."

Laura looked out the window at the Moscow suburbs below. *I'm hoping this is my last trip to Moscow ever*, she thought.

"Falcon five-zero, this is Sheremetyevo flight control. Maintain heading one-eight-zero. Increase speed to three-hundred knots and climb to fifteen-thousand feet."

"Flight control, this is Falcon five-zero. Roger that. Maintaining current heading of one-eight-zero. Increasing speed to three-hundred knots and climbing to fifteen-thousand feet."

Dmitri made his opening announcement over the intercom. "Good evening, everyone. This is Captain Polzin in the cockpit. My beautiful wife, Svetlana, will be serving you this evening. We are underway for our flight to Vienna, Austria this evening. Our flight time will be approximately two hours, fifty-five minutes. After we've reached our cruising altitude, you'll be free to move about the cabin. Svetlana will be coming through the cabin in a few minutes to take your drink order. She'll be serving sandwiches later, so relax and enjoy the ride. Captain out."

"Falcon five-zero, this is Sheremetyevo flight control. Please turn to heading two-two-five, increase speed to four-hundred knots and climb to thirty-five thousand feet."

"Roger, flight control. Turning to heading two-two-five, increasing speed to four-hundred knots and climbing to thirty-five thousand feet. Falcon five-zero, roger that, over."

Once the Falcon reached its cruise altitude, Svetlana headed to the galley where she prepared a light meal. The passengers relaxed and the mood became jovial. Laura used the restroom to change clothes. Gone was the mini-skirt and heavy make-up, replaced by jeans, sneakers and a light foundation. As she made her way up the aisle, Svetlana walked the other direction serving food. "Feeling more comfortable, Laura?"

"You know my name?"

"The Admiral told me," she said with a smile. "Would you like to take your dinner here on the sofa?" Svetlana asked.

"Please. I'm starving. It's been a rough day and I haven't eaten."

"Is a sandwich okay?"

"Perfect."

"Can I get you a glass of wine?"

"Please."

Laura watched Steve and Jack sitting in the front of the cabin. Steve leaned his head back and appeared to be asleep, but Laura knew better. *This was Steve's first opportunity to represent the agency at high level talks overseas*, she thought. *And I blew it for him. He's going to be angry for a while.* Jack was staring out the window, apparently still in shock at the brutality of the scene at the security station. *He's never seen anything like that*, she thought. *Even though I tried to prepare him for it in Prague, there's nothing like seeing it in person.*

The admiral sat next to Laura on the sofa. "How are you feeling, Laura? You look exhausted."

"It's been a long day, admiral."

"Vlad tells me it was rough."

"Yes, it was. Vlad was wonderful, by the way."

"Thank you. What you did today is the stuff of legends."

"Thank you, Admiral, but I was just doing my job."

"You certainly lived up to the stories one hears. Fedor speaks highly of you and so does my friend, Markus Wolf."

"You know Markus?"

"We've been friends for many years."

"Markus is like a father to me."

"When Fedor told me about you, I wanted another

opinion, so I called Markus. He told me you're the best intelligence agent he's ever met. You certainly lived up to that endorsement."

"Thank you. I'm flattered, but I'm wondering why you needed me at all. With your rank, didn't you have opportunities to leave on your own?"

"We're not allowed to travel with family. Families are used as leverage. Only the General Secretary can take family overseas. When Fedor mentioned you looked like the Secretary's daughter, it gave me an idea. Once I saw you, I knew it would work and you were clever enough to act the part perfectly."

Laura chuckled. "So, who did you call at the Customs booth?"

"Vlad's roommate and his girlfriend."

Both Laura and the Admiral burst out laughing. "Sometimes, the little things work the best, Admiral," she said.

Two hours into the flight, the radio became active. "Falcon five-zero, this is Warsaw Air Traffic Control. We need you to go to VHF one-two-one point five for an emergency transmission."

"Roger that, Warsaw Control."

Polzin switched the radio frequency. "This is Falcon five-zero reporting over."

"We read you, Falcon five-zero. This is Colonel General Garin, Soviet Air Defense Forces Command. Whom am I speaking with?"

"This is Captain Third Rank Dmitri Polzin, Soviet Naval Aviation speaking, Sir."

"What's the status of your flight?"

"All systems are nominal. We're on schedule according to flight plan."

"Is Admiral of the Fleet Tonov aboard?"

"Yes, Sir."

"The flight manifest lists six passengers besides yourself and the Admiral. Is that correct?"

"Yes, Sir. That's the head count."

"What's your ETA, Captain?"

"We're forty minutes out of Vienna International."

"Very good, Captain. We were worried about you. There's been trouble at Sheremetyevo this evening. We're contacting all flights to check status."

"We're good, General. The aircraft is performing well and passengers are behaving themselves."

"Thank you, Captain. Continue your flight plan. Over and out."

Polzin turned on the intercom. "Admiral, could you come to the cockpit for a moment?" Tonov stuck his head into the cockpit. "Everything okay, Dmitri?"

"I just had an unusual conversation with Soviet Air Defense Command. They're checking status on all flights that left Moscow this evening."

"What did you tell them?"

"The truth. All systems are nominal and we're on our scheduled flight plan."

"Is there anything to be worried about?"

"Not this close to Vienna. FAB CE is due to take us any minute. I do have a suggestion, though."

"Go ahead."

"Vienna is crawling with KGB. They could have people waiting for us when we deplane. It could be a trap.

I suggest we do a touch-and-go and fly on to Paris this evening."

"Do we need to refuel?"

"No. The fuel level's good."

Tonov patted Polzin on the back. "Go right ahead, Dmitri. Good thinking."

Warsaw Flight Control turned the tracking over to FAB CE Control a few minutes later and following that, Vienna Flight Control for the Falcon's approach into Vienna. After receiving permission for the touch and go maneuver, Polzin made the announcement to his passengers. "Ladies and gentlemen, we've had a change in plans. We're not stopping at Vienna International. We've decided to do a touch-and-go and continue on to Charles de Gaulle in Paris this evening. We're on approach at the present time, so please fasten your seat belts. Svetlana and I will keep you informed as to our progress. Captain out."

***

Reports kept streaming into Petrovsky's office during the evening hours. First, the forensics team at the warehouse concluded that as many as four people had been murdered. Next, a railroad worker found four bodies dumped in the rail yard behind a maintenance shed at the Kazansky Rail Station. The police connected the bodies to the murders on Basmannyy. The latest report came from Sheremetyevo Airport, where three murders took place at the security station in the International Terminal.

Leo Moldova returned from the warehouse and walked into Petrovsky's office. "Sir, the bodies from the rail yard are being taken to Central Morgue. They need someone who can identify them."

"We'll wait for morning to do that."

"Very good, Sir. I heard the news about Director Pasternik coming in the building."

"He was a good man, Leo. Grisha left a wife and two small children at home. What a shame."

"He wasn't the only one."

"That's right. There were two more. The criminals seem to have vanished. We can't find the computer people from Paris, we can't find Postl, and the only lead we have is that one of the Americans left the talks earlier today on the excuse of a family emergency. He seems to have vanished, too. We just don't know much at this point."

"Perhaps, they used a private plane."

"We thought of that. Only three took off this evening from Sheremetyevo. We contacted each one in the air and nothing out of the ordinary was found. The only odd occurrence was a touch-and-go by Admiral Tonov's plane at Vienna International. He was reportedly on his way to Salzburg for some kind of conference. We had people in place to meet the plane, but it didn't work out. Go on home, Leo, and we'll see what news the morning brings."

"Thank you, Sir. Have a good evening."

Petrovsky removed his coat and hat from the closet. He threw the coat over his arm, put on his hat and walked into the outer office. "Irina, I'm going home for the evening. Can you close up for me?"

"Certainly, Sir. Have a good evening."
"You, too."

***

Captain Polzin came on the intercom once the Falcon was at its cruise altitude again. "Thanks for your patience, everyone. We're currently en route to Paris, France. You're now free to unbuckle your seat belts and move about the cabin. Our flight time this evening will be about ninety minutes. The current weather condition in Paris is clear and 15 degrees Celsius. Relax and enjoy the ride, everyone. Captain out."

Laura walked to the front of the cabin and sat down next to Steve. "I guess you're still angry with me," she started.
"Not angry. Disgusted is the word I'd use."
"I didn't mean for the mission to affect you."
"I don't think you cared," Steve replied tersely.
"Of course, I cared."
Steve finally looked at her. "One thing I learned about you today is you're going to do whatever you damn well please without regard for anyone else."
"That's not fair, Steve."
"Look, could we skip the conversation?"
"You're right. We'll have plenty of time to talk back in D.C."
"If Bates doesn't throw you in jail."
Laura began to get angry. "You want to have a little

tantrum, go right ahead. I'm fine with that."

Steve gave her a harsh look. "Go back and talk to your new friends."

Laura moved to the opposite side of the cabin and sat down by Jack. "How are you doing, Jack?"

Jack looked at her. "What do you think?"

"I'm not sure. That's why I'm asking."

"I didn't realize people were going to die, Ms. Messier."

"Cut the horseshit, Jack," she said, getting angry again. "I told you in Prague it could get rough."

"You didn't tell me you were going to kill people."

"I risked my life to get you out, you ungrateful ass. I should have left you. You want to complain? Fine. We'll turn you over to the Soviet Embassy when we get to Paris."

"Dammit to hell!" Laura said under her breath as she got up. She moved to the back of the plane where the mood was far different. Arkady, Vlad, Jean and Svetlana were holding an impromptu celebration. "Mademoiselle, come sit with us," Jean said. "The Admiral and I are becoming great friends."

"We're telling old war stories," Arkady said, laughing.

"We're both great heroes no one ever heard of," Jean said.

"Quite right, Jean. Let's have a toast to Shewolf."

"Boss lady is the best!" Vlad said, lifting a glass.

"Here, here," Jean said raising his glass.

"Thank you, guys. I wish everyone felt that way," Laura said, nodding toward the front of the plane.

Arkady waved his hand toward the front. "Nonsense!

Today was a great day. Come sit with us," he said, motioning to one of the chairs. "Svetlana, would you be a sweetheart and open another bottle of wine?"

"Of course. I'll be right back."

Arkady turned to Laura. "Why would you be sad at a moment like this?"

"I may have lost my job and, perhaps, my husband, too," Laura said.

"In affairs of the heart, Mademoiselle, we are of little help," Jean said. "But we can help with the job loss," Jean said. "What do you think, Arkady?"

"Vlad, would you hand me my briefcase?"

Vlad reached under the seat, lifted the Admiral's briefcase and handed it to his father. Arkady opened it and pulled out a checkbook.

"Now, here's a question, Vlad. What amount of money is our freedom worth? For the happiness you and I will share in the West for the rest of our lives. What do you think?"

"Seven figures," Vlad said.

"I agree. You have a pen, Vlad?"

"Right here, Admiral," Vlad said.

The Admiral's check was drawn on Credit Suisse Bank in Zurich from a firm called 'Tonov Family Investments.' He wrote the check for one million dollars and handed it to Laura. "Does this compensate you for risking your life getting Vlad and me out?"

Laura looked at the check with disbelief. "Is this a joke?"

"I told you he had money, boss lady," Vlad quipped.

"Accept the money, Shewolf," Arkady said. "You did a

wonderful job, just as Fedor told me you would."

Laura finally smiled. "Yes, thank you."

"Aha!" the admiral said. "And now you're happy again?"

"Very."

Arkady looked at Jean. "You see, Jean, women are the same all over the world. Give them money and they're happy." Both of them broke out in chauvinistic laughter. "Allow me to increase your happiness a bit more," he said to Laura. "I have something else to give you."

"Nothing is necessary, Arkady. Actually, I should be thanking you. We wouldn't have gotten out without your plane."

"It's not my plane."

"Well, that's true. How do you plan to return it?"

"The Soviet Union sold the plane today. We should probably ask the owner what she wants to do with it."

The admiral handed Laura a receipt for a Dassault Falcon 50 jet aircraft, tail number 1908. The receipt contained a hand stamp with a long string of registration numbers handwritten underneath. It was counter-signed by the Director of Administration for the Ministry of Civil Aviation. Laura was stunned.

"You just gave me the plane?"

"No. That's what your $50,000 bought you."

"Isn't it worth millions?"

Tonov laughed. "Cash speaks loudly in a country that has little hard currency, Shewolf. Especially when people can put a little in their pocket during the transaction. You stack fifty grand on someone's desk, they're liable to sign whatever you want."

"Is it legal?"

"You see the signature by the minister underneath?" Tonov pointed to the signature. "And the 'Registered' stamp with the handwritten number? It's a registered receipt. That's all the proof you need that you're the owner."

Laura pointed to her name in the 'Sold To' box. "That's what you needed my name for?"

"Precisely. So, are you going to return it?"

"Hell, no," Laura said to everyone's laughter.

"You see, Jean, all beautiful women are alike. You shower them with gifts and they love you for it."

"Indeed," Jean replied.

"But in this case, you've given Vlad and me something far more valuable than I can ever pay for. Our freedom. For that, we're in your debt."

Chapter Twelve

WHEN THE PLANE landed at Charles de Gaulle airport, Polzin taxied to the private aircraft terminal where the group walked across the tarmac to the terminal doors. Inside the terminal, neither Jean nor Laura saw Jacques Martin waiting. "We didn't tell him of our change in plans," Jean said. "He's probably waiting at Air France."

Laura gathered the group together. "It's been a long, hard day. I'm sure all of us could use a good night's sleep before we fly to Washington. French officials will be here momentarily and let's see what they're willing to do for us." Jean returned from using a pay phone in the lobby area. "I got a hold of him. He's on his way here with Henri and a security team."

Laura turned to Dmitri. "What's involved in getting the plane ready to fly to the States tomorrow?"

"I'll have to file a flight plan, refuel and we should stock the galley. It would also be a good idea to have a mechanic go over the plane in the morning to make sure we're in good shape for a trans-Atlantic flight. Oh, and I'll have to pick up a co-pilot."

"How do we get a co-pilot?"

"In a big airport like this, there's always someone looking to pick up work. We'll find someone."

"Can we go non-stop from Paris?"

"To Washington? No, it's too far. We'll have to stop at Gander to refuel."

"Gander?"

"Newfoundland."

"I suppose I should think about where to park the plane once we get to the States. Washington's probably really expensive. What about, say, Harrisburg, Pennsylvania?"

"I don't know much about airfields in the United States. Do you know the runway length?" Dmitri asked.

"I have no idea."

"I'll check in the morning, but if it's a regional airport, it shouldn't be a problem.

"How much money will you need tomorrow?" Laura asked.

"Can you give me five thousand?"

"Of course."

"I'll return what I don't use, Ms. Messier. You've been more than fair to us."

Jacques Martin, Henri Thomas and a four man security team arrived within minutes. The relief on Jacques' face was palpable. "We had someone watching in Moscow and when you didn't board the Air France flight, we thought you'd run into trouble."

"Just a change in plans, Jacques. Sorry," Jean said. There wasn't time to notify you."

"Everyone seems to have survived," Jacques said, looking around at the group.

Jacques looked at Laura. "I heard you took care of business," Jacques said.

"Yes, but it wasn't pleasant."

"I'm sure it wasn't. We'll talk more in the morning. I'm

assuming you'll want to leave for D.C. tomorrow?"

"Yes."

"Let's do a short debrief in the morning and have you on your way by noon."

"Great. As you can see," she said, nodding to the group, "we've brought an entourage with us."

"We always welcome friends, Mademoiselle. Would you make the introductions?"

After introductions were made, Jacques went to work. "I'd like to ask everyone for their patience at customs. It's going to take a few minutes to get the paperwork in order, but we'll distribute temporary visas and put everyone up for the night at the downtown Marriott. Mr. Thomas and his team will protect you. I'd like to emphasize we're not taking anyone into custody. Each of you is free to go outside the hotel and enjoy the city. Just make sure Henri knows where you're going."

"Thank you, Jacques," Laura said.

"Jean, Laura and Mr. Tilton have residences in Paris, so they'll provide their own accommodations. Tomorrow, I'd like Jean, Laura and Mr. Postl to meet me at headquarters to debrief at 9:00 am. Jean, can you make sure that Mr. Postl finds his way to DST headquarters in the morning?"

"Of course, Jacques."

"Very good. Everyone please follow me and we'll get the paperwork started."

***

Laura and Steve were silent on the taxi ride to their apartment. They discovered the management company had changed the linens, towels and cleaned while Laura had been away. The apartment had a pleasant smell. "It's nice to be back," she said, as a conversation starter walking through the front door. "It's been a rough couple of days."

She tossed her bags onto the bed in the large bedroom and went to the kitchen to prepare a light dinner. Steve followed her, not content to allow the issues between them drop for the evening. He looked at his watch. "It's still only 4:30 in Washington. I'll call Langley and do some damage control before we arrive. If I were you, I'd hire an attorney before you set foot on U.S. soil tomorrow."

"You really think that's necessary?" she asked.

Steve gave her a cold look. "Yes, I do."

"I have no idea who to call."

"Rick Gleason. He's handled cases for members of Congress. Hang on a second, I might have his number." He rummaged through his billfold and pulled out a business card. "Yes, here it is. Give him a call right now, explain what happened and have him meet you at the airport tomorrow."

Steve insisted on sleeping in the second bedroom, which Laura found unnecessary, to prove a point. Steve rose early the following morning still upset at the events of the day before. "Hi, honey," Laura said, walking into the kitchen in her bathrobe. Steve mumbled an acknowledgement, but avoided eye contact as he prepared breakfast. "Here, let me help," she said, hoping Steve had forgiven her. She walked over and picked up the spatula he was using to cook eggs.

"I think I can manage to fix my own damn breakfast," he said angrily, grabbing it back.

"Fine!" She sat down at the kitchen table, exasperated at Steve's attitude. "Did you at least make enough coffee for both of us?"

"Here." He reached in the cupboard and handed her a cup.

"What are your plans today?" she asked.

"I'm running over to the embassy this morning to get a passport, then I've booked myself on a flight back to D.C."

"Okay."

"I managed to get hold of Bates at home last night. He wasn't pleased when I told him you pulled me out of the meeting."

"I'm sure he wasn't. Did you tell him about Tonov?"

"No. That's between you and Bates," Steve said.

"Will Bates have me arrested?"

"I have no idea. Did you get in touch with Gleason?"

"No. I left a message. I'll call him during the layover at wherever the hell the plane lands in Canada."

"Gander."

"I thought a gander was a male goose," Laura said.

That brought a smile to Steve's face. "It's an airport in Canada."

"Look, I know we've got a lot to work through, but ..."

Steve interrupted her. "Let's get back home first."

"Okay, honey."

"Don't call me 'honey.' Let's not pretend everything's fine. I've got to hurry or I'll miss my flight."

"Have a good flight."

"Goodbye," Steve said coldly. Laura began to realize

how badly she'd hurt Steve. She'd always heard that relationships between agency employees were a bad idea. Now she knew why.

***

Laura, Jean and Jack met with Jacques at DST headquarters the next morning in a small conference room upstairs. "Good morning. Is everyone feeling better?"

"Yes, definitely," Jean said.

"Mr. Postl, it's nice to finally get to know you. I hope Laura and Jean weren't too rough on you during your escape."

"I was shocked at seeing people killed right in front of me, Mr. Martin, but I'll get over it."

Jacques paused and looked at Jack before continuing. "Mr. Postl, would it be fair to say that you broke a number of laws trying to get out of the Soviet Union?"

"I guess that's true."

"So explain to me why we should accept a criminal into the Republic of France or the United States if that's where you want to go?"

"I'm not sure what you want me to say, Sir."

"I want you to stop complaining about the people who risked their lives to help you, Mr. Postl."

Jack looked at the floor, embarrassed at the comment. "I apologize, Mr. Martin."

"In what country would you like to establish residency?"

"The United States."

"Ms. Messier, do you have any thoughts?" Jacques asked.

Laura shrugged, suggesting she wasn't sure what to do. "If the intel's good enough, I might be willing to help him. Here are the disks he gave me." Laura handed Jacques the computer disks Jack passed to her in the box of chocolates.

Jacques picked up the phone and asked for a computer technician to come to the room. "Mr. Postl, I agree with Ms. Messier. We'll analyze the information you've given us. If it's of sufficient value, we may allow you to leave the country. Otherwise, we'll turn you over to the Soviet authorities."

A technician knocked and then opened the door. "You need something, Sir?"

"Yes. Would you access these disks, make two copies of whatever's on them and return everything to me?"

"Yes, Sir."

"I need it done right away."

"Certainly, Sir."

Jack was worried that he was about to be shipped back to Moscow. "Mr. Martin, I'm truly sorry for the comment I made."

"One moment, Mr. Postl," Jacques said brusquely.

Jacques phoned the security department. Almost immediately, there was a knock on the door. "Yes, Sir?"

"I'd like you to take this man," Jacques said pointing at Jack, "and lock him in a room. Put an armed guard outside the door. If he tries to escape, shoot him. Otherwise, we'll hold him until we determine his disposition."

The guard motioned to Jack. "Sir, would you come with me?"

After Jack left, Jacques smiled. "That ought to shut him up."

"You scared the hell out of him," Jean said, chuckling.

"Better to shut him up now than have him run to Le Monde or the New York Times with an exclusive."

"True."

"This is going to be really short," Jacques said. "We won't record anything. Just tell me what happened."

Laura and Jean related the details of the mission; their dinner with the Minister, the Ilitch killings, Postl's escape from the KGB, the change in flights, the touch-and-go in Vienna and the Admiral's involvement. Laura conveniently left out the money Tonov gave her and the gift of the plane, figuring it was none of Jacques' business.

"Congratulations," Jacques said. "The mission was a success. The two of you make quite a team."

"Thank you, Jacques," Jean said. "Will there be diplomatic issues coming out of this?"

"I doubt it. The official position of the French government is a private plane landed at de Gaulle last night from Vienna. The plane refueled and left French airspace. That's the only information we have."

"What about Inline Computers?" Laura asked.

"Inline closed suddenly for unknown reasons. They no longer exist."

"And their employees?"

"We have no information on their employees," Jacques said with a shrug.

"Perfect."

"For reasons of safety, though, it might be advisable for the two of you to disappear for a while. We'd like to pay your service time, plus hazard pay and add four weeks' vacation pay. Take some time off. You've earned it."

Coffee and tea service arrived and the three chatted while awaiting the results from the computer disks. Henri Thomas called to report that Dmitri Polzin and his wife, Svetlana, were at the airport preparing the plane for takeoff. Admiral Tonov and his son enjoyed breakfast at the hotel and were currently sightseeing.

"I'm assuming the admiral, his son, the pilot and his wife all desire to emigrate to the States?" Jacques asked Laura.

"I'm assuming so, but I don't think I asked them directly."

The computer technician knocked again. "Sir, I have the results from the computer disk scan. Sorry it took so long. Here are two copies of the printout and the original disks."

The three of them were stunned at the information contained on the disks. "Can you believe what's here?" Jacques asked.

"This is what we've always needed," Jean said.

"I need a favor, Jacques," Laura began.

Jacques waved his hand and smiled. "There's no need to ask. Here's the official French position, Laura. CIA refused to participate in the mission. In fact, they tried to obstruct it. The French government has no obligation to share the intelligence afterwards. We're giving you a copy as a courtesy. What you do with it isn't our concern."

"Thank you, Jacques."

"As for Postl, he's free to leave. The others are free to leave as well."

Jacques requested Postl be brought into the room. He looked frightened when he entered.

"Mr. Postl, please take a seat," Jacques said, motioning to an empty chair. "We've reviewed the intel you provided. We find its value sufficient to have risked the lives of our agents. If you still desire to emigrate to the United States, we'll permit it."

"Thank you, Sir."

"I do have a question for you. Do the Soviets know you stole this information?"

"No."

"Would there be any way for them to find out?"

"Possibly."

"Then stay silent. You don't want them showing up at your front door."

"Thank you, Sir. I'll follow that advice."

"I think we're finished here. Mr. Postl, we'll give you a lift to the airport. There'll be a car waiting downstairs in back for you. We encourage you to leave France immediately. Jean and Laura, you're free to go. Thank you again for a fine job."

"Could I ask a question?" Jack asked.

"Of course," Jacques replied.

"Can I ride with Ms. Messier to America?"

Laura considered Jack's request. "If you're willing to keep this affair confidential, then yes. Meet me out back and we'll ride to the airport together."

As everyone rose to leave, Jacques asked, "Laura, could I have a word privately with you?"

Laura turned to Jean. "Would you wait for me so we can walk out together?"

"Certainly, Mademoiselle. I'll meet you in the front lobby."

Jacques closed the door. "Are you going to have problems at CIA over this?"

"I may lose my job. But that's better than waiting around for Ilitch to kill me."

"If there's anything we can do, just ask. You've got our total support."

"Thank you, Jacques."

"If you ever need a job, call me. We'd love to have you."

"That means a lot."

They hugged each other and Jacques kissed her on both cheeks. "Farewell, old friend," Jacques said. "Have a safe flight."

Laura took the elevator to the lobby where Jean was waiting. He hugged her. "Mademoiselle, I'll miss you. The next time we meet for coffee, you're picking the cafe," he said with a laugh.

"Take care, Jean. You mean an awful lot to me." As Jean walked toward the door, Laura had a premonition. "Wait!" she shouted. Jean stopped. He turned around looking puzzled. She walked over and grabbed his arm. "Come with me out back," she said. "We're riding together."

"What's wrong?"

"I've got a bad feeling. Don't go out the front."

Laura walked Jean to the back entrance where Jack was waiting for a car. The car pulled up shortly after. "I'm taking shotgun," Laura said abruptly.

"What's that mean?" Jack asked

"The front seat," Jean said.

She opened her bag and pulled out both shoulder holsters and put them on before opening the car door. She checked the clips and found them only partially full. She reached in her bag and found two fully loaded mags and popped them into her weapons. Then, she holstered them. "What are you doing?" Jack asked, worried he might watch another shooting.

Jean answered for her. "She senses danger. Let her do her job."

"Hi, I'm Laura," she said to the driver as she hopped in the front passenger seat.

"I'm Pierre. Where are we going?"

"We'll drop Jean off at his club, then Jack and I are going to the airport. When you pull around the building, stop in the drive before you turn onto the street. I want to make sure it's safe."

"Yes, Ma'am," the driver said.

He pulled almost to the street and stopped. "Is this good?"

"Yes. Wait here. I'll be right back."

She exited the car, leaving the car door open, walked to the side of the building and peeked around the corner. She walked back to the car and stuck her head inside. "Just what I was afraid of, Jean. Two men in a car across the street."

"It could be nothing," Jean replied.

"It could be Petrovsky sent men to find us."

"What do you suggest?"

"I'm going to walk over and have a friendly chat."

"Why don't we just leave?"

She tapped the window with her fingernail. "Is this bulletproof?" she asked the driver.

"No, Mademoiselle."

"We're not bulletproof, Jean. If they follow us and we get caught at a light? We could be in trouble. Let's find out now."

"You need help?" the driver asked.

"No. Just keep the engine running." She looked back at Jean. "Hopefully, it's nothing."

Laura loosened the weapons in her holsters to be sure she could remove them quickly. She turned the corner and began walking down the middle of the street toward the car parked on the opposite side. It was parked facing her. *Let them shoot first, if that's their intent*, she thought. *Remember, aim slow, shoot slow.*

The driver started his engine and backed up as Laura approached. He was in a small space. *He'll have to go back and forth a few times to get out*, she thought. She walked up to the front of the car and stood in the street. The driver rolled down his window.

"You waiting for someone?" she asked loudly. The driver turned and spoke to the man in the back seat. The driver turned back and reached into his jacket. She saw the gun as he stuck it out the window. He fired without aiming. Laura heard the bullet whiz by her. He fired again, this time steadying his hand on top of the outside mirror. She moved to her left before he fired. He missed.

She moved with the speed of a gunfighter in an old black and white western, drawing both her weapons simultaneously. Moving to her left to force the driver to shoot through the windshield, she began to fire. *Twenty rounds*, she thought, counting as she fired through the windshield. *One-two-three-four-five-six-seven-eight-nine-ten*, never pausing as the windshield crumbled and fell into the car. The man in back opened the passenger door and dove onto the sidewalk. The driver appeared to be dead, although Laura could not see clearly through the remains of the broken windshield. She moved quickly around the car to the sidewalk where the man stood upright and fired over the top of the car door he'd left open. Laura bent down to use the door as a shield. He missed. *He's left-handed*, she thought. She lunged forward and slammed the open car door into him, pinching his gun hand between the door and the frame of the car. The gun fell to the ground at her feet.

Laura aimed both weapons at the man. He had blood splattered on his face and clothing, but he did not appear to be hurt. She spoke in Russian.

"Don't move or you're dead."

He smiled. "I kill you bitch," he replied in broken English.

"Don't move or you're dead," she repeated in English.

He glanced down at his gun lying on the sidewalk. Laura kicked it away.

She laid her weapons on the hood of the car. "You want to kill me? Come and try," she taunted.

"I play with you, then kill you," he hissed.

"Come to Mother, Spetsnaz boy."

He didn't. He continued to talk. "I rape you and kill you."

"What are you waiting for?"

"You woman. You make baby. You go to kitchen."

"Come to Mother, Spetsnaz boy. Mama will teach you some manners."

This was the banter of two opponents sizing up each other's strengths. He looked around. "Tell friends stay away."

DST lobby guards ran from the building after hearing gun shots. They took positions behind cars parked across the street, guns drawn.

"DST," she shouted, "don't shoot! Stay where you are!" The guards trained their guns on Laura's attacker, but did not fire. She dared not look at them, instead keeping her eyes trained on her opponent. She slowly walked around the car door until she faced him. He had the look of a military man, she thought. Very strong; confident in his strength. On the other hand, her speed and flexibility had proven more than a match against larger male opponents. She attacked.

Laura began with the move she had used so often in hand to hand combat, the roundhouse kick with her left foot, hitting him in his left cheekbone. He did not see it, nor expect it, because he watched her eyes. It stunned him momentarily and she used those few seconds to follow with a flurry of kicks and punches which pummeled his head and body. He fell backwards against the car. Although he gained his senses after a few seconds and tried to block her attack, he was too slow. A front kick hit him underneath his chin and threw his head back against the car. It dazed him again. This time, she closed with a vicious downward sidekick that broke his kneecap and he began to collapse. As he fell, she grabbed his left arm and twisted it while moving her hip into his body. She threw him over her shoulder onto the sidewalk where his head bounced off the concrete. She walked over to him. "Get up, Spetsnaz boy. Mother wants to continue the lesson."

The man tried to focus his eyes on her. "What's the matter, Spetsnaz boy?" she growled. She bent down, locked her right wrist and smashed his nose with her knuckles. His head, lying on concrete, absorbed the full force of the blow and his face exploded in blood. She recoiled to follow with another punch when someone from behind grabbed her.

"Stop, Laura!" It was Jacques' voice. "Stop! We need him alive," he said. He shouted to the officers, "Get an ambulance! Fast!" Jacques pulled her away. "Look at me." Laura took her eyes from her opponent, but it took seconds for her to understand. "Look at me" he repeated.

She had difficulty shifting her attention away from her opponent. "Jacques?" she asked.

"Laura, it's over. Walk with me." Jacques led her away and sat her down on the curb.

The ambulance arrived quickly. The paramedics immediately began working to save the man's life. Checking on the driver, they found him dead. Jacques pulled one of the paramedic's aside. "Please look at her, too."

"Are you okay, Ma'am?" one of the men asked her. He examined her briefly.

"I'm fine, thank you." She began to get up.

"Not yet." The paramedic put his hand on her shoulder. "Please stay seated and rest for a few minutes."

Laura watched as the man lying on the sidewalk was put on a stretcher and rolled to the back of the ambulance.

The Paris Police arrived. Paul Perrin stepped out of a squad car and approached Jacques. He saw Laura. "How is she, Jacques?"

"She'll be fine, Paul. Help me get her inside."

Jacques leaned over her. "Let's get you up now." He helped her to stand. "Can you walk across the street?"

"I'm fine, Jacques. Really, I am."

Jacques and Perrin each took an arm and escorted her back into the headquarters building. Jean walked toward them. "The driver and I saw the whole thing, Jacques. They opened fire at her as she walked toward their car."

"The guard at the door saw it, too," Jacques said. "Let's get everyone off the street. We'll take statements inside.

Paul Perrin took witness statements and questioned Laura. The statements were consistent. Laura walked up to the car and the occupants opened fire without provocation.

"Laura, do you need to go to the hospital?" Perrin asked.

"No, Paul. I'm fine."

"I think we have everything we need. You're free to go. If we need to contact you further, where can we reach you?"

"I'll be at my home in Washington."

"Are you traveling today?"

"Yes."

"Very good. Just as long as we can reach you."

"Thank you, Paul."

Jean and Jacques helped Laura to the car. "Are we still dropping you off somewhere, Sir?" the driver asked Jean.

"No, I've decided to fly to Washington with the Mademoiselle," Jean replied.

"And you, Sir?" the driver asked Jack.

"I'm going with Ms. Messier."

***

Laura's group met at the airport where Dmitri and Svetlana had finished preparations for a departure to Gander, Newfoundland. Arkady and Vlad came to offer their final goodbyes. They would travel to Switzerland where they would establish residency. After a final instrument check, Dmitri, Svetlana, plus Laura, Jean, Jack and a co-pilot took off bound for Canada. The six hour trip was uneventful. Svetlana served a light lunch and snacks, after which the passengers slept.

After arriving at Gander, Dmitri began the refueling process while passengers welcomed the opportunity to deplane during the layover. Laura headed for the telephone. She dialed Rick Gleason, who happened to be in his office. After relating her story, Gleason made a verbal commitment to represent her.

"What time are you arriving in Harrisburg?"

"Hang on a second," she said. She motioned for Dmitri to come to the phone. "Dmitri, how long will the flight take?"

"It's going to be another 30 minutes here before we leave," Dmitri replied. "The flight will take about an hour and a half, so I'd say, maybe two hours."

"Thanks."

She spoke to Gleason again. "Mr. Gleason, we'll be there by 5:00 pm."

"I'll be there, but it's a two hour drive and I'll need to check whether you've got pending warrants. Don't approach customs until I arrive. I want to walk you through."

"Great."

"I'll see you later today."

Laura's next call was to Rick Williams in Georgetown. "Rick?"

"Hey Laura. I've been waiting to hear from you. What happened?"

"I'll tell you about it when I get home today. Right now, I need a favor."

"Whatever you need."

"Can you rent a passenger van? You know, like the airport shuttles."

"Sure. Where should I bring it?" Rick asked.

"Bring it to the private aircraft building at the Harrisburg, Pennsylvania airport. I'll pay you back when you get here."

"No problem. Forget about the money. What time

should I be there?"

"Five."

Rick looked at his watch. "I better hurry then. I'll see you later this afternoon."

"Thanks, Rick. You're the best."

The last call was to the FBI headquarters in Washington, a call Laura hesitated to make. Laura had become romantically involved with Dan Jenkins during her time in Paris. It was a short, intense affair; the kind that produces passion, but not necessarily commitment. Laura had avoided contact with Dan since her marriage. Nevertheless, she was in trouble and needed to reach out to her allies, so she placed the call. "Is Dan Jenkins in the office? It's Laura Messier calling."

"One moment." The receptionist came back on the line shortly after. "Connecting you to Assistant Director Jenkins."

"Hi Laura. I haven't talked to you in ages," Jenkins said. "Since Paris a year ago, wasn't it? How the heck are you?"

"Well, I'm not sure, Dan. That's why I'm calling. I might need your help."

"Anything. You name it."

Laura explained she was entering the country accompanied by Soviet citizens requesting political asylum. Jenkins agreed to meet her in Harrisburg with a friend from the Immigration and Naturalization Service. "I'll have to run background checks to make sure they can get in the country. If you give me their names now, I'll do it before I leave."

Laura read off the names.

"Got it,' Dan said. "We'll see you around five. Don't go through customs until we get there."

"Thanks, Dan."

"You bet."

Dmitri told the co-pilot he was no longer needed and booked him a return flight to Paris. Once the refueling had been completed, the group boarded again and the plane departed for Harrisburg. During the short connecting flight, Laura studied the intel again. It contained a listing of all covert Soviet agents operating in the world, along with various correspondences from KGB headquarters in Moscow to embassies around the world. It was the largest security breach coming from the Soviet intelligence community she'd ever seen, she thought.

Upon landing at Harrisburg, Dmitri set out to secure a hanger spot for the plane. He brought Laura a registration form. "I found a copy machine in one of the offices. I need a copy of your aircraft receipt to reserve the hanger spot." Laura dug through her bag and gave him the receipt. "You also need to fill out this form to register the plane with the Federal Aviation Administration." While Laura completed paperwork, Dan Jenkins arrived from Washington. He found Laura in the terminal office.

"Hi, Laura," Jenkins said with a smile as he walked in

"Hi, Dan. Thank you for coming." They hugged each other. It had been months since they'd seen each other, but Laura still remembered the way he touched her. She looked in Dan's eyes and wondered whether he was still hurt by her breaking off the affair.

"It's great to see you," Dan said. "You're looking well.

How's that husband of yours?"

"Steve's doing well."

"You're still working for the agency?" Dan asked.

"Both of us are."

"I hate to bring this up, but did you know there's a warrant out on you?"

"I didn't know for sure, but I asked an attorney to meet me here just in case."

"The complaint lists several aliases. The agency must be behind it. No one else would know your covers. Do you have something else you can come in on?" he asked.

"I have a Soviet passport."

"Good. In my official capacity, I'm allowing you to enter the country on the grounds that you're working a clandestine mission. Having said that, you'll have to deal with the warrant pretty damn soon. Tomorrow, if you can."

"Have you seen someone who looks like an attorney?" Laura asked. "His name is Gleason."

"Is that him?" Dan asked, pointing to a gray haired man wearing an expensive gray suit standing outside in the terminal area. He carried a brown satchel; *a dead giveaway* Laura thought.

"Could be." Laura walked out of the office and into the lobby. "Mr. Gleason?"

"Yes, I'm Rick Gleason."

"Laura Messier. Thanks for driving out to meet me. This is Dan Jenkins, Assistant Director of the FBI," Laura said, gesturing to Jenkins."

Gleason nodded to Jenkins. "Director Jenkins."

Jenkins smiled. "Mr. Gleason."

"I assume you're here to take Ms. Messier into custody?" Gleason asked.

"Oh, no," Jenkins said, shaking his head. "I'm helping her with other business."

Gleason looked confused. "Ms. Messier, is there somewhere we can talk privately?"

"Sure. Walk with me to the empty office over there," she said, pointing.

"I'll get my INS guy working on your people, Laura," Jenkins said. "Here, give me your passport I'll get him going on yours, too." Laura dug through her bag and pulled out the red Soviet passport. "I'll have this back in a few minutes."

Gleason watched Laura hand over the passport. He frowned, but didn't interfere. Once Jenkins left, he said, "You're in quite a bit of trouble, Ms. Messier. The Justice Department has issued a warrant for your arrest."

"Yes, I'm aware of it."

"My advice is surrender to the authorities and ..." he looked at his watch, "... its five o'clock, but I'll try to get a judge to rule on your bond this evening and we can have you on your way home tonight."

"Thanks for the advice, Mr. Gleason, but that's not what I had in mind," Laura said.

"I couldn't help but notice you handed the FBI a passport from another country. Is that a legitimate passport of yours?"

"Not really. It's a clandestine ID."

"You do know it's illegal to gain access to the United States under false pretenses. I don't advise it. You're in enough trouble already."

"Once again, thank you for that, but as a CIA field agent, I'm permitted to use aliases in clandestine work," Laura replied.

"Then, I'm not sure why you asked me here."

Laura proceeded to work out a plan with Gleason who, as it turned out, was cooperative once he heard an explanation. By the time Laura and Gleason had finished their discussion, the INS official had completed the paperwork for the group and everyone was ready to proceed through Customs.

Dan walked back into the room. "We're ready to walk everyone through, Laura. Do you have transportation and accommodations arranged for these folks?" he asked.

"I should have someone waiting with a van. I'll work on temporary living quarters once we're through Customs."

"Good. I do have one suggestion. Would you allow me to sit down with the Attorney General and tell him your story? He's a college friend. Once I explain what's going on, he's got the authority to drop the charges."

"I'd appreciate any help you can give me."

"No problem. We go way back, Laura."

Laura and Dan hugged. "Thanks, Dan."

With entry into the U.S. approved by the INS and an assistant director of the FBI accompanying the entourage through the airport, the group entered the country without difficulty. Once in the outer terminal, Laura found Rick sitting in the lobby. He immediately walked over. "I was worried about you. Are you okay?"

They hugged; one of those tight, passionate hugs between close friends. "I'm fine, Rick," Laura said, smiling. "It's good to be back. Here are my guests," she said, pointing to the group. "We can make the introductions in the van. Right now, let's get the hell out of here."

They walked outside onto the sidewalk. "I had to park in short term parking," Rick said, "so we've got a bit of a walk. Anyone hungry?"

Laura looked around the group. "Anyone ready for a genuine American cheeseburger?" she asked in Russian. The group seemed pleased at the idea. "All right then. Rick, once we get going, would you pull in a drive through for us?"

"You got it."

The group loaded into Rick's van and headed for D.C., stopping for burgers, fries and soft drinks along the way. As they drove around the west side of the city, they stopped at a hotel in Tysons where Jean, Jack and Laura checked in. Laura handed Jean a banded stack of hundred dollar bills. "We can settle up later, but take this for tonight."

"Thanks," Jean said, "I'll babysit Jack for you."

"I'll be back late tonight. I've got to take Dmitri and Svetlana somewhere else."

"Very good. Call me when you get back," Jean said.

It was after midnight when the van pulled up to Fedor Belkin's cabin. The place was well lit by a pole light shining brightly in the yard. Belkin's door was open as though he expected company. When he heard the van coming up the drive, he came out the door with his arms wide open, smiling broadly. Dmitri hopped out and the two men embraced, laughing and pounding each other's back. Belkin turned to Laura, "Thank you, Laura."

"You and Dmitri know each other?"

"Sure. Dmitri's been my pilot plenty of times." He

turned to Dmitri. "Did Arkady stay in Europe?"

"He and Vlad traveled on to Switzerland," Dmitri said.

"He told me they might. He'll call me in a few days. Borys and I have the guest cabin ready for you."

Laura dug into her bag and gave Fedor money. "This is for expenses."

It was difficult to get Fedor to accept it. "No, no, it's not needed."

"Take it, Fedor." She pushed it into his hand. "For the next couple of days, let's keep their whereabouts unknown. Avoid using the telephone and don't take them out in public. People could be looking for them. It won't be safe."

"I understand."

"Before we leave, I want to introduce you to Captain Rick Williams, U.S. Marine Corp on assignment to the CIA. He could be useful to you, Fedor."

Rick offered his hand. "Colonel, it's an honor."

"Captain," Fedor said, taking Rick's hand with a firm grip. "I can reach you through Ms. Messier?"

"Yes, Sir. Don't hesitate to call."

"We've got a long trip back to D.C.," Laura said. "I'll be in touch."

"Thank you, again, Laura, for everything you've done," Fedor said.

Laura walked over to Dmitri and Svetlana. "Relax and enjoy springtime in Virginia."

"Thank you, Ms. Messier," Dmitri said to Laura.

"Nice move avoiding trouble in Vienna. Wonderful job."

"Thank you, Ma'am."

Laura fell asleep on the drive back to D.C. Rick decided to wake her as they approached the city. "Laura?"

"Yes?"

"Where we going?"

"Sorry. I fell asleep," she replied. "Can you take me by the house? I want to pick up the SUV and pack a few things. I'll go back out to Tysons and stay at the hotel for a few days. Probably safer."

"Good idea. You ready to tell me what happened?"

"Not much to tell," she said. "We caught them flat-footed. Ilitch had no idea the French had surveillance on him. He posted no sentries or guards at the warehouse where he met his team. I walked in on them during a meeting. Killed all four, including Ilitch and Khozin."

"By yourself?"

"Yes. The French team stayed outside while I went in alone."

Rick whistled. "Pretty gutsy move."

"By the time we got to the airport, Petrovsky had sort of figured out what we were doing. The KGB had Jack Postl in an interrogation. I had to kill three more at airport security to get him out of there."

"Fuck. You were lucky."

"Very. We managed to stay one step ahead of them and got out, but barely. What's the situation at the house?"

"Steve hasn't said much since he got back. He's sleeping in the basement."

"He's angry. I had to pull him out of his meeting with the Soviets. We were on the run and I was afraid. He was as angry as I've ever seen him."

"He'll get over it."

"I hope so."

They pulled up to Laura's Georgetown home, where she packed a few things and Rick helped her load the SUV. "Call me tomorrow if you need help returning the van," she said. "And, if that FBI fellow or the lawyer calls, go ahead and tell them I'm staying out in Tysons."

"Will do. Drive safe," Rick said, before she backed out the drive.

Chapter Thirteen

RICK GLEASON DROVE to CIA headquarters Wednesday morning. He was cleared through security, and escorted to the office of Greg Smithson, General Counsel for the Central Intelligence Agency. After waiting in Smithson's outer office for a few minutes, Smithson opened his door, walked over and greeted Gleason. "Mr. Gleason, I'm Greg Smithson. Why don't you come in?"

"Good to meet you, Sir."

"Please, take a seat," Smithson said, motioning to one of the chairs in front of Smithson's desk. "My secretary said you represent Laura Messier. Is that correct?"

"Yes, Sir. I want to inquire as to the nature of the complaint that originated in your office yesterday."

"You need to talk to the federal prosecutor."

"No, I don't. Ms. Messier is an employee of this agency and, frankly, your charges are frivolous."

"It's fairly straightforward, Mr. Gleason. Three counts. One, she disobeyed a direct order from the Director of Central Intelligence and participated in an unauthorized mission outside the United States. Two, while on that mission, Ms. Messier committed acts contrary to the CIA Code of Conduct. And three, she obstructed official negotiations between the United States and the Soviet Union. The details are listed in the complaint."

"Ms. Messier is a French citizen and works for the French government, Mr. Smithson. Neither the CIA, nor the United States government have any jurisdiction in the matter."

"She's an American citizen and as you said, she's an employee here at the agency," Smithson said. "Her actions fall under the governance of the Central Intelligence Agency and the laws of the United States."

"You do admit she was working for the French government, don't you?"

"There will be no negotiation until she surrenders, Mr. Gleason. This meeting was a courtesy. Is she currently in the United States?"

"She's at an undisclosed location," Gleason responded.

"Tell your client to turn herself in. These are serious charges, Mr. Gleason. Count two is a capital offense. The third count is treason. If abroad, she can surrender at any embassy. If she's Stateside, she can turn herself in at any police station. Once she's in custody, you'll have the opportunity to discuss the charges with the federal prosecutor."

"Your charges are, to put it bluntly, a pile of horseshit, Mr. Smithson. You have one charge. She disobeyed her supervisor. That doesn't rise to the level of federal charges. The second count, if it happened at all and we deny it did, took place outside the United States. The third count is rubbish. Press statements by the Secretary of State indicate the negotiation was a success. What you're doing, Mr. Smithson, is harassing my client. If you pursue this, we'll countersue. Don't embarrass yourself and the agency."

Smithson stood up. He offered his hand across the desk. "It's nice to meet you, Mr. Gleason. Anything else?"

Smithson isn't going to give an inch, Gleason thought.

He was accustomed to the tactic. Gleason's only option was a counter attack. "I give you fair warning to expect a countersuit."

"Thanks for stopping by," Smithson said coldly. He watched Gleason leave. *Typical defense attorney*, Smithson thought. *She hasn't told him the entire story. We've caught her red handed. She'll be prosecuted to the full extent of the law.*

***

Dan Jenkins took the elevator at the Department of Justice to the office of the Attorney General of the United States, Ron Middleton. He entered the outer office. "Yes, can I help you?" the receptionist asked.

"I have an appointment with Ron this morning. I'm Dan Jenkins."

The receptionist picked up her phone. "Mr. Middleton, Dan Jenkins is here."

Middleton walked out of his office with a big smile. "Hey Dan, great to see you. It's been awhile." He gave Dan a vigorous handshake and motioned him toward the inner office. Once he shut his door, he said. "How about those Patriots! Those guys are awesome."

"Lot different than when we played, eh? What was our record as seniors? Something like 12 and 48?"

"54 and 6 this year. They've got the best pitching staff in the league."

"George Mason goes from the outhouse to the penthouse," Dan said with a chuckle. "That was the headline the other day in the paper." Dan looked around the office at the sports memorabilia, including a number of sports related pictures on the wall. "You've got our team picture."

"That's the first picture I put up wherever I work." Middleton walked over and stood beside it. "There's you and there's me," he said, pointing.

Dan laughed, looking at the picture. "I hardly recognize us. You remember those two girls we dated our senior year?"

"You mean Vicki and Vicki?" Middleton asked. They both started laughing.

"Wild times."

"You been out to any games this year?"

"I can't find time. How about you?" Dan asked.

"I've seen a couple of double-headers. We ought to go to the conference tournament. You and me. A couple of dogs, a soft drink. It'd be fun."

"Let's do it," Dan said.

They sat in two chairs in front of the desk. "What's on your mind today?" Middleton asked.

"I'm here regarding a criminal complaint issued in the D.C. Circuit yesterday against Laura Messier."

Middleton thought for a minute. "Let me see if we have a copy yet." Middleton pushed his intercom button. "Susan, would you see if we've got a copy of a complaint filed in D.C. against, wait a second. Dan, how are you spelling the last name?"

"M-E-S-S-I-E-R."

"Did you hear that, Susan?"

"Yes. One moment." She came back on the line almost immediately. "Yes, Sir. I'll bring it in."

The receptionist handed it to Middleton. "Dan, give me a minute to read it."

"Sure."

Middleton read it and then looked up. "Seems kind of thin. Is this CIA's idea of harassment?"

"I worked with Laura in Paris for years, Ron. I know her well. She's a good girl. She worked under an agreement between the CIA and the French. She split her time working for both. The actions in this complaint were at the behest of the French government."

Middleton considered that for a minute. "Are you saying there's an employment agreement somewhere?"

"Yes."

"I wonder if Langley has a copy of it." He took a phone directory from his middle drawer and looked through it. "Let's find out." He dialed the number.

Bill Bates picked up his private line. "Bates."

"Bill, it's Ron Middleton over at Justice."

"What's going on in your neck of the woods, Ron?"

"I'm doing a little digging on a complaint filed yesterday in the D.C. Circuit against one of your employees. The name is Laura Messier. Does CIA have an employment agreement for her with the French government?"

"I'm not aware of it."

"Can you have someone look for me?" Middleton asked. "If something's out there, I need to see it."

"Sure. If we've got it, it's yours."

"Thanks, Bill."

Middleton hung up and looked at Dan. "Let's pick a

date for the conference tournament."

Bates called Roger Wilson, the CIA Chief of Staff.
"Roger Wilson here."
"Roger, its Bill.   Do you have Laura Messier's employment file in your office?"
"Yeah. What do you need?" Wilson asked.
"Was there ever an agreement between the French and us regarding her employment?"
"Sure. I helped negotiate it."
"What was in it?"
"We embedded her in the French government. To make her cover real, we decided she'd be employed by the French. You want to see it?"
"If you can find it, it would be helpful, yes," Bates said.
"I'll have someone make a copy and run it up to you."
"Thanks."

The fax came through to Middleton's office within 15 minutes.   His receptionist carried in.   "A fax marked 'Urgent' just came through."
"Who's it from?"
"Bill Bates.'"
"Yes, thank you, Susan."
Middleton looked at Dan. "This may be what you're talking about."

After reviewing the document for a couple of minutes, Middleton looked up and smiled. "Your girl may be off the hook, Dan.   This employment agreement gives her full autonomy to work for the French and doesn't seem to have an end date. Let's check one more thing." He punched his intercom button. "Susan, I need to call the Director of the French Intelligence Service in Paris. Can you set up the call for me?"

"Yes, Sir. You need an interpreter?"

"Maybe. Let's see if anyone over there speaks English first."

"I speak pretty good French if you need help."

"Great." After a couple of minutes, Middleton's receptionist came back on the intercom.

"Ron, I have the Director of French Intelligence waiting on hold for you. His name is Francois Picquet and he does speak English."

"Thank you, Susan. Connect us." She made the connection.

"Director Picquet, this is the Attorney General of the United States, Ron Middleton, calling. Thank you for taking my call."

"My pleasure, Mr. Attorney General. How may I be of service to you?"

"I'm investigating a legal proceeding involving Laura Messier here in the States. Can you confirm she works for you?"

"Yes, she works for the DST under an agreement with the Central Intelligence Agency."

"Has she worked for you recently?"

"Yes. She's been working on a national security matter. That work culminated in a classified operation this week in a foreign country."

"That operation was under the direction of the DST?"

"Yes. Under the direction of myself."

"And her actions were approved by you?"

"Yes, of course. Would you like a written statement to

that effect?"

"No, Sir. That won't be necessary. Thank you for your time, Sir."

"Very good."

"Thank you, again."

"Somebody over at CIA owes your girl an apology, Dan. Hang on; I've got to call the prosecutor's office." He picked up his phone again.

"Hank?" Middleton asked. "It's Ron."

"What's up?" Hank Banning asked.

"I have new information about that Laura Messier complaint you filed. Were you aware she was working under an employment agreement with the French government?"

"Nope. Did that asshole Smithson hang me out to dry again?"

"Yep."

"That's the third time he's fucked me over in two years, Ron."

"I'll fax the thing over to you, but the agreement clearly states Messier works for the French government. I just got off the phone with the French right now. They confirmed it. Everything Messier did in that complaint was at the direction of the French government. We have no jurisdiction and I need that complaint dropped with prejudice."

"Fax over the employment agreement so I have a copy and I'll get it done this afternoon."

"Thanks."

Middleton ended the call and looked at Dan. "That was

easy. By the way, do you play golf?"

"Sure."

"I'm in a regular foursome with the President, the Chief of Staff, me and a different fourth man each time. Maybe you'd like to play sometime. If you want to be in the mix for FBI Director, you really ought to meet the President."

"I'd love to," Dan said. "Thanks for the help on Messier."

"No problem."

"I'd like to call her and let her know. You got a phone I can use?"

"Sure. Conference room down the hall. Dial nine for an outside line."

Dan called Laura's home in Georgetown and persuaded Rick Williams to reveal where she was staying. He called the Hilton hotel in Tysons and asked to be connected to her room. Laura answered.

"Laura, its Dan."

"Hi Dan."

"You getting some rest?"

"Yes. It's been a tough week."

"Well, I've got good news. I met with Ron Middleton. They've agreed to drop the charges."

"Wow! I don't know how to thank you."

"Ron saw it for what it was. The charges were a pile of crap. The dismissal will be filed later today. I'll run over and get a copy. Are you going home?"

"No. Things aren't going too well on the home front."

"I'm sorry. Are you going out to Langley anytime soon?"

"Yes. I've got some housekeeping matters to attend to."

"If you want to go tomorrow, why don't I take you? I can hand deliver a copy of the dismissal."

"What time?"

"Late morning sound okay?"

"Perfect. Dan, thank you. I mean that."

"You're welcome. Talk with you tomorrow."

That call was followed shortly after by another, this time from Rick Gleason. "Ms. Messier, its Rick Gleason."

"Hi Rick."

"I've got bad news. I was at Langley this morning. I spoke with Greg Smithson, the CIA counsel. They're not budging on the charges. We may have to countersue."

"The problem's solved, Rick. Dan Jenkins was able to speak with the Attorney General this morning over at Justice. They're dismissing the complaint."

"Terrific. One problem solved."

"Thanks for the help."

"There is another matter. Your husband filed for divorce yesterday afternoon. The paperwork was delivered to my office. Would you like me to handle it?" Laura was silent for a long time. Her eyes began to tear and she reached for the box of tissues on an end table. "Ms. Messier, are you still there?" She didn't answer. "Are you okay?" he asked.

"What happens now?" Laura asked slowly.

"We don't have to answer the filing immediately. Take a few days before you respond."

"Can you handle it?"

"Of course. I'm sorry, Ms. Messier. Bad things happen to good people."

"It's been a tough week."

"Rest and take care of yourself. I'll be in touch."

Laura hung up the phone and collapsed on the bed.

***

Laura halfheartedly accepted Jean's invitation to dinner that evening. Jean, early as usual, was already seated at the hotel restaurant when Laura came downstairs. "Mademoiselle, you're the most beautiful woman in the world. I'm honored to take dinner with you."

That brought a smile to her face. "You always make me feel better, Jean. Thank you."

"You're welcome," he said in Dutch.

"You're going to make me work this evening?"

"My apologies," Jean said in English. "Is this more comfortable?"

"Definitely. Where's Jack?"

"I have no idea. He can't go far. He doesn't have any money," Jean said with a smile. "He'll turn up eventually."

"He upset me on the plane."

"He's just naïve, Mademoiselle. Don't take it personally."

"I suppose you're right."

After a few minutes talking with Jean, Laura was smiling and laughing again. *Jean has that effect on people*, Laura thought. *Superb people skills, smart, funny. He's the perfect person to be around when you're having problems.*

"I have a suggestion, if you're interested," he said.

"Of course, I'm interested."

"Your relationship with CIA is none of my concern. I'm only mentioning this as an alternative. Perhaps, you've already thought of it yourself. If you were to resign from CIA, you could begin taking private business. Certain individuals and governments would pay handsomely for the type of work you do."

"I've already decided to resign from the agency, Jean, but I have no idea what I'll do."

"It is not my place, Mademoiselle, to convince you one way or the other, but I would point out that if you were to act now, you have many of the pieces you need already in place."

"I have another problem, Jean. Steve filed for divorce."

Jean was surprised. He had no idea what to say. After some hesitation, he said, "I'm terribly sorry."

Her words came slower. "Thank you. It hurts."

"Rejection hurts worst coming from those we love," Jean said gently.

Tears came to Laura's eyes. Jean was patient, allowing her time to collect her thoughts.

"Yes, it does," she finally said, nearly inaudible.

Jean's words were softer. "He didn't understand the urgency of Ivan Ilitch."

Laura paused again, struggling to control her emotions. "I did what I thought was right. I defended my family."

"Sometimes it's the people closest to us who have the most difficult time understanding us."

"I guess I got in the way of Steve's career," she said.

Jean smiled and gave Laura the passionate look a father might give a daughter. "Give it time, Mademoiselle."

Laura paused again. Jean waited for her to find her

next thought. "I hated the way I felt after killing Ilitch. It was an execution, Jean. Cold blooded."

"You would have felt better if he had shot back?"

Laura smiled at that. "No."

"Remember, as long as you feel something, you're not like them."

"I'm afraid I'll become like them," she said.

"It is always good to question one's motives, Mademoiselle. But you're not like them. And you never will be."

Laura smiled and wiped the tears from her face. "Thank you for saying that."

"It wasn't like this in the beginning, was it?"

"No."

"It never is," Jean said. "We're led into this kind of work slowly over time. It happens in small steps until, all of a sudden, we find ourselves doing things we never dreamed of."

"That's it, exactly," she said. "When CIA hired me, my first job was processing visa applications at the French Consulate in Chicago. It was fun. Then, I had an opportunity to transfer to Paris and work in the Foreign Ministry. Working in Paris was like a dream come true."

"Take some time, Mademoiselle."

"You mean step away for a while?" she asked.

"Yes. Go somewhere warm and sunny. Stay there until you feel an urge to come back."

"What if I never want to come back?"

"Then don't."

***

Dan Jenkin's call on Friday morning woke an exhausted Laura Messier. She looked at the clock on the end table. It was almost noon. "Hello," she said softly.

"Hi, it's Dan. Are you still planning to go out to Langley?"

"Yes."

"I faxed Bates a copy of the dismissal. He wants to talk. He suggested we meet at 1:30."

"Can you pick me up at 1:00?"

"I'll be waiting out front. Black Chevy SUV."

"Thanks."

During the short drive out to Langley, Laura prepped Dan for the worst. "You have a security clearance?"

"Of course."

"Bates wants to talk about intel."

"What about it?"

"We took intel off KGB computers when we left. I suspect the French refused to give him a copy."

"Why would they refuse? Aren't we allies?"

"CIA sat on the sidelines. They've got more assets than anyone over there, but wouldn't use them. They were afraid the mission would compromise one of their precious high level meetings. In retaliation, the French are probably refusing to share the intel."

"The French gave you a copy?" Dan asked.

"Yes."

"Are you willing to share it with Bates?"

"Sure, if he pays my expenses. Everyone's got to have a little skin in the game. Nothing's free in life."

Upon arrival at Langley, they pulled through the gate and parked in the front lot. "I'm getting angry just walking in the building," she said. "I'm glad you're here."

While Dan was getting his visitor badge at the security station, one of the guards looked a little too long at Laura. "What the fuck are you looking at?" she asked, too loudly for comfort.

"We're under orders to arrest you."

Dan heard the exchange and walked over. "What's the problem?" Dan asked the officer.

"I'm sorry, Sir, but we've got orders to arrest Ms. Messier."

Dan pulled the dismissal from his briefcase. "Here is a dismissal of all the alleged charges against Ms. Messier. With all due respect, she cannot be arrested." He pulled out his FBI badge and showed it to the guard. "I'm Dan Jenkins, Assistant Director of the Federal Bureau of Investigation. Ms. Messier is under my protection. If you've got a problem, go get your supervisor so we can straighten this out right now."

The supervisor of the security station heard the discussion and walked over. "Sorry. There's no problem, Sir," he said to Dan. "We just got word of Ms. Messier's dismissal a few minutes ago. I hadn't told my employees yet. Ms. Messier is free to enter the building without interference." He looked at Laura. "My apologies, Ma'am. This was my fault."

Walking toward the bank of elevators, Dan asked, "What floor are we going to?"

"Seven. Thanks for coming, Dan. I needed you back there. Now, if you'll just prevent me from throwing Bates out the damn window, things will be perfect."

Dan pushed the seven button. "You're funny."

"You think I'm joking?"

"You know, for all your reputation as a hand-to-hand specialist, I've never actually seen you fight."

She gave him a mischievous look. "I'll try to restrain myself."

Bill Bates' secretary gave them a warm smile when they entered the office. "Hi Laura. Just a moment. I'll tell the Director you're here." Bates heard them enter and walked out of his office. "Come on in," he said, motioning with his hand. Bates offered Dan a handshake. "Bill Bates."

"Dan Jenkins, FBI."

"Good to meet you. Good afternoon, Laura."

"You're trying to be nice now?" she asked.

Bates frowned. "Let's try to be civil. Have a seat," he said pointing at the chairs in front of his desk. He sat behind his desk.

"Here's my resignation." Laura began, pulling the letter from her purse. She handed it to Bates as they settled into chairs. "I'll stop at Personnel on my way out and sign whatever they need."

"There are things we need to discuss," Bates said.

"There's nothing we need to discuss."

"I want you to understand something. The blowback from that mission was severe. You pissed off a cabinet officer, Laura. He wants your head. I'm sorry, but I was forced to respond. It wasn't personal."

"Wasn't personal?" she asked cynically.

Bates glared at her. "You really don't understand how things work, do you? Shit flows downhill."

"You don't really defend your staff, do you?"

"Picquet says you have our copy of the intel."

"Not your copy," Laura said. "I've got my copy. It was a French mission, Bill. You want the intel? Get it from them."

"Don't get yourself in deeper trouble."

"Is that a threat?" Laura asked.

"We can make life very difficult for you."

"I doubt that. I can send it to the Post. I guarantee it'll be embarrassing for you. The Soviets operating freely in D.C. A Soviet safe house in Georgetown. Two informants working at State. Two more here in this building. You'll lose your job."

"It's illegal to disclose classified information."

"Pardon me for interrupting, Director Bates," Dan said. "With all due respect, the United States doesn't own the information in her possession. You can request a copy and ask her to keep the information confidential, but you can't force her."

"If you publish one word of that intel, I'll have you arrested." Bates said to Laura.

"You don't have the authority to arrest me. He does," Laura said, motioning to Jenkins. Laura looked at Dan. "Come on, Dan, I'm done here."

"Hang on a minute," Dan suggested, looking at Laura. "Bill, why don't you stop playing hardball for a minute?"

Bates considered that for a few seconds. "Okay. What does she want?"

"I'm right here, Bill. Talk to me directly."

"What do you want?"

"I want reimbursement for my personal expenses during the mission."

"That's ridiculous. It was a French mission," Bates said. "Get your reimbursement from them."

"Fuck you then," Laura said. "You'll get nothing from me." Laura wasn't going to allow Bates to push her any farther.

Bates exploded in anger. "Dammit! Who the hell do you think you are?" He stood, slamming his chair into the back wall. "I can get the intel another way." He grabbed his telephone.

Dan watched Laura begin to stand up. He laid his hand on her arm and shook his head. "Just relax." Dan stood up instead.

Bates began to punch a number into the phone. Dan pressed the button disconnecting the line. "I certainly hope you're dialing your comptroller to arrange a payment for her," Dan said, "because if you're contacting security, I'll have armed FBI agents here within minutes. She's under federal protection."

That threat stopped Bates. Before he could respond, his phone rang. Dan took his finger off the line connecting the call. "Yes?" Bates asked.

"Sorry to interrupt your meeting, but the Attorney General's in the outer office. He says he needs to speak with you. Would you like me to show him in?"

Bates hesitated, wondering why the Attorney General would be in his outer office. He finally said, "Yes. Send him in."

Ron Middleton immediately sensed the tension when he entered the room. He looked at Bates, then Dan, Laura and then back at Bates. "Am I interrupting something?" he asked.

"This is Laura Messier, Ron," Dan said.

Middleton smiled. "It's a pleasure to meet you, Ma'am. Do I need to wait outside?" Middleton asked.

"No," Dan said. "I'm glad you're here. How did you know we were meeting today?"

"I didn't. I'm here on another matter. Is there a problem?"

"Ms. Messier seems to feel she can withhold intelligence that was intended to be passed on to the agency," Bates said. "She's threatening to publish it in the Post."

"Okay. Everyone just sit down and relax. Let's talk. What intelligence?" Middleton asked.

Bates and Jenkins sat down, but Middleton didn't. He was the highest ranking legal officer in government. He took control of the meeting. "What intelligence," he asked again, looking back and forth between them.

"Intelligence from the mission mentioned in the complaint, Ron," Dan said.

"Who owns the information?"

"Technically, that would be the French," Laura said. "Except, I own my copy."

"Why'd they give you a copy?" Middleton asked Laura.

"Professional courtesy."

Middleton thought for a moment. "I'm not familiar with protocol in the intelligence community. Help me out here. If intelligence is meant to be passed directly to CIA, how do they send it?"

"They send it via diplomatic bag," Laura said.

"That's not necessarily true," Bates said.

"Hang on a minute, Bill. You have something else to add, Ms. Messier?"

"The chain of custody with classified material is important. They wouldn't hand a copy to someone and tell them to give it to their boss."

"I understand." Middleton, a former federal prosecutor, thought for a minute. "Allow me to clarify the issue. You brought the information out of the Soviet Union and gave it to the French. If they intended to forward it to CIA, they'd have used a secure procedure. They didn't, so CIA wants your copy which was given to you by the French as a courtesy. Is that right?"

"Yes, exactly," Laura answered.

"Why wouldn't you give CIA a copy? That seems a reasonable thing to do."

"Actionable intelligence needs to follow a chain of custody. But as a courtesy, I'd be happy share my unofficial copy. What I'm asking is for Director Bates to pay the personal expenses I incurred to obtain it."

Middleton looked at Bates. "Bill, why wouldn't you pay her expenses? That seems reasonable."

"It was a French operation. She should seek reimbursement from them."

"CIA refused to participate in the mission ..." Laura said, but Middleton interrupted.

"Pardon me, Ms. Messier. One moment." Middleton turned to Bates. "Did you ask the French for the intel directly?"

"Yes. They refused," Bates said.

"Why?"

"We have no official security arrangement with the French. They don't participate in the military part of NATO," Bates said.

Middleton looked at Laura. "What amount of money are you asking for?"

"I have receipts totaling $75,000."

"So, this dispute is about money?"

"Yes," Laura said.

Middleton smiled, amused that a lowly field agent had beaten the Director of the CIA. "Looks like she's got you over a barrel, Bill. She's willing to sell you the information. Pay her the money, get a copy and move on."

Bates didn't react. He just stared at Middleton. "Is there a problem?" Middleton asked.

"I don't have a budget line for extortion."

"Oh come on, Bill," Middleton said sarcastically. "From what I hear, you shovel buckets of money out the door to guys running around Central America. Seventy-five grand is chump change to you guys."

Without saying another word, Bates picked up the phone and asked the comptroller to write a check in the amount of $75,000 to Laura Messier. "It'll be available at the comptroller's office in fifteen minutes," he said to Laura. "Where's the intel?"

Laura dug through her shoulder bag and produced an oversize brown envelope. She handed it over.

"Are you satisfied with the outcome, Ms. Messier?" Middleton asked.

"Yes."

"Bill?"

"Yes," Bates said, although it was obvious he wasn't pleased about the agreement.

"Good," Middleton replied. "Problem solved. Oh, by the way, Dan, I got you in a foursome with POTUS Saturday morning. You in?"

"Sure."

"Great."

Bates tried to return Laura's resignation. "You want to take this back?"

"Fuck you, Bill."

"I think that means, '*no*,' Bill," Middleton said with a smile.

"That's it, then?" Bates asked.

"That's it," Laura replied

"How can we reach you?"

"You can't." Laura looked at Dan. "You ready to leave?"

"If that's the way you want to end it, yes," Dan said.

Laura and Dan rose to leave. "It's a pleasure to meet you Mr. Middleton," Laura said.

"The pleasure's mine, Ms. Messier. Dan, meet us in the clubhouse at Andrews, eight thirty, Saturday."

"See you then," Dan answered.

Laura and Dan walked down the hall toward the elevators. "I need to stop at Personnel and the Comptroller's office. Do you mind waiting?"

"Not at all. Are you sure you made the right decision back there?"

"Bates is such an asshole. I can't work with him."

"Do you mind if I make an observation?"

"Of course not."

"I'm playing golf on Saturday with the President of the United States, Laura. I didn't get there by busting down doors in cheap motels arresting drug suspects. I learned early on that I needed to play politics. You've got extraordinary talent, Laura. Everyone recognizes that. But you'll always be busting down doors in cheap motels unless you learn how to play the game."

They got on the elevator and Laura pressed the bottom floor. She was embarrassed by her own inadequacy. "You're right, Dan," she admitted. "Of course, you're right. I just don't know how to do it."

After Laura and Dan left, Ron Middleton sat down opposite Bill Bates. "Tough lady," he said referring to Laura.

"The toughest."

"What'd she do over there, anyway?"

"In the Soviet Union?"

"Yes."

"According to Picquet, she killed a four man Soviet assassination team and three more KGB agents rescuing a man she brought out of the country. Then, she was attacked in Paris yesterday by two more Soviet agents. She killed one and badly injured the other."

Middleton whistled. "Damn! That sounds like someone you'd like to have working for you, Bill."

"Maybe. Uncontrollable is how I'd describe her."

"The best ones always are, aren't they? Take my advice, Bill. Give her some time and invite her back."

"What's on your plate today, Ron?"
"Iran Contra."

***

Driving out of the complex, Dan asked, "Can I drop you somewhere? I've got to get back to work."

"Downtown," Laura said. "Gleason, Roush and Simmons. Do you know where it is?"

"It's just a few blocks from headquarters."

A half-hour later, Jenkins pulled to the curb outside Rick Gleason's office. "Anything I can do for you, let me know," he said as a way of goodbye. He leaned over and kissed her.

"I'm married, Dan."

"I know. I'm just letting you know how I feel."

Laura looked down, old feelings intruding into her thoughts. She didn't know what to say. Finally looking up, she said, "You're in a no parking zone," she said. "You should go."

"Keep in touch."

"I will."

Walking into Gleason's office, Laura thought about Dan Jenkins. She'd considered their affair in Paris to be a mistake; one of those awkward situations that happen from time to time when people work in close quarters with each other. On the heels of her break-up with Steve, it was too soon; far too soon to contemplate getting involved again.

The receptionist at the front desk gave her a quick smile when she entered. "May I help you?"

"I'm Laura Messier. I don't have an appointment. I wonder if Mr. Gleason is available."

"He's in the office somewhere. Let me find him." She picked up the phone briefly and then hung up. "He's on a phone call, Ms. Messier. He said to tell you he'll be out in a few minutes. Can I get you something? Coffee? A soft drink?"

"No, I'm fine. Thank you."

She sat in the lobby and continued to think about her personal life. She recognized that Steve had become distant the last few months. He was consumed by advancement at CIA. The closer he came to the top job, the less he needed her. Perhaps a divorce was best for both of them.

Gleason appeared in the lobby fifteen minutes later. "I'm sorry, Laura. I got stuck on a conference call. Come on back." Laura followed him down a long hallway, past a bustling office full of clerks and attorneys. They sat in Gleason's office, an overly large room with dark, padded furniture and expensive wood paneling. One wall was taken up with shelves of legal volumes giving the room a serious look. *Typical lawyer's office*, she thought.

Gleason placed the file bearing Laura's name on his desk. "I took a look at Steve's filing. I know his attorney. He's fair. I don't think they'll be a problem. Have you talked with Steve yet?"

"No."

"Good. Don't. One of you should move immediately."

"It'll be me. Steve owned the house before we got married. I'll run over before he gets off work and pack the rest of my things."

"Do you have a temporary residence?"

"I've been staying at a hotel out in Tysons."

"Do you need help in arranging something?"

"No, I don't think so. I'm thinking about living abroad."

"Make sure we're able to contact you."

"I will. I'll be here for another few days, anyway. What's he offering in a property settlement?" she asked.

"Your husband is worth a lot of money, Laura."

"I had no idea of his assets. He never told me."

"With the real estate, personal property and stock portfolio, he's worth in excess of thirty million dollars."

"I'm shocked."

"A judge won't consider splitting the assets 50-50. You've only been married a year."

"I'm not interested in half his assets, Rick. I want to walk away feeling I've been treated fairly."

"He wants the house and furnishings in Georgetown. He wants the vacation home in Colorado. And he wants to keep the investment portfolio he received from his parents. He's offering you the building in Paris, one of the cars and a two million dollar cash buy-out."

"Which car?"

Gleason looked down at the file. "The SUV."

"I'm already driving that car. I'll just keep it. About the other, I'd like you to make a counter offer. The building in Paris, a five million cash buy-out and the car."

"Sounds fair to me. I'll call his attorney and make the counter. I need you to fill out these forms and return them to me." He handed Laura a stack of paperwork. "I'll file your response and we'll see."

"Good," Laura said, taking the forms. "How soon will we go to court?"

"Are you claiming any abuse or abandonment? Anything other than his claim of irreconcilable differences?"

"No."

"Thirty days. You don't have to show up. I can handle it for you."

"Thanks, that makes it much easier for me."

"Where can I reach you?"

"I'll be at the Hilton out in Tysons for the next few days. I'll drop the forms off tomorrow."

"Once again, I'm sorry, Laura."

"Thanks, Rick, but things will be fine."

"Yes, they will. You'll have plenty of money and a nice career."

Laura left Gleason's office and hailed a taxi back to the hotel. From there, she drove back into the city, to what was now her former home in Georgetown. Neither Steve nor Rick was there. She found boxes in the basement and packed her belongings. There wasn't much; most of it was in Paris. Laura had only a few pictures, clothing and personal items at the house. She loaded the boxes into the SUV and while checking the house one last time, she found a note by the phone.

"Laura, unknown caller – just said 'Wanglestrasse' and hung up – Rick"

Markus, she thought. I'll call him back in a day or two. She stopped at a storage facility, took a few clothing items and loaded the rest into a small unit.

***

She met Rick, Jean and Jack for dinner at the hotel. Jean mentioned starting their own private security firm again. "I'll need a crew for the plane," Laura said. "Would you have a problem with Dmitri and Svetlana?" she asked Jean.

"They'd be perfect."

"I'm driving out to Lake Anna in the morning. I'll ask them. I'm thinking of spending some time in the Bahamas. Anyone interested in going?"

"I'd like to move on to California," Jack said, "but I'd be happy to work for you from there. I'm as close as a computer terminal."

"That's fine with me," Laura said. "If you don't mind flying out there commercial, I'll give you some money to get started. What about you, Jean?"

"The Bahamas are just what I had in mind."

"I think I'll come, too," Rick said. "I'm pretty sure my employment's ending at CIA and I'm no longer welcome at the house."

"Good. We'll have plenty of time to talk later. I'm pretty sure my mood will improve sitting on a beach drinking rum and coke."

"Excellent, Mademoiselle," Jean replied with a smile.

Laura returned to her room, opened the mini-bar and turned on the television. She had drifted off to sleep when the phone rang at eleven. She awoke startled until she realized the sound was the telephone. *Who would call at this hour*, she asked herself. "Hello?"

"Laura, it's Dan."

"Something wrong?"

"No. I was just driving by your hotel and thought I'd stop in and see if you'd like a nightcap."

"You're here?"

"Yeah, downstairs in the bar."

"Give me a couple of minutes and I'll be down."

Laura hung up and looked in the mirror. *I look like shit*, she said to herself. She combed out her hair, did a quick make-up job, put on tight jeans, heels and a silk blouse. She found earrings and a few bracelets. *Better, but not great*, she thought. She dabbed her favorite perfume on her wrists, grabbed her purse and went downstairs. *Why am I trying to look nice for him*, she asked herself?

She found Dan sitting at the bar watching a ballgame on television. She put her hand on his shoulder. "Dan?"

He spun around on his bar stool and smiled. "Hi," he said gently.

"What brings you all the way out here so late at night?"

Dan laughed. "Golf. I was at a nearby driving range until dark, then stopped for dinner and realized I was right by your hotel. I thought I'd stop in and say hello."

He moved to kiss her and she turned her cheek. "If you were French, Dan, you'd kiss me on both cheeks," she said with a smile.

"Let's try this again." This time, he air kissed her on both cheeks.

"Now you're kissing like a French gentleman."

"I'm not French, but I'd like to think I'm a gentleman."

"You're definitely that. Thanks again for getting me out of that legal jam."

"Forget about it. What are you drinking?"

"Scotch and soda."

He motioned to the bartender and ordered for her. "I heard something about you today."

"What'd you hear?" Laura responded.

"Your husband filed for divorce. I'm sorry."

"Where'd you hear that?"

"FBI flagged you as a person of interest when the Soviet passport was processed."

"The FBI's going to follow me?"

"No, no. I took you off the list. Someone wrote a report that came across my desk this morning."

"Well, it's true," Laura admitted.

"Relationships are a casualty of what we do for a living, I guess. You didn't ask for my advice, but here it is anyway. Take some time off, slow down and get some perspective on things. You've been through a lot lately."

"That's good advice."

The bartender set another round in front of them. "I thought you'd want one more," he said. "It's last call. We close at midnight."

Dan smiled at the barkeep. "Not a problem." He looked at his watch and then returned his attention to Laura. "Before we get kicked out of here, I'd like to make a confession."

"Okay," Laura said, wondering whether it would be something she didn't want to hear.

Dan looked away as he spoke. "I've always felt that what happened in Paris meant more to me than it did to you."

Laura put her hand on his. "I don't know what my feelings are. There's so much going on in my life right now, I don't know what to say."

"I just wanted you to know how I feel." He glanced at the clock above the bar. "I wish we had more time."

She looked into his eyes. "Dan, I can't do this right now. It's not you; I've got too much going on in my life. Can we put this on hold until I've had time to straighten things out?"

Dan smiled. "Sure. Will you call me?"

"I will."

Dan kissed her. "I'm counting on it."

***

The next morning, Laura showered and prepared herself for the day. She walked out to the SUV with a bagel and a cup of coffee. *Get on with the day's business*, she thought, as she pulled out of the hotel lot. *Stop thinking about Dan; stop thinking about Steve. Put them out of your mind and get back to work.* By the time she had traveled halfway to Lake Anna, she felt rejuvenated.

Arriving at Lake Anna an hour and a half later, she found Fedor Belkin working around his dock. He waved as she walked down to meet him. "It's really pretty down here," she said. "I see why you like it. I came to check on Dmitri and Svetlana. I hope they're still here."

Fedor laughed. "I was hoping you'd be in a position to suggest something. Let me call over to the guest cabin and tell them you're here."

Dmitri and Svetlana showed up within minutes and were receptive to Laura's offer of employment. "We don't speak good English," Dmitri said. "American jobs will be hard for us. We'd be grateful if you'd hire us."

"Any problem taking care of the plane?"

"Not at all. Will you base your operations out of Harrisburg?"

"No, I'm thinking about Nassau."

"You mean the Bahamas?" Dmitri asked with an incredulous look.

"Yes. Would that be a problem?"

"Where would we live?" Svetlana asked.

"Well, we'd have to find you a house somewhere on the island. I was hoping you wouldn't mind."

Svetlana and Dmitri looked at each other and smiled. "Perfect," Svetlana said. "We accept."

Laura drove back later that afternoon. Early the next morning, she remembered the 'Wanglestrasse' message and placed a return call from her hotel room. She left the code word, 'Wanglestrasse,' on the answering machine, along with her hotel number. The call was immediate. "Hello Markus," she said.

"My dear girl, I hope you are well."

"Yes, I'm well and I hope you are, too."

"Yes, I'm fine," Marcus said. "My compliments on your recent success."

"I survived, Markus; nothing else. Survival is a victory, is it not?"

"To outlive one's enemies is a great accomplishment."

"Will there be any retaliation?"

"None that I know about yet. I'll let you know if I hear something."

"I'd appreciate that. Thanks for the name. I wouldn't have found him otherwise."

"Yes, you would," Markus said. "He was careless, overconfident."

"Maybe."

"Make yourself difficult to find for a while."

"I intend to do that. Keep in touch."

"I will. Goodbye, Shewolf."

After the clandestine call to East Germany, Laura thought it best to check out immediately. She used cash to pay the hotel charges. She drove downtown and dropped off legal forms at Gleason's office, then headed to Lake Anna to pick up Dmitri and Svetlana.

They traveled on to Harrisburg where Dmitri and Svetlana prepared the plane for a trip to the Bahamas. After waiting for Rick and Jean to arrive, they flew to Freeport on Grand Bahama Island. They relaxed for a couple of weeks at beach front resort. Sitting on the beach each day, they realized their desire to stay together was stronger than a desire to separate.

Exploring the eastern side of the island, Laura spotted an estate for sale near Pelican Point. Set on a hill between Grand Bahama Highway and the beach, the secluded property included a long stretch of private beach, a large main house and several outbuildings. The house offered a beautiful view of the ocean. An uncontrolled air strip nearby had over 7,000 feet of asphalt runway, perfect for

Laura's jet. After a couple of weeks in the Bahamas, she decided it'd be a nice place to live. What began with a gun battle on the streets of Paris ended on a pretty beachfront in the Caribbean. Life does have happy endings.

Epilogue

OVER THE NEXT few weeks, Laura, Jean and Rick began to build their new company, Security Associates of the Bahamas, headquartered on Grand Bahama Island. Once Laura's divorce was finalized, she flew to Paris and sold her apartment building. She put Rick in charge of the property renovations necessary to accommodate the group. The main house was completely renovated and a large outbuilding was converted to extra living space. Two other buildings became a security station and maintenance building. Rick bought two all-terrain vehicles to travel around the property. Electric fencing and security cameras were installed. Rick built a smaller security station at the entrance to the compound with a gate across the long gravel drive. A bulldozer cut paths through the dense undergrowth and dump trucks filled the paths with wood chips. Lighting was installed along the pathways, making the entire property accessible by foot.

Laura and Dmitri created a private airline company with an office in Freeport to ferry tourists to and from the States using Laura's jet. That would provide immediate income while Laura and Jean began to give notice that their security company was ready to accept business. Jack flew on to California where he sought work in Silicon Valley, but also promised to work for Laura as her computer expert.

Jean sold his Paris club and moved to the Bahamas location, although he didn't live at the compound. He purchased a condominium near the beach in Freeport. The six para-military guards Jean brought from his club added greatly to their payroll, but they were necessary to provide security and a quick response team for future missions. Some of them used the extra living space at the compound while others rented apartments in Freeport.

They hired a dozen part-time informants, unemployed local men who welcomed the extra cash in exchange for providing information. They were spread throughout the island and served as the eyes and ears of the company. Very little escaped their attention.

One surprise was the addition of Jack Mason, who joined them after retiring from CIA. He sought to retire somewhere warm and sunny and Grand Bahama Island was as good a location as any. He bought a beachfront cottage not far from the compound.

Another of the security measures Laura incorporated was the purchase of four Doberman Pincher pups. She named them Dasher, Dancer, Prancer and Vixen. Although she treated them as pets and one or more often slept with her, they quickly grew into fierce creatures. They roamed freely about the property. Even Jean's para-military guards feared them.

Like any firm, Laura found she needed an office so she

rented space at a downtown Freeport location. Jean and Jack Mason kept regular office hours. Inquiries began to dribble in, one by one. Some were blind inquires, people needing to find a loved one, wanting bodyguards to accompany them around the islands or asking for help in righting some injustice done to them. None seemed quite right until a man named Jason Schmitt called and asked for a meeting. He flew in from the States. Jean and Jack Mason met him at the office. They listened to his problem and decided he ought to meet Laura. Rick drove him to the compound.

Rick headed east on Grand Bahama Highway past High Rock and turned right onto the unmarked gravel road that led to the compound. They approached the gate where one of the French guards stepped out of the guardhouse and held up his hand motioning the car to stop.

"Hello, Monsieur Williams," he said. "Bringing someone into the compound today?"

"Yes, Pierre. His name is Jason Schmitt."

The guard looked in the car at Schmitt. "I'm sorry, Monsieur, but I must ask you to step out of the car for a moment."

Rick's guest got out and stood by the vehicle while the guard frisked him. Once he was satisfied Schmitt posed no danger, he lifted the gate and the car drove through. Driving past the guard's living quarters and the maintenance and security buildings, they finally came to the main house. As they turned off the car, Dasher and Dancer got up off the veranda and ambled toward the car. They knew Rick, but were wary of the other man.

"It's okay, boys," Rick said, petting both of them. "He's

just visiting." The dogs followed the two up the stairs onto the veranda where another guard rose from his chair.

"Morning, Monsieur Williams. Looking for the Mademoiselle?"

"Yes."

"She's down at the beach."

They walked around the house and down a path that led to the beach. Laura was asleep in a shaded hammock just off the beach. Vixen, who lay underneath, lifted her head and began to growl. Laura reached down and patted her. "Hear something, girl?" Vixen crawled out from under the hammock and stood in the path. "Somebody coming?" Laura threw the beach towel over her Sig and waited.

Rick saw Vixen standing in the path and knew Laura would be nearby. "Ms. Messier," he called out loudly. "We have a visitor."

"Come ahead, Rick." Laura got up and stood by Vixen. She reached down and patted the dog. "It's okay, girl. Sit. They're friendly." Vixen stopped growling and sat when she saw Rick.

"Morning," Rick said.

Laura nodded. "Rick."

"We have a visitor. This is Jason Schmitt."

Schmitt stepped forward. "Nice to meet you, Ms. Messier. Your reputation precedes you." He offered his hand.

Laura didn't accept the handshake. He withdrew it, slightly embarrassed. Instead, she studied Schmitt, sizing him up. American. Early fifties. Thin, slight of build. Five-ten. Glasses, short black hair. *Must be an office worker*, she thought. *Expensive suit; too heavy for this climate*. He stood as though he knew nothing about fighting. Laura decided he was harmless. "Can I help you, Mr. Schmitt?"

"Is there somewhere we can talk?"

"Right here is fine."

Laura listened while Schmitt explained his problem. "You met my partner, Mr. Broussard?" she asked.

"Yes, Ma'am."

"And he sent you out here?"

"Yes, Ma'am."

"I see you've met Mr. Williams."

"Yes."

Laura stared at Schmitt for a few moments. "One million dollars, Mr. Schmitt, plus expenses. The resources needed to solve your problem are expensive."

Schmitt started to reach into the breast pocket of his jacket. Laura immediately raised the Sig underneath her beach towel. Rick touched Schmitt's arm. Schmitt froze. "He's clean, Laura," Rick said.

"Go ahead, Mr. Schmitt," Rick said. Schmitt pulled out a checkbook. "Would you take a check?"

Laura nodded. "Go back up to the house with Mr. Williams. He'll give you a contract to sign. We'll be in touch."

"Thank you, Ma'am," Schmitt said. Rick led Schmitt back up the path. Laura lay down again and fell asleep. Vixen crawled underneath the hammock to lay in the shade. Security Associates of the Bahamas had their first client.

About the Author

Lawrence Scofield holds degrees from the University of Missouri at Kansas City and Northwestern University in Evanston, Illinois. Early in his career, he enjoyed performing with major symphony orchestras and opera companies. He has appeared on Grammy Award winning recordings and has international touring experience. Following a career in the performing arts, Mr. Scofield served in the administrations at colleges and universities. After retirement, he turned his attention to the written word and now writes novels, articles and columns.

If you enjoyed this novel, please leave a review on Amazon, Goodreads, or wherever possible. Your feedback and support are greatly appreciated.

Visit Lawrence's web page at www.lawrencescofield.com, Twitter account at @lscofieldauthor, and Facebook page at https://www.facebook.com/lawrencescofieldauthor.

Sneak Peek

Next in "The Laura Messier Files" Series

Three Days in Tripoli

A Spy Thriller

By Lawrence Scofield

Prologue

Sunday, April 13th, 1986

Located beneath the White House, the Situation Room's only contact with the outside world comes through video, telephone and telex. One heavily guarded elevator is the room's only access point. The video screens were turned off that morning and the insulated quiet of the environment served to amplify the conversation around the conference table.

Senior staff came into the building underground through the White House tunnels to avoid alerting the press. There was a certain tension in the air, the kind that could be expected given the gravity of a situation where military action was imminent. Secretary of State George Shultz, Chief of Staff Don Regan, National Security Advisor John Poindexter, Chairman of the Joint Chiefs Admiral William Crowe, Director of the Central Intelligence Agency William J. Casey, and National Security Agency Head General William Odom, all sat at the conference table talking quietly among themselves awaiting President Ronald Reagan. Secretary of Defense Caspar Weinberger, who would normally have been present, was traveling abroad that day. Vice-President George H.W. Bush would arrive late, having just returned from a trip to Saudi Arabia.

As President Reagan entered the room a few minutes late, he flashed his signature smile. "Good morning," he said, shaking his head. "Sorry I'm late, guys. Nancy and her damn questions." That caused a fair amount of amusement around the table, but the comment served a purpose for Reagan wanted to put his colleagues at ease. Reagan carried himself with an air of confidence which projected onto his staff. He had sound judgment and made clear and convincing decisions. Reagan was a big picture president and his people liked that about him.

"Okay, fellas, let's run Operation Eldorado Canyon from top to bottom," Reagan said as he lay a briefing book on the table. He sat, opened the folder and studied it while his subordinates waited for the President to speak. He raised his head and looked around the table. "Let's go around the room and ask everyone if we're ready. Mr. Secretary?" Reagan asked the Secretary of State George Shultz.

"Yes, Sir," Shultz responded. "Prime Minister Thatcher gave her permission to use the bases in England last week and diplomatically, all that's left is to notify our allies tomorrow morning. It would be wise to avoid informing the Soviets until shortly before the bombing commences."

Reagan said, "I agree. It would be just like those bastards to inform Gaddafi in advance. What about Congress?"

"We're required to brief Congressional leaders, Mr. President, but if we want a surprise attack, we should brief them late tomorrow afternoon after the planes are in the air. White House meetings attract the press."

"What about the press on this, Don?" the President asked his Chief of Staff, Don Regan.

"Mr. President, as you know, there has been speculation about an attack for weeks. The networks and wire services already have people in Tripoli. They'll begin reporting as soon as the attack begins. We should be prepared to have you address the nation shortly afterward."

"Good," Reagan said, nodding his head. "Get Larry Speakes to write something for me. Wait until late tomorrow to reserve time on the networks. We don't want rumors coming out of the Press Office."

"Yes, Sir," Regan answered.

Reagan looked at Joint Chiefs Chairman Admiral William Crowe. "Bill, how are we doing on the military side?"

"Mr. President," Crowe replied, "we're ready to go. NATO has scheduled a joint military exercise called 'Salty Nation' starting tomorrow in Britain. We'll use those maneuvers as cover for our aircraft. We should be able to take off without being noticed. France will deny overflight permission, but we've planned for that. We'll be flying around the continent and through the Strait."

"That'll be one hell of a long bombing run, won't it?" Reagan asked.

"The longest bombing run in history, Sir. But we're confident we can execute it. The Air Force has practiced for it and our pilots are ready."

"Good," Reagan said. "What about the NSA, Bill?" Reagan asked William Odom.

"Mr. President, we've heard nothing in our phone intercepts that lead us to believe the Libyans know anything about our plans. At the present time, only the British have advance knowledge of the mission. Our concern is Gaddafi could receive a last minute warning of the attack from aircraft flying through the Strait or carriers moving into position near Malta. Gaddafi will want a radar confirmation before he calls a full alert. If we're able to shut down Libyan long range radars, they'll probably be caught by surprise."

"It's my understanding we have someone from CIA in Libya this weekend working on that. Is that right, Bill?" Reagan asked CIA Director William Casey.

"Yes, Sir," Casey replied. "She's coming out of the country today."

"She?" Reagan asked. Reagan paused for a few seconds as though he didn't hear Casey properly. "You have a woman in there?" That raised eyebrows around the room.

Luckily, Casey brought Messier's file with him in case the subject came up. "This is Laura Messier, Mr. President, the agent we sent into Libya," Casey said as he slid the file across the table.

Reagan began thumbing through the pages. "She's pretty, Bill," Reagan said, looking at her pictures. "Isn't it dangerous to send a woman?"

"That was the point, Mr. President. Women are one of Gaddafi's weaknesses."

Reagan passed some of the pictures around the table for the others to see. SecState looked at Messier's modeling pictures. "This is her as a model, Bill?"

"Yes," Casey said, hoping the entire subject would go

away. "She was a runway model before she joined CIA."

"Wow," Shultz said. That raised the interest of others and parts of Messier's file were spread across the table.

"These are recent pictures of her?" the President asked.

"Yes, Sir," Casey said. "In the first one, she's walking into the American Embassy in Paris. That was taken just a few months ago. Her cover job is an aide to the French Minister of Foreign Affairs in Paris."

"I remember this girl, Mr. President," Shultz said to Reagan. "Every time we have meetings with the French, she's in the room on the French side. She acts as a kind of personal aide to the Minister. I always thought she was a clerical employee."

Reagan smiled when he spoke to Casey. "You mean we have people on both sides of the table when we talk to the French?"

"Yes, Sir," Casey replied.

Reagan laughed, "Too bad we don't have someone in the Libyan government."

"We do, Mr. President," Casey said. Every person in the room stopped, looked up and stared at Casey.

There was a pause in the room before the President said, "Go on, Bill."

"Well, he's not American. He's a French double agent positioned inside the Libyan government. Messier will bring the radar and missile codes out of Libya today. We'll relay them to the double agent. He'll be the one who shuts down the radars."

"Well, I'll be damned," Reagan said with a smile. He sat back and slapped the table with his hand. "Gentlemen, this is how you win wars. Nice job, Bill."

"Thank you, Mr. President."

The Vice-President entered the room with appropriate apologizes. "Mr. President, I apologize for being late. I just got back. Barbara insisted I change my clothes before I came over," he said. That brought a few chuckles from the group.

"You're lucky, George. Nancy would have asked me to walk the damn dogs," Reagan said with a smile. Bush sat down next to the President.

Reagan directed his next question to Secretary of State Shultz. "How's the world going to react to this?" Shultz hesitated before he answered. "Mr. President," he finally said, "the Canadians, Australians, Israelis and the British will support us. The rest of NATO will, too, although they'll appear neutral in the press. The Italians and the French are big trading partners with Libya so they'll issue mild condemnations, but the French, as we heard from Bill Casey, are helping behind the scenes. The Chinese, Soviets and East Germans will offer strong criticism, but it's unlikely to go further than that. We don't believe they'll interfere."

"George?" the President asked the Vice President, "what about the Saudis?"

"Mr. President, I spoke with King Fahd yesterday. He feels Gaddafi's had a destabilizing effect on the Middle East. They'll support us even though they'll publicly condemn the raid."

"That's good news; thanks."

Reagan heard what he needed to hear. "Gentlemen, here's what we're going to do. If our agent gets out of Libya," Reagan hesitated. "What's her name again, Bill?" Reagan asked, looking at Bill Casey.

"Messier. Laura Messier."

"If Ms. Messier gets out with the codes, that's great, but whether she does or not, we're moving ahead with the attack. Tomorrow morning, I'll call the allies to inform them of our plans. I'll brief Congress later in the day. What's the timetable from there, Bill?" Reagan asked Joint Chiefs Chairman William Crowe.

"Our bombers in Britain will leave around 6:00 pm tomorrow local time, twelve noon here," Crowe replied. "We'll fly around the continent and through the Strait of Gibraltar. That will put our forces in Libyan airspace about 2:00 am local time, 8:00 pm here in Washington. They'll get in and out within fifteen minutes, after which they'll return to base."

"Very good. Caspar will be back this afternoon," Reagan said to Crowe. "I want you and Caspar over at the Pentagon running the show. Keep me informed as it unfolds. And, gentlemen, let's keep this quiet. Everyone continue their normal routine today and tomorrow. Okay?"

"Yes, Sir," everyone answered nearly in unison.

"Bill?" the President asked William Casey.

"Yes, Sir, Mr. President."

"I want to know Messier's status. Call Don with any information about her, day or night."

"Yes, Sir," Casey replied.

"Gentlemen, we stand adjourned. Good luck and may God Bless the United States of America."